Follow My Leader
The Boys of Templeton

by

Talbot Baines Reed

Follow My Leader
The Boys of Templeton
by Talbot Baines Reed

Copyright © 2024

All Rights reserved.

ISBN: 978-93-61424-78-6

Published by

DOUBLE 9 BOOKS

2/13-B, Ansari Road
Daryaganj, New Delhi – 110002
info@double9books.com
www.double9books.com
Tel. 011-40042856

ABOUT THE AUTHOR

British author and writer Talbot Baines Reed (3 April 1852 – 28 November 1893) is best known for his children's books, especially school stories. Reed was born into a family of writers and publishers in Hackney, London. Charles Reed, his father, was a well-known publisher and benefactor. Talbot Baines Throughout his writing career, Reed mostly wrote tales set in schools and featuring schoolboy escapades. His paintings frequently portrayed the difficulties, camaraderie, and moral teachings that young boys encountered at school. Reed's books became well-known because of their compelling storylines, likeable characters, and moral lessons they offered. Among his most well-known compositions are "A Dog with a Bad Name" (1886), "The Adventures of a Three-Guinea Watch" (1883), and "The Fifth Form at St. Dominic's" (1881). Reed's books had a significant impact on the school story genre and helped shape children's literature in the late 1800s. Sadly, Talbot Baines Reed passed away at the age of 41, ending his career. Even though he wrote for a relatively short period of time, he had a significant influence on children's literature, and his stories and moral lessons have endured.

CONTENTS

Chapter One
How our heroes enter upon more than one career

On a raw, damp morning in early spring, a rather forlorn group of three youngsters might have been seen on the doorstep of Mountjoy Preparatory School, casting nervous glances up and down the drive, and looking anything but a picture of the life and spirits they really represented.

That they were bound on an important journey was very evident. They were muffled up in ulsters, and wore gloves and top hats—a vanity no Mountjoy boy ever succumbed to, except under dire necessity. Yet it was clear they were not homeward bound, for no trunks encumbered the lobby, and no suggestion of *Dulce Domum* betrayed itself in their dismal features. Nor had they been expelled, for though their looks might favour the supposition, they talked about the hour they should get back that evening, and wondered if Mrs Ashford would have supper ready for them in her own parlour. And it was equally plain that, whatever their destination might be, they were not starting on a truant's expedition, for the said Mrs Ashford presently came out and handed them each a small parcel of sandwiches, and enjoined on them most particularly to keep well buttoned up, and not let their feet get wet.

"It will be a cold drive for you, boys," said she; "I've told Tom to put up at Markridge, so you will have a mile walk to warm you up before you get to Templeton."

A waggonette appeared at the end of the drive, and began to approach them.

"Ah, there's the trap; I'll tell Mr Ashford—"

Mr Ashford appeared just as the vehicle reached the door.

"Well, boys, ready for the road? Good bye, and good luck. Don't forget whose son Edward the Fifth was, Coote. Keep your heads and you'll get on all right. I trust you not to get into mischief on the way. All right, Tom."

During this short harangue the three boys hoisted themselves, one by one, into the waggonette, and bade a subdued farewell to their preceptor, who stood on the doorstep, waving to them cheerily, until they turned a corner and found themselves actually on the road to Templeton.

Not to keep the reader further in suspense as to the purpose of this important expedition, our three young gentlemen, having severally attained the responsible age of fourteen summers, and having severally absorbed into their systems as much of the scholastic pabulum of Mountjoy House as that preparatory institution was in the habit of dispensing to boys destined for a higher sphere, were this morning on their way, in awe and trembling, to the examination hall of Templeton school, there to submit themselves to an ordeal which would decide whether or not they were worthy to emerge from their probationary state and take their rank among the public schoolboys of the land.

Such being the case, it is little wonder they looked fidgety as they caught their last glimpse of Mr Ashford, and realised that before they came in sight of Mountjoy again a crisis in the lives of each of them would have come and gone.

"Whose son was he?" said Coote, appealingly, in about five minutes.

His voice sounded quite startling, after the long, solemn silence which had gone before.

His two companions stared at him, afterwards at one another; then one of them said—

"I forget."

"Whose son was he?" said Coote, turning with an air of desperation to the other.

"Richard the Third's," said the latter.

Coote mused, and inwardly repeated a string of names.

"Doesn't sound right," said he. "Are you sure, Dick?"

"Who else could it be?" said the young gentleman addressed as Dick, whose real name was Richardson.

"Hanged if I know," said the unhappy Coote, proceeding to write an R and a 3 on his thumb-nail with a pencil. "It doesn't look right I believe because your own name's Richardson, you think everybody else is Richard's son too."

And the perpetrator of this very mild joke bent his head over his learned thumb-nail, and frowned.

It was a point of honour at Mountjoy always to punish a joke summarily, whether good, bad, or indifferent. For a short time, consequently, the paternity of Edward the Fifth was lost sight of, as was also Coote himself, in the performance of the duty which devolved on Richardson and his companion.

This matter of business being at last satisfactorily settled, and Tom, the driver, who had considerably pulled up by the road-side during the "negotiations," being ordered to "forge ahead," the party returned to its former attitude of gloomy anticipation.

"It's a precious rum thing," said Richardson, "neither you nor Heathcote can remember a simple question like that. I'd almost forgot it, myself."

"I know I shan't remember anything when the time comes," said Heathcote. "I said my Latin Syntax over to Ashford, without a mistake, yesterday, and I've forgotten every word of it now."

"What I funk is the *vivâ voce* Latin prose," said Coote. "I say, Dick, what's the gender of 'Amnis, a river?'"

Dick looked knowing, and laughed.

"None of your jokes," said he, "you don't catch me that way—'Amnis,' a city, is neuter."

Coote's face lengthened, as he made a further note on his other thumb-nail.

"I could have sworn it was a river," said he. "I say, whatever shall I do? I don't know how I shall get through it."

"Through what—the river?" said Heathcote. "Bless you, you'll get through swimmingly."

There was a moment's pause. Richardson looked at Coote; Coote looked at Richardson, and between them they thought they saw a joke.

Tom pulled up by the road-side once more, while Heathcote arranged with his creditors on the floor of the waggonette. When, at length, the order to proceed was given, that trusty Jehu ventured on a mild expostulation. "Look'ee here, young gem'an," said he, touching his hat. "You've got to get to Templeton by ten o'clock, and it's past nine now. I guess you'd better save up them larks for when you're coming home."

"None of your cheek, Tom," said Richardson, "or we'll have you down here, and pay you out, my boy. Put it on, can't you? Why don't you whip the beast up?"

The prospect of coming down to be paid out by his vivacious passengers was sufficiently alarming to Tom to induce him to take their admonition seriously to heart; and for the rest of the journey, although several times business transactions were taking place on the floor of the vehicle, the plodding horse held on its course, and Markridge duly hove in sight.

With the approaching end of the journey, the boys once more became serious and uncomfortable.

"I say," said Coote, in a whisper, as if Dr Winter, at Templeton, a mile away, were within hearing, "do tell me whose son he was. I'm certain he wasn't Richard the Third's. Don't be a cad, Dick; you might tell a fellow. I'd tell you, if I knew."

"I've told you one father," said Dick, sternly, "and he didn't have more. If you want another, stick down Edward the Sixth."

Coote's face brightened, as he produced his pencil and cleaned his largest unoccupied nail.

"That sounds more—, Oh, but, I say, how can Edward the Sixth be Edward the Fifth's father? Besides, he had no family and— Oh, what a howling howler I shall come!"

His friends regarded him sympathetically, and assisted him to dismount.

"We shall have to step out," said Richardson; "it's five-and-twenty to ten, and it's a good mile. Look here, Tom; you've got to come and fetch us at the school, do you hear? We're not going to fag back here after the exam."

"My orders was to wait here till you pick me up, young gentlemen," said Tom, grinning. "Mind what you're up to in them 'saminations."

With which parting sally our heroes found themselves alone, with their faces towards Templeton.

To any wayfarers less overwhelmed with care, that mile walk from Markridge to Templeton over the breezy downs, with the fresh sea air meeting you, with the musical hum of the waves on the beach below, and the glimmer of the spring sun on the ocean far ahead, would have been bracing and inspiriting. As it was, it was not without its attractions even for the three boys; for did they not stand on the precincts of that enchanted ground occupied and glorified by the heroes of Templeton? Was not this very road along which they walked a highway along which Templeton walked, or peradventure raced, or it may be bicycled? Were not these downs the hunting-ground over which the Templeton Harriers coursed in chase of the Templeton hares? Was not that square tower ahead the very citadel of their fortress? and that distant bell that tolled, was it not a voice which spoke to Templeton in tones of familiar fellowship every hour?

They trembled as they heard that bell and came nearer and nearer to the grand square tower. They eyed furtively everyone who passed them on the road, and imagined every man a master and every boy a Templetonian.

A shop with "mortar-boards" displayed in its window seemed like a temple crowded with shrines; and a confectioner's shop, in which two young gentlemen in gowns sat and refreshed themselves, was like a distant glimpse of Olympus where the gods banqueted.

A boy with a towel over his shoulder lounged past them, and surveyed them listlessly as he went by.

How they cowered and trembled beneath that scrutiny! How they dreaded lest their jackets might be too long, or that the studs in their shirts might not be visible! How they hated themselves for blushing, and wished to goodness they knew what to do with their hands!

How their legs shook beneath them as they came under the shadow of the great tower and looked nervously for the porter's lodge! They would have liked to look as if they knew the place; it seemed so foolish to have to ask any one where the porter lived.

"Just go and see if it's up that passage," said Richardson to Coote, pointing out a narrow opening on one side of the tower.

Coote looked at the place doubtfully.

"Hadn't we better all try?" said he.

"What's the good? Beckon if it's right, and we'll come."

The unfortunate Coote departed on his quest much as a man who walks into a cave where a bear possibly resides.

His companions meanwhile occupied themselves with examining the gateway and trying to appear as if architectural curiosity and nothing else had been the object of their passing visit to Templeton.

In a few minutes Coote reappeared with a long face.

"Well? is it right?"

"No; it's a dust-bin."

The great clock above them began to boom out ten.

"We must find out somehow," said Richardson. "We'd better ask at this door."

And, to the alarm of his companions, he boldly tapped on a door under the gate.

A man in uniform opened it.

"Well, young gentlemen, what's your pleasure?"

"Please can you tell us where the porter's lodge is?" said Richardson, in his most persuasive tone.

"I can. I'm the porter, and this is the lodge. What do you want?"

"Please we're Mr Ashford's boys, come for the examination. Here's a note from Mr Ashford for Dr Winter."

The porter took the note, and bade the panic-stricken trio follow him across the quadrangle.

What a walk that was! Across that noble square, with its two great elm-trees laden with noisy rooks; with its wide-fenced lawn and sun-dial; with its cloisters and red brick houses; with its sculptures and Latin mottoes.

And even all these were as nothing to the few boys who loitered about in its enclosure—some pacing arm-in-arm, some hurrying with books under their arms, some diverting themselves more or less noisily, some shouting or whistling or singing—all at home in the place; and all unlike the three trembling victims who trotted in the wake of the porter towards the dreadful hall of examination.

At the door, Richardson felt a frantic clutch on his arm.

"Oh! I say, Dick," gasped Coote, holding out a shaking ringer, with a legend on its nail, "whatever is this the date for—1476? I put it down, and—Oh! I say, can't you remember?"

But Richardson, though he scorned to show it, was too agitated even to suggest an event to fit the disconsolate date, and poor Coote had to totter up the stairs, hopelessly convinced that he had nothing at his fingers' ends after all.

They found themselves walking up a long, high-ceilinged room, with desks all round and a few very appalling oil portraits ranged along the walls, to a table where sat a small, handsome gentleman in cap and gown.

He took Mr Ashford's letter, and the boys knew they stood in the presence of Dr Winter.

"Richardson, Heathcote, Coote," said the Doctor. "Answer to your names—which is Richardson?"

"I am, please, sir."

"Heathcote?"

"I am, sir, please."

"Coote?"

"I am, if you please, sir."

"Richardson, go to desk 6; Heathcote, desk 13; Coote, desk 25."

Coote groaned inwardly. It was all up with him now, and he might just as well throw up the sponge before he began. With a friend within call he might yet have struggled through. But what hope was there when the nearer of them was twelve desks away?

For two hours a solemn silence reigned in that examination hall, broken only by the scratching of pens and the secret sighs of one and another of the victims. The pictures on the walls, as they looked down, caught the eye of many a wistful upturned face, and marked the devouring of many a penholder, and the tearing of many a hair.

In vain Coote searched his nails from thumb to little finger. No question fitted to his painfully collected answers. Edward the Fifth was ignored, the sex of "Amnis" was not even hinted at, and "1476" never once came to his rescue. And yet, he reminded himself over and over again, he and Heathcote had said their Latin syntax to Mr Ashford only the day before without a mistake.

"Cease writing," said the Doctor, as the clock struck two, "and the boys at desks 1 to 10 come up here."

This was the signal for the cruellest of all that day's horrors. If the written examination had slain its thousands, the *vivâ voce* slew its tens of thousands. Even Richardson stumbled; and Heathcote, when his turn came, gave himself up for lost. The Doctor's impassive face betrayed no emotion, and gave no token, either for joy, or hope, or despair. He merely said "That will do" after each victim had performed; and even when Coote, after a mighty effort, rendered "O tempora! O mores!" as "Oh, the tempers of the Moors," he quietly said, "Thank you; now the next boy."

At last it was all over, and they found themselves standing once more in the great quadrangle, not very sure what had happened to them, but feeling as if they had just undergone a surgical operation not unlike that of flaying alive.

However, once outside the terrible portal of Templeton, their hearts gradually thawed within them. The confectioner's shop, now crowded with "gods," held them in awe for a season, and as long as the road was specked with mortar-boards they held their peace, and meditated on their shirt-studs. But when Templeton lay behind them, and they stepped once more on to the breezy heath, they shook off the nightmare that weighed on their spirits and were themselves again.

"Precious glad it's over," said Richardson. "Beast, that arithmetic paper was."

"I liked it better than the English," said Coote. "I say, is 'for' a preposition or an adverb? I couldn't remember."

"Oh, look here! shut up riddles now," said Richardson, "we've had enough of them. Let's talk about our three and not your 'for,' you Coote you."

Whereupon Richardson started to run, a proceeding which at once convinced his companions that his last observation had been intended as a joke. As in duty bound they gave chase, but the fleet-footed Dick was too many for them; and when at last they came up with him he was strongly intrenched on the box-seat of the empty waggonette at Markridge, with Tom's whip in his hand, beyond all attack.

"I say," said he, after his pursuers had taken breath and granted an amnesty, "it would be great fun to drive home by ourselves. Tom's not here. I asked them. He's gone to see his aunt, or somebody, and left word he'd be back at three o'clock. Like his cheek. I vote we don't wait for him."

"All serene," said the others, "but we shall want the horse, shan't we?"

"Perhaps we shall," said Dick, with a grin, "unless you'd like to pull the trap. The horse is in the stable, and we can tip the fellow to put him in for us."

The "fellow" was quite amenable to this sort of persuasion, and grinningly complied with the whim of the young gentlemen; secretly enjoying the prospect of Tom's dismay.

"'Taint no concern of mine," said he, philosophically. "If you tells me to do it, I does it."

"And if we tells you to open your mouth and shut your eyes, and you'll find sixpence in your hand,—you'll find it there," said Dick.

"Of course you knows how to drive," said the stableman.

"Rather! Do you think we're babies? Here, shy us the reins. Come along, you fellows, there's room for all three on the box. Now then, Joe, give her her head. Come up, you beast! Swish! See if we don't make her step out. Let her go!"

With some misgivings, Joe obeyed, and next moment the waggonette swayed majestically out of the yard very much like a small steam-tug going out of harbour in half a cap of wind.

"Rum, the way she pitches," said Dick presently; "she didn't do it when we came."

"Looks to me as if the horse wasn't quite sober," suggested Coote.

"Perhaps, if you pulled both reins at the same time, instead of one at a time," put in Heathcote, "she wouldn't wobble so much."

"You duffer; she'd stop dead, if I did that."

"Suppose you don't pull either," said Heathcote.

Richardson pooh-poohed the notion, but acted on it all the same, with highly satisfactorily results. The trap glided along smoothly, and all anxiety as to the management of the mare appeared to be at an end.

"I left word for Tom," said Richardson, "if he stepped out, he'd catch us up. Ha, ha! Won't he be wild?"

"Wonder if he'll get us in a row with Ashford?" said Heathcote.

"Not he. What's the harm? Just a little horse-play, that's all."

Heathcote and Coote became grave.

"Look here," said the former, "we let you off last time, but you'll catch it now. Collar him that side, Coote, and have him over."

"Don't be an idiot, Heathcote," cried the Jehu, as he found himself suddenly seized on either hand. "Let go, while I'm driving. Do you hear, Coote; let go, or there'll be a smash!"

But as "letting go" was an accomplishment not taught at Mountjoy House, Richardson had to adopt stronger measures than mere persuasion in order to clear himself of his embarrassments.

Dropping the reins and flinging his arms vehemently back, he managed to dislodge his assailants, though not without dislodging himself at the same time, and a long and somewhat painful creditors' meeting down in the waggonette was the consequence.

The mare, whose patience had been gradually evaporating during this strange journey, conscious of the riot behind her, and feeling the reins dropping loosely over her tail, took the whole matter very much to heart, and showed her disapproval of the whole proceedings by taking to her heels and bolting straight away.

The business meeting inside stood forthwith adjourned. With scared faces, the boys struggled to their feet, and, holding on to the rail of the box-seat, peered over to ascertain the cause of this alarming diversion.

"It's a bolt!" said Richardson, the only one of the three who retained wits enough to think or speak. "Hang on, you fellows; I'll try and get the reins. Help me up!"

As well as the swaying of the vehicle would allow it, they helped him hoist himself up on to the box. But for a long time all his efforts to catch the reins were in vain, and once or twice it seemed as if nothing could save him from being pitched off his perch on to the road. Luckily the mare kept a straight course, and at length, by a tremendous stretch, well supported from the rear by his faithful comrades, the boy succeeded in reaching the reins and pulling them up over the mare's tail.

"Hang on now!" said he; "we're all right if I can only guide her."

Chapter Two
How our heroes fall out and yet remain friends

Mountjoy House had a narrow escape that afternoon of losing three of its most promising pupils.

The boys themselves by no means realised the peril of their situation. Indeed, after the first alarm, and finding that, by clinging tightly to the rail of the box-seat, they could support themselves on their feet on the floor of the swinging vehicle, Heathcote and Coote began almost to enjoy it, and were rather sorry one or two of the Templeton boys were not at hand to see how Mountjoy did things.

Richardson, however, with the reins in his hands, but utterly powerless to check the headlong career of the mare, or to do anything but guide her, took a more serious view of the situation, and heartily wished the drive was at an end.

It was a flat road all the way to Mountjoy—no steep hill to breathe the runaway, and no ploughed field to curb her ardour. It was a narrow road, too, so narrow that, for two vehicles to pass one another, it was necessary for one of the two to draw up carefully at the very verge. And as the verge in the present case meant the edge of rather a steep embankment, the prospect was not altogether a cheering one for an inexperienced boy, who, if he knew very little about driving, knew quite well that everything depended on his own nerve and coolness.

And Richardson not only had a head, but knew how to keep it. With a rein tightly clutched in each hand, with his feet firmly pressed against the footboard, with a sharp eye out over the mare's ears, and a grim twitch on his determined mouth, he went over the chances in his own mind.

"If she goes on like this, we shall get to Mountjoy in half an hour. What a pace! We're bound to smash up before we get there! Perhaps these fellows had better try and jump for it. Hallo! lucky we didn't go over that stone! Wonder if I could pull her up if I got on her back? She might kick up and smash the trap! Wonder if she will pull up, or go over the bank, or what? Tom—Tom will have to run hard to catch us. Whew! what a swing! I could have sworn we were over!"

This last peril, and the involuntary cry of the two boys clinging on behind him, silenced even this mental soliloquy for a bit. But the waggonette, after two or three desperate plunges, righted itself and continued its mad career at the heels of the mare.

"What would happen if we went over? Jolly awkward to get pitched over on to my head or down among the mare's feet! She'd kick, I guess! Those fellows inside could jump and— By Jove! there comes something on the road! We're in for it now! Either a smash, or over the bank, or— Hallo! there's a gate open!"

This last inward exclamation was caused by the sight of an open gate some distance ahead, through which a rough cart-track branched off from the road towards the sand-hills on the left. Richardson, with the instinct of desperation, seized upon this as the only way of escape from the peril which threatened them.

"Look out, you fellows!" cried he; "hang on tight on the right side while we turn, and jump well out if we go over."

They watched him breathlessly as they came towards the gate. The vehicle which was meeting them and their own were about equal distance from the place, and it was clear their fate must be settled in less than a minute.

Richardson waved to the driver of the approaching cart to pull up, and at the same time edged the mare as far as he could on to the off-side of the road, so as to give her a wide turn in.

"Now for it!" said he to himself, pulling the left rein; "if this don't do, I'll give up driving."

The mare, perhaps weary, perhaps perplexed at the sight of the cart in front, perhaps ready for a new diversion, obeyed the lead and swerved off at the gate. For a moment the waggonette tottered on its left wheel, and, but for the weight of the two passengers on the other side, would have caught the gate post and shattered itself to atoms in the narrow passage.

As it was, it cleared the peril by an inch, and then, plunging on to the soft, rough track, capsized gently, mare and all, landing its three occupants a yard or two off with their noses in the mud.

It was an undignified end to an heroic drive, and Richardson, as he picked himself up and cleared the mud from his eyes, felt half disappointed that no bones were broken or joints dislocated after all. Coote did certainly contribute a grain of consolation by announcing that he *believed* one of his legs was broken. But even this hope of glory was short-lived, for that young hero finding no one at leisure to assist him to his feet rose by himself, and walked some distance to a grass bank where he could sit down and examine for himself the extent of his injuries.

"Wal, young squire," said a voice at Dick's side, as that young gentleman found eyesight enough to look about him, "you've done it this time."

The owner of the voice was the driver of the cart, and the tones and looks with which he made the remark were anything but unflattering to Richardson.

"It was a close squeak through the gate," said the latter, "not six inches either side; and if it hadn't been for the ruts we should have kept up all right till now. I say, do you think the trap's damaged, or the mare?"

The mare was lying very comfortably on her side taking a good breath after her race, and not offering to resume her feet. As for the waggonette it was lying equally comfortably on its side, with one wheel up in the air.

"Shaft broken," said the driver, "that's all."

"That's all!" said Dick, dolefully, "we shall catch it, and no mistake."

The man grinned.

"You can't expect to play games of that sort without scratching the varnish off," said he. "No fault of yours you haven't got your necks broke."

"Suppose we try to get her up?" said Richardson, looking as if this last information had very little comfort in it.

So among them they unharnessed the mare and managed to disengage her from the vehicle and get her to her feet.

"She's all sound," said the man, after a careful overhauling.

"She's a cad," said Dick, "and I shouldn't have been sorry if she'd broken her neck. Look at the smash she's made."

The trap was indeed far worse damaged than they supposed as first. Not only was a shaft broken, but a wheel was off, and the rail all along one side was torn away. It was clear there was no more driving to be got out of it that afternoon, and the boys gave up the attempt to raise it in disgust.

"Do you know Tom, our man—Ashford's man?" said Dick.

"Who? Tom Tranter? Yes, I knows him."

"Well, you'll meet him on the road between here and Markridge, walking, or perhaps running. Tell him we've had a spill and he'd better see after the trap, will you? We'll go on."

"What about the horse, though?" said Heathcote.

"I suppose we shall have to take the beast along with us. We can't leave her here."

"I think we'd better stop till Tom comes, and all go on together," suggested Heathcote.

"I suppose you funk it with Ashford," said Dick whose temper was somewhat ruffled by misfortune. "I don't. If you two like to stop you can. I'll go on with the mare."

"Oh, no, we'll all come," said Heathcote. "I'm not afraid, no more is Coote."

"All serene then, come on. Mind you tell Tom, I say," added he to the carter. "Good-bye, and thanks awfully."

And they departed in doleful procession, Dick, with the whip in his hand, leading the mare by the mouth, and Heathcote and Coote following like chief mourners, just out of range of the animal's heels.

"What shall we say to Ashford?" asked Heathcote, after a little.

"Say? What do you mean?" said Dick.

"He's sure to ask us what has happened."

"Well, we shall tell him, I suppose."

"There'll be an awful row."

"Of course there will."

"We shall get licked."

"Of course we shall. What of it?"

"Only," said Heathcote, with a little hesitation, "I suppose there's no way of getting out of it?"

"Not unless you tell lies. You and Coote can tell some if you like—I shan't."

"I'm not going to tell any," said Coote, "I've told quite enough in my exam. papers."

"Oh, of course, I don't mean telling crams," said Heathcote, who really didn't exactly know what he did mean. "I'll back you up, old man."

"Thanks. I say, as we are in a row, mightn't we just as well take it out of this beastly horse? If Coote led him you and I could take cock shots at him from behind."

"Oh, yes," said Coote, "and hit me by mistake; not if I know it."

"We might aim at Coote," suggested Heathcote, by way of solving the difficulty, "and hit the mare by mistake."

"Perhaps it would be rather low," said Dick. "I don't see, though, why she shouldn't carry us. She's a long back; plenty of room for all three of us."

"The middle for me," said Coote.

"Think she'd kick up?" asked Heathcote.

"Not she, she couldn't lift with all of us on her. Come on. Whoa! you beast. Give us a leg up, somebody. Whoa! Hold her head, Coote, and keep her from going round and round. Now then. By Jove! what a way up it is!"

By a mighty effort of combined hoisting and climbing, the boys, one after the other, scaled the lofty ridge, and perched themselves, as securely as they could, well forward on the mare's long back.

Luckily for them, the patient animal endured her burden meekly, and plodded on in a listless manner, pricking her ears occasionally at the riot which went on on her back, and once or twice rattling the bones of her riders by a mild attempt at a trot, but otherwise showing no signs of renewing her former more energetic protest.

In this manner, after a weary and not altogether refreshing journey, the three jaded, tightly-packed heroes came to a standstill at the door of Mountjoy House, where, one after the other, they slid sadly from their perches, and addressed themselves to the satisfying of Mrs Ashford's natural curiosity, only hoping the interview would not be protracted, and so defer for long the supper to which they all eagerly looked forward.

"Why, what's all this?" said the matron.

"Where's the waggonette, and Tom?" chimed in Mr Ashford, appearing at the same moment.

"Please, sir," said Dick, "we didn't wait for Tom, and drove home, and there was a little accident. I was driving at the time, sir. We got spilt, and the trap was a little damaged. We left word for Tom to see to it, and I'll write and get my father to pay for mending it. We're all awfully sorry, sir. Dr Winter sends his regards, and we shall hear the result of the exam. on Thursday. One of the wheels came off, but I fancy it will go on again. It was a rut did it. We were coming along at a very good pace, and should have been here an hour ago if it hadn't been for the accident. We're sorry to be late, sir."

After which ample explanation and apology the boys felt themselves decidedly aggrieved that they were not at once ushered in to supper. Mr Ashford, however, being a mortal of only limited perception, required a good deal more information; and a painful and somewhat petulant cross-examination ensued, the result of which was that our heroes were informed they were not to be trusted, that both Mr and Mrs Ashford were disappointed in them, that they ought to be ashamed of themselves, and that they would hear more about the matter to-morrow.

And what about the supper?—that glorious spread of coffee and hot toast, and eggs and bacon, the anticipation of which had borne them up in all the perils and fatigue of the day, and had shone like a beacon star to guide them home? The subject was ignored, basely ignored; and the culprits were ordered to join the ordinary school supper and appease their hunger on bread and cheese and cold boiled beef, and slake their thirst on "swipes."

Then did the spirits of Richardson, Heathcote and Coote wax fierce within them. Then did they call Mr Ashford a cad, and Mrs Ashford a sneak. Then did they kick all the little boys within reach, and scowl furiously upon the big ones. Then did they wish the mare was dead and Templeton a ruin!

As, when Jove frowns and Mercury and Vulcan scowl, the hills hide their heads and the valleys tremble beneath the storm, so did the youth of Mountjoy quake and cower that evening as it raised its eyes and beheld those three gloomy heroes devour their beef and drink their swipes. No one ventured to ask how they had fared, or wherefore they looked sad; but they knew something had happened. The little boys gazed with awe-struck wonder at the heroes who had that day been at Templeton, and contended for Templeton honours. The elder boys wondered if gloom was part of Templeton "form," and when their turn would come to look as black and majestic; and all marvelled at the supper those three ate, and at the chasm they left in the cold boiled beef!

"Come on, you fellows," said Richardson, as soon as the meal was finished. "I'm going to bed; I'm fagged."

"So am I," said Heathcote.

"So am I," said Coote.

And the triumvirate stalked from the room, leaving Mountjoy more than ever convinced something terrific had happened.

If Coote had had his way, he would rather have stayed up. He slept in a different room from Richardson and Heathcote, and it was rather slow going to bed by himself at half-past seven. But as it was evident from Dick's manner that this was the proper course to take under the circumstances, he took it, and was very soon dreaming that he and Edward the Fifth's father were trotting round the Templeton quadrangle on the mare, much to the admiration of the Templeton boys, who assembled in their thousands to witness the exploit.

Next day the uncomfortable topic of the mare and the waggonette was renewed in a long conference with Mr Ashford.

As supper was no longer pending, and as a night's rest had intervened, the boys were rather more disposed to enter into details. But they failed to satisfy Mr Ashford that they were not to blame for what had occurred.

"I am less concerned," said he, "about the damage done to the waggonette than I am to think I cannot trust you as fully as I ought to be able to trust my head boys. I hope during the week or two that remains of this term you will try to win back the confidence you have lost. I must, in justice to my other boys, punish you. Under the circumstances, I shall not cane you, but till the end of the term you must each of you lose your hour's play between twelve and one."

Mr Ashford paused. Perhaps he expected an outburst of gratitude. Perhaps he didn't exactly know what to say next. In either case, he found he had made a mistake.

The boys, with an instinct not, certainly, of self-righteousness, but of common justice, felt that they had had punishment enough already for their sin. Mr Ashford took no account of those few seconds when the waggonette was dashing through the gate and reeling to its fall. He reckoned as nothing the weary jolt home, the indignity of that supper last night, and the suspense of that early morning. He made no allowance for an absence of malice in what they had done, and gave them no credit—although, indeed, neither did they give themselves credit—for the regret and straightforwardness with which they had confessed it. He proposed to treat them, the head boys of Mountjoy, as common delinquents, and punish them as he would punish a cheat, or a bully, or mutineer.

It wasn't fair—they knew it; and if Ashford didn't know it, too—well, he ought.

"We'd rather be caned, sir," said Richardson, speaking for all three.

Mr Ashford regarded the speaker with sharp surprise.

"Richardson, kindly remember I am the best judge of what punishment you deserve."

"It's not fair to keep us in all the term," said Dick, his cheeks mounting colour with the desperateness of his boldness.

Mr Ashford changed colour, too, but his cheeks turned pale.

"Leave my sight, sir, instantly! How do you dare to use language like that to me!"

Fortunately for the dignity, as well as for the comfort, of the three boys, Dick made no attempt to prolong the argument. He turned and left the room, followed by his two faithful henchmen, little imagining that, if any one had scored in this unsatisfactory interview, he had.

Don't let the reader imagine that any mystical glory belongs to the schoolboy who happens to "score one" off his master. If he does it consciously, the chances are he is a snob for doing it. If he does it unconsciously, as Dick did here, then the misfortune of the master by no means means the bliss of the boy.

Dick felt anything but blissful as he stalked moodily to the schoolroom that morning and growled his injuries to his allies.

But Mr Ashford, as soon as his first burst of temper had evaporated, like an honest, sensible man, sat down and reviewed the situation; and it occurred to him, on reviewing it, that he had made a mistake. It was, of course, extremely painful and humiliating to have to acknowledge it; but, once acknowledged, it would have been far more humiliating to Mr Ashford's sense of honour to persist in it.

He summoned the boys once more to his presence, and they trooped in like three prisoners brought up on remand to hear their final sentence.

The master's mouth twitched nervously, and he half repented of the ordeal he had set before himself.

"You said just now, Richardson, that the punishment I proposed to inflict on you was not fair?"

"Yes, sir, we think so," replied Dick, simply.

"I think so, too," said Mr Ashford, equally simply, "and I shall say no more about it. Now you can go."

The boys gaped at him in mingled admiration and bewilderment.

"You can go," repeated the master.

Richardson took a hasty survey of his companions' countenances, and said—

"Will you cane us instead, please sir?"

"No, Richardson, that would not be fair either."

Richardson made one more effort.

"Please, sir, we think we deserve something."

"People don't always get their deserts in this world, my boy," said the master, with a smile. "Now please go when I tell you."

Mr Ashford rallied three waverers to his standard that morning. They didn't profess to understand the meaning of it all, but they could see that the master had sacrificed something to do them justice, and with the native chivalry of boys, they made his cause theirs, and did all they could to cover his retreat.

Two days later, a letter by the post was brought in to Mr Ashford in the middle of school.

Coote's face grew crimson as he saw it, and the faces of his companions grew long and solemn. A sudden silence fell on the room, broken only by the rustle of the paper as the master tore open the envelope and produced the printed document. His eyes glanced hurriedly down it, and a shade of trouble crossed his brow.

"We're gone coons," groaned Heathcote.

"Don't speak to me," said Dick.

Coote said nothing, but wished one of the windows was open on a hot day like this.

"This paper contains the result of the entrance examination at Templeton," said Mr Ashford. "Out of thirty-six candidates, Heathcote has passed fifteenth, and Richardson twenty-first. Coote, I am sorry to say, has not passed."

Chapter Three
How our heroes gird on their armour

Our heroes, each in the bosom of his own family, spent a somewhat anxious Easter holiday.

Of the three, Coote's prospects were decidedly the least cheery. Mountjoy House without Richardson and Heathcote would be desolation itself, and the heart of our hero quailed within him as he thought of the long dull evenings and the dreary classes of the coming friendless term.

"Never mind, old man," Dick had said, cheerily, as the "Firm" talked their prospects over on the day before the holidays, "you're bound to scrape through the July exam.; and then won't we have a jollification when you turn up?"

But all this was sorry comfort for the dejected Coote, who retired home and spent half his holidays learning dates, so determined was he not to be "out of it" next time.

As for Heathcote and Richardson, they were neither of them without their perturbations of spirit. Not that either of them realised—who ever does?—the momentous epoch in their lives which had just arrived, when childhood like a pleasant familiar landscape lies behind, and the hill of life clouded in mist and haze rises before, all unknown and unexplored.

Heathcote, who was his grandmother's only joy, and had no nearer relatives, did hear some remarks to this effect as he girded himself for the coming campaign. But he evaded them with an "Oh, yes, I know, all serene," and was far more interested in the prospect of a new Eton jacket and Sunday surplice than in a detailed examination of his past personal history.

The feeling uppermost in his mind was that Dick was going to Templeton too, and beyond that his anxieties and trepidations extended no further than the possibility of being called green by his new schoolfellows.

Richardson had the great advantage of being one of a real family circle.

He was the eldest of a large family, the heads of which feared God, and tried to train their children to become honest men and women.

How far they had succeeded with Dick, or—to give him his real Christian name, now we have him at home—with Basil, the reader may have already formed an opinion. He had his faults—what boy hasn't?—and he wasn't specially clever. But he had pluck and hope, and resolution, and without being hopelessly conceited, had confidence enough in himself to carry him through most things.

"Don't be in too great a hurry to choose your friends, my boy," said his father, as the two walked up and down the London platform. "You'll find plenty ready enough, but give them a week or two before you swear eternal friendship with any of them."

Dick thought this rather strange advice, and got out of it by saying—

"Oh, I shall have Georgie Heathcote, you know. I shan't much care about the other fellows."

"Don't be too sure. And, remember this, my boy, be specially on your guard with any of them that flatter you. They'll soon find out your weak point and that's where they'll have you."

Dick certainly considered this a little strong even for a parent. But somehow the advice stuck, for all that, and he remembered it afterwards.

"As to other matters," said the father, "your mother, I know, has spoken for us both. Be honest to everybody, most of all yourself, and remember a boy can fear God without being a prig— Ah, here's the train."

It was a dismal farewell, that between father and son, when the moment of parting really came. Neither of them had expected it would be so hard, and when at last the whistle blew, and their hands parted, both were thankful the train slipped swiftly from the station and turned a corner at once.

After the bustle and excitement of the last few days, Dick found the loneliness of the empty carriage decidedly unpleasant, and for a short time after leaving town, was nearer moping than he had ever been before.

It would be an hour before the train reached X—, where Heathcote would get in. It would be all right then, but meanwhile he wished he had something to do.

So he fell to devouring the provisions his mother and sisters had put up for his special benefit, and felt in decidedly better heart when the meal was done.

Then he hauled down his hat-box, and tried on his new "pot," and felt still more soothed.

Then he extricated his new dressing-case from his travelling-bag, and examined, with increasing comfort, each several weapon it contained, until the discovery of a razor in an unsuspected corner completed his good cheer, and he began to whistle.

In the midst of this occupation the train pulled up, and Heathcote, with *his* hat-box and bag invaded the carriage.

"Hallo, old man," said Dick with a nod, "you've turned up, then? Look here, isn't this a stunning turnout? Don't go sitting down on my razor, I say."

"Excuse me a second," said Heathcote, putting down his traps and turning to the window, "grandma's here, and I've got to say good-bye."

"Good-bye, grandma," added the dutiful youth, holding out his hand to a venerable lady who stood by the window.

"Good-bye, Georgie. Give me a kiss, my dear boy."

Georgie didn't like kissing in public, especially when the public consisted of Dick. And, yet, he couldn't well get out of it. So he hurried through the operation as quickly as possible, and stood with his duty towards his relative and his interest towards the razor, wondering why the train didn't start.

It started at last, and after a few random flickings of his handkerchief out of the window, he was able to devote his entire attention to his friend's cutlery.

One exhibition provoked another. Heathcote's "pot" was produced and critically compared with Dick's. He had no dressing-case, certainly, but he had a silver watch and a steel chain, also a pocket inkpot, and a railway key. And by the way, he thought, the sooner that railway key was brought into play the better.

By its aid they successfully resisted invasion at the different stations as they went along, until at length Heathcote's watch told them that the next station would be Templeton. Whereat they became grave and packed up their bags, and looked rather wistfully out of the window.

"Father says," remarked Dick, "only the new boys go up to-day. The rest come to-morrow."

"Rather a good job," said Heathcote.

A long silence followed.

"Think there'll be any one to meet us?" said Dick. "Don't know. I wish Coote was to be there too."

Another pause.

"I expect they'll be jolly enough fellows," said Dick.

"Oh yes. They don't bully now in schools, I believe."

"No; they say it's going out. Perhaps it's as well."

"We shall be pretty well used to the place by to-morrow, I fancy."

"Yes. It'll be rather nice to see them all turn up."

"I expect, you know, they'll have such a lot to do, they won't bother about new fellows. I know I shouldn't."

"They might about the awful green ones, perhaps. Ha, ha! Wouldn't it be fun if old Coote was here!"

"Yes, poor old Coote! You know I'm half sorry to leave Mountjoy. It was a jolly old school, wasn't it?"

The shrieking of the whistle and the grinding of the brake put an end to further conversation for the present.

As they alighted, each with his hat-box and bag and umbrella, and stood on the platform, they felt moved by a sincere affection for the carriage they were leaving. Indeed, there is no saying what little encouragement would not have sufficed to send them back into its hospitable shelter.

"Here you are, sir—this way for the school—this cab, sir!"—cried half a dozen cabmen, darting whip in hand upon our heroes, as they stood looking about them.

"Don't you go along with them," said one confidentially. "They'll charge you half-a-crown. Come along, young gentlemen, I'll take you for two bob."

"Go on. You think the young gentlemen are greenhorns. No fear. They know what's what. They ain't agoin' to be *seen* drivin' up the Quad in a Noah's Ark like that. Come along, young gents; leave him for the milksops. The like of you rides in a hansom, I know."

Of course, this artful student of juvenile nature carried the day, and there was great cheering and crowing and chaffing, when the hansom, with the two trunks on the top, and the two anxious faces inside, peering over the top of their hat-boxes and bags rattled triumphantly out of the station.

As Templeton school was barely three minutes' drive from the station, there was very little leisure either for conversation or the recovery of their composure, before the gallant steed was clattering over the cobbles of the great Quadrangle.

They pulled up at a door which appeared to belong to a bell of imposing magnitude, which the cabman, alighting, proceeded to pull with an energy that awoke the echoes of that solemn square, and made our two heroes draw their breath short and sharp.

"Hop out, young gentlemen," said the cabman, helping his passengers and their luggage out. "It's a busy time, and I'm in a hurry. A shilling each, and sixpence a piece for the traps; that's two and three makes five, and leave the driver to you."

Considering the distance they had come, it seemed rather a long price, and Heathcote ventured very mildly to ask—

"The other man at the station said two shillings."

"Bah!" said the cabman in tones of unfeigned disgust, "you are green ones after all! He'd have charged a bob a piece for the traps, and landed you up to eight bob, and stood no nonsense too about it. Come, settle up, young gentlemen, please. The Templeton boys I'm used to always fork out like gentlemen."

Dick took out his purse, and produced five-and-sixpence, which he gave the driver, just as the door opened and the school matron presented herself.

"Is that your cab?" said she, pointing to the receding hansom.

"Yes, ma'am."

"How much did he charge you?"

"Five shillings, ma'am."

The lady uttered an exclamation of mingled wrath and contempt. "It's double his right fare. Run quick, and you'll catch him."

Heathcote started to run, shouting meekly, and waving his hand to the man to stop.

But the man good-humouredly declined the invitation, raising his hat gallantly to the lady, and putting his tongue into his cheek, as he touched the horse up into a trot, and rattled out of the square.

Heathcote returned rather sheepishly, and the two friends followed the lady indoors feeling that their entry into Templeton had been anything but triumphant.

"The idea!" said the matron, partly to herself and partly to the boys, "of his landing you and all your luggage on the pavement like that, and then going off, before I came. He knew well enough I should have seen he only got his right fare. The wretch!"

The boys did not know at the time, but they discovered it afterwards, that Mrs Partlett, the matron, had a standing feud with all the cabmen of Templeton, whose delight it was to enjoy themselves at her expense—a pastime they could not more effectively achieve than by fleecing her young charges, so to speak, under her very nose.

"Now," said she, when presently she had recovered her equanimity, "if you'll unlock these things, you can go and take a walk round the Quadrangle and look about you, while I unpack. The bell will ring for new boys' tea in half an hour."

They obeyed, and took a melancholy, but interested stroll round the great court. They read all the Latin mottoes, and were horrified to find one or two which they could not translate.

Fancy a Templeton boy not being able to understand his own mottoes!

They read the names on the different masters' doors; and dwelt with special reverence on the door-plate of Mr Westover, in whose house they were to reside. They deciphered the carvings on the great gate, and shuddered as they saw the name of one "Joe Bolt" cut rude and deep across the forehead of the cherub who stood sentinel at the chapel portal.

All was wonder in that strange walk. The wonder of untasted proprietorship. It was *their* school, *their* quadrangle, *their* chapel, *their* elm-trees; and yet they scarcely liked to inspect them too closely, or behave themselves towards them too familiarly.

One or two boys were taking solitary strolls, like themselves. They were new boys too—nearly all of them afflicted with the same uneasiness, some more, some less.

It was amusing to see the way these new boys held themselves one to another as they crossed and passed one another in that afternoon's promenade. There was no falling into one another's arms in bursts of mutual sympathy. There was no forced gaiety and indifference, as though one would say "I don't think much of the place after all." No. With blunt English pride, each boy bridled up a bit as a stranger drew near, and looked straight in front of him, till the coast was clear.

At length the bell above the matron's door began to toll, and there was a general movement among the stragglers in its direction.

About twenty boys, mostly of our heroes' age, assembled in the tea room. Their small band looked almost lost in that great hall, as they clustered, of one accord, for warmth and comfort, at one end of the long table.

The matron entered and said grace, and then proceeded to pour out tea for her hungry family, while the boys themselves, at her injunction, passed round the bread-and-butter and eggs.

A meal is one of the most civilising institutions going; and Dick, after two cups of Templeton tea, and several cubic inches of Templeton bread-and-butter, felt amiably inclined towards his left-hand neighbour, a little timorous-looking boy, who blushed when anybody looked at him, and nearly fainted when he heard his own voice answering Mrs Partlett's enquiry whether he wanted another cup.

Apart from a friendly motive, it seemed to Dick it would be good practice to begin talking to a youth of this unalarming aspect. He therefore enquired, "Are you a new boy?"

The boy started to hear himself addressed; then looking shyly up in the speaker's face, and divining that no mischief lurked there, he replied—

"Yes."

Dick took another gulp of tea, and continued, "Where do you live—in London?"

"No—I live in Devonshire."

Dick returned to his meal again, and exchanged some sentences with Heathcote before he resumed.

"What school were you at before?"

"I wasn't at any—I had lessons at home."

"A tutor?"

The boy blushed very much, and looked appealingly at Dick, as though to beg him to receive the disclosure he was about to make kindly.

"No—my mother taught me."

Dick did receive it kindly. That is, he didn't laugh. He felt sorry for the boy and what was in store for him when the news got abroad. He also felt much less reserved in continuing the conversation.

"Heathcote here and I were at Mountjoy; so we're pretty well used to kicking about," said he, patronisingly. "I suppose you didn't go in for the entrance exam, then?"

"Yes, I did," said the boy.

"Poor chap," thought Dick, "fancy a fellow who's never left his mammy's apron-strings going in for an exam. How did you get on?" he added, turning to his companion.

"Pretty well, I think," said the boy shyly.

"I was twenty-first out of thirty-six," said Dick, "and Heathcote here was fifteenth—where were you?"

Again the boy made a mute appeal for toleration, as he replied, "I was first."

Dick put down his cup, and stared at him.

"Go on!" said he.

"It was down on the list so," said the boy with an apologetic air. "They sent one with the names printed."

Dick made a desperate onslaught on the bread-and-butter, regarding his neighbour out of the corners of his eyes from time to time, quite at a loss to make him out.

"How old are you?" he demanded presently.

"Thirteen."

"What's your name?"

"Bertie Aspinall."

"Whose house are you going to live in?"

"Mr Westover's."

"Oh!" said Dick, abruptly ending the conversation, and turning round towards Heathcote.

In due time the meal was over, and the boys were told they could do as they liked for the next hour, until the matron was at leisure to show them their quarters.

So for another hour the promenade in the Quadrangle was resumed. Not so dismally, however, as before. The tea had broken the ice wonderfully, and instead of the studied avoidance of the afternoon, one group and another fell now to comparing notes, and rehearsing the legends they had heard of Templeton and its inmates. And gradually a fellow-feeling made every one wondrous kind, and the little army of twenty in the prospect of to-morrow's battles, drew together in bonds of self-defence, and felt all very like brothers.

Aspinall, however, who knew no one, and had not dared to join himself to any of the groups, paced in solitude at a distance, hoping for nothing better than that he might escape notice and be left to himself. But Dick, whose interest in him had become very decided, found him out before long and, much to his terror, insisted in introducing him to Heathcote and attaching him to their party.

"There's nothing to be in a funk about, young 'un," said he. "I know I don't mean to funk it, whatever they do to me."

"I'll back you up, old man, all I can," said Heathcote.

"I expect it's far the best way not to kick out, but just go through with it," said Dick. "That's what my father says, and he had a pretty rough time of it, he said, at first."

"Oh, *yes*; I'm sure it's all the worse for a fellow if he funks or gets out of temper."

All this was very alarming talk for the timorous small boy to overhear, and he longed, a hundred times, to be safe back in Devonshire.

"I'm afraid," he faltered. "I know—I shall be a coward."

"Don't be a young ass," said Dick. "Heathcote and I will back you up all we can, won't we, Georgie?"

"Rather," said Heathcote.

"If you do, it won't be half so bad," said the boy, brightening up a bit; "it's dreadful to be a coward."

"Well, why are you one?" said Dick. "No one's obliged to be one."

"I suppose I can't help it. I try hard."

"There goes the bell. I suppose that's for us to go in," said Dick, as the summons once more sounded.

They found the matron with a list in her hand, which she proceeded to call over, bidding each boy answer to his name. The first twelve were the new boys of Westover's house, and they included our two heroes and Aspinall, who were forthwith marched, together with their night apparel, across the court to their new quarters.

Here they were received by another matron, who presided over the wardrobes of the youth of Westover's, and by her they were escorted to one of the dormitories, where, for that night at any rate, they were to be permitted to sleep in the comfort of one another's society.

"New boys are to call on the Doctor after breakfast in the morning," announced she. "Breakfast at eight, and no morning chapel. Good-night!"

It was not long before the dormitory was silent. One by one, the tired boys dropped off, most of them with heavy hearts as they thought of the morrow.

Among the last was Dick, who, as he lay awake and went over, in his mind, the experiences of the day, was startled by what sounded very like a sob in the bed next to his.

He had half a mind to get up and go and say something to the dismal little Devonshire boy.

But on second thoughts he thought the kindest thing would be to let the poor fellow have his cry out, so he turned over and tried not to hear it; and while trying he fell asleep.

Chapter Four
How our heroes are put through their paces

"The Assyrian came down like a wolf on the fold" early next day. The twenty innocent lambs whom, in the last chapter, we left sweetly folded in slumber had barely had time to arise and comb their hair when the advance-guard of the hungry tyrant appeared in their midst.

This was no other than a truck-load of trunks, portmanteaux, bags and hat-boxes sent up from the station, the owners of which, so the alarming rumour spread, were on the road.

It was an agitated meal our heroes partook of with the spectacle of that truck before their eyes, and many an anxious ear was pricked for the first sound of the approaching horde.

But the horde, being aware that nothing was expected of it till mid-day, by no means saw the fun of surrendering its liberty at 10 o'clock, and went down to bathe in the harbour on the way up, so that the fate which impended was kept for two good hours in suspense.

Meanwhile, the interview with the Doctor was accomplished. It was not very alarming. Your new boy would sooner face twenty doctors than one hero of the middle Fifth. The head master asked a few kindly questions of each boy, and, so to speak, took stock of him before adding his name formally to the school list. He also added a few words of advice to the company generally, and enlightened them as to a few of the chief school rules. The others, he said, they would learn soon enough.

Whereat they all said, "Thank you, sir," and retired.

Dick and Heathcote, with young Aspinall in tow, walked back to Westover's house together, and were nearly half-way there, when Aspinall suddenly clutched Dick's arm and whispered—

"There's one!"

They all stood still and gazed as if it was a spectre, not a human being, they expected.

What they really did see was a rather nice-looking boy of sixteen or seventeen lounging in at the great gateway, looking about him with a familiar air, and apparently bending his steps straight for Westover's.

It was an awkward situation for our three new boys. Every step brought them nearer under the observation of the "Assyrian," and at every step they felt more awkward and abashed.

Dick did his best to put on a little swagger. He stuck one hand in his pocket, and twitched his hat a trifle on one side. Heathcote, too, instinctively let slip his jacket button so as to betray his watch-chain, and laughed rather loudly at something which nobody said. Poor young Aspinall attempted no such demonstration, but slipped under the lee of his protectors, and wondered what would become of him.

The old boy and the new foregathered just at the door of Westover's, and it was not till they actually stood face to face that the former gave any sign of being aware of the presence of the trio. He then honoured them with a casual survey as they stood back to let him enter first.

"New kids?" he asked.

"Yes."

"Westover's?"

"Yes."

The hero grunted and passed in, and they heard him shouting to the matron to ask if his traps had come from the station, and whether anybody had come yet.

Anybody come! He didn't count them, that was plain.

Not knowing exactly what to do, they determined on another walk round the Quad, preferring to be reconnoitred by the enemy in the open, and not indoors—possibly in a corner.

The enemy reconnoitred in force. After the first arrival, boys dropped in in twos and threes, in cabs, in omnibuses, in high spirits, in low spirits. The old square began to get lively. The echoes which had slept soundly for the past fortnight woke up suddenly, and the rooks in the elms began to grow uneasy, and summoned a cabinet council to discuss what was going on in the lower world.

"Hallo, Duff, old man," cried one boy near to our heroes, as he caught sight of a chum across the square. "Seen Raggles?"

"Yes; he's got a cargo down. He's asked me."

"Tell him I'm up, will you?"

"What's a cargo?" asked Heathcote, as the speaker went past.

"Goodness knows," said Dick—"perhaps it's a crib."

"My brother Will used to call a hamper a cargo," said Aspinall.

"Humph," said Dick, who never liked to be corrected, "there's something in that."

"I hope there is," said Heathcote.

It said a great deal for the solemnity of the occasion that Dick did not at once proceed to administer condign punishment. He took note of the offence, though, and punished the offender quietly in bed some days after. Just at the present moment, had he been inclined to square accounts, he had no leisure; for a sudden cry of "Dredger!" was raised, whereat they noticed a number of boys step off the pavement on to the grass. Before they could conjecture what this sudden manoeuvre might mean, a rush of steps arose behind, and next moment they were caught up in the toils of a net constructed of towels knotted together, stretching across the path, and held at each end by two swift runners who swept them along at a headlong pace, catching up a shoal of stray fish on the way until even the stalwart dredgers were compelled, from the very weight of their "take," to slacken speed.

A crowd collected to witness the emptying of the net. One by one the trembling small fry were grabbed and passed round to answer a string of questions such as—

"What's your name?"

"Are you most like your father or your mother?"

"Who's your hatter?"

"Can you swim?"

"Who was the father of Zebedee's children?"

"Are you a Radical or a Tory?"

All of which questions each luckless catechumen was required to answer truly, and in a loud, distinct voice, amid the most embarrassing cheers and jeers and hootings of the audience.

Dick got through his fairly well till he came to the political question, when he made the great mistake of saying he didn't know whether he was a Radical or a Tory. For, as he might have expected, every one was down on him, and he was sent forth a marked man to make up his mind on the question.

Heathcote, whose sorrow it was to be separated from his friend in the landing of the catch, was less lucky. He professed himself like his mother, which was greatly against him. His hatter also was a country artist instead of a Londoner, and that he discovered was an extremely grave offence. And as for his politics, he made a greater mistake even than Dick, for he professed himself imbued with opinions "between the two," an announcement which brought down a torrent of abuse and scorn, mingled with cries of "kick him for a half-and-half prig!" an observation which Heathcote was very sorry indeed to hear.

As the reader may guess, poor young Aspinall had a very bad time of it. He began to cry as soon as the first question was propounded. But this demonstration failed to shelter him. A general hiss greeted the sound of his whimper, and cries of, "Where's his bottle?"

"Meow!"

"Hush-a-bye baby!" His ruthless tyrants, who knew no distinction between the tears of a crocodile and the tears of a terrified child, made him go through his catechism to the bitter end. They howled with delight when they heard him call himself Bertie, and paused in dead silence to hear him say whether he was like "papa or mamma" — "or nurse?" as some one suggested. He took refuge in tears again, with the result that his inquisitors were more than ever determined to get their answer.

"Hang it, you young ass," said one boy, whom the child, even in his flutter and misery, recognised as the boy who had accosted them at the door of Westover's that morning, "can't you answer without blubbering like that? Nobody's going to eat you up."

This friendly admonition served to set the boy on his feet, and he stammered out, "Mother."

"You weren't asked if you were like your mother," shouted some one, "are you most like 'papa or mamma?'"

"Mamma," faltered the boy. Whereat there was great jubilation, as there was also when he described his hatter as *Mr.* Smith of Totnes.

"Can you swim?"

"N–no, I'm afraid not."

"That's a pity, with the lot you blubber. You'll get drowned some day."

Terrific cheers greeted this sally, in the midst of which the boy was almost forgotten.

But the political test remained.

"Now, Bertie dear, are you a Radical or a Tory?" he was asked.

The boy took a deep breath, and said—

"I'm a Radical."

At which straightforward and unlooked-for reply there were great cheers and counter-cheers, in the midst of which the scared little Radical was hustled down from his perch and sent flying to join his friends, and calm the fluttering of his poor little heart.

It being evidently unsafe to remain longer in the Quadrangle, the dejected trio betook themselves with many misgivings, to their house.

Westover's presented a striking contrast to the quiet scene of yesterday evening. It being still a quarter to twelve, and term not being supposed to commence till mid-day, the short interval of freedom from school rules was being made use of to the best advantage.

The matron, shouted at and besieged on all sides, already stood at bay, with her hands to her ears, having abandoned any attempt to do anything for anybody. The house porter was in a similar condition of strike. He had once been knocked completely over by rival claimants on his assistance, and he had several times been nearly pulled limb from limb by disappointed employers. He, therefore, stood with his back to the wall and his arms folded, waiting till the storm should blow itself out.

Upstairs, in the studies, riot scarcely less exuberant was taking place. Bosom friends, reunited after three weeks' separation, celebrated their reunion with paeans of jubilation and war-whoops of triumph. "Cargoes" were being unladen here; Liddell-and-Scott was officiating as a cricket ball there; a siege was going on round this door, and a hand-to-hand scrimmage between the posts of that. A few of the placid ones were quietly unpacking in the midst of the Babel, and one or two were actually writing home.

Our heroes, fancying the looks neither of the matron's hall nor of the lobby upstairs, deemed it prudent to retreat as quickly as possible to the junior schoolroom, there to await, in the calm atmosphere of expectant scholarship, the ringing of the twelve o'clock bell.

Has the reader ever visited that famous resort of youth, the Zoo? Has he stood on that terrace five minutes before dinner-time and listened to the deep-mouthed growl of the lion, the barking of the wolf, the shriek of the hyaena, as they pace their cages and await their meal? Then, turning on his heel, has he quitted that stately scene and pushed back the door of the monkey house?

Even so it was with our heroes. The junior schoolroom was as the matron's hall and the studies thrown into one.—At first, to the untutored eyes of the visitors, it looked like a surging sea of unkempt heads and waving elbows; then, as their vision grew accustomed to the scene, they beheld faces and legs and boots; then, amid the general din, they distinguished voices, and perceived that the sea was made up of human beings.

At the which they would fain have retreated; but, as old Virgil says— and we won't insult our readers by translating the verses—

"Facilis descensus Averni, Sed revocare gradum Hoc opus, hic labor est."

Their retreat was cut off before they were well in the room, and, amid loud cries of "New kids!" "Bertie!" "Scrunch!" they were escorted to the nearest form, where they forthwith received a most warm and pressing welcome into their new quarters. The top boy of the form, in his emotion, planted his feet against the wall and began to push inwards. The bottom boy, equally overcome, planted his feet in the hollow of a desk and also pushed inwards. Every one else, in fellow-feeling, pushed inwards too, except our heroes, who, being in the exact centre, remained passive recipients of their schoolfellows' welcome until the line showed signs of rising up at the point where Aspinall's white face pointed the middle; whereupon the bottom boy considerately let go with his feet, and the occupants of the form were poured like water on the floor.

After being thus welcomed on some half-dozen forms, our heroes began to feel that even good fellowship may pall, and were glad, decidedly glad, to hear the great bell beginning to sound forth.

School that morning was rather a farce; the master was not in the humour for it, nor were the boys. After calling over names and announcing the subjects which would engage the attention of the different classes, and reading over, in case any one had forgotten them, the rules of Westover's house, the class was dismissed for the present, all except the new boys being permitted to go out into the court or playing-fields till dinner.

It was a welcome relief to our new boys to find themselves together once more with the enemy beyond reach.

Their ranks showed signs of severe conflict. One boy, who had rashly worn a light blue necktie in the morning, wore no necktie now; Heathcote's jacket was burst under the arm; Dick bore no scars in his raiment, but his nose was rather on one side and his face was rather grimy; Aspinall was white and hot, and the "skeery" look about his eyes proclaimed he had had almost enough for one day.

After dinner, at which our heroes rejoiced to find "the Assyrians" had something more serious to do than to heed them, Templeton went out into the fields to air itself. There was nothing special doing. A few enthusiastic athletes had donned their flannels, and were taking practice trots round the half-mile path. Another lot were kicking about a football in an aimless way. Others were passing round a cricket ball at long range. But most were loafing, apparently undecided what to turn themselves to thus early in the term.

One or two of the Fifth, however, appeared to have some business on hand, in which, much to their surprise, our new boys found they were concerned.

The senior whose arrival they had witnessed in the morning came up to where they were, and said:

"You're all three new boys, aren't you?"

"Yes," they replied.

"Well, go up to the flag-staff there, and wait for me."

With much inward trepidation they obeyed, wondering what was to happen.

Swinstead, for that was the name of the Fifth-form fellow, continued his tour of the field, accosting all the new boys in turn, and giving them the same order.

At length, the long-suffering twenty clustered round the flag-staff, and awaited their fate.

It was simple enough. Every new boy was expected to race on his first day at Templeton, and that was what was expected of them now.

"Let's have your names—look sharp," said one Fifth-form fellow, with a pencil and paper in his hand, who seemed to look upon the affair as rather a bore. "Come on. Sing out one at a time."

They did sing out one at a time.

"Twenty of them," said the senior, running down his list. "Four fives, I suppose?"

"Yes," said Swinstead. "Clear the course, somebody, and call the fellows."

So the course was cleared, and proclamation made that the new boys were about to race. Whereat Templeton lined the quarter-mile track; and showed a languid interest in the contest. Swinstead called over the first five names on his list.

"Take off your coats and waistcoats," said he.

They obeyed. Dick, who was not in the first heat, took charge of Heathcote's garments, and secretly bade him "put it on."

"Toe the line," said Swinstead. "Are you ready? Off!"

They started. It was a straggling procession. Two of the boys could scarcely use their legs, and of the other three Heathcote was the only one who showed any pace, and, greatly to Dick's delight, came in easily first.

Dick's turn came in the second round, and he, greatly to Heathcote's delight, won in a canter.

In the fourth heat Aspinall ran; but he, poor fellow, could scarcely struggle on to the end, and had literally to be driven the last fifty yards. For no new boy was allowed to shirk his race.

Templeton evinced a more decided interest in the final round. It had looked on as a matter of duty on the trial heats; but it got a trifle excited over the final. The winner of the fourth round, the youth who had been robbed of his light blue tie, commanded the most general favour. Swinstead on the other hand secretly fancied Dick, and one or two others were divided between Heathcote and the winner of the third round.

"Keep your elbows in, and don't look round so much," whispered Swinstead to Dick, as the four champions toed the line.

Dick nodded gratefully for the advice.

"Now then. Are you ready?

"Go!" cried the starter.

The hero of the blue tie led off amid great jubilation among the sportsmen. But Swinstead, who trotted beside the race, still preferred Dick, and liked the way he kept up to the leader's heels in the first hundred yards. Heathcote, in his turn, kept well up to Dick, and had nothing to fear from the other man.

"Pretty race," said some one.

"Good action number two," replied another.

"Swinstead fancies him, and he knows what's what."

"I should have said number three, myself."

Two hundred yards were done, and scarcely an inch had the position of the three runners altered.

Then Swinstead called.

"Now then, young 'un."

Dick knew the call was meant for him, and his spirit rose within him. He "waited on his man," as they say, and before the next hundred yards were done he was abreast, with Heathcote close on the heels of both.

Frantic were the cries of the sportsmen to their man. But his face was red, and his mouth was open.

"He's done!" was the cry of the disgusted knowing ones. And the knowing ones were right. Dick walked away, as fresh as a daisy, in the last hundred yards, while Heathcote blowing hard stepped up abreast of the favourite. It was a close run for second honours; but the Mountjoy boy stuck to it, and staggered up a neck in front, with ten clear yards between him and the heels of the victorious Dick.

Chapter Five
How Heathcote nearly catches cold

Dick felt decidedly pleased with himself, as he walked back arm-in-arm with Heathcote, after his victory.

He felt that he had a right to hold up his head in Templeton already, and although he still experienced some difficulty in managing his hands and keeping down his blushes when he met one of the Fifth, he felt decidedly fortified against the inquisitive glances of the juniors.

In fact, in the benevolence of his heart, he felt so anxious lest any of these young aspirants to a view of the hero who had won the new boys' race should be disappointed, that he prolonged his walk, and made a circuit of the great square with his friend, so as to give every one a fair chance.

At tea, to which Templeton trooped in ravenously after their first afternoon's blow in the open air, he sat with an interesting expression of langour on his face, enduring the scrutiny to which he was treated with an air of charming unconsciousness, from which any one might suppose he harboured not the slightest desire to hear what Swinstead was saying to his neighbour, as they both looked his way. It was a pity he could not hear it.

"Look at that young prig," said Swinstead's neighbour. "He can't get over it. It's gone to his head."

"Young ass!" said Swinstead; "ran well too."

"It would be a good turn to take him down a peg."

"What's the use? He'll come down soon enough."

For all that, the two friends could not resist the temptation, when, after tea, they caught sight of Dick and his chum going out into the Quad, of beckoning to the former to come to them.

"Those fellows want me," said Dick to his friend, in a tone as much as to say, "I'm so used to holding familiar converse with the Fifth that it's really almost beginning to be a grind. But I don't like to disappoint them this time."

"Well, how do you feel?" said Swinstead.

"Oh, all right," replied Dick, showing unmistakeable signs of intoxication.

"Capital run you made," said the other. "Middling," said Dick, deprecatingly. "I hadn't my shoes, that makes a difference."

"It does," said the two elders.

"Rather a nice turf track you've got," said the boy presently, by way of filling up an awkward gap.

"Glad you like it. Some of the fellows growl at it; but we'll tell them you think it good."

It was rather an anxious moment to see how the fish would take it. But he swallowed it, hook and all.

"We used to run a good deal at our old school, you know," said he. "Some of us, that is."

"Ah, you're just the man we want for the Harriers. They're badly off for a whipper-in; and we had to stop hunting all last term because we hadn't got one."

"Oh!" said Dick.

"Yes. But it'll be all right if you'll take it—won't it be, Birket?"

"Rather!" said Birket. "He'd be a brick if he did."

"I don't mind trying," said Dick modestly.

"Will you really? Thanks, awfully! You know Cresswell? No, by the way, he's not here yet. He's in the Sixth, and has been acting as whipper-in till we got a proper chap. He'll be here in the morning. Any one will tell you where he hangs out. He'll bless you, I can tell you, for taking the job out of his hands. You never saw the pace he goes at when he tries to run, eh, Birket?"

"Rather not," said Birket. "It's a regular joke. A snail's nothing to him."

"How has he managed to whip in?" asked Dick, rather amused at the idea of this Sixth-form snail.

"Bless you, we've had no runs lately, that's why. But we shall make up now you've come."

Dick heartily wished he *had* run in his shoes that afternoon. He was sure he could have done the distance two or even three seconds better if he had.

"If you'll really go in for it," said Birket, "go to him early to-morrow, and tell him who you are; and say you are going to act as whipper-in, and that you have arranged it all with us."

Dick looked a little concerned.

"Hadn't you better come with me?" he asked, "I don't know him."

"We shall be in class. But he'll know if you mention our names. Say we sent you, and that you won the new boys' race. Do you twig?"

"All right," said Dick, beginning to feel he had something really big on hand.

"You're a young trump," said Birket, "and, I say don't forget to ask him to give you the whip. We might manage a run to-morrow. Good-night. Glad you've come to Templeton."

"Look here, by the way," said Swinstead, as they parted, "don't say anything about it to anybody. There's such a lot of jealousy over these things. Best to get it all settled first. Don't you think so?"

"Yes," said Dick, feeling a good deal bewildered, and doubtful whether after all he had not been foolish in undertaking so important a task.

He returned to his chum in an abstracted frame of mind. He had certainly expected his achievement that afternoon would give him a "footing" in Templeton, but in his wildest dreams he had not supposed it would give him such a lift as this.

Whipper-in of the Templeton Harriers was rapid promotion for a new boy on his first day. But then, he reflected, if they really were hard up for a fellow to take the office, it would be rather ungracious to refuse it.

"What did they want you for?" asked Heathcote.

"Oh, talking about the race, don't you know, and that sort of thing," said Dick, equivocally.

"Did they say anything about me?"

"Not a word, old man."

Whereat Heathcote turned a little crusty, and wondered that ten yards in a quarter of a mile should make such a difference.

Dick was bursting to tell him all about it, and made matters far worse by betraying that he had a secret, which he could on no account impart.

"You'll know to-morrow, most likely," said he. "I'm awfully sorry they made me promise to keep it close. But I'll tell you first of all when its settled; and I may be able to give you a leg up before long."

Heathcote said he did not want a leg up; and feeling decidedly out of humour, made some excuse to go indoors and hunt up young Aspinall.

On his way he encountered a junior, next to whom he had sat at dinner, and with whom he had then exchanged a few words.

"Where are you going?" demanded that youthful warrior.

"Indoors," said Heathcote.

"No, you aren't," replied the bravo, standing like a wolf across the way.

It was an awkward position for a pacific boy like Heathcote, who mildly enquired—

"Why not?"

"Because you cheeked me," replied the wolf.

"How? I didn't mean to," replied the lamb.

"That'll do. You've got to apologise."

"Apologise! What for?"

"Speaking to me at dinner-time."

The blood of the Heathcotes began to tingle.

"Suppose I don't apologise?" asked he.

"You'll be sorry for it."

"What will you do?"

"Lick you."

"Then," said Heathcote, mildly, "you'd better begin."

The youthful champion evidently was not prepared for this cordial invitation, and looked anything but pleased to hear it.

"Well, why don't you begin?" said Heathcote, following up his advantage.

"Because," said the boy, looking rather uncomfortably around him, "I wouldn't dirty my fingers on such a beast."

Now if Heathcote had been a man of the world he would have divined that the present was a rare opportunity for catching his bumptious young friend by the ear, and making him carry out his threat then and there. But, being a simple-minded new boy, unlearned in the ways of the world, he merely said "Pooh!" and walked on, leaving his assailant in possession of the field, calling out "coward!" and "sneak!" after him till he was out of sight.

He was rather sorry afterwards for his mistake, as it turned out he might have been much more profitably and pleasantly employed outside than in.

Aspinall, whom he had come to look after, was nowhere visible, and, feeling somewhat concerned for his safety, Heathcote ventured to enquire of a junior who was loafing about in the passage, if he knew where the little new fellow was.

"In bed, of course," said the junior, "and I'd advise you not to let yourself be seen, unless you want to get in an awful row," added he solemnly.

"What about?" asked Heathcote.

"Why, not being in bed. My eye! it'll be rather warm for you, I tell you, if any of the Fifth catch you."

"Why, it's only half-past seven?"

"Well, and don't you know the rule about new boys always having to be in bed by seven?" exclaimed the junior in tones of alarm.

"No. I don't believe it is the rule," said Heathcote.

"All right," said the boy, "you needn't believe it unless you like. But don't say you weren't told, that's all," and he walked off, whistling.

Heathcote was perplexed. He suspected a practical joke in everything, and had this junior been a trifle less solemn, he would have had no doubt that this was one. As it was, he was sorry he had offended him, and lost the chance of making quite sure. Dick, he knew, was still out of doors, and he, it was certain, knew nothing about the rule.

But just then a Fifth-form fellow came along, and cut off the retreat.

He eyed the new boy critically as he advanced, and stopped in front of him.

"What's your name?" he demanded.

"Heathcote."

"A new boy?"

"Yes."

"How is it you're not in bed? Do you know the time?"

"Yes," said Heathcote, convinced now that the junior had been right, "but I didn't know—that is—"

"Shut up and don't tell lies," said the Fifth-form boy, severely. "Go to bed instantly, and write me out 200 lines of Virgil before breakfast to-morrow. I've a good mind to send your name up to Westover."

"I'm awfully sorry," began Heathcote; "no one told me—"

"I've told you; and if you don't go at once Westover shall hear of it."

The dormitory, when he reached it, was deserted. Not even Aspinall was there; and for a moment Heathcote began again vaguely to suspect a plot. From this delusion, he was, however, speedily relieved by the appearance of a boy, who followed him into the room, and demanded.

"Look here; what are you up to here?"

"I was—that is, I was told to go to bed," said Heathcote.

"Well, and if you were, what business have you got here? Go to your own den."

"This is where I slept last night," said Heathcote, pointing to the identical bed he had occupied.

"You did! Like your howling cheek."

"Where is my bed room then?" asked Heathcote.

"Why didn't you ask the matron? I'm not going to fag for you. There, in that second door; and take my advice, slip into bed as quick as you can, unless you want one of the Fifth to catch you, and give you a hundred lines."

Heathcote whipped up his night-gown and made precipitately for the door, finally convinced that he was in a fair way of getting into a row very early in his Templeton career.

The door opened into a little room about the size of a small ship's cabin, and here he undressed as quickly as he could, in the fading daylight, and slipped into bed, inwardly congratulating himself that no one had detected him in the act, and that he had a good prospect, contrary to his expectations, of getting to sleep comfortably. The thought of the 200 lines, certainly, was unpleasant. But "sufficient unto the day," thought the philosophic Heathcote. He was far more concerned at the fate of the unsuspecting Dick. What would become of him, poor fellow?

Amid these reflections he fell peacefully asleep. The next thing he was conscious of, in what seemed to him the middle of the night, was the sudden removal of the clothes from the bed, and a figure holding a light, catching him by the arm, and demanding fiercely—

"What do you mean by it?"

His first impulse was to smile at the thought that it was only a dream, but he quickly changed his mind, and sat up with his eyes very wide open as the figure repeated—

"What do you mean by it? Get out of this!"

The speaker was a big boy, whom Heathcote, in the midst of his bewilderment, recognised as having seen at the Fifth-form table in Hall.

"What's the matter?" faltered the new boy.

"The matter! you impudent young beggar. Come, get out of this. I'll teach you to play larks with me. Get out of my bed."

Heathcote promptly obeyed.

"I didn't know—I was told it was where I was to sleep," he said.

"Shut up, and don't tell lies," said the senior, taking off his slipper and passing his hand down the sole of it.

"Really I didn't do it on purpose," pleaded Heathcote. "I was told to do it."

The case was evidently not one for argument. As Heathcote turned round, the silence of the night hour was broken for some moments by the echoes of that slipper-sole.

It was no use objecting—still less resisting. So Heathcote bore it like a man, and occupied his leisure moments during the ceremony in chalking up a long score against his friend the junior.

"Now, make my bed," said the executioner when the transaction was complete.

The boy obeyed in silence—wonderfully warm despite the lightness of his attire. His comfort would have been complete had that junior only been there to help him. The Fifth-form boy insisted on the bed being made from the very beginning—including the turning of the mattress and the shaking of each several sheet and blanket—so that the process was a lengthy one, and, but for the occasional consolations of the slipper, might have become chilly also.

"Now, clear out," said the owner of the apartment.

"Where am I to go?" asked Heathcote, beginning to feel rather forlorn.

"Out of here!" repeated the senior.

"I don't—"

The senior took up the slipper again.

"Please may I take my clothes?" said Heathcote.

"Are you going or not?"

"Please give me my trou—"

He was on the other side of the door before the second syllable came, and the click of the latch told him that after all he might save his breath.

Heathcote was in a predicament. The corridor was dark, and draughty, and he was far from home; what was he to do? "Three courses," as the wise man says, "were open to him." Either he might camp out where he was, and by the aid of door-mats and carpet extemporise a bed till the morning; or he might commence a demonstration against the door from which he had just been ejected till somebody came and saw him into his rights—or, failing his rights, into his trousers; or he might commence a house-to-house canvass, up one side of the corridor and down the other, in hopes of finding either an empty chamber or one tenanted by a friend.

There was a good deal to be said for each, though on the whole he personally inclined to the last course. Indeed he went so far as to grope his way to the end of the passage with a view to starting fair, when a sound of footsteps and a white flutter ahead sent his heart to his mouth, and made him shiver with something more than the evening breeze.

He stood where he was, rooted to the spot, and listened. An awful silence seemed to fall upon the place. Had he hit on the Templeton ghost?— on the disembodied spirit of some luckless martyr to the ferocity of a last century bully? Or, was it an ambuscade prepared for himself? or, was it some companion in—

Yes! there was a sob, and Heathcote's soul rejoiced as he recognised it.

"Is that you, young 'un?" he said in a deep whisper.

The footsteps suddenly ceased, the white flutter stopped, and next moment there rose a shriek in the still night air which made all Westover's jump in its sleep, and opened, as if by magic, half the doors in the long corridor. Aspinall had seen a ghost!

Amid all the airily-clad forms that hovered out to learn the cause of the disturbance, Heathcote felt comforted. His one regret was that he was unable to recognise his friend the junior, in whose debt he was in nocturnal garb; but he recognised Dick to his great delight, and hurriedly explained to him as well as to about fifty other enquirers, the circumstances—that is, so much of them as seemed worth repetition.

Between them they contrived to reassure the terrified Aspinall, who, it turned out, had been the victim of a similar trick to that played on Heathcote.

"Where are you sleeping?" said the latter to Dick.

"The old place. Where ever did you get to?"

"I'll tell you. Has any one got my bed there?"

"No. Come on—here, Aspinall, catch hold—look sharp out of the passage. Are you coming, too, Heathcote?"

To his astonishment, Heathcote darted suddenly from his side and dived in at an open door. Before his friend could guess what he meant, he returned with a bundle of clothes in his arms, and a triumphant smile on his face.

"Hurrah!" said he. "Got 'em at last!"

"Whose are they?" asked Dick.

"Mine, my boy. By Jove, I *am* glad to get them again."

"*Cave* there! Westover!" called some one near him. And, as if by magic, the passage was empty in a moment, our heroes being the last to scuttle into their dormitory, with Aspinall between them.

Dick lay awake for some time that night. He was excited, and considered, on the whole, he had made a fair start at Templeton. He had won the new boys' race, and he was the whipper-in-elect of the Templeton Harriers. Fellows respected him; possibly a good many of them feared him. Certainly, they let him alone.

"For all that," meditated he, "it won't do to get cocked up by it. Father said I was to be on my guard against fellows who flattered me, so I must keep my eyes open, or some one will be trying to make a fool of me. If Cresswell's a nice fellow, I'll have a talk with him to-morrow about young Aspinall, and see if we can't do anything to give him a leg up, poor young beggar. I wonder if I'm an ass to accept the whipping-in so easily? Any how, I suppose I can resign if it's too much grind. Heigho! I'm sleepy."

Chapter Six
How our heroes begin to feel at home

Heathcote awoke early the next morning with his friend the junior seriously on his mind. One or two fellows were already dressing themselves in flannels as he roused himself, amongst others the young hero who had threatened to fight him the evening before.

"Hallo!" said that young gentleman, in a friendly tone, as if nothing but the most cordial courtesies had passed between them, "coming down to bathe?"

"All serene," said Heathcote, not, however, without his suspicions. If any one had told him it was a fine morning, he would, in his present state of mind, have suspected the words as part of a deep-laid scheme to fool him. But, he reflected, he had not much to fear from this mock-heroic junior, and as long as he kept him in sight no great harm could happen.

"Come on, then," said the boy, whose name, by the way, was Gosse; "we shall only just have time to do it before chapel."

"Wait a second, till I tell Dick. He'd like to come, too," said Heathcote.

"What's the use of waking him when he's fagged? Besides, he's got to wash and dress his baby, and give him his bottle, so he wouldn't have time. Aren't you ready?"

"Yes," said Heathcote, flinging himself into his hardly-regained garments.

The "Templeton Tub," as the bathing place was colloquially termed, was a small natural harbour among the rocks at the foot of the cliff on which the school stood. It was a picturesque spot at all times; but this bright spring morning, with the distant headlands lighting up in the rising sunlight, and the blue sea heaving lazily among the rocks as though not yet awake, Heathcote thought it one of the prettiest places he had ever seen.

The "Tub" suited all sorts of bathers. The little timid waders could dip their toes and splash their hair in the shallow basin in-shore. The more advanced could wade out shoulder-deep, and puff and flounder with one foot on the ground and the other up above their heads, and delude the world into the notion they were swimming. For others there was the spring-board, from which to take a header into deep water; and, further out still, the rocks rose in ledges, where practised divers could take the water from any height they liked, from four feet to thirty. Except with leave, no boy was permitted to swim beyond the harbour mouth into the open. But leave was constantly being applied for, and as constantly granted; and perhaps every boy, at some time or other, cast wistful glances at the black buoy bobbing a mile out at sea, and wondered when he, like Pontifex and Mansfield, and other of the Sixth, should be able to wear the image of it on his belt, and call himself a Templeton "shark?"

Heathcote, on his first appearance at the "Tub," acquitted himself creditably. He took a mild header from the spring-board without more than ordinary splashing, and swam across the pool and back in fair style. Gosse, who only went in from the low ledge, and swam half-way across and back, was good enough to give him some very good advice, and promise to make a good swimmer of him in time. Whereat Heathcote looked grateful, and wished Dick had been there to astonish some of them.

One or two of the Fifth, including Swinstead and Birket, arrived as the youngsters were dressing.

"Hallo!" said Swinstead to Heathcote, "you here? Where's your chum?"

"Asleep," said Heathcote, quite pleased to think he should be able to tell Dick he had been having a talk with Swinstead that morning.

"Have you been in?"

"Yes."

"Can you swim?"

"Yes, a little," said Gosse, answering for him. "We're about equal."

Heathcote couldn't stand the barefaced libel meekly.

"Why, you can't swim once across!" he said, scornfully, "and you can't go in off the board!"

The Fifth-form boys laughed.

"Ha, ha!" said Swinstead, "he's letting you have it, Gossy."

"He's telling beastly crams," said Gosse, "and I'll kick him when we get back."

"I'll swim you across the pool and back, first!" said Heathcote.

The seniors were delighted. The new boy's spirit pleased them, and the prospect of taking down the junior pleased them still more.

"That's fair," said Birket. "Come on, strip."

Heathcote was ready in a trice. Gosse looked uncomfortable.

"I'm not going in again," he said; "I've got a cold."

"Yes, you are," replied Birket; "I'll help you."

This threat was quite enough for the discomfited junior, who slowly divested himself of his garments.

"Now then! plenty of room for both of you on the board."

"No," said Gosse; "I've not got any cotton wool for my ears. I don't care about going in off the board unless I have."

"That's soon remedied," said Swinstead, producing some wool from his pocket and proceeding to stuff it into each of the boy's ears.

Poor Gosse was fairly cornered, and took his place on the board beside Heathcote, the picture of discontent and apprehension.

"Now then, once across and back. Are you ready?" said Birket, seating himself beside his friend on a ledge.

"No," said Gosse, looking down at the water and getting off the board.

"Do you funk it?"

"No."

"Then go in! Hurry up, or we'll come and help you!"

"I'd—I'd rather go in from the *edge*," said the boy.

"You funk the board then?"

The boy looked at the board, then at his tyrants, then at the water.

"I suppose I do," said he, sulkily.

"Then put on your clothes and cut it," said Swinstead, scornfully. Then, turning to Heathcote, he shouted. "Now then, young 'un, in you go."

Heathcote plunged. He was nervous, and splashed more, perhaps, than usual, but it was a tolerable header, on the whole, for a new boy, and the spectators were not displeased with the performance or the swim across the pool and back which followed.

"All right," said Swinstead; "stick to it, young un, and turn up regularly. Can your chum swim?"

"Rather!" said Heathcote, taking his head out of the towel. "I wish I could swim as well as he can."

"Humph!" said Swinstead, when presently the two Seniors were left to themselves. "Number Two's modest; Number One's cocky."

"Therefore," said Birket, "Number Two will remain Number Two, and number One will remain Number One."

"Right you are, most learned Plato! but I'm curious to see how Number One gets out of his friendly call on Cresswell. Think he'll cheek it?"

"Yes; and we shan't hear many particulars from him."

Birket was right, as he very often was.

Dick, on waking, was a good deal perplexed, to find his friend absent, and when he heard the reason he was more than perplexed—he was vexed. It wasn't right of Heathcote, or loyal, to take advantage of him in this way, and he should complain of it.

Meanwhile he had plenty to occupy his mind in endeavouring to recover his "baby's" wardrobe, a quest which, as time went on and the chapel bell began to sound, came to be exciting.

However, just as he was about to go to the matron and represent to her the delicate position of affairs, a bundle was thrown in through the ventilator over the door, and fell into the middle of the dormitory floor. Where it came from there was no time to inquire.

Aspinall was hustled into his garments as quickly as possible, and then hustled down the stairs and into chapel just as the bell ceased ringing and the door began to close.

Heathcote was there among the other new boys, looking rather guilty, as well he might. The sight of him, with his dripping locks and clear shining face, interfered a good deal with Dick's attention to the service—almost as much as did the buzz of talk all round him, the open disorder in the stalls opposite, and the look of undisguised horror on Aspinall's face.

As Dick caught sight of that look his own conscience pricked him, and he made a vehement effort to recall his wandering mind and fix it on the words which were being read. He flushed as he saw boys opposite point his way and laugh, with hands clasped in mock devotion, and he felt angry with himself, and young Aspinall, and everybody, for laying him open to the imputation of being a prig.

He glanced again towards Heathcote. Heathcote was standing with his hands in his pockets looking about him. What business had Heathcote to look about him when he (Dick) was standing at attention? Why should Heathcote escape the jeers of mockers, while he (Dick) had to bear the brunt of them? It wasn't fair. And yet he wasn't going to put his hands in his pockets and look about him to give them the triumph of saying they laughed him into it. No!

So Dick stood steadily and reverently all the service, and was observed by not a few as one of the good ones of whom good things might be expected.

When chapel was over fate once more severed him from his chum, and deferred the explanation to which both were looking forward.

The matron kidnapped Master Richardson on his way into the house, in order to call his attention to a serious inconsistency between the number of his shirts in his portmanteau, and the number on the inventory accompanying them, an inconsistency which Dick was unable to throw any light on whatever, except that he supposed it must be a mistake, and it didn't much matter.

It certainly mattered less than the fact that, owing to this delay, he had lost his seat next to Heathcote at breakfast, and had to take his place at the lowest table, where he could not even see his friend.

There was great joking during the meal about the escapade in the lobby last night, the general opinion being that it had been grand sport all round, and that it was lucky the monitors weren't at home at the time.

"Beastly grind," said one youngster—"all of them coming back to-day. A fellow can't turn round but they interfere."

"Are all the Sixth monitors?" asked Dick.

"Rather," replied his neighbour, whom Dick discovered afterwards to be no other than Raggles, the hero of the "cargo," whose fame he had heard the day before.

"What's the name of the captain?"

"Oh, Ponty! He doesn't hurt," said the boy. "It's beasts like Mansfield, and Cresswell, and that lot who come down on you."

Dick would fain have inquired what sort of fellow Cresswell was, but he was too anxious not to let the affair of the whipper-in leak out, and refrained. He asked a few vague questions about the Sixth generally, and gathered from his companion that, with a very few exceptions, they were all "beasts" in school, that one or two of them were rather good at cricket, and swimming, and football, and that the monitorial system at Templeton, and at all other public schools, required revision. From which Dick argued shrewdly that Master Raggles sometimes got into rows.

By the time he had made this discovery the bell rang for first school, and there was a general movement to the door.

The two chums foregathered in the hall.

"Pity you weren't up in time for a bathe," said Heathcote, artfully securing the first word.

"I heard you went. Too much fag getting up so early. I mean to go down in the afternoon, when most of the fellows turn up."

"Swinstead and Birket were there. I wish you'd been there."

"Not worth the grind. You can come with me this afternoon, if you like. Some of the 'sharks' will be down as well."

Heathcote began to discover he had done a foolish thing; and when he found his friend launching the "sharks" at his head in this familiar way he felt it was no use holding out any longer.

"It was awfully low of me not to call you this morning," said he, "but you looked so fast asleep, you know."

"So I was," said Dick, unbending. "I'm glad you didn't rout me up, for I was regularly fagged last night."

"What time will you be going this afternoon?"

"Depends. I've got to see one of the Sixth as soon as he turns up, but that won't take long."

Heathcote retired routed. His friend was too many for him. He (Heathcote) had no one bigger than Swinstead and Birket to impress his friend with. Dick had "sharks," and behind them "one of the Sixth." What was the use of opposing himself to such odds?

"Wait for us, won't you?" was all he could say; and next moment they were at their respective desks, and school had begun.

Dick's quick ears caught the sound of cabs in the quadrangle and the noise of luggage in the hall while school was going on, and his mind became a little anxious as the prospect of his coming interview loomed nearer before him. He hoped Cresswell was a jolly fellow, and that there would be no one else in his study when he went to call upon him. He had carefully studied the geography of his fortress, so he knew exactly where to go without asking any one, which was a blessing.

As soon as class was over he made his way to the matron's room.

"Do you know if Cresswell has come yet, please."

"Yes, what do you want with him?"

"Oh! nothing," said Dick dissembling, "I only wanted to know."

And he removed himself promptly from the reach of further questions.

Little dreaming of the visit with which he was to be so shortly honoured, Cresswell, the fleetest foot and the steadiest head in Templeton, was complacently unpacking his goods and chattels in the privacy of his own study. He wasn't sorry to get back to Templeton, for he was fond of the old place, and the summer term was always the jolliest of the year. There was cricket coming on, and lawn tennis, and the long evening runs, and the early morning dips. And there was plenty of work ahead in the schools too, and the prospect of an exhibition at Midsummer, if only Freckleton gave him the chance.

Altogether the Sixth-form athlete was in a contented frame of mind, as he emptied his portmanteau and tossed his belongings into their respective quarters.

So intent was he on his occupation, that it was a full minute before he became aware of a small boy standing at his open door, and tapping modestly. As he looked up and met the eyes of the already doubtful Dick, both boys inwardly thought, "I rather like that fellow" —a conclusion which, as far as Dick was concerned, made it still more difficult for him to broach the subject of his mission.

Cresswell was still kneeling down, so it was impossible to form an opinion of his legs, but his arms and shoulders certainly did not look like those of a "snail."

"What do you want, youngster?" said Cresswell.

"Oh," said Dick, screwing himself up to the pitch, "Swinstead told me to come to you."

"Oh," said the other, in a tone of great interest, "what about?"

"About the—I mean—something about the—the Harriers," said Dick, suddenly beginning to see things in a new light.

"About the Harriers?" said Cresswell, rising to his feet and lounging up against the mantel-piece, in order to take a good survey of his visitor. "What does Mr Swinstead want to know about the Harriers?"

The sight of the champion there, drawn up to his full height, with power and speed written on every turn of his figure, sent Dick's mind jumping, at one bound, to the truth. What an ass he had been going to make of himself, and what a time he would have had if he hadn't found out the trick in time! As it was, he could not help laughing at the idea of his own ridiculous position, and the narrow escape he had had.

"What are you grinning at?" said Cresswell sharply, not understanding the little burst of merriment in his presence.

Dick recovered himself, and said simply, "They've been trying to make a fool of me. I beg your pardon for bothering you."

"Hold hard!" said Cresswell, as the boy was about to retreat. "It's very likely they have made a fool of you—they're used to hard work. But you're not going to make a fool of me. Come in and tell me all about it."

Dick coloured up crimson, and threw himself on the monitor's mercy.

"You'll think me such an ass," said he, appealingly. "It's really nothing."

"I do think you an ass already," said the senior, "so, out with it."

Whereupon Dick, blushing deeply, told him the whole story in a way which quite captivated the listener by its artlessness.

"They said you were an awful muff, and couldn't run any faster than a snail, you know,"—began he—"and as I had pulled off the new boys' race, they said they'd make me Whipper-in of the Harriers instead of you, and told me to come and tell you so, and ask you to *give* me the whip."

Cresswell laughed in spite of himself.

"Do you really want it?" he asked.

"Not now, thank you."

"I suppose you'd been swaggering after you'd won the race, and they wanted to take the conceit out of you?"

"Yes, I suppose so."

"And have they succeeded?"

"Well—yes," said Dick. "I think they have."

"Then, they've done you a very good turn, my boy, and you'll be grateful to them some day. As for the whip, you can tell them if they'll come here for it, I'll give it to them with pleasure. There goes the dinner bell—cut off, or you'll be late."

"Thanks, Cresswell. I suppose," said the boy, lingering a moment at the door, "you won't be obliged to tell everybody about it?"

"You can do that better than I can," said the Sixth-form boy, laughing.

And Dick felt, as he hurried down to Hall, that he was something more than well out of it. Instead of meeting the fate which his own conceit had prepared, he had secured a friend at court, who, something told him, would stand by him in the coming term. His self-esteem had had a fall, but his self-respect had had a decided lift; for he felt now that he went in and out under inspection, and that Cresswell's good opinion was a distinction by all means to be coveted.

As a token of his improved frame of mind, he made frank confession of the whole story to Heathcote during dinner; and found his friend, as he knew he would be, brimful of sympathy and relief at his narrow escape.

Swinstead and Birket, as they watched their man from their distant table, were decidedly perplexed by his cheerful demeanour, and full of curiosity to learn the history of the interview.

They waylaid him casually in the court that afternoon.

"Well, have you settled it?" said Birket.

"Eh? Oh, yes, it's all right," replied Dick, rather enjoying himself.

"He made no difficulty about it, did he?"

"Not a bit. Jolly as possible."

It was not often that two Fifth-form boys at Templeton felt uncomfortable in the presence of a new junior, but Swinstead and Birket certainly did feel a trifle disconcerted at the coolness of their young victim.

"You told him we sent you?"

"Rather. He was awfully obliged."

"Was he? And did he give you the whip?"

"No, he hadn't got it handy. But I told him he could give it to you two next time he met you—and he's going to."

And to the consternation of his patrons the new boy walked off, whistling sweetly to himself and watching attentively the flight of the rooks round the school tower.

"Old man, we shall have some trouble with Number One," said Swinstead, laughing.

"Yes, we've caught a Tartar for once," said Birket. "You and I may retire into private life for a bit, I fancy."

Chapter Seven
A General Election

The return of the Sixth, our heroes discovered, made a wonderful change in the school life of Templeton. The Fifth, who always made the best use of their two day's authority while they had it, retired almost mysteriously into private life in favour of their betters. All school sports, and gatherings, and riots had to depend no longer upon the sweet will of those who sported, or gathered, or rioted, but on the pleasure of the monitors. The school societies and institutions began to wake up after their holiday, and generally speaking the wheels of Templeton which, during the first two days had bumped noisily over the cobbles, got at last on to the lines, and began to spin round at their accustomed pace.

In no part of the school was this change more felt than among the juniors. They liked being off the line now and then, and they always rebelled when the iron hand of the law picked them up and set them back on the track. It wasn't only that they couldn't run riot, and make Templeton a bear-garden. That was bad enough. But in addition to that, they had to fag for the Sixth, and after a week or two of liberty the return to servitude is always painful.

"You kids," said Raggles, two days after the return of the Sixth, "mind you show up at Den after Elections this evening."

"What is Den, and who are Elections?" asked Dick.

"What, don't you know? Awful green lot of new kids you are. Elections is after tea in the hall, and Den's directly after that."

Raggles was very much affronted, when, after this lucid explanation, Dick again enquired—

"What do you mean by Den and Elections?"

"Look here, what a howling idiot you must be if you've got to be told half a dozen times. I'll spell it for you if you like."

"All serene," said Heathcote. "Two to one you come a cropper over Elections."

"Who do they elect?" asked Dick.

"Why, everybody, of course. The captains of the clubs, and all that. Hang it, you'll be there. What's the use of fagging to tell you?"

"And what about the Den? Who lives in it?"

"Look here! I shall lick you, Richardson, if you go on like that. You green kids are a lot too cheeky."

And the offended envoy went off in a huff, leaving his hearers in a state of excited uncertainty as to the nature of the ceremony to which their company had been invited.

As the reader may like to have a rather more definite explanation than that afforded by Mr Raggles, let him know that unlike most public schools, the school year at Templeton began after the Easter holidays, instead of after the summer holidays. The new boys came up then for the most part (though a few "second chances," as they were called, straggled in in the autumn term), and the various appointments to offices of honour and duty, the inauguration of the clubs, and the apportionment of the fags always formed an interesting feature of the new term. The whole of the business was transacted in a mass meeting of the school, known by the name of "Elections," where, under the solemn auspices of the Sixth, Templeton was invited to pick out its own rulers, and settle its own programme for the ensuing year.

Elections, as a rule, passed off harmoniously, the school acquiescing on most points in the recommendations of the Sixth, and, except on matters of great excitement, rarely venturing to lift up its voice in opposition. The juniors, however, generally contrived to have their fling, usually on the question of fagging, which being a recognised institution at Templeton, formed a standing bone of contention. And, as part of the business of Elections was the solemn drawing of lots for new boys to fill the vacancies caused by removal or promotion, the opportunity generally commended itself as a fit one for some little demonstration.

The Juniors' Den at Templeton, that is, the popular assembly of those youthful Templetonians who had not yet reached the dignity of the Fourth Form, had always been the most radical association in the school. Though they differed amongst themselves in most things, they were as one man in denouncing fagging and monitors. Their motto was—down with both; and it pleased them not a little to discover that though their agitation did little good in the way of reforming Templeton, it served to keep their "Den" well before the school, and sometimes to cause anxiety in high places.

Such was the state of school politics at Templeton, when Dick and Heathcote obeyed the summons to attend their first Elections, on the first Saturday of the new term.

They found the Great Hall crowded with benches, rather like chapel, with a raised dais at the upper end for the Sixth, a long table in front for the 'reporters,' and the rest of the space divided into clusters of seats, occupied by members of the various school organisations represented. Of these clusters, by far the largest was that devoted to the accommodation of the Den, towards which our heroes, actively piloted by Raggles and Gosse, and a few kindred spirits, were conducted in state, just as the proceedings were about to begin.

"Come and squash up in the corner," said Raggles; "we're well behind, and shan't be seen if we want to shine."

"Shine," as our heroes discovered in due time, was a poetical way of expressing what in commonplace language would be called, "kicking up a shine."

"Shall you cheer Ponty?" asked Gosse of his friend.

"Rather. He's a muff. I shall howl at Mansfield, though, and Cresswell."

"I shan't howl at Cresswell," said Dick boldly.

"Why not? He's a beast. You'll get kicked, if you don't, I say."

"I suppose they'll make him Whipper-in again," said another boy near them. Dick looked uncomfortable for a moment. But the indifferent looks on his neighbours' faces convinced him the story had not yet reached the Den.

"Cazenove thinks he ought to get it," said Gosse, amid a general laugh, for Cazenove was almost as round as he was high. "Shall I put you up, old man? Hullo, here they come! There's Ponty. Clap up, you fellows."

A big cheer greeted Pontifex, the captain of the school, as he strolled on to the dais, and took the chair of state.

The new boys eyed him curiously. He was a burly, good-humoured, easy-going fellow, with an "anything for a quiet life" look about him, as he stretched himself comfortably in his seat, and looked placidly round the hall. The cheering had very little effect on his composure. Indeed, he may not have taken in that it was intended for him at all; for he took no notice of it, and appeared to be quite as much amused at the noise as any one else.

A great contrast to Pontifex was Mansfield, the vice-captain, who, with quick eye, and cool, determined mouth, sat next, and eyed the scene like a general who parades his forces and waits to give them the word of command.

Like Pontifex, he seemed but little concerned, either with the cheers of his friends or the few howls of his mutinous juniors. He was used to noises, and they made very little difference to him one way or another. Cresswell, on the contrary, seemed decidedly pleased, when cheers and cries of "Well run!" greeted his appearance; and most of the other monitors—Cartwright, the quick-tempered, warm-hearted Templeton football captain; Freckleton, the studious "dark man;" Bull, the "knowing one," with his horse-shoe pin; Pledge, the smirking "spider;" of the Sixth, and others—seemed to set no little store by the reception the school was pleased to accord them.

At last all were in their places, the door was shut—a traditional precaution against magisterial invasion—and Pontifex lounged to his feet.

"Well, you fellows," said he, with a pleasant smile and in a pleasant voice, "here we are again at another Election. We're always glad to see one another after the holidays—at least I am (cheers)—and I hope we've got a good year coming on. They tell me I'm captain of Templeton this year. (Laughter and cheers.) I can tell you I'm proud of it, and only wish I wasn't going to Oxford in the autumn. (Cheers and cries of 'Don't go.') The comfort is, you'll have a rattling good captain in Mansfield when I'm gone. (Cheers and a few howls.) I don't wonder some of the young 'uns howl, for he'll make some of you sit up, which I could never do. (Great laughter among the Seniors, and signs of dissension in the Den.) But I've not got to make a speech. There's a lot of business. The first thing is the cricket captain. There's only one man fit for that, and I won't go through the farce of proposing him. Those who say Mansfield's the right man for cricket captain, hold up your hands."

A forest of hands went up, for even the malcontents who didn't approve of Mansfield as a monitor had nothing to say against his cricket, which was about as perfect as any that had been seen in the Templeton fields for a dozen years.

With similar unanimity Cresswell was re-elected Whipper-in of the Harriers, and no one held up his hand more enthusiastically for him than did Dick, who shuddered to think how he could ever have imagined himself on such a lofty pedestal.

Then followed in quick succession elections to the other high offices of state in Templeton—Cartwright to the football captaincy, Bull to the keepership of the fives and tennis, Freckleton to be warden of the port—a sinecure office, supposed to imply some duties connected with the "Tub," but really only the relic of some ancient office handed down from bygone generations, and piously retained by a conservative posterity.

All these were re-elections and passed off without opposition, and as a matter of course.

When, however, Pontifex announced that the office of Usher of the Chapel was vacant, the duties of which were to mark the attendance of all boys and present weekly reports of their punctuality, and proceeded to nominate Pledge for the post, the first symptoms of opposition showed themselves, much to the delight of the Den.

"I move an amendment to that," said Birket, looking a little nervous, but evidently in earnest. "I don't think Pledge is the proper man. (Cheers.) I don't like him myself—(loud cheers)—and I don't think I'm very fastidious. (Great applause from the Den.) We want an honest, reliable man—(hear, hear)—who'll keep our scores without fear or favour. (Applause.) You needn't think I'm saying this for a lark. I'm pretty sure to catch it, but I don't care; I'll say what I think. (Cries of 'We'll back you up,' and cheers.) You're not obliged to have a monitor to be Usher of the Chapel, and I propose Swinstead be appointed."

Birket sat down amid loud cheers. It had been a plucky thing for him to do, and very few would have undertaken so ungracious a task; but, now he had undertaken it, the meeting was evidently with him.

"Everybody here," said Pontifex, "as long as he's in order, has a right to express his opinion without fear. Two names have now been proposed—Pledge and Swinstead. Any more?"

No one broke the silence.

"Then I'll put up Swinstead first. Who votes for Swinstead?"

Everybody, apparently. The Den, to a man, and the Middle school scarcely less unanimously.

"Now for Pledge."

About a dozen, including Bull and one or two of the Sixth, a select few among the juniors, and a certain unwholesome-looking clique among the Fourth and Fifth.

It rather surprised our heroes to notice that Pledge, so far from appearing mortified by his reverse, took it with a decidedly amiable smile, which became almost grateful as it beamed into the corner where Birket and Swinstead, both flushed with excitement, sat.

"By Jingo! I wouldn't be those two for a lot!" said Raggles.

"Now *I* think Pledge takes it very well," said Heathcote.

Whereat there was a mighty laugh in the Den as the joke passed round, and the phenomenon of the "green new kid" blushing scarlet all over attracted general curiosity, and stopped the proceedings for several minutes.

As soon as order was restored, other elections were proceeded with, including the school librarian and the post fag, the duty of which latter office was to distribute the letters which came by the post to their respective owners. For this office there was always great competition, each "set" being anxious to get one of its own members, on whom it could depend.

The contest this year lay between Pauncefote, of Westover's, and Duffield of Purbeck's, and ever since the term opened canvassing had been going on actively on behalf of the respective candidates. I regret to say the laws relating to elections at Templeton were not as rigid as those which regulate public elections generally, and bribery and corruption were no name for some of the unscrupulous practices resorted to by the friends of either party to secure a vote. If a small boy ventured to express so much as a doubt as to his choice, his arm would be seized by the canvassing party and screwed till the required pledge was given. And woe to that small boy if an hour later the other side caught him by the other arm and begged the favour of his vote for their man! Nothing short of perjury would keep his arm in its socket. Nor was it once or twice only that the youth of Templeton would be made to forswear itself over the election of post fag. Several times a day the same luckless voter might be made to yield up his promise, until, at the end of a week, he would become too confused and weary to recollect for which side his word of honour had last been given. Nor did it much matter, for his vote in Hall depended entirely on the company nearest within reach of his arm; and if, by some grim fatality, he should chance to get with one arm towards each party, the effort of recording his vote was likely to prove one of the most serious undertakings of his mortal life.

Our heroes, luckily for them, found themselves planted in the midst of Pauncefote's adherents, so that they experienced no difficulty at all in making up their minds how they should vote. They either did not see or did not notice a few threatening shouts and pantomimic gestures addressed to them by some of Duffield's supporters in a remote corner of the room, and held up their hands for his opponent with the clear conscience of men who exercise a mighty privilege fearlessly.

"Stick up both hands," said Gosse. "We shall be short."

"It wouldn't be fair," said Dick, boldly.

"Howling prig!" said Gosse, in disgust, "canting young hypocrite; you'll get it hot, I can tell you, if—"

"Shut up!" shouted Dick, rounding on him with a fierceness which astonished himself. It was a show to see the way in which Gosse collapsed under this thunderclap of righteous indignation. He looked round at Dick out of the corners of his eyes, very much as a small dog contemplates the boot that has just helped him half-way across the road, and positively forgot to keep his own grimy hand raised aloft till the counting was finished.

"Pauncefote has 108 votes. Now those who are in favour of Duffield?"

There was great excitement, and no little uproar, as the rival party made their show. Cries of, "Cheat! both hands up!" rose from the shocked adherents of Pauncefote; and a good deal of quiet service, in holding the arms of weaklings down to their sides, was rendered on the frontier. Finally, it was found that Duffield had in votes; whereat there were tremendous cheers and counter-cheers, not unmixed with recriminations, and imputations and threats, which promised our heroes a lively time of it when finally they adjourned to the Den.

Before that happened, however, a solemn ceremony had to be gone through, in which they were personally interested. The chairman read out a list of new boys, and ordered them to answer to their names, and come forward on to the platform. It was a nervous ordeal, even for the most self-composed, to be thus publicly trotted out in the presence of all Templeton, and to hear the derisive cheers with which his name and appearance were greeted as he obeyed.

"Look at his legs!" cried one, as Dick, inwardly hoping he was making a favourable impression, passed up the hall and mounted the steps. Whereupon Dick suddenly became conscious of his lower limbs—which, by the way, were as straight and tight a pair of shanks as any boy of fourteen could boast—and tried to hide them behind a chair.

"I can see them still!" cried a shrill voice, just as he thought he had succeeded; and poor Dick, who, an hour ago, had almost forgotten he was a new boy, had to endure a storm of laughter, and look as much at his ease as he could, while all Templeton mounted on chairs, and stretched its necks to catch a glimpse of his unfortunate legs.

Heathcote came in for a similar trial on account of his blushes, and poor Aspinall positively staggered, and finally broke down under allusions to the "bottle," and "soothing syrup," and "mamma" and "sister Lottie."

The Sixth had the sense not to attempt to quell the disorder till it had had a fair chance of blowing itself off. Then Pontifex ordered the names to be put into a hat, and handed round for each of the monitors to draw. Each monitor accordingly drew, and announced the name of his future fag. In the first round Heathcote's name and Aspinall's both came up—the former, much to his disgust, falling to the lot of Pledge, the latter to that of Cresswell. Dick boiled with excitement as the hat started on its second round. Suppose he, too, should fall to the lot of a cad like Pledge, or a brute like Bull! Or, oh blissful notion! suppose Cresswell should draw him, too, as well as Aspinall.

The hat started; Pontifex drew a stranger; so did Mansfield. Then Cresswell drew, and, with a bound of delight, Dick heard his own name, and marked the gleam of pleasure which crossed his new master's face as he turned towards him. He forgot all about his legs, he even missed Heathcote's doleful look of disappointment, or the thankful sigh of young Aspinall. He felt as if something good had happened to him, and as if his star were still in the ascendant.

At the end of the Elections a cry of "three groans for fagging!" was proposed by some member of the Den, who took care to keep himself well concealed, and, as usual, was lustily responded to by all the interested parties. Which little demonstration being over, Pontifex announced that the meeting was over, and that "captain's levée" would be held on that day week at 5:30.

Our heroes were promptly kidnapped, as they descended from the platform, by the emissaries of the Den, who hurried them off to the serene atmosphere of that dignified assembly, where, for an hour or more, they took part in denouncing everybody and everything, and assisted in a noble flow of patriotic eloquence on the duty of the oppressed towards the oppressor, and the slave towards his driver. The Sixth, meanwhile, rather glad to have Elections over, strolled off to their own quarters.

"More row than ever this year," said Mansfield, as he followed Cresswell into his study. "Ponty's too easy-going."

"I don't know. If you keep them in too tight they'll burst. I think he's right to give them some play."

"Well, perhaps you're right, Cress; but I'm afraid I shan't be as easy with them as Ponty. My opinion is, that if you give them an inch they'll take an ell. By the way, that was a queer thing about Pledge. Did you expect it?"

"No, but I'm not surprised. He's a low cad—poor Forbes owed his expulsion last term to him, I'm positive. He simply set himself to drag him down, and he did it."

"Pity he's such a good bowler, one's bound to keep him in the eleven, and the fellows always swear by the eleven. By the way, I hear we have our work cut out for us at Grandcourt this year. They're a hot lot, and we play them on their own ground this time."

"Oh, we shall do it, if only Ponty will wake up."

These two enthusiasts for the good of Templeton would have been a good deal afflicted had they seen what the burly captain of the school was doing at that moment.

He was sitting in his easy-chair, the picture of comfort, with his feet up on the window-ledge, reading "Pickwick," and laughing as he read. No sign of care was on his brow, and apparently no concern for Templeton was weighing on his mind; and even when a fag entered and brought him up a list of names of boys requiring his magisterial correction, he ordered him to put it on the table, and never even glanced at it for the next hour.

Pontifex, it is true, did not do himself justice. He passed for even more easy-going than he was, and when he did choose to make an effort—few fellows could better deal with the duties that fell to his lot. But, unfortunately, he didn't make the effort often enough either for the good of Templeton or his own credit.

He was getting to the end of his chapter when the door opened again, and Pledge entered.

"Hallo," said the captain, looking up after a bit, "you came a cropper, I say, this afternoon. What have you been up to?"

"That's what I came to ask you," said Pledge, with an amiable smile.

"Goodness knows! I was as much surprised as you. You know, between you and me, I don't think you did Forbes much good last term."

"Quite a mistake. I befriended him when everybody else was cutting him. He told me when he left I was the only friend he had here."

"A good friend?" asked Pontifex, looking hard at his man.

"Really, Ponty, you don't improve in your manners," said Pledge, with a slightly embarrassed laugh.

"No offence, old man," said the captain. "But, seriously, don't you think you might do a little more good, or even a little less well, harm, you know, in Templeton than you do?"

"Most noble captain, we must see what can be done," said Pledge, colouring a trifle, as he left the room.

"I've lost my pull on him, I suppose," said the captain, taking up his "Pickwick."

"By Jove! I wish I could make up my mind to kick him!"

Chapter Eight
In which Heathcote becomes interesting

Pledge was a type of fellow unfortunately not uncommon in some public schools, whom it is not easy to describe by any other word than dangerous. To look at him, to speak to him, to hear him, the ordinary observer would notice very little to single him out from fifty other boys of the same age and condition. He was clever, good-humoured, and obliging, he was a fine cricketer and lawn tennis player, he was rarely overtaken in any breach of school rules and he was decidedly lenient in the use of his monitorial authority.

For all that, fellows steered clear of him, or, when they came across him, felt uncomfortable till they could get out of his way. There were ugly stories about the harm he had done to more than one promising simple-minded young Templetonian in days past who had had the ill-luck to come under his influence. And although, as usual, such stories were exaggerated, it was pretty well-known why this plausible small boys' friend was called "spider" by his enemies, who envied no one who fell into his web.

Heathcote accordingly came in for very little congratulation that evening after Elections when he was formally sworn in to the Den as the "spider's" fag and was thoroughly frightened by the stories he heard and the still more alarming mysterious hints that were dropped for his benefit.

However, like a philosopher as he was, he determined to enjoy himself while he could, and therefore entered with spirit into the lively proceedings of that evening's Den.

That important institution was, our heroes discovered, by no means an assembly of one idea. Although its leading motive might be said to be disorder, it existed for other purposes as well; as was clearly set forth in the articles of admission administered to each new boy on joining its honourable company.

Terrible and sweeping were the "affirmations" each Denite was required to make on the top of a crib to Caesar's Commentaries.

(1) "I promise to stick by every chap of the Den whenever I am called upon."

(2) "I promise never to sneak, or tell tales of any chap of the Den, under any circumstances."

(3) "I promise never to fag for anybody more than I can possibly help."

(4) "I promise to do all I can to make myself jolly to the Den."

(5) "If I break any of these rules, I promise to let myself be kicked all round by the chaps of the Den, as long as I am able to stand it."

Our heroes and young Aspinall were called upon solemnly to subscribe to each of these weighty promises, under threat of the most awful vengeance if they refused. And, as it seemed to each he might safely venture on the promise required, they went dutifully through the ceremony, and had the high privilege of exercising their new rights, ten minutes later, in kicking a couple of recalcitrant Denites, one of whom, as it happened, was the high-minded Mr Gosse, who had been detected in the act of telling tales to a monitor of one of his companions.

Mr Gosse availed himself on this occasion of the last clause of Rule 5, and lay down on the ground, after the first kick. He was, however, persuaded to resume his feet, and finally had the inward satisfaction of feeling that he had obeyed the requirements of the rule to the utmost.

This little matter of business being disposed of, and the usual patriotic speeches having been delivered, the Den, which was nothing if it was not original, proceeded to its elections—a somewhat tedious ceremony, which it was very difficult for a stranger to understand.

A vicious-looking youth, called Culver, was elected president of the club, Pauncefote (the rejected post fag) and Smith were appointed treasurers, and, greatly to the surprise of the new boys, but of no one else, Mr Gosse, still barely recovered from his loyalty to Rule 5, was elected secretary, and made a very amiable and highly-applauded speech, in returning thanks for the compliment paid to him.

After this, the Den resolved itself into a social gathering, and became rather tedious.

Dick was interrupted in a yawn by Messrs Pauncefote and Smith, who politely waited upon him for his subscription, a request which Culver, as president, and Gosse, as secretary, were also in attendance to see complied with.

"How much?" said Dick.

"Threepence," said Smith, but was instantly jostled by a violent nudge from Gosse.

"How much tin have you got?" demanded that official.

Dick, who had long ere this lost any reverence he might be expected to entertain towards the secretary of the Den, replied:

"Threepence."

"Howling cram!" observed Gosse. "I know you've more than that."

"Ah! you've been putting your hands in my pockets then?"

Whereat there was a mighty cheer, and the Den was called to order to hear the joke, which it did with genuine merriment; and then and there passed a resolution unanimously, requesting Mr Gosse once more to comply with Rule 5. That young gentleman got out of it this time by making a public apology, and in no way abashed by the incident, proceeded to attend the treasurers during the remainder of their business circuit. Culver stayed behind, and said to Dick:—

"Awfully well you shut him up. I say, by the way, I suppose you don't want a knife, do you?"

"Yes, I do. Have you got one?"

"Rather! but I'd sooner have a dog's-head pin instead. I suppose you've not got one."

Considering that Dick's dog's-head pin, the gift of his particular aunt, was all this time within a few inches of Culver's nose, the inquiry was decidedly artless.

"Yes, I have," said Dick, pointing to his scarf; "a jolly one, too."

"How'd you like to swop?"

"Let's see the knife," replied the business-like Dick.

Culver produced the knife. Rather a sorry weapon, as regarded its chief blades. But it had a saw, and a gouge to remove stones from one's boot.

"It's a jolly fine knife," said Culver, seeing that it was already making an impression; "and I'd be sorry to part with it."

Dick mused on the weapon, and lightly rubbed his chin against his aunt's dog's-head.

"All right," said he, putting the knife into his pocket, and slowly pulling out the pin. His conscience half smote him, as he saw his treasure being transferred to Culver's scarf. But he was too proud to try to revoke his bargain, and consoled himself as best he could by fondling the knife in his pocket, and thinking how useful the gouge would be.

, Before the evening was over he made the discovery that "swopping" was a favourite pastime of the leisure hours of the Den. He was startled at one period of the evening to notice Heathcote's steel chain adorning the waistcoat of Gosse, and an hour later to find it in the possession of Raggles, who came over to Dick with it, and asked casually.

"I suppose you wouldn't care to swop a knife for this?"

Dick was proof against the temptation. He didn't want a steel chain. But he wished Culver would be moved to transfer the dog's-head to some one who wanted a knife. That, however, Culver did not do. He seemed, as indeed his experience in business justified him in being, a good judge of a good bargain; and stuck very faithfully to his new pin, in spite of a considerable number of offers.

After joining in a few songs the airs of which were somewhat vague, the Den adjourned. As its proceedings had consisted in an uninterrupted uproar for two consecutive hours, the new boys, none of whom were seasoned to it, were all more or less tired.

Poor young Aspinall, in particular, was very tired. He had had a rough time of it; and had tremblingly complied with every demand any one chose to make of him. He had parted with all his available "swoppable" goods; he had stood on a form and sung little hymns to a derisive audience; he had answered questions as to his mother, his sister, and other members of his family; he had endured buffeting and kicks, till he was fairly worn out, and till it ceased to be amusing to torment him.

When finally he was released, and found himself on his way to the dormitory, under Dick's sheltering wing, he broke down.

"I wish I was dead," he said, miserably, "it's awful here."

"Don't talk like that," said Dick, a trifle impatiently, for with all his good heart he got tired of the boy's perpetual tears. "You'll get used to it soon. Haven't you got any pluck in you?"

"It's all very well for you," said the boy; "fellows seem to let you alone, and not care to touch you; but they see I can't stand up for myself."

"More shame if they do," said Dick bluntly; "I don't believe you when you say so. I call it cant. How do you know? You can't tell till you try."

"Oh, don't be angry, please," said the boy. "I know you are right; I really will try, if you stick up for me."

"Never mind me," said Dick, getting into bed.

Aspinall did not pursue the topic; but as he lay awake that night, feeling his heart jump at every footstep and word in the room, he made the most desperate and heroic resolves to become a perfect griffin to all Templeton. For all that, he also nearly made up his mind to steal out of bed and peep from the window, to see if there were any possibility of escaping home, while Templeton slept, to Devonshire.

The new boys all obeyed the summons of the half-past-six bell next morning with nervous alacrity. For it was something more than a mere call to shake off "dull sloth"—it was a reminder that they were fags, and that their masters lay in bed depending on them to rouse them in time for morning chapel.

The old fags smiled to see the feverish haste with which the new ones flung themselves into their garments, and started each on his rousing mission. These veterans had had their day of the same sort of thing. Now they knew better, and as long as they could continue occasionally to be found by their seniors with a duster in their hands, or toasting a piece of bread before the fire, the "new brooms" could be left to do all the other work, for which the old ones reaped the credit.

Heathcote, with very dismal forebodings, knocked at Pledge's door.

"It's time to get up, please," said he.

"All right. Fetch me some hot water, will you? and brush my lace boots."

Heathcote, as he started off to fetch the water, thought that the voice of his new master was certainly not as repulsive as he had been led by his numerous sympathisers to expect.

"However," said he to himself, "you can't always judge of a fellow by his voice."

Which was very true, as he found immediately afterwards, when, as he was kneeling down at the tap, trying to coax the last few drops of hot water into his can, a voice behind him said—

"Look sharp, you fellow, don't drink it all up," and he looked up and saw Dick, and Dick's can, bound on the same errand as his own.

"Hallo," he said, "you won't find much left."

"You'll have to give me some of yours then," said Dick.

"I can't, I've only got half a can-full as it is."

"But Cresswell sent me, I tell you."

"And Pledge sent me."

"Pooh! He doesn't matter. He's a beast. Come, go halves, old man."

Of course Heathcote went halves, and enquired as he did so whether Dick had got any boots to clean.

"I've put the young 'un on to that," said Dick, rather grandly. "I left him crying on them just now."

"How many fags has Cresswell got?"

"Us two," said Dick, "at least I've not seen any more."

"I believe I'm the only one Pledge has got."

"Poor beggar! Thanks, Georgie. Get next to me at chapel."

And the two friends went each his own way.

Pledge seemed, on the whole, agreeably surprised to get as much as a quarter of a can of hot water; and Heathcote, as he polished up the lace boots, felt he had begun well. His new master said little or nothing to him, as he put the study tidy, arranged the books, and got out the cup and saucer and coffee-pot ready for the senior's breakfast.

"Is there anything else?" he asked as the chapel bell began to toll.

"No, that's all just now. You can come and clear up after breakfast, and if you've got nothing to do after morning school, you can come and take a bat down at the nets, while I bowl."

At the very least Heathcote had expected to be horrified, when this terrible ogre did speak, by a broadside of bad language; and he felt quite bewildered as he recalled the brief conversation and detected in it not a single word which could offend anybody. On the contrary, everything had been most proper and considerate, and the last invitation coming from a first eleven man to his new fag was quite gratuitously friendly.

"I don't think he's so bad," he remarked to Dick, as they went from chapel to breakfast.

"All I know is," said Dick, "Cresswell was asking me if it was my chum who had been drawn by Pledge, and when I told him, he told me I might say to you, from him, that you had better be careful not to get too chummy with the 'spider;' and the less you hang about his study the better. I don't think Cresswell would say a thing like that unless he meant it."

"I dare say not," said Heathcote. "But I wish to goodness some one would say what it all means. I can't make it out."

After breakfast he repaired to his lord's study, and cleared the table.

"Well," said Pledge. "What about cricket?"

"Thanks, awfully," said the fag, "I'd like it."

"All serene. Come here as soon as school is up." Which Heathcote did, and was girt hand and foot with pads, and led by his senior down into the fields, where for an hour he stood gallantly at the wickets, swiping heroically at every ball, and re-erecting his stumps about once an over, as often as they were overturned by the desolating fire of the crack bowler of Templeton.

A few stragglers came up and watched the practice; but Heathcote had the natural modesty to know that their curiosity did not extend to his batting, gallant as it was. Indeed, they almost ignored the existence of a bat anywhere, and even failed to be amused by the gradual demoralisation of the fag who wielded it, under the sense of the eyes that were upon him.

"Pledge is on his form this term," said Cresswell, one of the onlookers, to his friend Cartwright.

"Tremendously," said Cartwright. "Grandcourt won't stand up to it, if it's like that on match day. Who's the kid at the wicket?"

"His new fag—poor little beggar!"

"It's a pity. Poor Forbes was just like him a couple of years ago."

"Never mind," said Cresswell, "Mansfield has got his eyes open, and I fancy he'll be down in that quarter when he's captain. Old Ponty won't do it. He's worse than ever. Won't even come to practice, till he's finished 'Pickwick,' he says."

And the two friends strolled off rather despondently.

In due time Heathcote was allowed to divest himself of his armour, and accompany his senior indoors.

"You didn't make a bad stand, youngster," said Pledge, as they walked across the field, "especially at the end. Have you done much cricket?"

"Not much," said Heathcote, blushing at the compliment.

"You should stick to it. You'll get plenty of chance this term."

"And yet," said Heathcote to himself, "this is the fellow everybody tells me is a beast to be fought shy of, and not trusted for a minute." He was almost tempted to interrogate Pledge point-blank on what it all meant; but his shyness prevented him.

Nothing occurred during the day to solve the mystery. There was comparatively little to be done in the way of fagging; and what little there was, was amply compensated for by the help Pledge gave him in his Latin composition in the evening.

Later on, while Pledge was away somewhere, Heathcote was putting the books away on to the shelves, and generally tidying up the study, when the door partly opened, and a small round missive was tossed on to the floor of the room.

Heathcote regarded the intruder in a startled way, as if it had been some infernal machine; but presently took courage to advance and take the missive in his hand. It was a small round cardboard box, about the size of a tennis ball, which, much to his surprise, bore his own name, printed in pen and ink, on the outside. He opened it nervously, and found a note inside, also addressed to himself, which ran thus:—

> "Heathcote.—This is from a friend. You are in peril. Don't believe anything Pledge tells you. Suspect everything he does. He will try to make a blackguard of you. You had much better break with him, refuse to fag for him and take the consequences, than become his friend. Be warned in time.—Junius."

This extraordinary epistle, all printed in an unrecognisable hand, set Heathcote's heart beating and his colour coming and going in a manner quite new to him. Who was this "Junius," and what was this conspiracy to terrify him? "Suspect everything he does." A pretty piece of advice, certainly, to anybody. For instance, what villainy could be concealed in his bowling for an hour at the wickets, or rescuing young Aspinall from his tormentors? "He will try to make a blackguard of you." Supposing Junius was right, would it not be warning enough to fight shy of him when he began to try? Heathcote had reached this stage in his meditations when he heard Pledge approaching. He hurriedly crushed the letter away into his pocket, and returned to the bookcase.

"Hullo, young fellow," said Pledge, entering. "Putting things straight? Thanks. What about your Latin verses? Not done, as usual, I suppose. Let's have a look. I'll do them for you, and you can fetch them in the morning. Good-night."

Heathcote retired, utterly puzzled. He could believe a good deal that he was told, but it took hard persuasion to make him believe that a senior who could do his Latin verses for him could be his worst enemy.

Chapter Nine
A Literary Ghost

For two whole days Heathcote let "Junius's" letter burn holes in his pocket, not knowing what to think of it, or what to do with it. For him to take Dick into his confidence was, however, a mere matter of time, for Heathcote's nature was not one which could hold a secret for many days together, and his loyalty to his "leader" was such that whenever the secret had to come out, Dick's was the bosom that had to receive it.

"It's rum," said the latter, after having read the mysterious document twice through. "I don't like it, Georgie."

"The thing is, I can't imagine who wrote it. You didn't, did you?"

Dick laughed.

"Rather not. I don't see the good of hole-in-the-corner ways of doing things like that."

"Do you think Cresswell wrote it? He's about the only senior that knows me, except Pledge."

"I don't fancy he did; it's not his style," said Dick, who seemed quite to have taken the whipper-in under his wing.

"He might know. I wonder, Dick, if you'd mind trying to find out? It maybe a trick, you know, after all."

"Don't look like it," said Dick, glancing again at the letter. "It's too like what everybody says about *him*."

"That's the worst of it. He's hardly said a word to me since I've been his fag, and certainly nothing bad; and he writes my Latin verses for me, too. I fancy fellows are down on him too much."

"Well," said Dick, "I'll try and pump Cresswell; but I *wish* to goodness, Georgie, you weren't that beast's fag."

Every conversation he had on the subject, no matter with whom, ended in some such ejaculation, till Heathcote got quite used to it, and even ceased to be disturbed by it.

Indeed, he was half disappointed, after all the warning and sympathy he had received, to find no call made upon his virtue, and no opportunity of making a noble stand against the wiles of the "spider." He would rather have enjoyed a mild passage of arms in defence of his uprightness; and it was a little like a "sell" to find Pledge turn out, after all, so uninterestingly like everybody else.

Dick duly took an opportunity of consulting Cresswell on his friend's behalf.

"I say, Cresswell," said he, one morning, as the senior and his fag walked back from the "Tub."

"Who was Forbes?"

"Never mind," said Cresswell, shortly.

This was a rebuff, certainly; but Dick stuck to his purpose.

"Heathcote asked me," he said. "He's Pledge's fag, and everybody says to him he'll come to grief like Forbes; and he doesn't know what they mean."

"You gave your chum my message, did you?" said Cresswell.

"Oh, yes; and, do you know, the other evening he had a letter thrown into him, he doesn't know where from, saying the same thing?"

Cresswell whistled, and stared at his fag.

"Was it signed 'Junius,' and done up in a ball?" he asked, excitedly.

"Yes. Did *you* send it?"

"And was it in printed letters, so that nobody could tell the writing?"

"Yes. Do you know about it, I say?"

"No," said Cresswell; "no more does anybody. Your chum's had a letter from the ghost!"

"The what?"

"The Templeton ghost, my boy."

"I don't believe in ghosts," said Dick.

"That's all right. No more do I. But those who do, say its a bad sign to get a letter from ours. Forbes got one early last term."

"Do you really mean—?" began Dick.

"I mean," said Cresswell, interrupting him, and evidently not enjoying the topic, "I mean that nobody knows who writes the letters, or why. It's been a mystery ever since I came here, three years ago. It happens sometimes twice or thrice a term; and other times perhaps only once in six months."

"What had Heathcote better do?" asked Dick, feeling anything but reassured.

"Do! He'd better read the letter. There's no use going and flourishing it all round the school."

With this small grain of advice Dick betook himself to his friend, and succeeded in making him more than ever uncomfortable and perplexed. Nor was his perplexity made less when, during the next few days, it leaked out somehow, and spread all over Templeton, that Heathcote had had a letter from the ghost.

Interviewers waited on him from all quarters. Seniors cross-examined him, Fifth-form fellows tried to coax the letter out of him, and the Den called upon him, under threats of "Rule 5," to make a full disclosure of what had befallen him. He had a fair chance of losing his head with all the attention paid him; and, had it not been for Cresswell's advice, emphasised by Dick, he might, like the ass in the lion's skin, have made himself ridiculous. As it was, he was not more than ordinarily intoxicated by his sudden notoriety, and kept the ghost's letter prudently hidden in his own pocket.

One fellow, and one only besides Dick, saw it. And that was Pledge.

"What's all this about the ghost?" asked the senior of his fag one evening during preparation in their study. "Is it true you've had a letter?"

"Yes," said Heathcote, very uncomfortably.

"Do you mind letting me see it?"

"I'd rather not, please," said the boy.

"Don't you think it was meant for me to see?" asked Pledge.

Heathcote was puzzled. He had never thought so yet, and wished Dick was at hand to be consulted.

"I don't think so," he said.

"It says, doesn't it, that you are to be on your guard against me, and that I shall be sure and do you harm, and that the less you see of me the better, eh?"

"Yes; have you seen the letter?"

"No, or I shouldn't ask to see it.—How would you like to have letters written about you like that?"

"Not at all. Do you know who wrote it?"

"No. No one knows. And you believe it, of course?"

"No, I don't," said Heathcote, making up his mind at a bound on a question which had been distracting him for a week.

Pledge seemed neither pleased nor surprised by this avowal.

"Doesn't everybody say you ought to?"

"Perhaps they do," said Heathcote, getting into a corner.

"Doesn't your chum say so?"

"He only goes by what other fellows say."

"You mean Cresswell?"

"I daresay Cresswell may have said something," said the new boy, getting deeper and deeper, and beginning to shuffle in spite of himself.

"You *know* he has said something," said Pledge, sternly. "The ghost didn't tell you to tell falsehoods, did it?"

"No. Cresswell did say something."

"And you think it was very friendly of him, don't you?"

"No, I don't," said the unhappy Heathcote.

"Is Cresswell very fond of you?" asked Pledge.

"No. I hardly ever saw him."

"Why do you suppose he sent you that message, then?"

"I don't know. Perhaps he's got a spite against you."

The boy was fairly out of his depth now, and gave up trying to recover his feet.

"Would you like to know why; or don't you care?"

"I would like to know, please."

"I daresay you've heard of a fellow called Forbes?"

Heathcote had, from twenty different fellows.

"Forbes was a fag of mine last year—a nice boy, but dreadfully weak-minded. Any one could twist him round his thumb. As long as I kept my eye on him he was steady enough; but if ever I let him slide he got into trouble. I was laid up a month last autumn with scarlet fever, and, of course, Forbes was on the loose, and spent most of his time with Cresswell and his set. As soon as I got back I noticed a change in him. He had got into bad ways, and talked like a fellow who was proud of what he had learned. He used to swear and tell lies, and other things a great deal worse. I did all I could to pull him up, and before Christmas I fancied he was rather steadier.

But last term he broke out again as bad as ever. I could keep no hold of him. He was constantly cutting me for his other friend; and all the time I, as his senior, got the credit of his ruin. He was expelled in February for some disgraceful row he got into, and, because I stuck to him to the end, his other friend gets up a report that I was to blame for it all. I don't profess to be better than I ought to be, youngster; I know I should be better than I am; but I'm not a blackguard."

Heathcote was greatly impressed by this narrative. It cleared up, to his mind, a great deal of the mystery that had been tormenting him the last few days, and accounted for most of the stories and rumours which he had heard. The manner, too, in which Pledge defended himself, taking no undue credit for virtue, and showing such little bitterness towards his traducers, went far to win him over.

"It's hard lines on you," he said.

"You see, even a ghost can be wrong sometimes."

"Yes, he can," said Heathcote, resolutely.

"I should like to see the letter, if you have it."

And he did see it, and Heathcote watched the two red spots kindle on his cheeks as he read it and then crushed it up in his hand.

"You don't want it back, I suppose? You're not going to frame it?"

"No," replied the boy, watching the ghost's letter, rather regretfully, as it flared up and burned to ashes on the grate.

He wished the unpleasant impression caused in his own mind by the affair could come to an end as easily as that scrap of paper did.

Care, however, was not wont to sit heavily at any time on the spirit of George Heathcote, and as Pledge did not again return to the subject, and even Dick, seeing no immediate catastrophe befall his friend, began to suspect the whole affair as an intricate and elaborate practical joke at the expense of two new boys, the matter gradually subsided, and life went on at its usual jog-trot.

This jog-trot gave place, however, on one eventful afternoon to a more stately parade, on the occasion of the captain's levee, a week after Elections.

This ceremony, one of the immemorial traditions of Templeton, which fellows would as soon have thought of neglecting as of omitting to take a holiday on the Queen's birthday, was always an occasion of general interest after the reassembling of the school.

The captain of Templeton on this evening was "at home;" in other words, he stood on the platform at the top of "Hall" in his "swallows" and received the school, who all turned up in their very best attire to do honour to the occasion.

New boys were "presented" by their seniors, and the captain, if he was a fellow of tact and humour, usually contrived to say something friendly to the nervous juniors; and generally the occasion was looked upon as one on which Templeton was expected to make itself agreeable all round and do itself honour.

For some days previously our heroes had been carefully looking up their wardrobes in anticipation of the show. Dick, on the very evening of Elections, had put aside his whitest shirt, and Heathcote had even gone to the expense of a lofty masher collar, and had forgotten all about the ghost in his excitement over the washing of a choker which *would* come out limp, though he personally devoted a cupful of starch to its strengthening.

There was, as usual, keen competition among the members of the Den as to who should achieve the "showiest rig" on the occasion. For some days the owner of Heathcote's steel chain was mentioned as the favourite, until rumour got abroad that young Aspinall was a "hot man," and had white gloves and three coral studs. But Culver outdid everybody at the last moment by appearing in a real swallow-tail of his own, which he had secretly borrowed from a cousin during the holidays and kept dark till now.

This, of course, settled the contest in favour of the president of the Den, and so much enthusiasm prevailed over the discovery, that a Den levée was immediately proposed.

The idea took, and, after much debate, it was resolved that the honourable and original fraternity should take possession of the lower end of Hall on the captain's night, and, after doing duty at the top end, repair to the bottom, there to display their loyalty to their own particular "swallow." Due announcement was made to this effect, and Rule 5 carefully rehearsed in the ears of all waverers.

The evening came at last. Pontifex, surrounded by the Sixth, rambled up on to the daïs and waited good-humouredly for the show to begin, quite regardless of his own imposing appearance and of the awe which the array of senior shirt-fronts struck into the hearts of the new juniors who looked on.

In solemn order Templeton ascended the dais and rendered homage. With the Fifth the captain was affable, and with the Upper Fourth he exchanged a few jocular courtesies. With the Middle school he contented himself with a shake of the hand and a "How are you, Wright?"

"Ah, Troup, old man," and such-like greetings. Boys he had punished yesterday he received quite as warmly now as the most immaculate of the virtuous ones, and boys who had cheeked him two hours ago in the fields he shook hands with as cordially as he did with the most loyal of his adherents.

There was a pause as the last of the Middle school descended from the dais, and the Den, headed by the resplendent Culver, advanced. Templeton tried to look grave and remember its good manners, but it was an effort under such an array of glory. Culver himself, with his borrowed coat so tight under the arms that he could not keep his elbows down, and his waistcoat pinned back so far that the empty button-hole in his front quite put the studded ones to shame, might have passed in a crowd; but Gosse, with his hair parted in the middle and his "whisker" elaborately curled; Pauncefote, with his light blue silk handkerchief protruding half out of his waistcoat pocket; and Smith, with the cuffs that hid the tips of his fingers, were beyond gravity, and a suppressed titter followed the grandees up the hall and on to the platform.

Pontifex received them all with serene affability and good breeding.

"Hullo, youngster!" said he to Culver, not even bestowing a glance on his finery: "hope to see you in an eleven this season. Ah, Gosse, my boy; quiet as ever, eh? You're an inch taller than last levée. How are you, Pauncefote? How are you, Smith? How goes the novel? not dead, I hope?"

"No; it's going on," said Pauncefote, blushing.

"Put me down for a copy," said the captain. "Hullo! here come the new boys."

Time did not appear to have endowed our heroes yet with confidence or elegance in the art of ascending the Templeton platform. Dick still retained a painful recollection of his legs, and Heathcote was torn asunder by the cruel vagaries of his high collar, which would not keep on the button, but insisted on heeling over, choker and all, at critical moments to one side. Aspinall made a more respectable show, for he was too nervous to bestow a thought on his dress, or to notice the curious eyes turned upon him from remote corners.

New boys were always presented by their seniors, and it was a critical moment when Cresswell, taking Dick and Aspinall, one by each arm, said in an audible voice:—

"Captain, allow me to introduce Mr Richardson and Mr Aspinall, two new boys."

Dick bowed as gracefully as he could, and watched the captain's hand sharply, in case it might show signs of expecting to be shaken, which it did, with a cheery—

"Very glad to see you, Richardson. I hear you won the new boys' race. You've got a good trainer in Cresswell. How do you do, Aspinall? Feeling more at home here, aren't you? I recollect how lost I was the first time I tumbled into school."

"Captain, allow me to introduce Mr Heathcote," said Pledge.

Poor Heathcote, whose choker had now got round to his back, turned crimson, and said, "Thank you," and then made a grab at the captain's hand, by way of hiding his confusion.

"Ah, how are you, Heathcote?" said the magnate kindly. "Hope to see plenty of you in the 'Tub,' and down field. You new boys should show up out of doors all you can."

Mansfield was not the only senior standing by who heard and appreciated this delicate hint. Pledge heard it too, and knew what it meant.

"If old Ponty," said Mansfield to Cresswell, "would only follow it up, what a splendid captain he would be. There's not another fellow can go through levée the way he does. He strokes down everybody. Goodness knows, when my turn comes, I shall come a cropper."

"Your turn will come soon, if Ponty leaves this term. You're bound to have levée in your first week. Hullo! what's up down there?"

This last question was caused by the slight excitement of Den levée, which, according to programme, was in the act of being celebrated at the bottom of the hall.

Culver, who was really rather sore under the arms, with his long confinement in his cousin's "swallow," was mounted on a lexicon, and word being passed that he was ready to receive company, the Den proceeded to file past him, in imitation of the ceremony which had just been concluded on the upper dais.

The imitation in this case, however, was not flattery. Culver was not a dignified youth, and his sense of humour was not of that refined order which enables a man to distinguish between comedy and burlesque. He had a general idea that he had to make himself pleasant, which he accordingly did in his own peculiar style.

"Ah, Gossy, old chap!" he said, as the secretary of the Den presented himself with his whiskered cheek nearest to his chief. "It's coming on, my boy. You'll have a hair and a half before the Grandcourt match."

The titter which greeted this sally highly delighted the tight-laced president, who (especially as his audience consisted of a good sprinkling of the Middle school, attracted by the chance of sport), strained every nerve to sustain his reputation for wit.

"How do you do, Pauncefote, my lad?" said he, as the owner of the light blue silk handkerchief approached. "Why don't you show enough wipe? Stick a pin in one corner, and leave the rest hanging down. How's the novel, my boy?"

"Pretty well," said Pauncefote.

"Ah, my venerable chum, Smith," continued the president, holding out his hand to the joint secretary.

"Why don't you wash your face, and stick your hands up your sleeves. How's a fellow to flap you a daddle in those cuffs, eh?"

In this refined style of banter, Culver passed his followers in array, gradually degenerating in his humour as he went on, until the last few came in for decidedly broad personalities.

But he saved up his final effort for the new boys, of whom Aspinall happened to be pushed forward first.

"Booh, hoo! poor little baby. Did it come for a little drink of its 'ittle bottle? It should then. Hold out your hand, you young muff."

Aspinall obeyed, and next moment was writhing under the "scrunch" which the president in his humour bestowed upon it.

"Now make a bow," demanded that gentleman when the greeting was over.

Aspinall made obeisance, amid loud derisive cheers, and was called upon to repeat the performance several times.

"Now shake hands again."

The boy tried to escape, but his arm was roughly seized, and his hand once more captured in the ruthless grip of his host.

In vain he tried to get free. The more he struggled the tighter the grip became, till at last he fairly fell on his knees, and howled for pain.

Then Dick, who had gradually been boiling over, could stand it no longer.

"Let his hand go!" he shouted, stepping up to the president, and emphasising his demand with a slight push.

You might have knocked the Den down with a feather! They stared at one another, and then at Dick, and then at one another again, until their eyes ached.

Then Culver, utterly oblivious of his tight sleeves, or his dignified position, turned red in the face and said —

"What do you mean?"

"What I say," said Dick, a trifle pale, and breathing hard.

"Will you fight?" said Culver.

"Yes," said Dick, in a dream, for his head was swimming round, and he forgot where he was, and what the row was about.

"You mean it?" once more asked the president.

"Yes, I do," again retorted Dick.

"Very well," said Culver.

Instantly there was a stampede of the Den, and cries of "a fight!" shook the halls and passages of Templeton.

The Sixth heard it in their lofty regions, whither they had retired after the fatigue of levée.

"Pity to stop it," said Birket, who reported the state of the matter to the seniors. "It'll do good."

"Who's the better man?" asked Cresswell.

"Culver, I fancy."

"Humph!" said the captain, "you'd better be there to see fair play, Birket; and Cresswell will come down and stop it in ten minutes. Eh, Cress?"

"All serene," said Cresswell.

Chapter Ten
Describes a great battle, and what followed

Perhaps I ought to begin this chapter with an apology. Perhaps I ought to delude my readers into the belief that it gives me far more pain to describe a fight, than it gave Dick and his antagonist to take part in it. Perhaps I ought to go back and alter my last chapter, and call in the dogs of war. Perhaps I should solemnly explain to the reader how much more beautiful it would have been in Dick, if, instead of letting his angry passions rise at the sight of young Aspinall's wrongs, he had walked kindly up to the bully, and laying his hand gently on his shoulder, asked him with a sweet smile, whether he thought that was quite a nice thing for a big boy to do to a small one? whether his conscience didn't tell him he erred? and whether he wouldn't go and retire for a quiet hour to his study, and think the matter over with the said conscience? Then, if, at the end of that time he still felt disposed to use physical force towards the little new boy, would he allow him, Dick, on this occasion to bear the punishment in his young friend's place?

I say, I might, perhaps begin my chapter in this fashion, were it not for two trifling difficulties—one being that I should be a humbug, which it is not my ambition to be; the other, that Dick, too, would have been a humbug, which he certainly was not.

The truth about fighting is—if one must express an opinion on so delicate a subject—that its right and wrong depend altogether on what you fight about. There are times when to fight is right, and there are a great many more times when to fight is wrong. And for Dick at the present moment to hold up his hands and say, "Oh, no, thank you," when Culver asked him if it was a fight, would have been as bad every bit, as if he had picked a quarrel and fought with the man who caught him out at cricket.

Having relieved our minds so far, let us, reader, accompany Basil the son of Richard, as he strides; surrounded by his myrmidons, and most of all by the faithful Heathcote, to the Templeton "cock pit," where already the large-boned Culver, hemmed in no more by the envious grip of the toga of his mothers sister's son, awaits the fray.

For him Gosse holds the sponge, and bids him hit low, and walk his foeman over the tapes.

And now a score of officious voices cry out "A ring!" and the surging waves fall back, as when a whirlpool opens in mid-ocean.

Tall amid the crowding juniors stalks Birket, at sight of whom Dick's heart rejoices, and Gosse's countenance falls. For Birket will see fair play.

And now the faithful Heathcote staggers under the weight of his friend's discarded garments, and whispers words of brotherly cheer as the snowy sleeves of the hero roll up his arm, and his chafing collar falls from his swelling neck.

The crowd grows dumb and hearts beat quick, as those two stand there, face to face, the large-boned, solid Culver, and the compact, light-footed Dick, with his clean, fresh skin, and well-poised head, and tight, determined lips; and the signal goes forth that the battle has begun.

The knowing ones are there, who, with Birket, look close to see what the new boy is made of, and how he works his left. But the unknowing regard the size of their Culver, and prophesy fast and furiously.

Then do these two circle slowly round the tapes, attempting nothing great, but, by feint and parry, seeking each to unmask his man and discover where he is weak and where strong. The unknowing ones and Gosse murmur, and cry on their man to let out. And he, irresolute a moment, yields, and standing drives at his foeman's head. Up goes the right of Basil the son of Richard, and behold while all cry "a parry!" in goes his left, quick as a flash, and grazes the chin of the solid Culver.

Whereat the ring well-nigh breaks with applause, and the knowing ones nod one at another, and Heathcote leaps for joy and beams like the sun at mid-day as his hero returns to his knees and girds himself for the second round.

Birket looks up at the clock and groans to see five minutes gone. Gosse, too, groans as his man steps forward once more, unsteady and amazed at what had befallen him. "Hit low!" he whispers.

And now, once more, dead silence falls upon the ring, and all eyes turn to where Dick steps lightly up and meets his man. All mark the laugh in his eye, but the knowing ones like it not.

"Steady," says Birket; "don't be too sure."

But Basil the son of Richard heeds him not, and his eyes laugh still. This time, not Culver, but he is the pursuer, and the unknowing ones quake for their hero. Yet Culver stands as he stood before and deals his blow. Once more the new boy parries and drives home with his left. But, alas! Culver is ready for him, while he, unprepared, with his right still up, receives the fist of Culver on his chest. And the echo falls upon the ring like distant thunder.

Where, now, is the laughter in Basil's eyes, or who can see the sunlight on Heathcote's troubled face? Who now nod their heads but the unknowing ones? and who looks grave but Birket?

As when a mountain torrent rushes down its bed with huge uproar until it meet a fiercer, leaping headlong from the cliff, and drowning the lesser din with a greater, so do the shouts for Basil the son of Richard, grow faint beneath the shouts that rise for Culver, the large of bone. Nor when "time" is called, and from the trembling knees of their seconds those two arise and stalk into the ring, does the clamour cease, till Birket, with his eye on the clock, breathes threatenings and demands it.

Then you may hear a pin fall, as Basil, stern of eye and tight of lip, stands fast and waits his man. The knowing ones look anxiously to where the solid Culver squares, and take cheer; for he is flushed and eager, and his lips are open as he walks into the fray. And Heathcote calls loud upon his hero, and Birket bids him straight "go in and win." Gosse yet again bids the solid one "hit low!" and the unknowing ones cry "two to one on Culver."

The heroes meet, and Culver, gathering up his might, makes feint at Basil's head. Up goes the wary arm of Basil, which marking, Culver smites hard and low, a villain thrust hard on the hero's belt. Whereat Gosse cries aloud "bravo!" but Heathcote rages and shouts "belt!" and would himself spring into the fray, but Birket holds him back.

For Basil's eyes flash fire, and on the distant staircase stands already Cresswell, ready to stop the fight. "A minute more," cries Birket, and the ring is still as when Etna, ready to burst, sleeps.

Then does Basil the son of Richard gather himself together and draw breath, while Culver, sure of his man, steps back for a mighty blow. Dick sees it coming, and marks with a quick cool eye its fierce descent. With half a step he avoids it, and as the solid form sways past he greets it right and left with well-aimed blows, which send it headlong to the dust two long yards distant.

Then, as when the swelling torrent breaks with one furious bound into the vale below, does the crowd burst into the ring, and, with mighty shouts, proclaim a victory to the light-footed son of Richard. And, behold, as they do so, the towering form of Cresswell comes in view and bears down upon the scene.

Never did swarm of mice, spying Grimalkin afar, scamper quicker to their holes than do the youths of Templeton vanish before the distant view of Cresswell. Victor and vanquished, knowing and unknowing—all but one, fade to sight, and ere the monitor can stop the fight, the fight is over.

Birket alone remained to meet the senior.

"Well," said the latter, "is it all over?"

"Rather," said the Fifth-form boy. "I'm awfully glad you didn't come sooner."

"Bless you," said Cresswell, "I've been watching it for the last five minutes, so I ought to know when to turn up."

"You have? Then you saw the finish? The youngster made as neat a job of it as I ever saw."

"It was rather pretty," said Cresswell. "He'd something to make up for, though, after making such an ass of himself in the second round. By-the-way, was that last shot of Culver's below the belt?"

"It was precious close to the wind, anyhow. You leave that to me, though. I'll make that all right."

"Thanks," said the monitor. "Something ought to be said about it, or we shall have more of it. Well, I suppose they'll shake hands after a bit. You might see to that, too. Ponty's sure to ask, and there ought to be an end of it."

When Birket, half an hour later, descended to the Den he found a revolution in active progress. Dick was the hero of the hour. His valiant stand against solid odds, his last victorious blow, but, most of all, the cowardly blow of his opponent, had suddenly raised him to a pinnacle of glory which took away his breath. Culver, despite his dress-coat, despite his exertions at levee, despite his seniority and long service, had been ignominiously deposed from office, and subjected to the rigour of rule 5 by an indignant and resentful populace. The unknowing ones, who had backed him the loudest, now answered the soonest to Heathcote's demand for retribution, and Gosse himself, who had an hour ago whispered nothing but "hit low," now denounced the coward and proclaimed his deposition.

By a single vote Culver was dethroned, and Dick, amid frantic cheers, elected president in his stead. Nor did popular clamour cease there, for Gosse was stripped of his office, too, and Heathcote unanimously chosen secretary; and, for the first time in history, the Den did homage to two week-old new boys, and called them its leaders.

It was scarcely possible that Dick, in the midst of all this glory, should remain unmoved. He tried to look modest, he tried to bear himself as though he had done nothing out of the common, he even tried to persuade himself he would rather not accept the office thrust upon him. But his heart swelled with pride, and his head grew light in its lofty atmosphere.

Nor did Birket's visit tend to sober him.

"Well, youngster," said the Fifth-form boy, "you managed it at last, then?"

"Oh, yes," said Dick, grandly, "he's not very good with his parries."

"Isn't he? He's good at coming in on your chest, my boy. Don't you be too cocky. You're not a Tom Sayers yet."

"The last blow was below the belt, though," said Dick.

"I know. I've come to see about that."

"You needn't bother. He's been licked for it. I didn't touch him, of course, but the other fellows did."

"Kind of you. Has he apologised?"

"Oh, never mind," said Dick, forgivingly, "it doesn't matter."

"Tut! do you suppose he's got to apologise to you? I was there to see fair play, and he's to do it to me."

At any other time Dick might have felt snubbed; but now he failed to see the rebuke, and gave order grandly that Culver should be brought.

"There he is," said he, as the unhappy ex-president of the Den was conducted into his presence.

"Culver," said Birket, "you are a cad; you hit below the belt."

"No, I didn't, it was an accident," pleaded the culprit. "Please, Birket, I've been licked already."

"Stand up on that form, and tell all the fellows you apologise for doing a cowardly action and disgracing Templeton."

Culver promptly obeyed, and repeated the apology word for word.

There were loud cries for Gosse at this point, and Birket yielded to the popular demand, and ordered the ex-secretary to go through the same ceremony. Which the ex-secretary cheerfully did.

"Now then," said the Fifth-form boy, turning again to Culver, "shake hands with Richardson and make it up. You've been licked, so there's nothing left to settle."

Culver may have secretly differed from Birket on this point, but he kept his secret to himself and held out his hand. Dick took it, and gave it an honest shake. It is one of the luxuries victors enjoy, to shake the proffered hand of the vanquished, and Dick enjoyed it greatly.

"It's all made up now," said Birket, addressing the Den, "and there'd better be no more row about it, or you'll have one of the Sixth down on you, and he won't let you off as easy as I have, I can tell you."

But although the fight was over, and the breach of the peace was healed, the consequences of the fray were of much longer duration.

Their effect on Dick was not, on the whole, beneficial to that doughty young warrior. Prosperity went harder with him than adversity. As long as he had his hill to climb, his foe to vanquish, his peril to brave, Dick had the makings of a hero. But when fortune smoothed his path, when the foe lay at his feet, when the peril had passed behind, then Dick's troubles began. Popularity turned his head, and laid him open to dangers twice as bad as those he had cleared. The more fellows cheered him, the more he craved their cheers; the more he craved their cheers, the more willing a slave he became.

"It strikes me, youngster," said Cresswell one day, when the term had turned the corner, and the Grandcourt match was beginning to loom very near in the future, "it strikes me you're not doing much good up here. You're always fooling about with those precious juniors of yours, instead of sticking to cricket and tennis and your books. Here's young Aspinall here, ahead of you, by long chalks, in classics, and getting a break on at tennis that'll puzzle you to pick up unless you wake up. You can do as you like; only don't blame me if you get stuck among the louts."

For a time, this friendly advice pulled Dick up in his profitless career. The dread of being considered a "lout" by your senior is a motive which appeals forcibly to most boys; and for a week or so Dick made a feverish show of returning to his outdoor sports, and doing himself justice.

But the effort died away under the claims of the Den. Den suppers, Den concerts, Den debates, and Den conclaves always somehow managed to clash with Templeton work and play; and even Heathcote found it next to impossible to keep up his batting and his secretarial duties to the honourable fraternity.

"I shall have to jack it up," said he, one day, dolefully to Dick, "Pledge always wants me just when things are going on here. Hadn't you better get some one else?"

"Bosh! Let Pledge get some one else," said Dick, warmly. "What right has he got to make you fag for him out of school; that's the very thing we want to stop."

"But I rather like the batting. Cartwright said I was improving."

"Oh, of course; just a dodge to make you stick to it. Don't you let them gammon you, Georgie. Stick to us, and hang Pledge."

And, of course, Heathcote obeyed, and his cricket suffered; and fellows who had hopes of him shrugged their shoulders when they saw him rioting in the Den, and letting another usurp his pads.

Had Dick known the bad turn he was doing his friend he would have hesitated before requiring him to give up a healthy sport, which, just then, was one of his chief safeguards against far less healthy occupations.

The "spider" had not had the fly in his web for five weeks without casting some light toils around him. Heathcote himself would have said that Pledge was as inoffensive to-day as he had been on the first day of the term, and would have angrily scouted the idea that "Junius," or any one else, had been right in his warnings.

And yet in five weeks Heathcote had begun not to be the nice boy he was. Not that Pledge, by any direct influence, incited him to evil-doing. On the contrary, he always corrected him when he prevaricated, and scolded him when he idled.

But the boy had begun a course of indirect training far more dangerous to his morals and happiness than any direct training could have been.

He discovered, very gradually, that Pledge's notions of persons and things were unlike any he had hitherto entertained. In the innocence of his heart he had always given every one credit for being honest, and virtuous, until he had good cause to see otherwise. When any one told him a thing, he usually believed it straight off. If any one professed to be anything, he usually assumed it was so. The small knot of boys at Templeton who called themselves religious, who said their prayers steadily, who refused to do what their conscience would not allow, who tried to do good in some way or other to their fellows, these Heathcote had readily believed were Christians, and more than once he had wished he belonged to their set.

But, somehow, Pledge's influence gave him altogether different ideas on these points. For instance, he would one evening hear a conversation somewhat as follows, between his senior and some friend—generally Wrangham of the Fifth, who usually associated with Pledge:

"I hear Holden is not going to try for the Bishop's scholarship, after all," says Wrangham, who, by the way, is aesthetic, and adopts an air of general weariness of the world which hardly becomes a boy of seventeen.

"Did he tell you so himself?" asked Pledge.

"Yes."

"Then, of course, we don't believe it. He'd like us to think so, I daresay."

"He knows what he is about, though. He got confirmed last week, you know, and that's bound to go down with Winter."

"Winter's pretty well bound to favour Morris, I fancy, though he's not pious," says Pledge. "There are three young Morrises growing up, you know."

Wrangham laughs languidly.

"Nice rotten state the school's in," says he. "Thank goodness, it doesn't matter much to me; but I've once or twice thought of joining the saints, just to save trouble."

"Ha, ha! I'd come and look at you, old man. Fancy you and Mansfield looking over the same hymn-book, and turning up your eyes."

"But," says Heathcote, who has been drinking in all the talk in a bewildered way, and venturing now, as he sometimes does, to join in it. "But I always thought Mansfield was really good."

His two hearers laugh till the boy blushes crimson, and wishes he had not made such an ass of himself.

"Rather," says Wrangham. "He is one of the elect. It's worth fifty pounds a year to him, so it would be a wonder if he wasn't."

"Yes, my boy," says Pledge, "if you want to get on at Templeton, take holy orders. Believe everybody's as good as he tries to make out, and you'll have no trouble at all. When a fellow cracks up your batting, don't on any account suspect he wants to borrow five shillings of you, and if he tells you it's naughty to look about in chapel, don't imagine for a moment he's got half-a-dozen cribs in his study. Bah! They're all alike. Thank goodness you're not a hypocrite yet, young 'un, whatever you may become. Now you can cut. Good-night."

And Heathcote obeys, and lies wide awake an hour, wondering how he can ever have remained a simpleton as long as he has.

Chapter Eleven
How Ponty takes his hand out of his pocket

The Grandcourt match was the only match of the season which Templeton played away from home. All its other matches, the house match, and even the match against the town, were played in the Fields, in the presence of the whole school. But once every other year, Templeton went forth to war in drags and omnibuses against its hereditary rival, and mighty was the excitement with which the expedition and its equipment were regarded by every boy who had the glory of his school at heart.

Seventy boys, and seventy only, were permitted to form the invading army, the selection of whom was a matter of intrigue and emulation for weeks beforehand. But for a few broad rules, which eliminated at least half the school, the task might have been still more difficult than it was. For instance, all juniors, to the eternal wrath and indignation of the Den, were excluded. Further, all boys who during the term had suffered punishment, either monitorial or magisterial, all boys who had not shown up at the proper number of practices in the Fields, all boys who had lost a given number of "call-overs" forfeited the chance of getting their names on the "Grandcourt List," as it was called.

Of the reduced company that remained, each member of the eleven had the right of nominating six, the remaining four being chosen by the patriarchal method of lot.

Altogether, it was admitted that the system of selection was on the whole impartial, although, as a matter of course, it involved bitter disappointments to many an enthusiastic and deserving cricketer.

Our heroes, being juniors, were of course out of it, and they warmly adopted the indignation of the Den against the gross tyranny of excluding the rising generation from taking part in the great school event.

But Dick was not a youth whose inmost soul could be satisfied with mere indignation. If a thing struck him as unjust, the desire to rid himself of the injustice took possession of him at the same time.

"Georgie," said he to Heathcote, the day before the match, "it's all rot! We *must* go, I tell you."

"How can we? We should get bowled out, to a certainty, before we started."

"But, Georgie, it's no end of a day, fellows say; you get put up like lords at Grandcourt, and the spread afterwards is something scrumptious."

"Yes, but what chance should we stand of that when every one will know we're mitching?"

"Oh, they wouldn't say anything if once we got there. I tell you, old man, I'd risk a good bit to do it. Think of the crow we'd have at the next Den."

"How should we get over, though?"

"Oh, I know some of the Fourth. They might smuggle us into their trap, or we could hang on somehow. Bless you! the fellows will be too festive to notice us. What do you say?"

"All right; I'm on to try it," said Heathcote, not feeling very sanguine.

"Right you are. Keep it quiet, I say, and come down to 'Tub' early to-morrow."

Which being arranged, the two dissemblers went down and addressed a monster meeting of the Den, denouncing everybody and vowing vengeance on the oppressor.

At "Tub time" next morning, Dick met his friend with a radiant face.

"It's all right," said he; "I've been over to the Mews and had a look at the traps, and one of them's got a bar underneath we can easily hang on to."

"Rather a grind hanging on to a bar for two hours!" suggested Heathcote.

"Bless you! that won't hurt. Besides, we might get a lift further on; in fact, one of the coachmen said for five bob he'd stow us away in the boot."

"That would be less dusty," said Heathcote; "but—"

"Look here," said Dick eagerly, as he and his friend stood side by side on the spring-board ready for a plunge, "what howling asses we are! Of course all the fellows will go on the top of the omnibuses, so if we cut round to the stables directly after breakfast, we can stow ourselves away inside one, under the seat, and then we shall have it all to ourselves."

"All right," said Heathcote, looking at last as if he saw his way to the venture.

And the two friends forthwith dived, and turned the plan over beneath the waves.

When, punctually at ten o'clock, the six coaches paraded in the great Quadrangle, no one noticed the absence of Dick and his henchman in the crowd that assembled to watch the departure of the lucky seventy. Nor when coach one had started with the Eleven, and coaches two, three, and four had carried off the rest of the Sixth and Fifth, did any one suspect that coach five had taken up two of its passengers already.

The Upper and Middle Fourth, who boarded this vehicle, had little idea, as they pitched their coats and wraps inside and mounted themselves to the top, that, like the birds who buried the babes in the wood beneath the leaves, they were hiding the light of day from two innocents who lay one under either seat, with their noses to the fresh air and their hearts very decidedly in their mouths.

"Chock full up here," cried a voice from the top, which Dick, even in his retirement, recognised as belonging to Duffield, the post fag, who, by virtue of his office, was just out of the Den; "you kids will have to go inside."

"Oh, I say, you might let us up," replied one of the "kids" in question, in tones of expostulation; "we won't take up much room. It's so jolly stuffy inside."

"So it is," inwardly ejaculated the two stowaways.

"Just the place for you. You can play oughts-and-crosses and enjoy yourselves. There's not standing room up here," cried Duffield.

"Can't we stand on the step?"

"No; Hooker's bagged the bottom step, and I've bagged the one half up this side as soon as we start."

The lurkers gasped. They had not reckoned on the steps being occupied and their snug retreat raked by the eyes of the bumptious Hooker.

"Can we stand on them till you're ready, I say?" once more asked the persevering Fourth-formers.

"Why can't you go inside? I say, though," added the post fag, "there's room for two on the next coach. Hop up, or you'll be out of it!"

To the relief of our heroes, the youngsters yapped off on the new scent; and they presently had the satisfaction of hearing their voices raised in a halloo of triumph from the box of coach six.

"All right!" cried a master, as the last man squeezed up to his perch.

Then arose great cheers and counter-cheers, not unmixed with yells, as the cavalcade drove off in style, followed by Templeton in full cry as far as the great gate, where they parted company, amid shouts that brought all the town to its windows.

Once clear of the school, our heroes breathed more freely in more senses than one. As long as Hooker kept guard of the lower step, and Duffield's legs swayed about on the other, they were unable to do more than quietly push back the coats and put their heads out. But both these amateur conductors were too much occupied in hailing passers-by and protecting their caps from the assaults of their own friends above to bestow much attention to the inside of a coat-strewn, stuffy vehicle; and in time our heroes found they might venture to whisper across the floor and attempt in a quiet way to make themselves more comfortable; "Beastly dusty," said Heathcote; "it gets in my mouth."

"Wouldn't mind that," said Dick, "if I didn't get pins-and-needles in my arms. I've a good mind to turn over."

Here they were sent back like rabbits to their holes by the scare of a free fight taking place on the lower step between Hooker and a town youth, whom he had aggrieved by discharging a broadside of peas on a tender portion of his visage.

The fight was a sharp one, for the burly town youth was a "tartar," and had more than one grudge to settle with the Templeton boys. He managed to get a footing on the step, and hooking one elbow securely over the door, worked his other arm with great effect on the unfortunate Hooker. The whole fray was so suddenly got up that those on the roof knew nothing about it, and Duffield was so occupied with kicking at the intruder with his one spare leg that he quite forgot to raise a war cry.

The town boy proved equal to his two antagonists. Duffield was early rendered *hors de combat* by his spare foot being captured and tucked under the arm by which the enemy hung on to the door. And Hooker himself was gradually getting ousted from his perch, and might have been finally dropped on to the road, had not an unexpected diversion in his favour rescued him.

This was made by no one less than Dick, who, having taken in with a quick eye the position of affairs, saw that Templeton demanded his services, cost him what they might. He, therefore, summoned Heathcote to back him up, and taking an overcoat from the pile, cast it adroitly over the head of the town boy just as he had edged Hooker on to the very margin of the step. This, of course, settled the business. Duffield got back his foot, and Hooker got his arm once more over the door. The former raised a cry of

"Cad hanging on!" The latter shouted, "Whip behind!" The occupants of coach six yelled, "Chuck him over!" And putting one thing with another, the town boy decided that he would be more comfortable on the pavement than where he was. So he dropped off, leaving his hat behind him, which trophy was immediately seized and passed aloft, amid universal triumph, and displayed proudly on the top of a bat, on coach five, until the cavalcade was clear of the town.

"Who scragged that fellow?" asked Hooker, as soon as the campaign was over, looking up and down.

"I don't know," said Duffield. "Is there any one inside?"

Dick, who had been gradually trying to edge back to his retreat, deemed it prudent to make a clean breast of it at once, while the two "step" men owed him their thanks.

"I say, Hooker," said he, putting up his head behind the pile of wraps in a manner that made the gentleman addressed almost fall off with fright, "don't say anything—I scragged him. Heathcote and I wanted so awfully to see the match. Keep it dark, I say."

Hooker put his head into the window, and whistled.

"You'll get in a frightful row," said he, consolingly; "never mind, I'll say nothing. Cover up, and don't let the chaps see you."

They took his advice as cheerfully as they could, and even endured pleasantly the occasional pea-shooter practice with which, by way of enlivening their solitude, he was good enough to favour them.

They had an anxious drive on the whole. For besides Hooker's pea-shooter and the dismal prophecies he kept calling in to them of the terrible fate that awaited them on their return to Templeton, they found the dust and heat very trying. All that, however, was as nothing to the panic produced by a sudden rumour of a shower, and the possible descent of the whole of coach five into the interior. Happily for them Jupiter Pluvius changed his mind at the last moment, and sheered off. But the two minutes they spent in expecting him were calculated considerably to curtail the natural life of both.

It was hard lines, too, to hear all the festivities going on above and be able to take no part in them. They dared not even sit up for fear of becoming visible to the occupants of the box-seat of coach six, who had a full view of their interior. So they lay low for two mortal hours, and by the time Grandcourt was reached discovered that their dusty heads and limbs ached not a little.

"You'd better come out and cheek it," said Hooker, as the coach pulled up; "you're bound to get into a row, so you may as well enjoy yourselves."

Dick's intention had been to get taken on under the seat to the stables, and there make his escape. But after all there was not much less risk that way than in following Hooker's advice. So they tumbled out with the crowd, and kept near Hooker, on whose support they felt entitled to rely, after the service rendered to him in the battle of the lower step.

Every one was so excited about the match, and so anxious to show off well to the Grandcourt boys, that no one took any notice of the two small interlopers, which was a matter of great thankfulness to our heroes.

Their spirits gradually rose as they found themselves sitting comfortably among a knot of Templetonians, in the glorious Grandcourt meadow, with a superb view of the match. They lost all their reserve, and joined wildly in the cheers for the old school, heedless of every consideration of prudence and self-preservation.

And they certainly had some excuse for their enthusiasm. For Templeton walked away from her enemy from the very first, in a style which amazed even her most ardent admirers.

In their first innings they put together 215 as smartly and merrily as if they were playing against an eleven of the Den. One after another the Grandcourt bowlers collapsed. No sort of ball seemed to find its way past the Templeton bats, and no sort of fielding seemed to hem in their mighty hits.

Pontifex—"dear old Ponty," as everybody called him to-day—who had been breaking his friends' hearts by his indolence and indifference all the term, stood up now, and punished the Grandcourt bowling, till the enemy almost yelled with dismay. The steady Mansfield was never steadier, nor Cartwright more dashing, nor Pledge more artful. Even Birket, who to-day fleshed his maiden bat on the Grandcourt meadow, knocked up his two and threes, with one cut for four into the tent, till it seemed to Templeton that cricket was in the air, and that even Hooker and Duffield could have pulled the match off single-handed.

But the batting was nothing to the play when Templeton was out and took the offensive. Pledge was more than dangerous, he was deadly, and knocked the balls about in a manner quite "skeery." Heathcote was perfectly sure he could have made as good a stand as the Grandcourt captain, and began to lay down the law to his hearers as to how this man should have taken one ball and that man "drawn" another, till he became quite amusing, and was recognised for the first time by several of his schoolfellows.

However, the general interest in the match was still too keen to give him the notoriety his indiscretion deserved; and lulled by his apparent immunity and the luxury of his present circumstances, he, like Dick, quite forgot he had no right to be where he was, and even expostulated with Duffield for squashing him and interfering with his view.

Grandcourt went out for a miserable 80; of which 30 had been put on by one man. Of course they had to follow on, and as the time was short, it was agreed to curtail the usual interval, and finish up the match straight away.

So Grandcourt went in again, and although it fared somewhat better, was still unable to stem the tide of defeat. With 135 to get in order to avoid a single innings defeat, it was only natural they did not settle down to their task very cheerfully or hopefully. Pledge still sent down a ruthless fire from one end; and seemed even to improve with exercise. Nor was he badly backed up at the other end by Cresswell; while Mansfield, at the wicket, and Ponty, at point, seemed, as it were, to help themselves to the ball off the end of the bat, whenever they liked. By painful, plodding hard work, Grandcourt put up their hundred, and it spoke well for the chivalry of the victorious seventy, that they cheered the three figures as loudly as any one.

It was uphill work trying to hold out for the remaining 35 runs. But the losers were Englishmen, and long odds brought out their good qualities. With solemn, almost ferocious, faces, the two last men in clung to their bats, and blocked, blocked, blocked, stealing now a bye, pilfering now a run out of the slips, and once or twice getting on the right side of a lob with a swipe that drew the hearts of Templeton into their mouths.

A score of runs did those two add on to their hundred, and the seventy groaned as the chances of a single innings victory dwindled run by run.

"Most frightful soak if they do us," said Dick, addressing the audience generally. "Why don't they try Mansfield?"

"Shut up. Lie down under the seat, and don't talk to me," said Hooker, flushed with excitement.

"Pledge has bowled four maidens running," said Heathcote, determined that no one should blame the bowler *he* had assisted to train.

"What's the use of bowling maidens? Why don't he bowl the boys, and have done with it?" said Duffield.

Dick looked at Heathcote; Heathcote looked at Dick; Duffield hummed a ditty. How could he do such a thing at such a time, and in such a place? Oh, had he been only in the Mountjoy waggonette on a lonely road, what a business meeting they could have held! As it was, there was only time to crush the debtor's hat down over his eyes, and dig him on each side in the ribs, when a general stir betokened some important movement on the field of battle.

"By George! they're going to change bowlers," said Hooker. "Quite time, too."

"No, they're not," replied Dick, "they're going to change ends. Awful low trick to put Cresswell with the light in his eyes."

"Pledge has had it in his all the last hour," said Heathcote.

"Shut up, you kids, and don't make such a row. You can talk when we're in at supper," said a Fifth-form fellow.

The allusion was a depressing one. More than once it had crossed our heroes' minds that supper was coming on; but the chances of their "cheeking in" (as they called it) to that part of the day's entertainment were, to say the least, narrow.

At any rate, the allusion made them sad, and they relapsed into silence as the bowlers changed ends, and Pledge prepared to attack from his new base.

There was a sudden uncomfortable silence all round the meadow. Grandcourt felt that if they could weather the storm a few overs longer they might yet avert the disgrace of a single innings defeat. Templeton felt, with decided qualms, that unless the change told quickly, it had better not have been made at all. The eleven stepped in a bit, and watched the ball with anxious faces. Ponty, alone, with one hand in his pocket, yawned, and looked somewhere else. "What's the odds to Ponty?" thought the seventy, marvelling how any one could look so unconcerned at such a crisis.

Pledge bowled one of his finest, awkwardest, most disconcerting slows. The cautious batsman was proof against its syren-like allurements, and stepped back to block what any one else would have stepped forward to slog. The ball broke up sharp against his bat, and Grandcourt began to breathe again as they saw its progress arrested.

But at that particular moment it appeared to enter dear old Ponty's head to take his hand out of his pocket and stroll forward a pace or two from his place at point in the direction of the wicket. And somehow or another it seemed to him that while he was there he might as well pick up the ball, as it dropped off the end of the bat on its way to the ground.

Which he did. And as every one looked on, and wondered what little game he was up to, it occurred to the umpire that it was a catch, and that the match was at an end.

Whereupon, the truth flashed round the field like an electric shock, and the crowds broke into the meadow in wild excitement, while the seventy, crimson with cheers, formed column and went for their men.

Poor Ponty had a hard time of it getting back to the tent, and half repented of his feat. But it did him and Templeton good, when they came upon the headquarters of Grandcourt, to hear the hearty cheers with which the vanquished hailed their victors.

Chivalry is infectious. For the next quarter of an hour the meadow was given up to cheers by Templeton for Grandcourt, and cheers by Grandcourt for Templeton, in which the gallant seventy-two, despite their numerical inferiority, held their own with admirable pluck.

Then, a mighty bell tolled out across the meads, and conqueror and conquered, united in the brotherhood of appetite and good fellowship, turned in to supper, carrying their cheers with them.

Now was the hour of our heroes' perplexity. For, be it said to their credit as gentlemen, that however easily they may have got over their scruples as to breaking Templeton rules, riding in Templeton coaches, and enjoying themselves in the Grandcourt meadows, they had some hesitation about making free with the Grandcourt supper without a rather more precise invitation than they were already possessed of.

So they lagged a little behind the seventy, put their Templeton badges conspicuously forward, and tried to look as if supper had never entered into their calculations.

"Aren't you two fellows coming to supper?" said a Grandcourt senior, overtaking them as they dawdled along.

"Thanks, awfully," said they; "perhaps there won't be room."

"Rather!" said the hospitable enemy, "you two won't crowd us out."

"We'll sit close, you know," said Dick.

"Better not sit too close to begin with," said the Grandcourt boy, laughing, "or it'll be real jam before supper's over. Cut on and join your fellows, and squeeze into the first seat you can find."

The first seat our heroes found was one between Ponty and the Grandcourt head master, which, on consideration, they decided not to be appropriate. They therefore made hard for the other end of the room, and wedged themselves in among a lot of jolly Grandcourt juniors, who hailed them with vociferous cheers, and commenced to load them with a liberal share of all the good things the hospitable table groaned under.

Happy for Dick and Heathcote had they taken advice and begun the orgy at half distance! But they survived the "jam;" and what with chicken pie, and beef and ham, and gooseberry pie and shandy-gaff, to say nothing of jokes and laughter, and vows of eternal friendship with every Grandcourt fellow within hail, they never (to quote the experience of the little foxes in the nursery rhyme) "they never eat a better meal in all their life."

They could have gone on all night. But alas! envious time, that turns day to night, and hangs its pall between our eyes and the light of our eyes, put an end to the banquet. The coaches clattered up to the Grandcourt gate; the seventy, with their wraps and coats, were escorted, by their hosts in a body, to the chariots; horns sounded; cheers answered cheers; caps waved; whips cracked, and in five minutes the Grandcourt gate was as silent as if it guarded, not a fortress of hearty schoolboys, but a deserted, time-ruined monastery.

Chapter Twelve
In which Nemesis has a busy time of it

Our heroes had all along had a presentiment that their troubles would begin some time or other. They had expected it at the very start; but it had been put off stage by stage throughout the day, until it really seemed as if it must make haste, if it was to come at all.

And yet everything had gone so smoothly so far; the day had been so successful, the match so glorious, the supper so gorgeous, that they could hardly bring themselves to think Nemesis would really pounce upon them.

That worthy lady, however, though she often takes long credit, always pays her debts in the long run, and our heroes found her waiting for them before Grandcourt was many miles behind them.

They had been baulked in their intention of getting back into the friendly shelter of coach five at the outset, by the very awkward fact that Mansfield would stand at the door of Grandcourt, talking to a friend, until coach five had received its passengers, and started. Coach six followed, and to the horror of our two skulkers the way was still blocked. Things were getting desperate. The top of number *six* was packed, and still Mansfield stood across the door.

Should they throw themselves on his mercy, or hurl themselves between his feet, and overturn him, if haply they might escape in the confusion? How they hated that Grandcourt fellow who talked to him. What business had he to keep a Templeton fellow there catching cold? Why hadn't all Grandcourt been ordered to bed directly after supper?

Horrors! Coach six shouted "All right!" and rattled off.

"We're done for," said Heathcote. "We may as well show up."

"Stay where you are," said Dick; "we shall have to hang on behind the coach the Eleven go in."

"But, Dick, they're all monitors!"

"Can't be helped," said Dick, peremptorily.

The Eleven's coach drove up, and all Grandcourt turned out with a final cheer for their conquerors. Mansfield shook hands with his friend, and climbed up on to the box. The rest followed. Ponty rambled out among the last. He looked up at the crowded roof, and didn't like it. It was far too much grind for the dear fellow to swarm up there.

"I'll go inside, Cresswell. Come on; we'll get a seat each, and make ourselves comfortable."

Cresswell laughed.

"If you hadn't made that catch, old man," said he, "I'd say you were the laziest beggar I ever saw. But as you've a right to give your orders, I'll obey. Lead on, mighty captain."

Our heroes shivered, and wondered if any sin in the calendar were equal to that of sloth! With all the Eleven on the top, they had had a chance yet of weathering "Mrs" Nemesis, and hanging on behind. But with the captain and whipper-in inside, they might as well try and hang on a lion's tail.

"All U P, old man," groaned Heathcote.

"Slip out sharp!" said Dick excitedly. "Our only chance is to get ahead of them, and pick them up on the road."

Scarcely any one noticed the two dismayed little Templetonians, as they squeezed out of the gate, with their caps drawn over their eyes, and their heads diligently turned away from the coach of the Eleven. One fellow, however, spotted them, and scared the wits out of them, by saying "Hallo! here are two youngsters left behind. Get inside this coach; there's lots of room. Look alive, they're starting."

"Oh, thanks!" said Dick, scarcely able to speak for the jumping of his heart, "we're going to do a trot the first mile or so. Thanks awfully! Good-bye." And to the amazement of the Grandcourtier, the small pair started to run with their heads down and their fists up, at the rate of seven miles an hour.

"By George," thought he to himself, "some of those Templeton kids go the pace."

The pleasant village of Grandcourt was startled that evening, as the shades of night fell, by the sight of two small boys trotting hard down the High Street, side by side, some three hundred yards in advance of the coach which carried the conquering heroes of Templeton; like eastern couriers who run before the chaise of the great man. But those two heeded neither looks nor jeers; their ears were deaf to the cry of "Stop thief," and shouts of "Two to one on Sandy," stirred no emotions in their fluttering breasts. Luckily for them the road began uphill, so they were able to get a fair start by the time the village was clear. When at last they pulled up breathless at the road-side, they could see the lamp of the coach a quarter of a mile down the road, advancing slowly.

"It's touch and go," said Heathcote, "if we do it without getting nabbed. That wretched light shows up everything."

"Yes, I don't like it," said Dick; "we'd better lie down in the ditch, Georgie, till it's got past. They'll trot as soon as they get up here on to the level, and we must make a shot at the step. Those fellows inside are sure not to be looking out."

It was an anxious few minutes as the light approached, and shot its rays over the prostrate bodies of the boys in the ditch. They dared not lift their faces as it passed, and it was only when, as Dick had predicted, the walk changed into a trot, that they started from their lurking-place, and gave chase.

"Why," groaned Heathcote, as they came up, "it's got no step!"

For once, Dick was gravelled. The idea that the coach was not like all the other coaches had never once crossed his mind; and he felt beaten. The two unhappy pursuers, however, kept up the chase, pawing the forbidding coach door, very much as kittens paw the outside of a gold-fish bowl.

Alas! there was nothing to lay hold of; not even a handle or a nail!

"Shall we yell?" gasped Heathcote, nearly at the end of his wind.

"Wait a bit. Is there anything underneath we could lay hold of?"

They groped, but, as it seemed, fruitlessly. Dick, however, stooped again, and next moment turned round radiant.

"There's a bit of string," said he. "Keep it up, old man, and we'll get hold of it."

With much diving he succeeded in picking up the end of a casual piece of string that had somehow got its other end fastened to a nut underneath the coach. As quick as thought he whipped out his handkerchief and looped it on to the string. Then Heathcote whipped out his handkerchief and looped it on to Dick's, and between them the two held on grimly, and tried to fancy their troubles were at an end.

The support of a piece of stray string at the tail of a coach, supplemented by two pocket-handkerchiefs, may be grateful, but for practical purposes it is at best a flimsy stay, and had it not been for occasional hills at which to breathe, our heroes might have found it out at once.

As it was, they were carried three or four miles on their way by the purely moral support of their holdfast until the last of the hills was climbed, and the long steady slope which led down to Templeton opened before the travellers and reminded the horses of corn and stable. Then a trot began, which put the actual support of the extemporised cable to the test.

Our heroes, worn out already, could not, try all they would, keep it slack. Every step it became tauter and tauter, until at last you might have played a tune upon it. They made one gallant effort to relieve the strain, but, alas! it was no good. There was a crack of the whip ahead, the horses, full of their coming supper, gave a bound forward, and that moment on the lonely road, five miles from home, sprawled Heathcote, with Dick in his lap, and two knotted pocket-handkerchiefs in the dust at their feet. They had no breath left to shout, no energy to overtake, so they sat there panting, watching the coach vanish into the night and humbly wondering—what next?

"Here's a soak!" said Heathcote at last, recovering speech and slowly untying his handkerchief from the cable in order to mop his face.

"Yes," said Dick, getting off his friend's lap and looking dismally down the road; "our ride home didn't come off after all."

"We came off, though!" said Heathcote. But he corrected himself as he saw Dick wearily round upon him. "I mean—I say, what must we do?"

"Stump it," said Dick. "It's about five miles."

Heathcote whistled.

"Pity we didn't cheek it into our own coach," said he. "I say, Dick, what a row there'll be!"

"Of course there will," said Dick. "Have you only just found that out? Come along; we'll be late."

Considering it was eight o'clock and they were yet five miles from home, this last observation was sagacious.

They strolled on for half an hour in silence, mending their pace as they recovered their wind, until at the end of that time they had settled down into a steady three-and-a-half miles an hour, and felt rather more like getting home than they had done.

"Another hour will do it," said Dick. "I say, we might smuggle in after all, Georgie. What a crow if we do, eh?"

Georgie inwardly reflected that there would be a crow of some sort or other whatever happened, but he prudently reserved his opinion and said, "Rather!"

"We ought to come to the cross-roads before long," said Dick. "I hope to goodness you know which one goes to Templeton."

"No, I don't; but there's bound to be a post."

There was a post, but, though they climbed up it and rubbed their eye-lashes along each arm, they could get no guiding out of it. They could see an L on one arm, and an N on another, and a full stop on each of the other two, but, even with this intelligence, they felt that the road to Templeton was still open to doubt, as, indeed, after their wanderings round and round the sign-post, they presently had to admit was the case with the road by which they had just come.

"We'd better make ourselves snug here for the night," said Heathcote, who fully took in the situation.

"That would be coming to a full stop with a vengeance!" said Dick.

"Shut up; I let you off—and, by Jove, here's somebody coming!"

The red embers of a pipe, followed by a hulking nautical form, hove slowly in sight as he spoke, and never did a sail cheer the eyes of shipwrecked mariners as did this apparition bring comfort to Dick and Heathcote.

"I say," said the former, advancing out of the shades and almost startling the unsuspecting salt, "we've lost our way. Which road goes to Templeton?"

The big sailor gave a grunt and lay to in an unsteady way, which convinced our heroes, unlearned as they were in such matters, that he wasn't quite sober.

"What d'yer want ter go ter Templeton fur?" demanded he.

"We belong to the school, and we've got left behind."

The sailor laughed an unsympathetic laugh and took his pipe out of his mouth.

"Yer belong to the school, do yer, and yer've lost yer way?"

"Yes; can you put us right?"

"Yes, I can put yer right," said the brawny young salt, putting his pipe back between his lips. "What'll yer stand?"

"We'll give you a shilling," said Dick.

"Yer will? Yer'll give me a sovereign apiece, or I'll bash yer!"

And he laid a hand on the arm of each of his victims, chuckling and smoking as he looked down on their puny efforts to escape.

"Turn out yer pockets, nobs!" said he, giving them a slight admonitory shake.

"I haven't got a sovereign," said Heathcote.

Dick did not even condescend to plead; he fell headlong on his huge opponent, shouting, in the midst of his blows —

"Let us go, do you hear? I know your name; you're Tom White, the boatman, and I'll get you locked up if you don't."

But even this valiant threat, and the still more valiant struggles of the two boys, availed nothing with the nautical highwayman, who smoked, and shook the bones of his wretched captives, till they were fain to call for mercy.

The mercy was dearly bought. Dick's half-sovereign, Heathcote's twelve shillings, the penknife with the gouge, among them did not make up the price. One by one their pockets were turned inside out, and whatever there took the fancy of the noble mariner went into the ransom. Pencils, india-rubber, keys, and even a photograph of Dick's mother were impounded; while resistance, or even expostulation only added bone-shaking into the bargain; till, at last, the unhappy lambs were glad to assist at their own fleecing, in order to expedite their release.

"There yer are," said Tom, when at last the operation was over, "that's about all I want of yer, my hearties; and if yer want the road to Templeton, that's she, and good-night to yer, and thank yer kindly. Next time yer want a sail, don't forget to give an honest jack tar a turn. Knows my name, do yer? Blessed if I ever see you afore."

"You're a beastly, low, tipsy thief," shouted Dick, from a respectful distance, "and we'll get you paid out for this."

And not waiting for a reply, the two unfortunates, less heavily weighted than ever, started down the road, snorting with rage and indignation and full of thoughts of the direst revenge.

Nemesis was coming down on them at last with a vengeance!

Two miles they went before speech came to the relief of their wounded feelings.

"It's transportation," said Heathcote.

"Cat-o'-nine-tails too," said Dick.

"Jolly good job," said Heathcote.

And they went on another mile.

Then it occurred to them this was not the road along which they had driven in the morning; and once more the villainy of Tom White broke upon them in all its blackness.

"He's sent us upon the wrong road!" said Heathcote, beginning at last to feel that Nemesis was a little overdoing it.

Dick gulped down something, and walked on in silence.

"Where are you going? What's the use of going on?"

"May as well," said Dick, striding on. "It's bound to lead somewhere."

In which comfortable conviction they accomplished another half-mile.

Then to their satisfaction, and somewhat to Dick's self-satisfaction, they heard a low noise ahead, which they knew must be the sea.

"I thought it would bring us out," said Dick. "When once we get at the sea, we can't help finding Templeton."

"Unless we take a wrong turn to start with, and then we shall have to walk all round England before we turn up."

"Shut up, Georgie, we've had foolery enough for one night."

Heathcote collapsed, and another mile brought the two wanderers to the sea.

Luckily for them, the rising moon came to their rescue in deciding whereabouts they were.

"Not far out," said Dick, "there's the Sprit Rock; two miles more will do it."

"I shan't be sorry when I'm in bed," said Heathcote.

"I shan't be sorry when I see Tom White hung. I say, we may as well have a dip before we go on."

So they solaced themselves with a plunge in the moonlit sea, which, after their dusty labours, was wonderfully refreshing. Having dressed again, all but their shoes and stockings, which they looped together and hung over their shoulders, they tucked up their trousers, and started to wade along the strand to their journey's end.

The tide had only just started to come in, so they had the benefit of the hard sand, which, combined with the soft, refreshing water and the bright moonlight, rendered their pilgrimage as pleasant as, under the circumstances, they could have desired. Their talk was of Thomas White, for whom it was well he was not within earshot. They arrested him, tried him, sentenced him, flogged him, transported him, and yet were not satisfied.

"You know, Georgie," said Dick, working himself into a fury, "he collared my mother's photograph! the low cad! I'd be a beast if I didn't pay him out."

"Rather! and I'll back you up, old man. I was going to get a tennis-bat with that twelve bob; the blackguard!"

About a mile from home the lights of Templeton hove in sight; but still our heroes' talk was of Tom White and the next assizes.

They had the beach to themselves, with only a few stranded boats for company, over whose anchors they had to pick their way gingerly.

"The tide's coming in at a lick," said Dick. "Half an hour later, we should have had to tramp on the soft sand — Lookout, you duffer!"

The last remark was caused by Heathcote tripping over a rope, and coming down all fours on the wet sand.

"Bother that rope," said he, "I never saw it. I say, it's rather a small one for that big boat, isn't it?"

"It is," said Dick, walking round to the stern of the boat in question, "its — Hallo, I say, Georgie, look here!"

Georgie looked in the direction of Dick's finger, and read the words, "'Martha,' Thomas White, Templeton" on the stern of the boat.

Both boys whistled. Then Dick marched resolutely up to the bows, over a thwart in which the anchor rope was hitched in a loop.

"Tom White must have been drunk when he anchored this boat," said Dick. "She'll never hold if the wind gets up."

"Good job, too," said Heathcote.

"So I think," said Dick, thoughtfully. "I say, Georgie," added he, with his fingers playing on the end of the loop, "Tom White's a frightful cad, isn't he?"

"Rather!"

"And a thief, too?"

"I should think so."

"It would serve him jolly well right if he lost his boat."

"He don't deserve to have a boat at all."

"This knot," said Dick, slipping the loop, "wouldn't hold against a single lurch. Why, it comes undone in a fellow's hand —"

And the end dropped idly on the floor of the boat as he spoke.

Heathcote nodded.

"Think of the cad having robbed two juniors like us, and collared mother's photograph, too, the brute!" said Dick, taking his friend's arm and walking on.

They talked no longer of Thomas White, but admired the moonlight, and wondered how soon the tide would be up, and speculated as to whether there wasn't a breeze getting up off the land. Once they turned back, and glanced at the black hull, lying, still aground, with the tide yards away yet. Then they thought a trot would warm them up before they put on their boots, and mounted the cliff to Templeton.

The clock struck half-past eleven as they knocked modestly at the porter's lodge. The porter was up, and evidently expected them.

"Nice goings-on, young gentlemen," said he. "The Doctor wishes to see you after chapel in the morning. In you go. I'm sorry for you."

With fluttering hearts they stole across the moonlit Quadrangle, and gazed round at the grim windows that peered down on them from every side. The housekeeper was up and ready for them, too.

"Bad boys," said she, as she opened the door; "go to bed quietly, and make no noise. The Doctor will be ready for you the moment chapel is over."

They mounted the creaking stairs, and crawled guiltily along the passage to their dormitory.

The dormitory monitor was sitting up in bed ready for them, too.

"Oh, you have turned up, have you?" said he. "I hope you'll enjoy yourselves with Winter in the morning. Most of the fellows say it's expulsion; but I rather fancy a licking, myself. Cut into bed, and don't make a noise."

And he curled himself up in his bedclothes, and slept the sleep of the just, which was more than could be said for the fitful slumbers of our heroes, which visions of Tom White's boat, and Ponty's pocket, and the piece of string at the tail of the Eleven's coach, combined to make the reverse of sound.

In the middle of the night Dick, as he lay awake, felt Heathcote's hand nudging him.

"I say, Dick!" said the latter, "the wind's got up. Do you hear it?"

"Shut up, Georgie. I'm just asleep."

Nemesis handed in her last cheque to our heroes after chapel next morning in the Doctor's study. I will spare the reader the harrowing details of that serious interview. Suffice it to say that the dormitory fag was right, and that Mrs Partlett was spared the trouble of packing up the two young gentlemen's wardrobes.

But they emerged from the study wiser and sadder men. They knew more about the properties of a certain flexible wood than they had ever dreamed of before. They also felt themselves marked men in high quarters, with a blot on their new boy's scutcheon which it would take a heap of virtue to efface.

"By George!" said Dick that afternoon, "we got it hot—too hot, Georgie."

"I think Winter might have let us down rather easier, myself," said Georgie.

There was a pause.

"Was it windy last night?" asked Dick.

"Rather!" said Georgie.

"Anything new down town?"

"Couldn't hear anything."

"Hum! I wonder what that beast's done with mother's photograph? I say, Georgie, what a howling brute he was!"

"He was; he deserves anything."

Strange, if so, that neither of our young heroes went to the police station and informed against their man. On the contrary, they went up on to the cliffs after school, and scanned the bay from headland to headland, doubtless lost in the wonders of the deep, and wishing very much they could tell what the wild waves were saying as to the whereabouts of the *Martha*.

Chapter Thirteen
Twixt Scylla and Charybdis

Perhaps no epoch of a schoolboy's life is more critical—especially if he be of the open-hearted nature of Dick and Heathcote—than that which immediately follows his first punishment at the hands of the law.

On the one hand he has the sense of disgrace which attends personal chastisement, as well as the discomfort of a forfeited good name, and the feeling of being down on the black books of the school authorities generally. On the other hand, he is sure to meet with a certain number of companions who, if they do not exactly admire what he has done, sympathise with him in what he has suffered; and sympathy at such a time is sweet and seducing. A little too much sympathy will make him feel a martyr, and a little martyrdom will make him feel a hero, and once a hero on account of his misdeeds, he needs a stout heart and a steady head to keep himself from going one step further and becoming a professional evil-doer, and ending a fool and his own worst enemy.

Dick and Heathcote ran a serious risk of being shunted on to the road to ruin after the escapade of the Grandcourt match.

The former discovered that his popularity with the Den was by no means impaired by adversity. In fact, he jumped at one bound to the hero stage of his ordeal. He was but a boy of flesh and blood, and sympathy is a sweet salve for smarting flesh and blood.

After the first burst of contrition it pleased him to hear fellows say—

"Hard lines on you, old man. Not another in a hundred would have cheeked it the way you did."

It pleased him, too, to see boys smaller than himself look round as they passed him, and whisper something which made their companions turn round too. Dick grew fond of small boys as the term went on.

It pleased him still more to be taken notice of by a few bigger boys, to find himself claimed by Hooker and Duffield as a crony, to be bantered by the aesthetic Wrangham, and patronised by the stout Bull.

All this made him go over the adventures of that memorable day often in his mind, and think that after all it wasn't a bad day's sport, and that, though he said so who shouldn't, he had managed things fairly well, and got his money's worth.

His money's worth, however, reminded him of his lost half-sovereign and his mother's photograph, and these reflections usually pulled him up short in his reminiscences.

Heathcote, in a more philosophical and dismal way, had his perils, and Pledge gave him no help through his difficulty. On the contrary, he encouraged his growing discontent.

"Dismals again?" said he, one evening. "That cane of Winter's must be a stiff one if it cuts you up like that."

"Winter always does lay it on thick to the kids, though," said Wrangham, who happened to be present. "His lickings are in inverse ratio to the size of the licked."

It did comfort Heathcote to hear his case discussed in such learned and mathematical terms, but that was all the consolation he got.

Dick was in far too exalted a frame of mind to give much assistance.

"What does it matter?" said he, recklessly. "I don't mean to fret myself."

And so the matter ended for the present. The two friends were bearing their ordeal in two such different ways that they might almost have parted company, had there not been another common interest of still greater importance to bind them together.

One day Heathcote came up from the "Tub" at a canter and caught his friend at the chapel door.

"Dick," he said, "it's all out! This bill was sticking on one of the posts by the pier. It was wet, so I took it off."

Dick read—"£2 reward. Lost or stolen from her moorings, on Templeton Strand, on the 4th inst, a lugger-rigged sailing boat, named the *Martha*. Any one giving information leading to the recovery of the boat—or if stolen, to the conviction of the thief—will receive the above reward. Police Station, Templeton."

Dick handed the ominous paper back with a long face.

"Here, take it. Whatever did you pull it off the post for?"

"I thought you'd like to see it," said Heathcote, putting the despised document into his pocket.

"So I did. Thanks, Georgie. We didn't steal the boat, did we?"

"Rather not. Not like what he did to our money."

"No. That was downright robbery."

"With violence," added Heathcote.

"Of course. It was really Tom White's fault the boat got adrift. It was so carelessly anchored."

"Yes. A puff of wind would have slipped that knot."

There was a pause.

"It's plain he doesn't guess anything," said Dick.

"Not likely. And he's not likely to say anything about it, if he does."

"Of course not. It would mean transportation for him."

"After all, some one may have gone off with the boat. We can't tell. It was there all right when we saw it, wasn't it?"

Dick looked at his friend. He could delude himself up to a certain point, but this plea wouldn't quite wash.

"Most likely they'll find it. It may have drifted round to Birkens, or some place like that. It'll be all right, Georgie."

But the thoughts of that unlucky boat haunted their peace. That Tom White had only got his deserts they never questioned; but they would have been more comfortable if that loop had slipped itself.

Days went on, and still no tidings reached them. The bills faced them wherever they went, and once, as they passed the boat-house with a crowd of other fellows, they received a shock by seeing Tom White himself sitting and smoking on a bench, and looking contemplatingly out to sea.

"There's Tom White," said one of the group. "I say," shouted he, "have you found your boat, Tom?"

Tom looked up and scanned the group. Our heroes' hearts were in their boots as his eyes met theirs. But to their relief he did not know them. A half-tipsy man on a dark night is not a good hand at remembering faces.

"Found her? No, I aren't, young gentleman," said he.

"Hard lines. Hope you'll get her back," said the boy. "I say, do you think any one stole her?"

"May be, may be not," replied the boatman.

"Jolly rum thing about that boat," said the spokesman of the party, as the boys continued their walk.

"I expect it got adrift somehow," said another.

"I don't know," said the first. "I was speaking to a bobby about her: he says they think she was stolen; and fancy they've got a clue to the fellow."

Heathcote stumbled for no apparent reason at this particular moment, and it was quite amusing to see the concern on Dick's face as he went to the rescue.

"Jolly low trick," continued the boy, who appeared to interest himself so deeply in Tom's loss, "if any one really took the boat away. Tom will be ruined."

"Who do they think went off with her?" asked another.

"They don't say; but they're rather good at running things down, are our police. Do you recollect the way they bowled out the fellow who tried to burn the boat-house last year, and got him six months?"

This police gossip was so alarming to our two heroes, that they gave up taking walks along the beach, and retired to the privacy of the school boundaries, where there was no lack of occupation, indoor and out, to relieve the monotony of life.

A week after the Grandcourt match, a boy called Braider came up to Dick and asked to speak to him. Braider was in the Fourth, and Dick knew of him as a racketty, roystering sort of fellow, very popular with his own set—and thought something of by the Den, on account of some recent offences against monitorial authority.

"I say," said he to Dick, confidentially, "what do you say to belonging to our Club?"

"What Club?" asked Dick, scenting some new distinction, and getting light-headed in consequence.

"You'll promise not to go telling everybody," said Braider. "We're called the 'Sociables,' It's a jolly enough lot. Only twenty of us, and we have suppers and concerts once a week. The thing is, it's *awfully* select, and a job to get into it. But your name was mentioned the other day, and I fancy you'd get in."

"I suppose Georgie Heathcote isn't in it?" said Dick.

"Rather not!" said the other, mistaking his meaning; "he'd have no chance."

"He's not a bad fellow," said Dick. "I wouldn't mind if he was on."

"Well, there are two vacancies. What do you say for one?"

"Do I know the other fellows?"

"Most of them," and Braider repeated a string of names, among which were those of a few well-known heroes of the Fifth and Fourth.

"They're all jolly fellows," said Braider, "and, back up one another like one o'clock. It was your plucky show up at Grandcourt that made them think of having you; and if you join you'll just be in time for the next concert. What do you say?"

Dick didn't like to say no; and not being a youth who dallied much between the positive and the negative, he said:

"All serene, Braider, if they really want it."

"Of course they do, old man," said Braider, in tones of satisfaction; "they'll be jolly glad. Mind you don't go talking about it to any one, you know. They're very select, and don't want all Templeton wanting to join."

"When's the election?" asked Dick.

"Oh! to-day week. There's one fellow, Culver, up against you; but he's got no chance. One black ball in six excludes, so it's always a close run."

"Do you think there would be any chance for young Heathcote?"

"Doubt it. But we might try when you're in. Ta, ta! old man. Mum's the word."

Dick spent a troubled week. He was uncomfortable with Heathcote, in whom he was bursting to confide. He was uneasy, too, in meeting the few members of the "Sociables" whom he knew, and felt that they were watching him critically, with a view to the election next Thursday. And he was vindictive in the presence of Culver, whose possible rivalry he regarded as little short of an insult.

Indeed, the effect of the suspense on him was bad all round. For having somehow picked up the notion from Braider's hints that "spirit" was a leading qualification for aspiring members of the club, he was very nearly increasing that qualification notoriously, before the week was out, by another row with headquarters.

He purposely shirked his work, and behaved disorderly in class, in order to show his patrons what he was made of; and what was worse, he egged the unsuspecting Georgie on to similar excesses by his example. Georgie, as far as "spirit" went, stood better qualified for membership of the club at the week's end than did the real candidate; for while the latter escaped punishment, the former was dropped upon to the tune of three hundred lines of Virgil, for throwing a book across the room during class.

"Just my luck," said he defiantly to his leader afterwards. "Everybody's down on me. I'm bound to catch it, so I may as well have my fling."

"You did have your fling, Georgie, and you caught it, too."

Georgie was too out of humour to notice the jest. "You don't catch me caring twopence about it, though," said he.

But his tones belied the valiant words, and Dick looked curiously at his troubled, harried face.

"Why, Georgie," said he, "you're down on your luck, old man."

"Blow my luck!" said Georgie, "perhaps I am down on it. It serves me worse than yours."

Dick didn't say anything more just then. Perhaps because he had nothing to say. But he didn't like this new state of things in his friend. Georgie was being spoiled, and would have to be looked after.

Dick was not the only Templetonian who had made this brilliant discovery. Ponty had dropped a casual eye on him now and then, so had Mansfield; and neither the captain that was, nor the captain that was to be, liked the look of things.

"He's going the way of all—all the Pledgelings," said Ponty. "Can't you stop it, Mansfield?"

"If I were captain of Templeton, I'd try, old man," replied the other.

"Really, Mansfield, you frighten me when you look so solemn. What can I do?"

"Do? Take him away from where he is, to begin with."

"On what grounds? Pledge hasn't done anything you or I could take hold of. And if the kid is going to the dogs, we can't connect it with Pledge, any more than we can with Winter himself."

And Ponty yawned, and wished Mansfield would not look as if somebody wanted hanging.

"It's curious, at any rate," said Mansfield, "that Pledge's fag should begin to go to the dogs, while his chum, who fags for Cresswell, and is quite as racketty, should keep all right."

"Do you call young Richardson all right?" asked Ponty. "I should say he and his friend are in the same boat, and he's holding the tiller."

Which was pretty 'cute for a lazy one like Ponty.

"Well," said Mansfield, who, with all his earnestness, felt really baffled over the problem, "things mustn't go on as they are, surely."

"Certainly not, dear boy, if we can make them better; but I don't see what's to be done. I'd bless you if you could put things right."

And he put his feet upon the chair in front, and took up his novel.

Mansfield took the hint. Nor did he misunderstand his indolent friend. Ponty's indolence wasn't all laziness. It was sometimes a cloak for perplexity; and the captain-to-be, as he said good-night, guessed shrewdly that not many pages of the novel would be skimmed that evening.

Ponty did, in fact, wake up a bit those last few weeks of the term. He rambled down once or twice to the Juniors' tennis court, and terrified the small fry there by sprawling at full length on the grass within sight of the play. It was a crowded corner of the fields and a noisy one, and, if the captain went there for a nap, he had queer notions of a snug berth. If, however, he went there to see life, he knew what he was about.

He saw Aspinall there, toughening every day, and working up his screwy service patiently and doggedly, till one or two of the knowing ones found it worth their while to get on the other side of the net and play against him. Culver was there, big of bone, bragging, blustering as ever, but keeping the colour in his cheeks with healthy sport. Gosse was there, forgetting to make himself a nuisance for one hour in twenty-four. The globular Cazenove was there, melting with the heat, but proclaiming that even a big body and short legs can do some good by help of a true eye and a patient spirit. These and twenty others were there, getting good every one of them, and atoning, every time they scored a point and hit out a rally, for something less healthy or less profitable scored elsewhere. And Ponty, as he lay there blinking in the sun, moralised on the matter, and came to the conclusion that there is hope for a boy as long as he loves to don his flannels and roll up his shirt-sleeves, and stand up, with his head in the air, to face his rival like a man. Even a Culver may look a gentleman as he rushes down to his corner and saves his match with a left-hander, and Aspinall himself may appear formidable when, as he stands up to serve, his foeman pulls his cap down and retreats with lengthened face across the service-line.

But where were Dick and Heathcote? For a whole week Ponty took his siesta in the Juniors' corner, blinking now at the cricket, now at the tennis, strolling sometimes into the gymnasium, and sometimes to the fives courts, but nowhere did Basil the son of Richard meet his eyes, and nowhere was Heathcote the Pledgeling.

One day he did find the latter wandering like a ghost in the Quadrangle, and saw him bolt like a rat to his hole at sight of a monitor; and once he saw Dick striding at the head of a phalanx of Juniors, with his coat off and his face very much on one side, and the marks of battle on his eye and lip.

Ponty sheered off before the triumphal army reached him and shrugged his shoulders.

That afternoon he encountered our heroes arm-in-arm in the Quadrangle and hailed them. They obeyed his summons uneasily.

"Go and put on your flannels, both of you," said the captain, "and come back here; I'll wait for you."

In trepidation they obeyed and went, while Ponty looked about for a cozy seat on which to stretch himself.

In five minutes they returned and presented themselves. Ponty eyed them both calmly, and then roused himself and began to walk to the fields.

Tennis was in full swing in the Junior corner, where all sorts of play, good, bad and indifferent, was going on at the nets. Ponty, followed by the two bewildered champions, strolled about till he came upon an indifferent set being played by Gosse and Cazenove against Raggles and another boy called Wade.

"Stop the game for a bit, you youngsters," said the captain. "Which two of you are the best?"

"I think I and Raggles are," said Gosse, with his usual modesty.

"Oh, then you can sit out. Give your rackets to these two; they're going to play against Cazenove and Wade."

Dick's heart sank within him as he took Gosse's racket and glanced up at the captain's face.

"I'm rather out of practice," faltered he.

"Come, are you ready? I'll umpire," said the captain.

It was a melancholy exhibition, that scratch match; all the more melancholy that the other courts gradually emptied and a ring of Juniors formed, who stared silently now at the players, then round at Pontifex, and wondered what on earth he found to interest him in a miserable show like this. For our heroes mulled everything. Two faults were not enough for them; the holes in their rackets were legion, and their legs never went the way they wanted. The Den blushed as it looked on and heard Ponty call, game after game, "Love—forty."

Of course the two wretched boys were scared—Ponty knew that well enough—but so were Cazenove and Wade. And yet Cazenove and Wade managed to keep their wind and get over their net, and no one could say they had less to be scared at than their opponents.

At length the doleful spectacle was over. "One—six" was the score in games.

"You must be proud of your one game," said Ponty, strolling off.

Our heroes watched him go, and felt they were hard hit. It was no use pretending not to understand the captain's meaning, or not to notice the still lingering blushes of the spectators on their account.

So they withdrew sadly from the field of battle, chastened in spirit, yet not without a dawning ambition to make Ponty change his mind concerning them before the term was quite run out.

Chapter Fourteen
How Dick has one Latin exercise
more than he bargained for

Dick did not often feel ashamed of himself. He had a knack of keeping his head above water, even in reverses, which usually stood him in good stead. But after that mournful scratch match with Cazenove and Wade, he certainly did feel ashamed.

And, be it said to the credit of his honesty, that he blamed the right offender. Ponty had been rough on him, but it wasn't Ponty's fault. Cazenove and Wade had knocked him and his chum into a cocked hat, but it wasn't Cazenove's or Wade's fault. Heathcote had mulled his game dreadfully, and done nothing to save the match, but it wasn't Heathcote's fault. Basil the son of Richard was the guilty man, and Basil the son of Richard kicked himself and called himself a fool.

Not publicly, though. In the Den, despite the blushes his tennis had caused, he did his best to keep up his swagger and restore confidence by a few acts of special audacity; and the Den was forgiving on the whole. They did feel sore for a day, and showed it; but gradually they came back to their allegiance, and made excuses for their hero of their own accord.

If truth must be told, Dick was far more concerned as to the possible effect of his public humiliation on his election at "the Sociables," which was now only a day off.

Braider told him, with rather a long face, that his chances had been rather shaken by the affair, and that there was again some talk of pushing Culver against him. This alarming news drove all immediate projects of virtue out of Dick's head. Not that membership of the club was his one ideal of bliss; but, being a candidate, he could not bear the idea of being defeated, particularly by a young ruffian like Culver. So he indulged in all sorts of extravagances on the last day of his probation, and led Heathcote on to the very verge of a further punishment in order to recover some of the ground he had lost with the "select" twenty.

After school he could settle to nothing till he knew his fate. He dragged the unsuspecting Heathcote up and down the great Quadrangle under pretext of discussing Tom White's boat, but really in order to keep his eye on the door behind which the select "Sociables" sat in congress.

Heathcote saw there was a secret somewhere, and, feeling himself out of it, departed somewhat moodily to Pledge's study. Dick, however, continued his walk, heedless if every friend on earth deserted him, so long as Culver should not be preferred before him behind that door.

He was getting tired of this solitary promenade, and beginning to wonder whether the "Select Sociables" had fallen asleep in the act of voting for him, when a ball pitched suddenly on to the pavement between his feet.

He couldn't tell where it came from—probably from some window above, for no one just then was about in the Quadrangle.

He stooped down to pick it up and pitch it back into the first open window, when, greatly to his surprise, he saw his name written across it, and discovered that the ball was not a tennis ball at all, but a round paper box, which came in two as he held it.

Dick was not superstitious. He had scoffed at the Templeton ghost when he first heard of it, and made up his mind long since it was a bogey kept for the benefit of new boys.

But it certainly gave him a start to find himself, at this late period of the term, when he had almost forgotten he ever was a new boy, pitched upon as the recipient of one of these mysterious missives.

The letter inside was written in printed characters, like those addressed to Heathcote.

"Dick," it began.

"Hallo," thought Dick to himself, "rather cheek of a ghost to call a fellow by his Christian name, isn't it?"

"Dick,—Don't be a fool. You were a fine fellow when you came. What are you now? Don't let fellows lead you astray. You can be a fine fellow without being a bad one. Let the 'Sociables' alone. They'll teach you to be a cad. If you don't care for yourself, think of Heathcote, who only needs your encouragement to make a worse failure than he has made already. Save him from Pledge. Then you'll be a fine fellow, with a vengeance. Your real friend,—

"Junius.

"P.S.—Translate 'Dominat qui in se dominatur.'"

The first thing that struck Dick about this extraordinary epistle was, that it was odd the ghost should write his letters on Templeton exercise paper. It then occurred to him that it was rather rough to put him through his paces in Latin idioms at a time like this. Couldn't the ghost get a dictionary, or ask a senior, and find out for himself?

It then occurred to him, who on earth was it who had written to him like this? Some one who knew him, that was certain; and he almost fancied it must be some one who liked him, for a fellow wouldn't take the trouble to tell him he was a fine fellow at the beginning of the term, and all that sort of thing, unless he had a fancy for him.

What did he mean by "What are you now?" It sounded as if he meant "You are not a fine fellow now." Rather a personal remark.

"What's it got to do with him what I am now?" reflected Dick, digging his hands into his pockets, and resuming his promenade. "And what does he mean by fellows leading me astray? Like to catch any one trying it on, that's all. Like to catch *him*, for the matter of that, for his howling cheek!"

Dick sat down on one of the stone benches, and pulled out the letter for another perusal.

"'Let the Sociables alone.' Oh, ah! most likely he's been blackballed himself, and don't like any one to—. Humph! wonder if they *are* a shady lot or not? What does he mean by saying they'll teach me to be a cad? Who'll teach me to be a cad? Not a muff like Braider."

At that moment a door opened at the end of the corridor, and a voice shouted—

"Richardson!"

It was Braider's voice, and Dick knew it.

He crumpled the letter up in his hand, and the colour came and went from his cheeks.

"Richardson! where are you?" called Braider again, for it was dusk, and our hero's seat was screened from view.

Dick coloured again, and bit his lips; and finally got up from the bench, and strolled off in an opposite direction.

"Richardson! do you hear?" once more shouted the invisible Braider.

Dick walked on in the dusk, wondering to himself whether Braider would get into a row for kicking up that uproar in the Quad.

At last, after one final shout, he heard the door slam. Then he quickened his pace, and made for Cresswell's study.

On the staircase he met Aspinall.

"I heard some one calling you out in the Quad.," said the small boy.

"Did you?" replied Dick. "I wonder who it can have been? Is Cresswell in his study?"

"No."

"All serene. Come back with me. Have you done your swot?"

"Yes, I did my lessons an hour ago."

"Oh!" said Dick, and strode on, followed somewhat dubiously by his young *protégé*.

"Shut the door," said Dick, sternly, as they entered the study.

"Whatever is going to happen to me?" ejaculated the small boy, inwardly, as he obeyed. Dick had never spoken to him like this before. Had he offended him unwittingly? Had he been disloyal to his sovereignty?

Dick walked to the fireplace, and, pulling a letter from his pocket, read it through twice, apparently heedless of his subject's presence. Then he looked up suddenly, and, crushing the paper viciously back into his pocket, stared hard at his perturbed companion.

"Young Aspinall," said he, sharply, "do you say I'm a fool?"

"Oh, no," replied the boy, staggered by the very suggestion, "I should never think of saying such a thing."

"Should you say I was a blackguard?"

"No, indeed, Dick. No one could say that."

The hero's face brightened. There was a warmth in Aspinall's voice which touched the most sensitive side of his nature. Dick would have liked the ghost to be near to hear it.

"Should you say I've let myself be led astray, and made a mess of it here, at Templeton?"

"No, Dick, I don't think so," said the boy.

"What do you mean? *don't think*. Have I, or have I not?" demanded Dick.

It was a delicate position for the timorous small boy. He had had his misgivings about Dick, and seen a change in him, not, as he thought, for the better. But the idea of telling him so to his face was as much as his peace was worth. Yet he must either tell the truth, or a lie, and when it came to that, Aspinall could not help himself.

"You are the best friend I've got," said he, nervously, "and I'd give anything to be as brave as you; but—"

"Well, wire in," said Dick, tearing to bits one of Cresswell's quill pens with his teeth; "but what?"

"You're so good-natured," said Aspinall, "fellows make you do things you wouldn't do of your own accord."

"Who makes me do things?" demanded Dick, sternly.

"I don't know," pleaded the boy, feeling that this sort of tight-rope dancing was not in his line; "perhaps some of your friends in the Fourth and Fifth. But I may be all wrong."

"What do they make me do?" said Dick.

"They make you," said Aspinall, feeling that it was no use trying to keep his balance any longer, and that he might as well throw down his pole and tumble into the net; "they make you break rules and get into rows, Dick, because you see it goes down with them, and they cheer you for it. You wouldn't do that of your own accord."

"How do you know that?"

"I don't think you would," said the boy.

If any one had told Aspinall, ten minutes ago, he would be talking to Dick in this strain, he would have scouted the idea as a bit of chaff. As it was, he could hardly believe he had said as much as he had, and waited, in an uncomfortable sort of way, for Dick's next remark.

"Oh! that's what you think, is it?"

"Please don't be angry," pleaded the boy, "you asked me."

"What about Heathcote?" demanded Dick, abruptly, after a pause.

"What do you mean, Dick?"

"I mean, is he making a mess of it, too?"

"Oh, Dick; I never said you were making a mess of it."

"Well, then, is Heathcote being led astray?"

"I don't know. He seems different; and talks funnily about things."

"Does what? I never heard Georgie talk funnily about things, and I've known him a good bit. Who's leading him astray? Am I?"

Poor Aspinall was on the tight-rope again, at the most ticklish part. For he did think Dick was running Heathcote into mischief, unintentionally, no doubt, but still unmistakably, "Am I?" repeated Dick, rounding on his man, and fixing him with his eyes.

"Heathcote's not so strong-minded as you are, Dick, and when he sees you doing things, I fancy he thinks he can do them too. But he can't pull up like you, and so he gets into rows."

"Oh!" said Dick, returning to his quill pen, and completing its demolition. Then he pulled out the letter, and read it to himself again, and this time, instead of returning it to his pocket, twisted it up into a spill, and lit the gas with it.

"What should you say was the English of 'Dominat qui in se dominatur,' young 'un," he asked, casually, when the operation was complete.

"Why, that's one of the mottoes in the Quad," said Aspinall, wondering what on earth this had to do with Heathcote's rows. "I always fancied it meant, 'He rules best, who knows how to rule himself.'"

"Which is the word for best," asked Dick, critically, rather pleased to have found a flaw in the motto.

"Oh, I suppose it's understood," said Aspinall.

"Why couldn't he say what he meant, straight out?" said Dick, waxing wondrous wroth at the motto-maker, "there's plenty of room in the Quad for an extra word."

Aspinall quite blushed at this small explosion, and somehow felt personally implicated in the defects of the motto.

"Perhaps I'm wrong," said he. "Perhaps it means a fellow can't rule at all, unless he can rule himself."

"That won't wash," said Dick, profoundly. "Where's the 'nisi?' Never mind. Good-night, young Aspinall. I'm going to do my work here."

And Aspinall departed, a good deal exercised in his mind as to Dick's latest humour, but thankful, all the same, that he didn't appear desperately offended with the answers he had extorted to his very home questions.

Dick did not do much "swot" that evening. He couldn't get the ghost out of his head, nor the slovenly Latin prose of the old Templeton motto-writer.

"Qui in se dominatur." What Latin! Dick pulled down Cresswell's dictionary and looked up "se" and "dominatur," and wished he had the fellow there to tell him he ought to be ashamed of himself. Why, it might mean "who is ruled by his inside!" Perhaps it did mean that.

But no, Dick couldn't get out of the hobble he was in. He tried every way, but the right way. He denounced the ghost, he denounced Heathcote, he denounced the Latin grammar, but they always sent him back to where he started; until, finally, in sheer desperation, he had to denounce himself.

He was just beginning this congenial occupation, in as comfortable an attitude as he could, in Cresswell's easy-chair, when the study door opened, and Braider entered.

"Hallo! You're here, are you?" said that youth. "Why ever didn't you come before? I told you to be in the Quad, and I'd call for you; didn't I? You've got in a nice mess!"

Here was another candid friend going to tell him he'd got into a mess!

"What mess? Who with?"

"Why, with the Club. They elected you by a close shave, and expected you'd come in. I yelled all over the place for you, and couldn't find you. So they thought you'd skulked, and were nearly going to take Culver after all, when I promised to find you, and bring you. They're waiting for you now."

"Awfully sorry, Braider," said Dick, in an embarrassed way. "I can't come."

"Can't come, you ass! What do you mean?"

This was just what Dick wanted. As long as Braider was civil, Dick had to be rational, but as soon as Braider began to threaten, Dick could let out a bit, and relieve his feelings.

"Look here! who are you calling an ass?" said he, starting up.

Fortunately for the peace, Cresswell at that moment entered the study.

"Hallo!" said he, looking round, "make yourselves at home in my study, youngsters. Can't you ask a few friends in as well? What's the row?"

"Braider's the row," said Dick; "I want him to cut, and he won't. He wants me to—"

"All right," said Braider, in sudden concern, lest the secret of the "Sociables" was to be divulged, "I'll cut. And don't you forget, young Richardson, what you've promised."

"Of course I shan't," said Dick.

The select "Sociables" sat in congress to a late hour that night. What passed, no one outside that worthy body exactly knew. But Braider, on the whole, had a busy time of it.

He did not visit Dick again, but he interviewed both Culver and Heathcote, and was extremely confidential with each. And both Culver and Heathcote, after preparation, lounged outside the door, as Dick had lounged two hours before. And the two loungers, neither of them fancying the intrusion of the other, came to words, and from words proceeded to personalities, and from personalities to blows.

And as, in the course of the combat, Heathcote made a mighty onslaught and caught his enemy round the body and wrestled a fall with him on the threshold of the "Sociable" door, it so happened that the door, not being securely latched, gave way beneath the weight of the two combatants, and swinging suddenly open, precipitated them both on to the floor of the apartment, just as the Club was proceeding to record its votes.

Be it said to their credit, the select "Sociables" had a soul above mere routine, and seeing the contest was even, and that blood was up on both sides, they adjourned the business and hospitably invited the two candidates to fight it out there and then.

Which the two candidates did, with the result that, on the whole, Heathcote got rather less of the worst of it than Culver. Then, having politely ejected them both, the Club returned to business, and elected George Heathcote as a fit and proper person to fill the vacancy caused by the unjust expulsion of the late Alan Forbes.

Heathcote was thereupon brought in and informed of the honour bestowed upon him; and after being sworn to secrecy, and promising to obey the Club in all things, was called upon for a speech.

Heathcote's speech was short and memorable:—

"All serene. Anything you like. I don't care a hang."

Every sentence of this brilliant oration was cheered to the echo, and Heathcote was installed into his new dignity with loud enthusiasm.

He had not a ghost of an idea who the "Sociables" were, what they did, or what they wanted; but he had a rough idea they were a select assembly not favoured by the monitors or the masters, in which a fellow was popular in proportion to his record of "rows."

And Heathcote, whose one ambition it was at present, under Pledge's influence, not to figure as a prig or a hypocrite, cast his lot in with them, and chanced the rest.

It did occur to him to enquire if Dick was a member.

"Yes, he's a member, rather," said Spokes, the president. "He was elected this evening, wasn't he, you fellows?"

"Rather," echoed the high-souled club, winking at one another. Whereupon Heathcote asked no more questions, and proceeded to enjoy himself.

As the Club was breaking up, Twiss, one of its leading spirits, came up to the new member and said—

"Look here, youngster, don't you forget you're on your honour not to say a word about the Club outside to anybody. Not to Pledge, or your chum, or anybody."

"But Dick's a member too," said Heathcote.

"That does not matter. You mayn't even speak about it to me, or pretend you belong to my set. Do you twig?"

"All right," said Heathcote, "it's a good job you told me, though, for I was going to tell Dick about my election."

"Well, you know now. You're on your honour, so are we all."

Noble society! Organised dishonour held together in bonds of honour! If boys were only to cast round what is right the same shield of honour which they so often cast round what is wrong, what a world this would be!

When Heathcote and Dick met that evening in the dormitory, they had something more important to talk about or to be silent about than the select "Sociables."

"Look here, old man," said Dick, thrusting a piece of newspaper into his friend's hand. "They wrapped up the notepaper I got in town to-day in this. It's a bit of last week's *Templeton Observer*."

Heathcote looked at the paragraph his friend pointed to, and read:—

> **The mysterious disappearance of a boat**.—Up to the present no news has been heard of the *Martha* of Templeton, which is supposed to have been stolen from its moorings on the night of the 24th ult. The police, however, profess to have a clue to the perpetrators of the robbery. It is stated that late on the evening in question a lad, without shoes or stockings, was seen on the strand in the neighbourhood of the boat, and as the lad has been lost sight of since, it is supposed he may be concerned. At present the police are unable to give a description of the suspected lad, but vigilant enquiries are being prosecuted, and it is hoped that before long the mystery may be solved and the culprit brought to justice.

Chapter Fifteen
In which our heroes do not
distinguish themselves

One result of the alarming paragraph in the *Templeton Observer* was, that Dick and Heathcote for the remainder of the term became models of virtue as far as going out of school bounds was concerned.

Other boys might stray down the High Street and look at the shops, but they didn't. Others might go down to the beach and become familiar with the boatmen, but our heroes were far too respectable. Others might "mitch" off for a private cruise round Sprit Rock in quest of whiting, or other treasures of the deep; but Dick and Georgie would not sully their fair fame with any such breach of Templeton rules.

They kept up early morning "Tub," but that was the limit of their wanderings from the fold, and it was often amusing to mark the diligence with which they always took to drying their heads with the towels on the way up, if ever a boatman happened to cross their path.

Heathcote on more than one occasion was compelled, politely but firmly, to decline Pledge's commissions into the town, although it sometimes cost him words, and, worse still, sneers from his patron.

Once, however, he had to yield, and a terrible afternoon he spent in consequence.

"Youngster," said the 'Spider,' "I want you to go to Webster's in High Street and get a book for me."

"Afraid I can't, Pledge," said Heathcote. "I must swot this afternoon."

"What have you got to do?"

"There's thirty lines of Cicero, and I haven't looked at them."

"I'll do it for you before you come back."

"And there are some Latin verses for Westover, too."

"Leave them with me, too."

Heathcote felt uncomfortable, and it occurred to him it was not right to accept another's help.

"I think I ought to do them myself," said he, "I don't like having them done for me."

"Quite right, my dear young friend. You're beginning to find out it pays to be a good little boy, are you? I always said you would. I only hope you'll make a good thing of it."

Heathcote coloured up violently.

"It's not that at all," said he, "it's only— would it do if I went after preparation this evening?"

"What! Saint George propose to break rules? Well, I am shocked; after all my pains, too. No, my child, I couldn't let you do this wicked thing."

"What book am I to ask for?" said Heathcote, giving it up.

"Thanks, old man. There's something better than the saint in you, after all. Tell Webster it's the book I ordered last week. It is paid for."

Heathcote started on his mission with a heavy heart. He had lost caste, he feared, with Pledge, and he was running into the enemy's country and perilling not only himself, but Dick, in the venture.

He made fearful and wonderful détours to avoid a few straggling policemen, or any figure which in the distance looked remotely like a British seaman. The sight of a shopkeeper sitting at his door and reading the *Templeton Observer* scared him, and the bill offering a reward for his discovery all but drove him headlong back to the school without accomplishing his mission.

At length, after an anxious voyage, he ran into Mr Webster's harbour, and for a little while breathed again.

The bookseller knew quite well what book Pledge had ordered.

"Here it is," said he, handing over a small parcel, "and I'd advise you to get rid of it as soon as you can. It would do you no good to be found in your pocket, or Mr Pledge either," he added.

"He says it's paid for," said Heathcote.

"Quite right." Then, noticing that the boy still seemed reluctant to launch forth once more into the High Street, he said—

"Perhaps you'd like to look round the shop, Mr Heathcote?"

Heathcote thought he would, and spent a quarter of an hour in investigating Mr Webster's shelves of books.

Just as he was about to leave, Duffield and the "sociable" Raggles entered the shop.

"Hullo, Georgie!" said the latter; "who'd have thought of seeing you in the town? Everyone says you're keeping out of the way of the police, don't they, Duff?"

"Yes," said Duffield, perceiving the joke, "for some burglary, or something like that."

Heathcote breathed again at the word burglary, and made an heroic effort to smile.

"Not at all," said Raggles, nudging his ally; "not a burglary, but boat-stealing, isn't it, Webster?"

"Ah," said Mr Webster, who was a good man of business and fond of his joke, "they never did find that young party, certainly."

"Shut up and don't be a fool!" said Heathcote, feeling the colour coming to his face, and longing to be out in the open air.

"What's this the description was?" said Duffield, perching himself on the corner of the counter and reading off the unhappy Heathcote's personal appearance. "Good-looking boy of fourteen, with fair hair and a slight moustache. Dressed in a grey tweed suit, masher collar, and two tin sleeve-links. Not very intelligent, and usually wears a smudge of ink under his right eye. Isn't that it?"

"That's something about the mark," said Mr Webster, laughing.

"Think of offering two pounds reward for a chap like that!" said Raggles. "They must be hard up."

"Look here," said Heathcote, seeing that his only refuge lay in swagger, "I'm not going to have any of your cheek, Raggles. Shut up, or I'll lick you!"

"No fighting here, young gentlemen, please," said the affable bookseller.

"Ha! ha!" said Raggles, enjoying himself under the security of Duffield's alliance; "he's in a wax because we said it was only a *slight* moustache. He thinks we ought to have said a heavy one!"

"He may think it ought to be, but it ain't," said Duffield. "I never saw such a slight one in all my days!"

It is rarely that any one sees reason to bless his own moustache, but on this particular occasion, when he perceived the welcome controversy to which it was giving rise, Georgie was very near calling down benedictions on his youthful hairs. With great presence of mind he recovered his good-humour, and diverted the talk further and further into its capillary course.

He backed his moustache against Duffield's and Raggles' spliced together, he upbraided them with envy, and called Webster to witness that the pimple on Raggles' lip, which he claimed as the forerunner of his crop, had been there for the last six months with never a sign of harvest.

Altogether, under shelter of his moustache, Georgie crept out of a very awkward hobble, and finally out of Webster's shop, greatly to the relief of his palpitating heart.

But his trials were not quite over. As he was running headlong round the corner of High Street, determined that no pretext should detain him a moment longer than necessary in this perilous territory, he found himself, to his horror, suddenly confronted with the form of the very British seaman whom, of all others, he hoped to avoid; and, before he could slacken speed or fetch a compass, he had plunged full into Tom White's arms.

Tom White, as usual, I am sorry to say, was half-seas-over. Never steady in his best days, he had, ever since the loss of the *Martha* made his headquarters at the bar of the "Dolphin." Not that the loss of the *Martha* was exactly ruin to her late owner. On the contrary, since her disappearance, Tom had had more pocket-money than ever he had when she was his.

For sympathetic neighbours, pitying his loss, had contributed trifles towards his solace; the Templeton boys, with many of whom he had been a favourite, had tipped him handsomely in his distress, and it was even rumoured that half of a collection for the poor at the parish church a few Sundays ago had been awarded to poor destitute Tom White.

On the whole, Tom felt that if he could lose a *Martha* twice a year, he might yet sup off tripe and gin-toddy seven times a week.

The "Dolphin" became his banker, and took very particular care of his money.

All this the boy, of course, did not know. All he knew was that the waistcoat into which he had run belonged to the man he had wronged, who, if he only suspected his wronger, could make the coming summer holidays decidedly tedious for Georgie and his friend.

"Belay there!" hiccupped Tom, reeling back from the collision and catching Heathcote by the arm. "Got yer, young gem'n! and I'll bash yer!"

"I beg your pardon," said Georgie, terribly scared, and seeing already, in his mind's eye, the narrowest cell of the county jail.

Tom blinked at him stupidly, holding him at arm's length and cruising round him.

"Bust me if it ain't a schollard!" said he. "What cheer, my hearty? Don't forget, the poor mariner that's lost his *Martha*. It's very 'ard on a honest Jack tar."

How Heathcote's soul went out to the poor British seaman as soon as he discovered that he did not recognise him! He gave him his all—two shillings and one penny—and deemed it a mite to offer to so deserving a cause. He hoped from his heart Tom would find his boat, or, if not, would get a pension from the Government, or be made an Inspector of Coastguards. Nothing was too good for the sweet, delectable creature, and he told him as much.

Whereat Tom, with the 2 shillings 1 penny in his hand and all the boy's blandishments in his ears, retired to the "Dolphin" to digest both; and once more Heathcote, with the perspiration on his brow and his chest positively sore with the thumping of his heart, sped like a truant shade from the fangs of Cerberus.

After that, neither threats, entreaties, or taunts could induce Heathcote to venture either alone or in company into Templeton.

Fortunately for him and his leader, the approaching close of the term gave every one at Templeton an excuse for keeping bounds, and sticking steadily to work. Pledge, among others, was in for a scholarship, which five out of six of those who knew him prophesied he would get, if he took a fortnight's hard work before the examination.

A fortnight before the examination, to the day, Pledge began to work, and Templeton put down the Bishop's scholarship to him, without further parley. Only two men were against him—Cartwright, who, fine fellow as he was, could not desert the cricket field and gymnasium even in the throes of an examination, and Freckleton, the hermit, whom half of Templeton didn't know by sight, and the other half put down as a harmless lunatic, who divided his time between theological exercises and plodding, but not always successful, study.

Our heroes, being new boys, were exempt from the general school examinations—their guerdon of reward being the general proficiency prize for new boys, a vague term, in which good conduct, study, and progress, were all taken into account. Dick sadly admitted that he was out of it. Still he vaguely hoped he might "pull off his remove," as the phrase went—that is, get raised next term to the serene atmosphere of the lower Fourth, along with the faithful Heathcote.

But nowhere was the studious fit more serious than in the upper Fifth, where Birket, Swinstead, Wrangham and one or two others, cast longing eyes on the vacant desk in the Sixth, and strained every nerve to win it. Cricket flagged, and it was hard during that fortnight to make up a set at tennis. The early "Tub" alone retained its attractions, and indeed was never more crowded than when Templeton was heart and soul in study.

One fellow regarded the whole scene half sadly, and that was Ponty. Indolent as he seemed to be, he loved the old school, and hated the thought of leaving it. He had friends there that were like brothers to him. There were nooks here and there where he had lounged and enjoyed life, which seemed like so many homes. He knew he had not done anything great for Templeton. He knew he had let the tares grow side by side with the wheat, and made no effort to uproot them. He knew that there were boys there whom he ought to have befriended, and others he ought to have scathed; and it made him sad now to think of all he might have done.

"I don't think they'll erect a statue to me in the Quad, old man," said he to Mansfield at the end of the examination.

"I know there isn't a fellow that won't be sorry to lose you," said Mansfield.

"Ah! no doubt. They've had quiet times under easy-going old Saturn, and don't fancy the prospect of Jove, with his thunderbolts, ruling in his stead. Eh?"

"If I could be sure of fellows being as fond of me as they are of you, I should—well, I should get something I don't expect," said Mansfield.

"Don't be too sure, old man," said Ponty. "But, I say, will you take a hint from a failure like me?" added the old captain, digging deep into his pockets, and looking a trifle nervous.

"Rather. I'd only be too thankful," said Mansfield.

"Go easy with them at first. Only have one hand in an iron glove. Keep the other for some of those juniors who may turn out all right, if they get a little encouragement and aren't snuffed out all at once. You'll have plenty of work for the iron hand with one or two hornet's nests we know of. Give the little chaps a chance."

This was dear old Ponty's last will and testament. Templeton looked back upon him after he had gone, as an easy-going, good-natured, let-alone, loveable fellow; but it didn't know all of what it owed him.

The examinations came at length. The new boys having been the last to come, were naturally the first to be examined; and once more the portraits in the long hall looked down upon Basil Richardson and Georgie Heathcote, gnawing at the ends of their pens, and gazing at the ceiling for an inspiration.

It was rather a sad spectacle for those portraits. Possibly they barely recognised in the reckless, jaunty, fair boy, and his baffled, almost wrathful companion, the Heathcote and Richardson who four months ago had sat there, fresh, and simple, and rosy, with the world of Templeton before them.

It had not been a good term for either. Thank heaven, as they sat there, they had honesty enough left to know it, and hope enough left to feel there might still be a chance. They were not to jump by one leap into the perfect schoolboy; still, with honesty and hope left, who shall say they had lost all?

As to their immediate care, the examination—their last lingering expectation of getting their remove slowly vanished before those ruthless questions, all of which they knew they ought to know, but many of which they discovered they knew nothing about.

Other boys, like Aspinall, who, with all his tears and terrors, had struggled through the term more of a hero than either of his doughty protectors, found the time only too short to answer all they had to answer; and our two dejected ones, as they looked round, and saw the fluency of every one else, felt themselves, like sediment, gradually sinking to their level. As long as the stir of term life had lasted, they had imagined themselves as well up, even better than most of their contemporaries; but now they began to find out it was not so.

The suspense, if they felt any, was not long. Two days after the examination, at the time when the Sixth and Fifth were passing through their ordeal, the new boys' list came out.

Aspinall was first, and got his well-deserved remove, with a compliment from the Doctor into the bargain, which made his pale face glow with pleasure. Dick, with a sturdy effort to look cheerful, waved his congratulations across the Hall, and then settled down to hear the almost interminable string of names before his or Georgie's broke the monotony.

In their own minds, and in the modesty of their own self-abasement, they had fixed on the twentieth place, or thereabouts, for Heathcote, and about the twenty-fifth for Dick. Alas! the singles grew into the teens, and the teens into the twenties, and the twenties into the thirties before the break came. After eighteen every one knew that the removes were exhausted, and that the list which followed was, if not a list of reproach, at any rate one neither of honour nor profit.

"31—Richardson," read the Doctor, making a pause on the announcement which cut the penitent Dick to the quick; "32—Fox; 33—Sumpter; 34—Whiles; 35—Heathcote; 36—Hooker, junior. That is all."

Poor Heathcote! He had buoyed himself up to the last. He had reminded himself that he was not a prig or a saint, that he didn't go in for conduct that "paid," that he called a spade a spade, and that he didn't profess to be what he wasn't; and yet all this failed to place him higher than last but one of thirty-six boys, among whom, only four months ago, he stood fifteenth! Even Dick had beaten him now, although Dick himself had fallen ten places down the list.

The two friends had a dreary walk round the deserted Fields that afternoon.

"I can't make it out," said Heathcote. "I knew I hadn't done well, but I expected to be higher than that. I wonder if Winter's got a spite against me."

"More likely got one against me. Did you hear the way he read out my name?"

"Yes; he may have been surprised you came out so high."

"It's nothing to joke about," said Dick. "We've both made a mess of it."

"I really thought I'd done my lessons pretty steadily," said Heathcote, loth to part with the idea that there must be a mistake somewhere.

"You mean Pledge did them for you. I tell you what, old man—I've had enough of this sort of mess. I don't like it."

"No more do I," said Heathcote, very truly.

"I mean to get my remove at Christmas, if I get brain-fever over it."

"Rather; so do I," said Heathcote.

"I shall have a go in at the irregular verbs during the holidays."

"Eh—will you?" asked Georgie, beginning to stagger a little at the new programme. "All serene; so will I."

"We might begin to-night, perhaps."

"Awfully sorry—I've an engagement to-night," said Heathcote.

"Where?"

This was the first occasion on which Dick had asked this very awkward question. It was the wind-up supper of the "Select Sociables" for the present term, and to Heathcote one of the chief attractions of the prospect had been that Dick, being a member, would be there too. He was, therefore, startled somewhat at the inquiry.

"Oh, you know. We don't talk about it," said he.

"So it seems," said Dick; "but it happens I don't know."

"Don't you? Then the fellows must have told me a cram."

"What fellows?"

"Why, do you mean to say you don't know, Dick?"

"How should I?"

"Haven't they asked you, too? Aren't you a— I mean, don't you know?"

At this particular moment, Cresswell came across the Quadrangle with a bundle of books in his hands, which he told Dick to take to his study.

And before Dick had time to perform his task and return to the Quad, Braider had pounced on Heathcote, and borne him away, in hot haste, to the orgy of the "Select Sociables," where he spent a very unprofitable evening in trying to square his conscience with all he saw and heard, and in trying to ascertain from every member of the Club he could get hold of, why Dick wasn't there, too. He was not released without a renewal of his promise of secrecy, and spent a very uncomfortable half-hour in the dormitory that evening, trying, as best he could, to parry the questions of his friend, into whose head it had never entered that the "Select Sociables," after ejecting him, should dream of such a thing as electing Heathcote. They might have quarrelled over the mystery, had not the approaching holidays, and an opportune note from Coote, announcing that he had just scraped through the pass examination for "second chances," and would be at Templeton after the recess, driven all other thoughts, for the time being, out of their heads. And the few remaining days of the term were devoted, not to irregular verbs, but to the devising of glorious schemes of welcome to old Coote, and anticipations of the joys of their reformed triple alliance.

The great result day found Templeton, as it always did, in the chaos of packing up. At the summons of the great bell, to come and hear the lists read in the Hall, fellows dropped collars and coats, rackets and rods, boots and bookstand rushed for a front seat.

Every one turned up to the summer list—even the housekeepers and the school porter. The masters were there in caps and gowns, and the Sixth, in solemn array, occupied the benches on the dais. The rest of the Hall was left to the first comers; and, as all Templeton, on this occasion, arrived first in a body, the scene was usually animated.

Dr Winter read the list himself, and every name rang through the Hall, being followed with cheers which made all the more striking the silence with which the next name was listened for.

"The Bishop's Scholarship has been won by Freckleton," said the Doctor.

Amazement, as well as approval, mingled with the applause which followed this most unexpected announcement.

"Which *is* Freckleton?" asked Dick of Swinstead, who sat in front.

"That dark fellow, talking to Mansfield."

"Silence! Pledge was second, and within a few marks. Cartwright was third."

"How pleased Winter must have been to find those marks the right way!" whispered Pledge, with the red spots on his cheeks, to Bull. "It's a funny thing that Freckleton should be a nephew of Winter's and yet just get the scholarship, isn't it? So very unusual, eh?"

"The Fifth-form remove has been gained by Swinstead," said the Doctor (loud cheers). "Wrangham was second, but not very close, and Birket was a few marks below Wrangham."

These announcements were the most interesting on the Doctor's list, and Templeton listened impatiently to the rest. It waited, however, in its place, in order to give a final cheer for Ponty at the close.

Which it did. And the dear old fellow, though he seemed very sleepy, and longed for his arm-chair, couldn't help hearing it and looking round at the old school, nodding his kindly head. When, however, somebody called out "Speech," he stretched himself comfortably and shrugged his shoulders; and they knew what that meant, and gave it up.

Twenty-four hours later, Templeton was scattered to the four winds, and our heroes' first term had become a chapter of ancient history.

Chapter Sixteen
In which a notable Triple Alliance is renewed

The six short weeks of holiday darted away only too quickly.

Dick, in the whirl of family life, a hero to his sisters, and a caution to his young brothers, forgot all the troubles of the term, and all its disappointments, all about the "Select Sociables," and all about Tom White's boat, in one glorious burst of holiday freedom.

He even forgot about his irregular verbs; and the good resolutions with which he had returned, he left packed up in his trunk until the time came to take them back to Templeton.

Still, it wasn't a bad time, on the whole, for Dick. Like some small boat that gets out of the rushing tide for a little into some quiet creek, he had time to overhaul himself and pull himself together, ready for another voyage. He was able, in the home harbour, to take some little fresh ballast on board and to rearrange what he at present had. He was able to stow away some of his useless tackle and bale out some of the water he had shipped in the last few rapids. Altogether, though Dick was not exactly a boy given to self-examination, or self-dedication, and although he would have scouted the notion that he was going in for being a reformed character, his little cruise in calm water did him good, and steadied him for his next venture on the tide, when the time should come.

It was not so with George Heathcote. He was a craft of flimsier build than his leader, and the tide had gone harder with him. There was a leak somewhere, and the tackle was a-twist, and the ballast rolled to one side. And, for him, the home harbour was no place for repairs.

Heathcote had neither father nor mother, and though his old relative did her best for him, the boy was more or less at a loose end at home, with no better guide than his own whims. The wonder was, considering his surroundings, that Heathcote was not utterly spoiled, that he was still honest and amiable, and amenable to good influence when he came across it.

He did not, however, come across much these holidays. For four weeks he kicked his heels about in any way that suited him, and began to long for Templeton again, and the face of a friend.

Then one day a letter came to him from Pledge.

"Dear Youngster,—You said something about wanting to see London these holidays. What do you say to coming here on a visit? My father and mother would be glad to see you, and we can go back to Templeton together. If you come to-morrow, you'll be in time for the last day of the Australian match at the Oval—Yours truly,—

"P. Pledge."

Heathcote jumped at the invitation. An invitation from anybody would have been welcome just then, but to be asked by his own senior, in this unexpected way, was both tempting and flattering.

So he took the letter to his grandmother, and indulged in a glowing account of Pledge's virtues and merits. The good lady, of course, gave her consent, and the very next day Georgie was in London.

The week slipped by in a round of pleasures for Heathcote. Pledge, the spoiled child of wealthy parents, was pretty much his own master, and spared no pains to make his young protégé at home, and gratify his every inclination. To Georgie, the life in which he found himself was bewildering in its novelty.

Pledge showed him London. They saw public buildings, and they saw the great streets; they went to theatrical entertainments, and concerts, and parties. They met friends, good and bad, and heard talk, good and bad. No one thought of making any distinction; no one seemed to admit that there was much distinction. It was all life. If some went in for the good, well, let them; if others went in for the bad, what right had any one to interfere? and if any went in for a little of both, well, wasn't the balance about straight, and who was any the worse for it?

Heathcote felt that he was in Liberty Hall—that he might do exactly as he liked without the awkwardness of feeling that any one was surprised, or that any one was shocked. Pledge did not distinctly tempt him to do anything; and yet, during that one short week, the boy's moral sense was more deeply undermined than during the whole of the term that had passed. The clear line between good and evil vanished. And, seeing the two side by side, and hearing his companion's constant sneers at "sanctity," it became natural to him to suspect the good and, of the two, prefer the evil.

So Georgie Heathcote went back to Templeton the worse for his holidays, and snared faster than ever in the "Spider's" web.

But the sight of Dick on the Templeton platform drove all his unhealthy philosophy for a time from his mind, and when, an hour later, the train from G— came in and discharged Coote and Coote's hat-box and travelling-bag, there was joy in the hearts of those three old Mountjoy boys, which could not find vent in mere smiles or words of greeting.

Coote was in a horrible flutter, despite the countenance of his two protectors. He could not trust himself out of their sight. As they walked up from the station and crossed the Quadrangle, he suspected a snare everywhere, and sniffed an enemy at every corner.

"Come on, old fellow," said Dick, in all the glory of an old hand, "stick your hat on the back of your head, and make a face at everybody you meet, and nobody will humbug you."

Coote had his doubts of this advice; but, it occurred to him, if it should be good, he had better make the experiment while his friends were there to protect him.

So he tilted his hat cautiously back, and timidly protruded his tongue at Culver, whom they met staggering under the weight of a carpet bag, near the housekeeper's door.

Culver regarded the demonstration with a certain amount of bewildered disfavour, and, to Coote's terror, looked for a moment like putting down his carpet bag. But the presence of Dick and Heathcote deterred him for the present, and he contented himself with a promise that tilted the new boy's hat back into its proper elevation with wonderful celerity.

"Never mind him," said Heathcote, "he always doubles up after five or six rounds."

"Do you mean he will fight me?" asked Coote.

"Bless you, yes!"

"To-day, do you think?"

"Don't know. Depends on what he's got in his bag. If it's a cargo, he won't be out for a couple of nights."

All this was very alarming to Coote, who devoutly hoped Culver's "cargo" might be big enough to keep him many nights in unloading it.

Dick and Heathcote led their junior partner rejoicing to the housekeeper, and assisted in counting out his shirts and socks. They then took him to show him off in the lobbies, deserting him once or twice, to his consternation, in order to greet some crony or take part in a mild shindy in the studies.

The presence of their "new kid" inspired them with a wonderful fund of humour and audacity. His astonishment flattered them and his panics delighted them. With a lively recollection of their own experiences last term, they took care he should be wandering in the Quad when the "dredger" came its rounds; and, for fear he should miss the warm consolations of a lower third "Scrunch," they organised one for his special benefit, and had the happiness of seeing him rising in the middle, scared and puffing, with cheeks the colour of a peony. All the while they tried to figure as his protectors, and demanded credit for getting him through his ordeals in a way he would by no means have got, if left, as they had been, to his own resources.

Nor were they wholly unoriginal in their endeavours to make him feel at home in his new surroundings.

"By George! it's ten minutes to dinner-time," said Dick, looking at the clock. "There'll be a frightful row if you are late first day, and you've barely time to dress."

"Dress! I am dressed," said Coote, in alarm.

"You muff, you're not in your flannels. Think of a new fellow turning up to Hall first day not in his flannels, eh, Georgie?"

"My eye!" said Georgie; "what a row there'd be!"

"Cut as hard as ever you can, and put them on. Better not show up till just as the clock strikes, in case fellows humbug you. We'll be near the door and show you where to sit."

"Whatever should I have done," thought the grateful Coote to himself, as he rushed off to don his brand-new flannels, "if it hadn't been for those two bricks?"

The "two bricks" waited somewhat anxiously near the door of the Hall for their "new kid," and as the clock began to strike they had the joy of seeing him dart resplendent across the Quad, keeping in the shade as much as possible, and looking nervously up at the clock.

"Lamm it on!" called Heathcote, as the bell ceased and the breathless athlete ran into their arms.

"Am I all right?" asked the victim.

"So-so," said they, surveying him critically, "but you'd better carry your coat over your arm. Look out, Winter will be coming in. You've got to sit up there at the top table, in that empty chair. Look alive, or he'll catch you."

And as the blushing innocent walked up the room, the observed of all observers, and made straight for the Head Master's table, our heroes became absorbed in admiration of the plates in front of them, and positively trembled with the emotion their beauty evoked.

Every one was most polite to the abashed new boy on his journey up the room. They ceased talking as they beheld him, and respectfully made room for him. Some even were good enough to assist his progress by word and gesture.

"Where are you going, my pretty maid?" asked Birket of the rosy youth, as he neared his destination.

The poetical suggestion was too much for the Fifth, who caught up the pastoral ditty, and accompanied the measured tread of the wanderer with an undertone chorus of—

"'Where are you going, my pretty maid?'
'I'm going to dinner, sir,' she said.
'May I go with you, my pretty maid?'
'Not if I know it, sir,' she said."

Coote got used to the pretty melody before the term was over, but just now his sense of music was deadened by the apparition of Dr Winter, who entered by a door at the upper end of the Hall, and walked straight for the chair which the modest novice had looked upon as the goal of his tedious journey.

"Cut back!" said Birket, coming to the rescue just in time, and turning the unhappy boy to the rightabout. "They've been making a fool of you."

Then might have been seen a spotless white figure flying like the wind down the Hall of Templeton, making the place rosy with his blushes, and merry with his hot haste.

Dick and Heathcote caught their brother as he made for the door, and squeezed him in between them at their table, where roast beef and good cheer restored some of his drooping spirits, while the applause of his patrons and the success of the whole adventure went far to reduce the tension which otherwise might have threatened the stability of the "Firm."

But after that, Coote felt his confidence in the "two bricks," on whom he had hitherto relied so implicitly, a trifle shaken, and was not quite sure whether, after all, a new boy might not get through his first few days as comfortably without the protection of two bosom friends as with it.

There being very few new boys this term compared with last, he found himself by no means neglected in his walks abroad, and it required all his wariness to elude the gins and pitfalls prepared for him. Indeed, his very wariness got him into trouble.

After chapel on his second morning Swinstead came to him and said —

"Youngster, you are to go to the Doctor at half-past nine."

"Oh, ah!" said Coote to himself, knowingly. "I know what that means."

"Do you hear?" asked Swinstead.

"I suppose you think I'm green," said the new boy.

Swinstead laughed.

"What on earth should make me think that?" said he.

Coote chuckled merrily to himself as he saw the senior depart.

"I'm getting over the worst of it," said he to himself. "They'll soon give up trying it on me. Ha, ha!"

And he went off to find his chums, who took him for a stroll in the Fields.

"Well, young 'un," said Dick, patronisingly, "getting used to it? Worn your flannels lately?"

"You're a beastly cad, Dick," said Coote; "but you don't catch me like that again."

"No, you're getting too knowing," said Georgie.

Coote laughed.

"I'm not quite as green as some fellows think," said he. "A fellow came to me this morning and told me to go to the Doctor at 9:30. A nice fool he thought he'd make of me. Ha, ha!"

"What fellow was he?" said Dick, looking rather serious.

"I don't know his name," said Coote. "The fellow who marked the names in chapel, I believe."

"What, Swinstead? Did he tell you to go?"

"Rather; and I told him I wasn't such a fool as I looked — I mean as he thought."

"By Jove!—you young ass! You've got yourself into a mess, if you like."

"How do you mean?" inquired the new boy, beginning to be alarmed at the concerned looks of his two friends.

"Why, he's Chapel usher," said Dick. "Do you mean to say you didn't go to the Doctor?"

"Rather not. I—"

"What's the time?" said Dick.

"A quarter to ten."

Without more ado they took the unhappy Coote between them and rushed him frantically back to the school, where they shot him in at the Doctor's door just as that gentleman was about to dismiss his new boys' class.

"How is this, Coote?" demanded the Head Master, sternly, as the breathless boy entered. "Were you not told to be here at half-past nine?"

"Yes, sir; I—I made a mistake. I'm very sorry, sir."

The genuine terror in his face procured his reprieve this time. Dr Winter may have been used to "mistakes" of this kind. At any rate, he contented himself with cautioning the new boy against unpunctuality generally, and, by way of punishment, gave him an examination all to himself, which resulted, much to his comfort, in his being placed in the upper third, of which Dick and Heathcote were already shining lights.

While he was thus engaged, Dick and Heathcote were holding a secret, and by no means cheerful, consultation over a recent number of the *Templeton Observer*.

"I made sure it was all blown over," said the latter, dejectedly.

"What a cad the fellow must be!" said the former.

"I think newspapers are a regular nuisance!" said Georgie.

"All I know is, he robbed us of all we had, and if we'd informed he'd have been in Botany Bay or somewhere this minute!" said Dick, working himself up into a passion.

The extract from the *Templeton Observer* which gave rise to this duet of wrath was as follows, dated some ten days before the close of the holidays:—

The recent mysterious disappearance of a Templeton boat.—Up to the present time nothing has been heard of the *Martha*, which, as our readers will remember, disappeared from the Templeton beach, on the 4th June last. The supposed clue with which the police professed to be provided has, so far, failed to bring the perpetrators of the outrage to justice; although the hope is by no means abandoned of tracing the missing lad. The matter is somewhat seriously complicated by the discovery that Thomas White, the reputed owner of the boat, was at no time its actual proprietor. The *Martha* was the joint property of White and three other men, one of them skipper of the brig *Julia*, and the other two well-known fishermen, of this town. It appears that an arrangement was made, whereby White should be the nominal owner of the boat, he undertaking to hand over monthly three quarters of the profits to his partners. In May last, during the absence of his other partners, White pawned the *Martha* representing her to be his sole property, and appropriated the whole proceeds of the transaction. For this act of fraud (which the recent loss of the boat and the return of its joint owners has brought to light) we understand a writ has been issued against White, and that he will be arrested immediately on his return to Templeton from his present cruise with the Fishing Fleet in the high seas.

"Tom White's a regular bad one," said Dick.

"Yes. It was a jolly mean trick to pawn what didn't belong to him."

"The thing is, who did it belong to when we—when it got adrift?"

"The pawnbroker, I suppose," said Heathcote. "Most likely Nash."

"No wonder Tom White didn't seem much cut up about losing her."

"No; he made a good thing by it. It's a comfort to think he'll get nabbed at last."

"Of course, we've nothing to do with his row," said Dick.

"Of course not. We had nothing to do with pawning the boat."

And yet, they concluded, if the *Martha* had never gone adrift, no one would have known of Tom White's fraud, and he might have been able to make money enough with her to clear himself.

It seemed unfair to rake up an old sore like this at the very beginning of the term, especially when, as they persuaded themselves, over and over again, the whole affair had very little to do with them.

"I vote we don't look at this wretched paper any more," said Heathcote, crumpling up the offending *Observer* into a ball, and giving it a punt across the path.

"Why not? We may as well see what becomes of Tom White," said Dick. "Young Aspinall can fetch us up a copy once a week."

And so one of the events of the new term was that the *Templeton Observer* had a new subscriber, and increased its circulation by two new and very diligent readers.

Chapter Seventeen
The new Captain draws a straight line

Mansfield returned to Templeton like a man who knows that his work is cut out for him, and who means to do it, *coûte qui coûte*, as the French say.

Any one else might have been afraid of the task before him, and doubtful of success. Mansfield was neither; at any rate, as far as any one else could see. He set himself up neither for a Hercules nor a Galahad. It never occurred to him what he was. But it did occur to him that Templeton wanted reform, and that the Captain of Templeton ought to reform it. And with that one clear purpose before him, Mansfield was the sort of fellow to go straight through thick and thin to reach it, or perish in the attempt.

They say that when a certain Russian Emperor wanted a railway made between the two chief cities of his dominion, and was asked what route it should take, so as to benefit the largest number of intervening towns and villages, he called for a map and ruler, and drawing a straight line between the two places, said, "Let it go that way."

That was pretty much the style of Mansfield. He didn't understand turning to right or left to give anybody a lift on the way. All he knew was that Templeton was not up to the mark, and that Templeton must be brought up to the mark. Between those points he ruled his straight line, and that way he meant to go.

If the line cut a snug little set of chums in half, if it turned one or two settled school customs out of house and home, if it sent one or two waverers hopelessly over to the wrong side—well, so be it. It was a pity, especially if the innocent had to suffer with the guilty. But the good of Templeton was at stake, and woe to the traitor who thought anything more important than that!

Dear old Ponty, whom Templeton had never loved so much as when it missed him, had curled his line about in snug, comfortable ins-and-outs, so as not to disturb anybody. Mansfield didn't think himself better than Ponty, whom he loved as a brother. But Mansfield couldn't draw curling in-and-out lines. He only knew one line, and that was a straight one; and so, for better or worse, Mansfield called for his map and his ruler, and dashed into his task.

"Give the little chaps a chance," Ponty had said, in his last will and testament, and the new Captain of Templeton was willing to make one little curve, in order to carry out his friend's wish.

On the fourth evening of the term, as the Den was assembled in full session, for the purpose of swearing in Coote and denouncing the powers that be, that honourable fraternity was startled out of its never superabundant wits by an apparition far more terrible than the Templeton Ghost.

Dick was in the chair at the time, and Heathcote was in the act of moving a resolution, "That this Den considers all the monitors ought to be hanged, and hopes they will be," when the Captain of Templeton suddenly entered the room.

Then fell there a silence on the Den, like to the silence of a kennel of dogs when the whip of the master cracks! The word "hanged" died half-uttered on the lips of Heathcote, and Dick slipped aghast from his eminence. The tongue of Coote clave to the roof of his mouth, and even Gosse's heart turned to stone in the midst of a "swop." Never did condemned criminals stand more still, or wax-works more dumb.

Mansfield closed the door behind him, and marched straight to the top of the room, where stood Dick's vacant chair. Was he going to drive them out single-handed? Was he going to arrest their leader? Or was he going to make a speech?

As soon as they perceived he was going to do neither the first nor the second, and knew he was going to do the last, they groaned. They could have endured a stampede round the Quad; they could have brought themselves to see their leader immolated in a good cause; but to have to stand still and hear Jupiter speak—what had they done to deserve that?

"Look here, you youngsters," began Mansfield, needing not even a motion of his hand to command silence, "I've not come as an enemy, but a friend."

"What will it be like," mused Coote, "when he comes as an enemy?"

"And I've only a very few words to say to you."

Was it a sigh of relief or disappointment that escaped the Den? Mansfield didn't know; he wasn't well up in sighs.

"There's a great deal goes on in the Den that isn't right. Some of you youngsters think the only use of school rules is to break them, and that it's a fine thing to disobey the monitors. You're wrong, and, unless you give up that sort of thing, you'll find it out. The school rules are made to be kept, and the monitors are appointed to see they *are* kept; and any boy that says otherwise is an enemy to Templeton, and he will be treated accordingly. Some of you don't approve of all that goes on here, and yet you don't like to stand up against it. That's not right. You can't be neutral. If you mean to be steady, you are bound to stand out and have nothing to do with the bad lot. I want you all to understand this once for all, and not say you've had no warning. I warn you now. Rules are made to be kept, and you must keep them. Pontifex—"

The Captain had to stop; for the Den, which had stood in breathless silence thus far, sprang, at the mention of the name, into a cheer which spoke quite as much for the tension of their own feelings at this moment as for their affection for the old Captain.

Mansfield let them have it out; he liked them none the worse for their love to his friend, and what he had to say would by no means spoil by keeping till the cheers were over.

They were over at last. The sight of the Captain there, tall, upright, determined, with his dark eyes bent on them, cut them short and brought the Den back to silence as deep as that which had just been broken.

"Pontifex was fond of you youngsters. He said to me a day or two before he went, 'Give the little chaps a chance.'"

They could not help it; Captain or no Captain, they must cheer again. And again Mansfield waited patiently and ungrudgingly till it was over.

"This is why I've come here to-night. You have your chance. Let everybody choose for himself, and don't let any one say he didn't know what to expect. There's to be a Captain's levée on Thursday. I don't want any one to come to it who is not prepared to stand by Templeton rules this term. Those who are prepared will do well to show up."

So ended Jupiter's speech to the Den. He stalked down the room and out of the door amid a solemn silence, which was not broken until his firm footsteps died away down the passage.

Then the Den looked at one another as much as to say—

"What do you think of that?"

"Pretty warm!" said Dick, relieving the general embarrassment by speaking first.

"Think he means it?" said one.

"Looks like it!" said Dick, gloomily.

There was a pause. The Den knew, somehow, it was no joke.

It was a case of life or death, war or peace, liberty or servitude, and they hesitated on the brink.

"I don't mean to knuckle under to him!" said Heathcote, speaking with the mantle of Pledge upon him. "It's all a dodge to curry favour with Winter."

The Den was thankful for the suggestion, and revived wonderfully under its influence.

"Catch me doing more for him than for old Ponty!" cried Gosse, who had never done anything for Ponty.

The reference was a popular one, and the Den took it up also. It fell to extolling Ponty to the very heavens, and abasing Mansfield to the opposite extremity, while it held up its hands in horror at the man who could seek to make the good order of Templeton the price of his favour with the Head Master.

But, when the little outburst had subsided, the awkward question still remained—What was to be done?

"Of course nobody will be cad enough to go to the levée after what he said," said Heathcote, who, warmed by the admiring glances of Coote and the success of his last observation, felt called upon to speak for the assembly in general.

"Rather not! You won't go, will you, Dick?" said Pauncefote.

"Don't know," said that hero, shortly.

The Den was startled. What did Dick mean by "Don't know"? Was he going to knuckle in after all and join the "saints?"

The uncertainty had a very depressing effect on Heathcote's enthusiasm, which had calculated all along on the countenance of his leader. Coote, too, cautiously separated himself from Gosse, who was shouting sedition at the top of his voice, and drew off to more neutral territory. Smith and Pauncefote kept up their cheers for Ponty, but gradually dropped the groans for Mansfield, and altogether the howls of the Den toned down to the roar of a sucking dove as it got whispered abroad that Dick Richardson "didn't know."

The two days that followed were days of suspense to the Den.

"Is Dick going?" was the question every one asked.

"He doesn't know," was the invariable answer.

Under these circumstances, it will be understood, but little enthusiasm could be called up over the rival toilets of the fraternity. Culver's dress-coat had been returned to its lawful owner long since, and for that reason, if for no other, he determined not to attend. Heathcote's choker and white gloves were the worse for wear, so he was not anxious; and Coote, whose one strong point was a watered ribbon watch-chain, was rumoured to be weak in collars, and, on the whole, not a "hot man" at all, or likely to show up.

As to Dick, opinions were divided as to what he could do if he went. It was known his "dicky" had fallen off, but, on the other hand, he had brought back a pair of patent leather pumps, which might make him feel it his duty to attend.

"Look here, old man," asked Heathcote, for about the hundredth time, the evening before the levée, "are you going, or are you not?"

"Don't know," replied Dick. "Are you?"

What a question for a leader to ask his lieutenant! Dick knew it was ridiculous, but he guessed shrewdly it might choke off further inquiry. And it did.

Heathcote, however, had other counsellors besides Dick, who were neither doubtful nor sparing in their advice on the great question. A hasty meeting of the "Select Sociables" was summoned, by means of Braider, that very evening, to take into consideration the action of the Club at the forthcoming levée, at which it was agreed unanimously that, after the Captain's threat, no member of that honourable body should, on any account, show up.

Heathcote held up his hand for the resolution with the others, and felt sure, in his own mind, Dick would have done the same.

"Mind, nobody shows up, on any pretext," said Spokes, as the meeting separated. "We're on our honour, and, of course, no one mentions the Club out-of-doors."

Of course, nobody would think of such a thing.

Heathcote felt a good deal concerned as the evening went on, and still no sign came from Dick. It wasn't exactly kind to keep a fellow in suspense like this. The only thing was to take the bull by the horns, and announce what *he* was going to do. Then, possibly, Dick might show his hand.

"I've decided not to show up at the levée," said Georgie, on the morning of the eventful day.

"Have you?" said Dick, with a most provoking indifference.

"Yes," said the cunning Georgie. "I tell you what, Dick; while it's going on, you and I can get the top court and play off our heat for the handicap. What do you say?"

"Don't know."

Whereupon, Heathcote wished that two words in the English language could be suspended, and went off to see if any comfort was going in the Den. But no.

"What's Dick going to do?" asked almost everybody.

"He doesn't know," groaned Heathcote.

Whereupon, the Den, as well as Georgie, wished ill to those two unlucky words.

The morning passed, and still no ray of light illumined the doubters. Dick got twenty lines from Pledge for jumping over the geranium bed in the Quad, and knocking off a flower in the act; and every one guessed this would decide him against the levée.

But at dinner-time a rumour spread, on the authority of Coote, that he had put on a clean collar since morning school, and public opinion immediately veered round to the opposite direction. No sooner, however, was dinner done than he was seen to fetch his tennis racket from his study; and once more it was surmised that he was going, after all, to play off his heat with Georgie instead of attending the ceremony. And that supposition was in turn dashed to the ground, when it was discovered that he had got the bat in order to give it to a messenger from Splicers, the racket maker, to be tightened up in the top cord.

Afternoon school dragged tediously on, and the Den grew desperate. Fellows went off to dress. But what was the use of Heathcote putting on his choker, or Smith and Pauncefote parting their hairs, when they didn't know whether they were going to the levée or not?

Heathcote made one final effort to "draw" the Sphinx.

"Come on," said he, "we'll bag the court if we are sharp, and get an hour's quiet play."

"I've got no racket," said Dick.

"I say, Dick, *are* you going to the levée—do tell us?"

"I don't know. What do you want to know for?"

"I—I vote we don't go," said Georgie, coaxingly. "I'm not going."

"I know that."

"Are you?" and there was a tone of desperate pathos in the boy's voice.

"Haven't I told you, a hundred and fifty times, I *don't know*?" replied Dick, scarcely less desperate.

Heathcote gave it up, and joined the Den, who were waiting about, in anxious groups, near the door of the Hall, with their ornaments in their hands, ready to put on at a moment's notice if necessary.

Presently Dick strolled up and joined them.

Hurrah! he had not got his patent leather boots on, after all! A weight fell from the minds of half the beholders as they cast their eyes down at his dusty double soles. And yet, if he wasn't going in, what was he hanging about there for?

Dick would have been very sorry if any of the Den had guessed what was passing in his mind. He didn't know what to do. If there had been no one but himself, it wouldn't have mattered. But there was that young ass Heathcote, and Coote too, who were certain to do as he did; and the fag of making up his mind for three people was not fair to a fellow.

And yet the Ghost's letter somehow stuck in his mind, and the ballast he had taken on board during the holidays made it harder to play pitch and toss with himself than it had been. He didn't like the way Mansfield had almost dared them to stay away. Because, if it came to that, he would just as soon let fellows see he wasn't going to be bullied. On the other hand, the Captain had as good as said it wanted some pluck to stand out against the rowdies, and that was an argument in favour of showing up at levee. The worst of it was, when once you showed up, you were committed to the steady lot, and couldn't well back out. If young Heathcote—no, he was bound to look after Heathcote.

So, to the amazement and consternation of the Den, after loafing about at the door for ten minutes, Dick strolled into the Hall, and made his way up to the platform.

One or two, including Coote, followed him immediately. Others remained long enough to put on their cuffs and chokers, and then followed suit. One or two looked at the door, and went back again, and a few talked about treason and Rule 5.

Heathcote alone was aghast and dumbfounded. For he had never seriously calculated on his leader's decision; and, being himself under vow not to present himself, his dilemma was terrible.

Perjury or treason? That was the problem he had to decide at half a minute's notice, and it was no joke.

As he watched Dick slowly advance up the room, dogged by the faithful Coote and supported by a bodyguard of loyal followers, his courage failed, and he could hardly restrain himself from rushing after him.

And yet, the memory of his promise to the "Select Sociables," and the vision of Braider watching him from a distance, held him where he was.

How he wished he could have a fit, or break his arm, or have his nose bleed; anything to get him out of this hobble!

But no. He saw Dick ascend the dais and shake hands with the Captain, who looked almost amiable as he spoke a few words to him. He saw Pauncefote and Smith and the other, loyal ones come in for the same greeting. He saw Coote and his watered ribbon being presented by Cartwright, and he caught sight of Pledge looking up and down the room, possibly in search of his Georgie.

All this he saw, and yet could not stir. Only when he saw Dick descend the platform and slowly return towards the door, did the spell yield and permit him to escape to the Quad.

There half an hour later he was found by Pledge.

"Hullo, youngster; you didn't turn up at the pantomime, then?"

"No," said Heathcote, "I didn't want to."

"What! not want to be shaken hands with and blessed by the holy Mansfield? You naughty boy, to neglect such a short cut to peace and plenty!"

"I don't want to toady to anybody," said Heathcote, bitterly.

"Of course you don't. But I'm afraid your courage will cost you something in impositions and detentions, and that sort of thing."

"What do I care? I'd sooner have any amount of them than be a humbug and truckle to anybody."

"Every one," said Pledge, with an approving smile, "made sure when your friend Richardson came to do homage, that you would come too. I was quite pleased to find I knew better and was right."

"I don't know what made Dick go," said Heathcote.

"No? Can't you guess? Isn't Dick a good boy, and doesn't he always do what good boys do?"

Heathcote laughed.

"I don't think he's very much in that line."

"Well, he imitates it very well," said Pledge, watching his man carefully, "and I've no doubt he will find it worth his while."

"What do you mean?" inquired Heathcote, looking up.

"I mean that Mansfield is picking his men for the 3rd Football Fifteen, and I'm afraid you won't be in it, my boy."

Heathcote said nothing, but walked on to the school door where he and his patron parted company; the latter proceeding to his study with a particularly amiable smile on his countenance; the former repairing to the adjourned meeting of the "Select Sociables," there to hear high praises of his loyalty and steadfastness, and to partake of a very select contraband supper, which, with the questionable festivities that followed, was good for neither the body nor the soul of our unheroic young hero.

Chapter Eighteen
Dick conspires to defeat the ends of Justice

Dick, on quitting the Captain's levée, retired in anything but exalted spirits to Cresswell's study.

He didn't care to face the Den that evening. Not that he was afraid of Rule 5, or cared a snap what anybody there had to say about his conduct. But he wasn't sure himself whether he had made a mistake or not. He hated being in a corner. He had no natural antipathy to doing what was right, but he didn't like being pinned down to it. He didn't go to the levée because he was desperately in love with law and order, and it was a shame for any one to suppose he had. He went because he knew Heathcote was waiting to see what he did. And now, after all, Heathcote had deserted his colours and not gone.

It was enough to make any one testy, and Aspinall, had he known it, would have been less surprised than he was to have his head almost snapped off as the two fellow-fags sat at work in their senior's study that evening.

"Can't you do your work without groaning like that?" said Dick, when the small boy, for about the fiftieth time, stumbled over his hexameters.

"I beg your pardon," said Aspinall, "I didn't mean to disturb you."

"Who said you did?" retorted poor Dick, longing for a quarrel with some one. "What's the use of flaring up like that?"

"I didn't mean—I'm sorry if I—"

"There you go. Why can't you swear straight out instead of mumbling? I can't hear what you say."

"I beg your pardon, Dick."

"Shut up, and get on with your work, and don't make such a noise."

After that the wretched Aspinall hardly dared dip his pen in the ink, or turn over a page, for fear of disturbing his badger companion. It was a relief when presently Cresswell entered and gave him a chance of escape.

"Well, youngster," said the senior, when he and Dick were left alone, "I'm glad you had the sense to turn up at the levée."

"I'm sorry I did," said Dick, shortly.

Cresswell knew his man too well to be taken aback by the contradiction.

"Yes? Is the Den going to lick you for it?"

"I'd like to see them try," said Dick, half viciously.

"So would I," said the senior, laughing.

"Mansfield will be trying to make out I've promised to back him up," said Dick.

Cresswell laughed.

"By Jove! he *will* be cut up when he finds you aren't. He'll resign."

Dick coloured up, and looked a little foolish. "I didn't mean that," he said.

"No very dreadful thing if you did back him up, eh?" said the monitor, casually. "It might disgust some of your friends in the Den, but you aren't obliged to toady to them."

"Rather not," said Dick.

"Besides, a fellow may sometimes do what's right and not be an utter cad. Perhaps you don't think so, though. You'd cut a nobler figure, wouldn't you, dragging down your chums from one row to another, than by anything so paltry as doing right because it is right? I quite understand that feeling."

"Why do you talk to me like that?" said Dick, feeling a sting in every word of the senior's speech. "You think I went to the levée to please myself. I didn't."

"And is that why you are sorry you went? Don't make yourself out worse than you are, Dick. You've done a plucky thing for once in a way, and got yourself into a row with the Den, and I really don't see that you have very much to reproach yourself with."

"I don't care a farthing for the Den," said Dick.

"But you do for yourself. If I were you, I wouldn't let myself be floored by one reverse. Stick to your man, and you'll get him out of the hands of the Philistines after all."

This little talk did Dick good, and cleared his mind. It put things in a new light. It recalled the Ghost's letter, and brought up in array once more the better resolutions that appeal had awakened. What was the use of his setting up as an example to his friends, when he was little better than a rowdy himself? Yes; Dick Richardson must be looked to. How, and by whom?

"*Dominat qui in se dominatur*," said Dick to himself, as he went off to bed, and closed a very uncomfortable and critical day.

When he went to call Cresswell next morning he found him already up and dressed.

"Ah, youngster, before you to-day! Have you forgotten it's a holiday?"

"So it is," said Dick, who, in his troubles, had actually overlooked the fact.

"What do you say to coming with Freckleton and me for a day's fishing in the Bay? Winter has given us leave if we keep inside the Sprit Rock, and I expect he'd let you come if I asked him."

"I'd like it frightfully," said Dick, glowing with pleasure at the invitation.

"All right. Set to work with the sandwiches. Make as many as the potted meat will allow, and get the matron to boil half-a-dozen eggs hard. I'll see Winter after chapel about you, and if it's all square we'll start directly after breakfast."

Dick went into raptures over the making of those sandwiches. Fishing was one of his great weaknesses, and a day of it, in such lovely weather as this, and in such distinguished company, was a treat out of the ordinary. The one drawback was that neither Heathcote nor Coote was in it. That, however, could not be helped; and he decided that, under the circumstances, it would be kindest not to tell them about it or raise their regrets.

After chapel he made straight for Cresswell's study and waited with some anxiety the result of his senior's application to the Head Master.

In due time Cresswell returned.

"All serene," said he. "He didn't much fancy it, I think; but I undertook to be responsible for you."

It occurred to Dick that he didn't see why he couldn't be responsible for himself; but he was too anxious not to mar the expedition, to raise any protest on behalf of his own independence.

"Take this can," said Cresswell, "and go down as quick as you can to Green's, next door to the 'Dolphin,' and tell him to fill it with worms for me, and bring them down to the beach. We're going to have Tug's boat, and we'll be there in half-an-hour, so look alive."

Dick, rather thankful to be able to get off unobserved, hurried off on his savoury errand. He had scarcely once gone down town since the affair of Tom White's boat, and certainly not since the alarming paragraphs in the *Observer* had taken to appearing. But he comforted himself with the reflection that Tom was at present on the high seas, and that no one else appeared to have any suspicion which would connect him (Dick) with the mysterious lad who had been seen on the Strand on the eventful night last June.

For all that, he dawdled not a moment longer than he could help. Green had the worms ready.

"So you're going for a day's sport, are you?" said he. "It's a good day, too, and the whiting ought to be plentiful off the rock."

"I hope they will," said Dick.

"They've been let alone the last week or two," said the bait merchant, "since our chaps have been out in the deep, so you've a fair chance."

"When will the boats be back?" asked Dick, rather nervously.

"We should have seen some of them this morning, but the wind's dropped. Maybe it will be afternoon before they come in."

"It's always a great day when they come in, isn't it?" asked the boy.

"Depends on the catch. When it's a bad catch no one cares to see them back."

Dick tried hard to keep down his next question, but it had a sort of fascination for him, and he could not smother it.

"I suppose," said he in the most careless tones he could assume, "Tom White's not likely to come back in a hurry?"

Green laughed. He was no friend of the double-dealing mariner.

"Not if he knows who's a-going to be down on the beach to welcome him. But, bless you, how's he to know? The sooner he comes home and gets his right lodgings, the better, so say I. What do you say, young squire?"

The "young squire" did not exactly know what to say, and took up his can of worms to depart, with something like precipitation.

He found Cresswell and Freckleton waiting for him down at the boat. Until this moment he had never seen the Templeton Hermit, except occasionally at a distance; and he glanced with some curiosity at the face of the fellow who had beaten Pledge for the Bishop's Scholarship. He didn't altogether dislike him. The stolid face and bright black eyes of the Hermit made him a little uncomfortable, but there was an occasional twitch at the corners of his mouth, and a music, when he chose to use it, in his voice, which reconciled the junior to his presence, and even interested him in the disposal of his new patron's good graces.

It didn't take long to get "all aboard." The precious worms were safely deposited in the hold, the three lines were stowed away under the seat, and the basket containing the sandwiches and hard-boiled eggs added ballast to the bows. Cresswell, who had an idea of doing things comfortably, had brought his ulster and made Freckleton bring his. The latter had armed himself also with a Shakespeare in case the fish didn't bite; and three towels, knowingly produced by the whipper-in, added a further pleasant suggestion for whiling away a dull half-hour.

The calmness of the day and the absence of any sign of wind induced the party to vote the mast and sails a useless encumbrance, and they were accordingly left ashore, and a spare pair of oars taken in their place. The irony of fate left it to Dick's lot to see the anchor was in proper trim and firmly secured—a task which he discharged with almost vicious solemnity.

"What time does the tide turn, Joe?" asked Cresswell of the boatman as they ran the boat down to the water.

"Half-past two about, mister. Yer'll need to bring her in close ashore and give the Fiddle-sand a wide berth while the tide flows."

"All right. Shove her off, Joe."

They had a glorious day. The sea had scarcely a ripple, and the sky scarcely a cloud. The fish seemed to vie with one another in falling upon the bait. The view of Templeton from the sea was perfect, and the sharp outline of the Sprit Rock above them was grandeur itself.

Dick, as he lolled over the side of the boat, slowly hauling up his line and speculating whether he had got two fish on each hook or only one, felt supremely at peace with himself and all the world. The sandwiches had been delicious, Cresswell and Freckleton had treated him like a lord, the pile of fish on the floor of the boat was worthy of a professional crew, the light breeze was just enough to keep the sun in his place, and the sofa he had made for himself with Freckleton's ulster in the bows was like a feather bed. Dick loved the world and everything in it, and when Cresswell said, "Walk into those sandwiches, young 'un," he really thought life the sweetest task in which mortal can engage.

Cresswell and Freckleton were scarcely more proof against the luxury of the morning. They chatted in a sort of sleepy undertone, as if they knew all Nature was taking a nap and didn't want to be disturbed.

"How did you think old Jupiter got through levée?" asked Cresswell.

"Well, for those who wish him well," said the Hermit.

"Ah, he's an uphill job before him, and I fancy he knows it. If he ever is down in the mouth, I think he was so last night after it was all over."

"I thought so too," said Freckleton; "that is, I shouldn't call it down in the mouth. He had headache; that's about the same thing."

"He's staked high. No one else would have dared to challenge the whole school in the way he did," said Cresswell, dropping his voice, but still, in the quiet air, not quite beyond Dick's hearing.

"It answered; it brought the right fellows to the front."

"And shut the wrong fellows hopelessly out?"

"I hope not. Many of them are only fools. They think it's plucky to defy the powers that be, and quite forget it's pluckier to defy themselves."

"That's a neat way of putting it, old man!"

"There's a big bite this time!" said the Hermit.

So there was—three fish on two hooks, and it was some time before the diversion was disposed of.

"It's a pity every one can't be made to see he's his own worst enemy; it would simplify matters awfully. If a youngster got it into his head that it wanted more pluck to go against himself than all the Templeton rules put together, we should get some surprises!"

"No chance of that, I'm afraid, while there are fellows like Pledge, who make it a business to drag youngsters down."

"You may say so. I should say there's not a youngster in Templeton in greater peril at this moment than Pledge's fag, and the worst of it is there is no one to help him."

Dick suddenly felt his sofa uncomfortable. The boards underneath cramped him; the sun, too, for some reason or other, became too hot, and the breeze fidgeted him; the last sandwich he had eaten had had too much mustard in it; he was getting fagged of fishing.

Although the talk of the two seniors had not been intended for his ears, it had been impossible for him to avoid overhearing it, even if he had tried, which he had not, and the Hermit's last words had stung him to the quick and spoilt his enjoyment.

"What's the matter, youngster?" asked Cresswell. "Getting sea-sick?"

"No," replied Dick, trying to compose himself.

"What do you say to a header?"

Dick was stripped in half a minute. Anything for a change. And what change more delightful than a plunge in the lovely green sea?

The seniors smiled at his hurry, as they proceeded in a more leisurely fashion to follow his example.

"Don't wait for us; over you go," said Cresswell, "and tell old Neptune we are coming."

Dick waited for no further invitation, and sprang from the gunwale. They watched the spreading circles that tracked his dive, and marked the white shining streak as it darted past, under the water.

"He'll be a shark, before long," said Cresswell. "Look at the distance he's dived."

"He has to thank the tide for part of this, though," said Freckleton, looking at his watch. "Why, it's—"

An exclamation from Cresswell stopped him. Dick had reappeared, but he was twenty yards at least astern of the boat, and drifting back every moment.

At first he did not seem to be aware of it; but, treading water, waved one hand exultantly to celebrate his long dive.

But when he began to swim, leisurely at first, but harder presently, he suddenly realised his position, and saw that instead of making way back to the boat, he was losing distance at every stroke.

Some of my readers may have been in a similar position, and know the horror of helplessness which, for a moment, comes over the swimmer at such a time. Dick was not given to panic, still less fear, but, for all that, the minute which ensued was one of the most terrible in his life.

At certain times of the tide, the current between the Sprit Rock and the long Fiddle-Sandbank rushed like a mill-race. The boys knew this; they had been reminded of it at starting. But the morning had passed so quickly that, until Dick had taken his header, and they saw him swept astern, it had never occurred to one of them that it could possibly be three o'clock. Freckleton was the first to see the danger, and almost as soon as Dick appeared above water, he flung off his coat and boots, and saying to Cresswell, "Come quick with the boat," plunged into the water.

He was soon at Dick's side; not to support him, for the boy was able to do that for himself, but to encourage him to keep cool, and not waste his strength in endeavouring to stem the tide. And Dick had sense enough to take the advice, and tread water quietly till the boat should come.

It seemed a long time coming. The anchor was fast in the bottom, and it wanted all Cresswell's strength to get it up. Indeed he would have been tempted to simplify matters by cutting the cord, had he had a knife at hand.

By the time it was free, the boys were almost a quarter of a mile away, and getting weary. But once free, their suspense was not prolonged. Cresswell bore quickly down upon them, and picked them up; and rarely did three friends breathe more freely than when they all stood once more on the floor of their boat.

There was no speech-making or wringing of hands, no bragging, no compliments. They knew one another too well for that, and dressed in silence, much as if the adventure had been an ordinary incident of an ordinary bathe.

"It strikes me," said Cresswell, who still had the oars out, "it will take us all our time to get back. Are you ready to take an oar, old man?"

Short as the time had been—indeed the whole incident had not occupied much more than five minutes—the boat was about a mile below her old moorings, and still in the rush of the current.

It was little the two rowers could do to keep her head up, much less to make any way; and finally it became clear that if they were to get back to Templeton at all that day, they must either anchor where they were, for six hours, with the risk of their rope not holding in the Race, or else let the current take them out to the open, and then make a long row back outside the Sprit, and clear of the Fiddle Bank.

They decided on the latter, and somewhat gloomily rested on their oars, and watched the backward sweep of the boat on the tide seaward.

The square tower of Templeton had become a mere speck on the coast-line, before they felt the tide under them relax, and knew they were out of the Race.

Then they manned their oars, and began their long pull home. Fortunately the water still remained quiet, and the breeze did not freshen. But after about a mile had been made, and the Sprit Rock seemed only midway between them and the shore, a peril still more serious overtook them. The sky became overcast, and a sea mist, springing from nowhere, came down on the breeze, blotting out first the horizon, then the rock, and finally the coast, and leaving them virtually blindfolded in mid-ocean.

"We may as well anchor, and wait till it clears," said Cresswell.

"I think we might go on slowly," said Freckleton. "If we keep the breeze on our left, and Dick looks sharp out in front, we are bound to come either on the Sprit or the shore. Try it for a bit."

So they tried; rowing gingerly, and steering by the breeze on their cheeks, while Dick, ahead, strained his eyes into the soaking mist.

They may have made another mile, and still the mist wrapped them round. They had no idea where, they were. They might be close to the Rock, or they might have drifted down the coast, or they might be coming on to the Race again.

Still, anything seemed better than lying idle, and they paddled steadily on, hoping against hope for a single glimpse of daylight through the veil.

Suddenly Dick held his hand above his head, and shouted—

"Easy! Hold hard!"

And they could just see a dark object ahead on the water.

It couldn't be the rock, for it was too small; and they could hardly imagine it to be part of the pier, or a boat on the beach.

They shouted; and, in a moment, an answer came, "Ahoy, there!" and they knew they had come upon a fishing-boat at anchor.

"It's one of the fleet, waiting to get in. We'd better go alongside, and wait with them," said Freckleton.

So Dick shouted to say they were coming, and they rowed carefully alongside.

The first sight that met Dick's astonished eyes, as he reached across to seize the gunwale of the friendly boat, was Tom White, sitting comfortably smoking in the stern.

"Good day, young gentlemen," said that worthy. "Can't keep away from us, can't yer?"

"Hullo, Tom! We've lost our way in the mist," said Cresswell. "Where are we?"

"Reckon you're in the bay, and a swim to the pierhead."

"So near! We made sure we were outside the Sprit. How long have you been here?"

"Come here when the tide turned, we did," said Tom, "with a boat full, and no mistake. Say, young gentlemen, you ain't forgot the poor mariner that lost his boat, have yer? It's cruel hard to lose your living and have to begin afresh."

"If you mean you want a shilling for piloting us ashore," said Cresswell, "here you are. Will you take us, or will your mate?"

Dick grew uncomfortable, and, under pretence of wanting to examine some of the fish on the floor of the lugger, he scrambled up the side, and got in.

"Come back, Dick; do you hear?" called Cresswell. "We must go back if one of those fellows will run us in. Will you come, Tom?"

Visions of the bar-parlour of the "Dolphin" hovered before Tom's mind as he looked down at the speaker and the shilling that lay in his hand.

He was just about to consent, when he felt his arm nudged by Dick, who was crouching down over the fish at his feet.

"Tom White," said the boy, looking up nervously, "don't go ashore. They are going to arrest you for pawning that boat that didn't belong to you. Tell your mate to see us ashore. There's another shilling for you!"

Tom took his pipe out of his mouth and gaped at the boy. Then he slowly pocketed the shilling. Then he relieved himself of an oath. Then he called his mate—

"Jerry, see the squires ashore."

With fluttering heart Dick scrambled back into the boat, followed by the hulking Jerry, who, in a very few minutes, ran them comfortably on to the beach, and made an end of all their perils for that day.

They reached Templeton just in time for call over; and no one knew, as they walked into Chapel that evening, through what adventures they had passed since they left Templeton in the morning.

Early next morning Dick could not resist the temptation of going down to call on Mr Green.

"Well, did the boats all come in?" he inquired.

"All, bar Tom White's. And they do say it will be long enough before any one sees him in these parts again. He's got wind somehow. It's wonderful the way news travels on water—so it is."

Chapter Nineteen
In which Heathcote mounts high and falls low

George Heathcote celebrated the early hours of his holiday by "sleeping in," until the boom of the Chapel bell shot him headlong out of bed into his garments.

Coote, who had not yet mastered the art of venturing into Chapel alone, grew more and more pale as the hand of the clock crawled on, and the desperate alternative loomed before him, either of sharing his unpunctual friend's fate, or else of facing the exploit of walking unaided into his stall in the presence of gazing Templeton.

He had almost made up his heroic mind to the latter course, when a sound, as of coals being shot into a cellar, broke the stillness of the morning air; and next moment, Heathcote descended the stairs at the rate of five steps a second.

"Come on, you idiot; put it on!" he cried, as he reached Coote, and swept him forward towards the Chapel.

It was a close shave. Swinstead was shutting the door as Heathcote got his first foot in, and, but that the usher was unprepared for the desperate assault of the two juniors, and lost a second in looking to see what was the matter, Coote would have scored his first bad mark, and Heathcote's name would have figured, for the fifth or sixth time that term, on the monitor's black list.

As the latter young gentleman had nothing but his trousers, slippers, and coat on over his nightshirt, he deemed it prudent to bolt as soon as chapel was over, so as to elude the vigilant eyes of the authorities. He, therefore, saw nothing of Dick as he came out; and Dick, as we have seen, had too much on hand, just then, to see him.

At length, however, when the toilet was complete, and the glorious liberty from lessons began to swell our heroes' breasts, Heathcote's thoughts turned to Dick.

"Where's old Dick?" said he to Coote; "did you see him at breakfast?"

"Yes; he was at the other table. But I didn't see where he went afterwards."

Heathcote didn't like it. Dick had done him a bad turn yesterday over that levee business, and the least he could have done to-day would have been to find him out and make things jolly again.

But, instead of that, he had vanished, and left it to Heathcote to find him out. "Go and see where he is," said he to Coote.

The meek Coote obeyed, and took a cursory trot round the School Fields in search of his leader. No Dick was there, and no one had seen him.

Heathcote's face grew longer as he heard the report. It was getting serious. Dick was not only ill-treating him; he was cutting him.

He went off to Cresswell's study, as a last chance. The study was empty; and even the caps were gone from the pegs. Base desertion!

As he left the study he met Pledge.

"Ah, youngster! Going to grind all to-day?"

"I was looking for Dick."

"Oh! David looking for Jonathan. Poor chap! Johnny has given you the slip this time."

"Where has he gone?" asked Heathcote, trying to appear indifferent.

"The saintly youth has gone for a day's fishing in the Bay, with the dearly-beloved Cresswell and the reverend Freckleton. They have got him an exeat from the Doctor, they have bought him lines and bait, they have filled his pockets with good things. So you see piety pays after all, Georgie. What a pity you are not pious, too! You wouldn't be left so lonely if you were."

Heathcote was too hard hit to reply; and Pledge was kind enough not to attempt any further consolation.

It had been coming to this for weeks past. Georgie had refused to believe it as long as he could. He had stuck to his chum, and borne all the rebuffs which had rewarded him, patiently. He had even made excuses for Dick, and tried to think that their friendship was as strong as ever.

But now he saw that all the time Dick had been falling away and cutting himself adrift. This was why he left the "Select Sociables" the moment Heathcote joined them. This was why he went to the levee as soon as he saw Heathcote was not going. And this was why he had hidden out of the way this morning, for fear Heathcote should find out where he was going, and want to come too.

Georgie laughed bitterly to himself, as he made the discovery. As if he cared for fishing, or boating, or sandwiches! As if he cared about being cooped up in a tarry boat the livelong day, with a couple of such fellows as Cresswell and Freckleton! As if he couldn't enjoy himself alone or with Coote—poor young Coote, who had come to Templeton believing Dick to be his friend, whereas Dick, in his eagerness to toady to the "saints," would let him go to the dogs, if it wasn't that he, Heathcote, was there to befriend him.

So Heathcote went forth defiant, with Coote at his heels, resolved to let Templeton see he could enjoy himself without Dick.

He laughed extravagantly at nothing; he feigned to delight himself in the company of every idler he came across; he scorned loudly such stupid sport as fishing, or tennis, or fives.

He meant to make his mark. And then Dick, when he came back, would gnash his teeth with *envy* and wish woe to the hour when he was fool enough to desert his noblest friend!

"Tell you what'll be a lark, Coote," said Heathcote, as the two strode on, arm in arm, followed by a small crowd of juniors, who, seeing they were "on the swagger," hoped to be in the sport as spectators. "Tell you what; we'll have a walk round the roofs. I know where we can get up. We can get nearly all round the Quad. Won't it be a spree?"

Coote looked as delighted as he could, and said he hoped they wouldn't be caught, or there might be a row.

"Bless you, no one's about to-day. Come on. Nobody's done it since Fitch fell off a year ago, and he only got half round."

Coote was inwardly most reluctant to deprive the late Master Fitch of his hard-earned laurels, and even hinted as much. But Heathcote was in no humour for paltering. He was playing a high game, and Coote must play, too.

So they gave their followers the slip, and dodged their way back to the Quad, and made for the first staircase next to the Great Gate. Up here they crept, hurriedly and stealthily. One or two boys met them on the way, but Georgie swaggered past them, as though bound to pay an ordinary morning call on some occupant of the top floor. The top floor of all was dedicated to the use of the maids, who at that hour of the day were too much occupied elsewhere in making beds and filling jugs, to be at all inconvenient.

Heathcote, who, considering he had never made the expedition before, was wonderfully well up in the geography of the place, piloted Coote up a sort of ladder which ended in a trap-door in the ceiling of the garret.

"I know it's up here," he said. "Raggles told me it was the way Fitch got up."

"Oh!" said Coote, hanging tight on to the ladder with both arms, and trusting that, whichever way they ascended, they might select a different mode of descent from that adopted by the unfortunate Fitch.

Horrors! The trap-door was padlocked!

Joy! The padlock was not locked!

They opened the flap, and scrambled into a cavernous space between the ceiling and the roof, from which, to Coote's relief, there seemed no exit, except by the door at which they entered.

Heathcote, however, was not to be put off, and scrambled round the place on his hands and knees, in search of the hole in the roof, which he knew, on Raggles' authority, was there.

It was there, at the very end of the gable: a little manhole, just big enough to let a small body through to clear the gutter, and no more.

"Hurrah, old man!" shouted Heathcote, in a whisper, to his follower, who still lingered at the trap-door. "I've got it. Shut that door down, and crawl over here. Mind you keep on the rafters, or you'll drop through."

"Hurrah!" said Coote, pensively, as he proceeded to obey.

In two minutes they were out upon the roof, and enjoying a wonderful bird's-eye view of Templeton and the coast beyond.

A moderately broad gutter ran round the roof on the inside of the Quadrangle, with a low stone parapet at the edge. Along this the two boys crawled slowly and cautiously, until they had reached about the middle of their side of the Quadrangle.

It was dizzy work, looking down from their eminence; but glorious. Even Coote, now the venture had been made, and no relics of the late Master Fitch had appeared, began to enjoy himself.

"What a pity Dick isn't here!" said he.

"Rather! Won't he look blue when he hears of it?" said Heathcote. "Hullo! there are some of the fellows in the Quad. There's Pauncefote, isn't it? I vote we yell."

"Perhaps somebody would hear. Hadn't we better chuck a stone."

Heathcote detached a piece of plaster from the gutter, and pitched it neatly down within an inch of the head of the unsuspecting Pauncefote. That hero started, and looked first at the stone, then at the sky. Finally his eyes met Georgie's triumphant face beaming over the parapet, side by side with the rosy countenance of Coote.

It was enough. In another two minutes the Den knew what was going on, and Georgie and Coote were the heroes of the hour.

Moved by a desire to afford their spectators an entertainment worthy of their applause, they proceeded to make the round of the Quadrangle at a smart, though not always steady, pace; for their attention was so much divided between the gutter before them and the upturned faces below them, that they were once or twice decidedly close on the heels of the luckless Fitch.

Once, when they came to a comparatively broad landing, they varied the entertainment by swarming a little way up the tiles and sliding gracefully down again, regardless of tailors' bills; and when the spectators got tired of that, they treated them to a little horse-play by pelting them with bits of plaster, and finally with Coote's hat.

Even the highest class of entertainment cannot thrill for ever, and after a quarter of an hour of this edifying exhibition, the Den found they had had enough of it, and began to saunter off, much to the amazement of the two performers.

"May as well cut down," said Heathcote, when at length the Quad was deserted, and nothing seemed likely to be gained by remaining.

Coote was quite ready to obey. He had enjoyed his outing pretty well, but was rather tired of standing with one foot in front of the other, and keeping his eyes on Georgie.

He was nearest to the trap-door and had already crouched through it when Heathcote, perceiving that one of the Den had come back for another look, decided, in the kindness of his heart, to take one last turn round before retiring.

He had accomplished half his journey, and was glancing down rather anxiously to see if the boy was enjoying it, when a second-floor window on the opposite side suddenly opened and Mansfield looked out.

This apparition nearly sent Georgie headlong over the parapet. He saved himself by dropping on his hands and knees. He wasn't sure whether the Captain had seen him or not. If he had, he was in for it. If he had not, why on earth did he stand there at the window?

Georgie's performance ended in a humiliating wriggle back along the gutter to the trap-door. He dared not show so much as his "whisker" above the parapet, and as the parapet was only high enough to conceal him as he lay full length on his face, the return journey was both painful and tedious.

At last he reached the door where the faithful Coote anxiously awaited him, wondering what had kept him, and not sure whether the peculiar manner in which he advanced to the door was to be regarded as a joke or a feat of agility.

As Heathcote did not gratify his curiosity on this point, he received the hero with a smile of mingled humour and admiration, and then followed him in his precipitate descent to the lower world.

At the bottom of the staircase, Duffield was comfortably lounging.

"Hullo, kids!" he said, "you've got down then? What a mess you're in! Mansfield wants you, Heathcote."

And the messenger departed, whistling a cheery tune, and dribbling Coote's cap, after the straightest rules of the Association, across the Quad before him.

Heathcote's face lengthened. This was the triumphal reception which was to greet him on his return to earth, the mention of which was to set Dick's teeth gnashing!

He walked sulkily to Mansfield's study, and knew his fate almost before he entered the room.

The Captain was stern and cutting. He wasted few words in inquiry, still fewer in expostulation.

"You're one of the boys it's no use talking to," he said, almost scornfully. "You'll be glad to hear I'm not going to talk to you. I'm going to thrash you."

And that beautiful holiday morning George Heathcote was thrashed in a manner which hurt and startled him.

He fled from the Captain's presence, sore both in body and mind. But, strange to say, his chief wrath was reserved not for the Captain, but for Dick. His mind, once poisoned, contrived to connect Dick with every calamity that came upon him. And it enraged him to think that at this moment, while he was smarting under the penalty of a straightforward honest breach of rules, inflicted by a senior whose chief quarrel with him was that he had had the pluck to stay away from levée, Dick was reaping the benefit of his toadyism and basking in the sunshine of the powers that were.

Pledge, as might be expected, did nothing to discourage this feeling. He was not a bit surprised. He had expected it, and he knew equally well it was but the beginning of a settled programme. Heathcote had better not keep up the contest. He had better knuckle under at once, as Dick had done, and enjoy a quiet time. Or, if he must break rules, let him remember that fellows could lie, and cheat, and sneak in Templeton, and never once be interfered with by the holy monitors; but when once they took to walking on the roofs—why, where could they expect to go to when they descended to such a depth of wickedness as that?

Heathcote spend a miserable afternoon, letting his misfortune and Pledge's words rankle in his breast till he hated the very name of Dick and goodness.

In due time the three fishers returned that evening tired with their hard day's work, and bronzed with the sun and breeze.

Dick looked serious and anxious as he followed his seniors into the Quadrangle, carrying the ulsters and the empty luncheon basket.

"Ah," thought Heathcote, as he watched him from a retired nook, "he's ashamed of himself. He well may be."

The two seniors turned in at Westover's door, leaving Dick to continue his walk alone.

Now was Heathcote's time. Emerging from his corner he put his hands carelessly in his pockets and advanced to meet his former friend, whistling a jaunty tune.

He was half afraid Dick might not see him, but Dick had a quick eye for a friend, and hailed him half across the Quadrangle.

"Hullo, Georgie, old man!" said he, running up. "So awfully sorry you couldn't come on our spree too. What's the matter?"

What, indeed? Georgie, with an elaborate air of unconsciousness either of the voice or the presence of his comrade, walked on looking straight in front of him and whistling more jauntily than ever.

Dick stood for a moment aghast. He would fain have believed his chum had either not seen him or was joking. But a sinking at his heart told him otherwise, and a rush of anger told him that whatever the reason might be it was an unjust one.

So he checked his inclination to pursue his friend and demand an explanation there and then, and strolled on, whistling himself.

Heathcote pursued his dignified walk until he concluded he might safely stop whistling and venture to peep round.

When he did so he was dismayed to see Dick walking arm in arm across the Quadrangle with Coote, laughing at some narration which that pliable young gentleman was giving.

Poor Georgie! This was the hardest blow of all. If Dick had appeared crushed, if he had even looked hurt, or said one word of regret, Georgie's heart would have been comforted and his wrath abated.

But to have his elaborate demonstration of rebuke ignored and quietly passed by in favour of Coote was too much! Georgie could not bear it. Pledge and all Pledge's sophistry vanished in a moment with the loss of his friend.

If Dick would only give him another chance!

Chapter Twenty
How Coote comes out as a
suspicious character

It would have been well for Heathcote if he had acted on the impulse of the moment, and made it up with Dick that same evening.

Dick had come back from his boating expedition better disposed towards his lieutenant than he had been for a long time. He had come determined to befriend him, and rescue him from his enemies, and set him up upon his feet. He had come, reproaching himself with his former neglect, and convinced that Georgie's fate was in his hands for good or evil; and that being so, he had determined to make a good job of his friend and turn him out a credit to Templeton.

But in all this modest programme it had never occurred to him that Georgie would be anything but delighted to be taken in hand and made a good job of.

Therefore, when in the fulness of his benevolence he had found his friend out immediately on his return, and been repulsed for his pains, Dick felt "gravelled."

All his nice little plan of campaign fell through. It was no use routing the Den, and putting Pledge and the "Sociables" to shame, when Georgie wouldn't be made a good job of. And so Dick, with some dismay and considerable loss to his self-conceit, had to order a retreat and consider whether the war was worth going on with under the circumstances.

He therefore did not meet Heathcote half-way, and curled himself up into bed, sorely perplexed, sorely crest-fallen, and sorely out of love with the world at large.

No news spreads so fast as the news of a quarrel, and before school was well launched next morning the noise of a "row" between Dick and Heathcote ran through Templeton from end to end.

The Den heard it, and hoped there would be a fight. The "Select Sociables" heard it, and voted it a good job. The Fourth and Fifth heard it, and said, "Young idiots!" The Sixth heard it, and shook their heads.

Pledge, however, regarded the matter with complacency.

"So it's a row, is it?" said he, as his *protégé* wandered disconsolately into his study after morning school. "Pistols for two, coffee for four, and all that sort of thing, eh?"

"He cuts me dead," said Heathcote.

"And you break your heart? Of course you do. I knew you couldn't get on without him."

"I don't break my heart at all!" said Heathcote, savagely.

"No; you look as if you were going to hang yourself! How glad he'll be to see dear Georgie sorrowing for his sins! If you'll take my advice, you'll go out next time you see him and lie down at his feet and ask him kindly to tread upon you."

"I'm not going to bother about him!" said Heathcote, miserably. "If he wants to make up, he'll have to come and ask me himself."

"And, of course, you'll fall on his neck, and weep, and say, 'Oh! yes, I loved you always.' Very pretty! Seriously, youngster—don't make a donkey of yourself! As long as it pays him to cut you, he will cut you, and when it pays him better to be friends, he'll want to be friends. Don't make yourself too cheap. You're better than a dirty halfpenny, to be played pitch and toss with."

These words sank deep in the boy's disturbed mind, and drove away any lingering desire for an immediate reconciliation.

Day after day the two old chums met and cut one another dead, and the spectacle of the "split" became a part of every-day life at Templeton.

At the end of a week fellows almost forgot that David and Jonathan had ever been on speaking terms.

Then an unlooked-for incident caused a diversion and upset the calculations of everybody.

Coote had, of all interested parties, least relished the falling-out of his two old comrades. It had not only pained him as a friend, but, personally, it had caused him the greatest discomfort.

For he found himself in the position of an animated buffer between the two. When Heathcote wanted to show off to Dick that he was not breaking his heart on his account, he got possession of Coote, and lavished untoward affection on that tender youth. And when Dick wanted to exhibit to Heathcote that he was not pining in solitude for want of an adherent, he attached Coote to his person and treated him like his own brother.

And Coote, when Heathcote had him, was all for Heathcote, and eloquent on the abominable sins of piety and inconstancy. And when he was with Dick he was all for Dick, and discoursed no less eloquently on the wickedness of deceit and poorness of spirit. Sometimes his bad memory, and the quick transitions of allegiance through which he was called upon to pass, made him forget his *rôle*, and condole with Dick on Heathcote's piety, or with Heathcote on Dick's poverty of spirit; and sometimes, when, in the company of the one, he happened to meet the other, he quite lost his head and made an ass of himself to both.

This course of double dissimulation at the end of a week began to lose its charms, and Coote, with all his good nature and desire to make things pleasant for everybody, began to get tired of his two friends and long for a breath of freedom.

So he took an early morning stroll along the cliffs one morning, finishing up with Mr Webster's shop in the High Street.

The gossiping Templeton stationer had suffered somewhat in temper since the reader saw him last, three months ago. The young gentry for whom he catered were not the "apples of his eyes" they had been. Not that he was at open war with them, but he had a grievance.

He didn't complain of the liberties they sometimes took with his shop — making it a general house of call and discussion forum. That was good for trade, and Mr Webster didn't object to anything that was good for trade. Nor did the occasional horse-play, and even fighting, that took place on his premises now and then sour his milk of human kindness more than was natural. But when it came to abusing, not himself, but his goods, with the result that a good many of the latter, in the course of a term, came to be damaged, and some, he had reason to suppose, pilfered, then Mr Webster thought it time to make a stand and assert himself. He was, therefore, more brusque and less obsequious to the junior portion of Templeton this term than he had been last.

So, when Coote, in the artlessness of his nature, feigned an earnest desire to know the price of an elegant ormolu inkpot, and modestly inquired it, the tradesman eyed him sharply and replied —

"Ten shillings. Do you want to buy it?"

Coote was one of those individuals who cannot say "no" to a shopman. Though nothing was further from his mind than putting his sadly reduced pocket-money into an ormolu inkpot, his tender heart could not bear to dash the stationer's hopes too rudely. He said he couldn't quite make up his mind, and would just look round, if he might.

Mr Webster had got tired of the young Templeton gentlemen "looking round." He knew what it meant, generally. The springs of all his inkpots got critically tested, pencils got twisted in and out till they refused to twist again, desks got ransacked, and their contents mixed in glorious and hopeless confusion, photographs got thumbed, books got dog-eared; and the sole profit to the honest merchant was the healthy exercise of putting everything tidy after his visitors had left, and the satisfaction of expressing his feelings in language strictly selected from the dictionary.

He was, therefore, by no means elated at Coote's proposal, and might have vetoed it, had not an important customer, in the shape of the Rev. Mr Westworth, the curate, entered at that moment, and diverted his attention. But even the reverend gentleman's conversation was unable entirely to engross the honest bookseller, who kept a restless corner of one eye on the boy's movements, while, with the rest of his features, he smiled deferentially at his customer.

Coote, meanwhile, unaware of the suspicion with which he was being regarded, enjoyed a pleasant five minutes in turning Mr Webster's stock of writing materials inside out. Being of a susceptible nature, he fell in love with a great many things in the course of his investigations, and the ormolu inkpot was several times eclipsed. What took his fancy most was a pretty chased silver penholder and pencil, which shut up into the compass of a date-stone, and yet, when open, was large and firm enough to write out the whole of Virgil at a sitting.

Whatever else he looked at, he always came back to this treasure; and finally, when he became aware that Mr Westworth was about to depart, he had almost to push it from him, in order to bring himself to the pitch of leaving too.

He had no desire further to lacerate Mr Webster's feelings by declining to purchase anything, and therefore quitted the shop hurriedly, not noticing, as he did so, that the unlucky little pencil, which he had put down with such affectionate reluctance, had shown its regret by rolling quietly and sadly off the tray on to the counter, till it reached a gap half-way, into which it plunged suicidally, and became lost to the light of day.

Mr Webster, who had seen as little of the catastrophe as the boy had, bowed his reverend guest out, and then turned to the disordered tray with a shrug of his shoulders.

His review of its contents had not lasted half a minute when he started and uttered an exclamation. The pencil was gone—so was Coote!

For once there was no shadow of a doubt in the honest stationer's mind; it was as clear as daylight. No one else had been in the shop except the curate, who had never been near the tray. Coote had; he had touched and fingered all its contents; he had had this very pencil in his hand, he had quitted the shop abruptly, and started running as soon as he got outside.

Mr Webster *did* know what two and two made, and it was quite a relief to him to feel absolutely and positively certain he had been robbed by a Templeton boy!

His one difficulty was that he did not remember having seen Coote before, nor did he know his name. However, he would find him, if he had the whole school marched one by one in front of him, and, when he had found him, he would make an example of him.

Blissfully unconscious of the cloud on the horizon, Coote had arrived at the school just in time for chapel. On his way out Heathcote came up and took his arm.

"Well, old fellow," said that youth in a loud voice, which made it perfectly clear to Coote that Dick must be somewhere within hearing, "come and have another jolly two-hander after school, won't you? You and I ought to be able to lick Raggles and Culver into fits now, oughtn't we?"

"It's a wonder to me," said Dick, walking off in another direction with Aspinall, "how Raggles and Culver play tennis at all; any fool could lick them left-handed."

Aspinall knew better than to dispute the assertion, and submitted to be taken down to the courts after morning school by Dick, where, in full view of Heathcote and Coote, the two played an exciting match, in which, of course, Dick came off victorious, for the simple reason that Aspinall had not the moral courage to beat him.

Towards the end of the game Cresswell and Cartwright walked up with their rackets. Finding all the courts occupied, Cresswell said to Dick—

"You two may as well make up a four with Heathcote and Coote; we want one of the courts."

Dick was delighted to give up the court, but he was far too fagged to play any more. So was Aspinall, wasn't he? Besides, they neither of them cared about four-handers.

Heathcote and Coote, for their part, were far too absorbed in their game to heed Cresswell's suggestion. They were playing best out of fifteen sets, Georgie announced, and had just finished the third. Which being known, the spectators fell away from that part of the field rapidly.

The two o'clock bell sounded before the fifth set was over, rather to Coote's relief, who had been getting just tennis enough during the last week.

The two champions were walking back lovingly to the school, when, as they approached the Quad gate, Heathcote said—

"Hallo! there's Webster! What's he hanging about for there?"

"Perhaps you owe him a bill," said Coote.

"Not I. I've jacked Webster up; he's a surly beast."

"I was in his shop this morning," said Coote. "There was such a stunning little shut-up penholder, about so big. I can't fancy how they make them shut up so small."

"Did you buy it?"

"No; I couldn't afford it. Hallo! what does he want? He's beckoning."

"Jolly cheek of him!" said Heathcote. "If he wants you, let him come. I wouldn't go to him if I were you. Call out and ask him what he wants."

Whereupon Coote called out:—

"What do you want?"

"I want you," said the bookseller, approaching.

"Tell him you're busy, and he'd better come again."

"I'm busy, I say," cried Coote; "come again."

"No, thank you," said Mr Webster, stepping before the boys. "Ah! good day to you, Mr Heathcote; quite a stranger, sir. If you'll allow me, I would like a word with your friend?"

"You know you'll get in a row, Webster, if you're seen up here," said Heathcote. "All the shop fellows have to stop at the gate."

Having delivered which piece of friendly caution, Georgie walked on, leaving Coote and the bookseller *tête-à-tête*.

"What do you want?" asked Coote.

"Come, none of your tricks with me, young fellow! I want that pencil-case, there!"

"Pencil-case! What pencil-case? I've not got any pencil-case!" said Coote.

Mr Webster had expected this; he would have been a trifle disappointed had the criminal pleaded guilty at once.

"Do you suppose I didn't see you with it in your hand in my shop, sir, this morning?" said he.

"But I didn't take it—I haven't got it—I wouldn't do such a thing," said Coote, beginning to feel very uncomfortable.

"You'd like me to suppose that some one else took it; wouldn't you?" said Mr Webster, feeling so sure of his ground as quite to enjoy himself.

"If you've lost it, somebody else did. I didn't," said the boy.

"Now, look here, young gentleman, that sort of thing may go down at home or here in school, but it's no use trying it on with me. If you don't choose to give me that pencil this moment, we'll see what a policeman can do."

At this threat Coote turned pale. "Really, I never took it! You may feel in my pockets. Oh, *please* don't bring a policeman, Mr Webster!"

"What's your name?" demanded Mr Webster, ostentatiously producing a pencil and paper.

"Coote—Arthur Dennis Coote," said the trembling boy.

"Address?"

"One, Richmond Villas, Richmond Road, G—."

"Very well, Mr Coote," said the stationer, folding up the paper and putting it into his pocket-book; "unless you call on me before this time to-morrow with the pencil, I'll have you locked up. Good morning."

Coote, with his heart in his shoes, watched the retreating figure till it was lost to view, and then turned, bewildered and scared, to the school.

Heathcote was waiting for him at the door.

"Well, what did the cad want?—what's the row, I say?" he demanded, catching sight of the dazed face of his chum.

"Oh, Georgie, a most frightful row!" gasped Coote. "He says I've stolen a pencil!"

"What, the one you were talking about?"

"Yes, the very one."

"I suppose you haven't, really?" asked Heathcote, with no false delicacy.

"No, really I haven't—that is, if I have I— Look here; do hunt my pockets, will you, old man?"

Georgie obeyed, and every pocket of the unhappy Coote was successively explored, without bringing to light the missing pencil.

"There," said the suspect, with a sigh of relief when the operation was over, "I was positive I hadn't got it. He says I was the only one in the shop, and that he missed it as soon as I had gone; but really and truly I didn't take it; I never did such a thing in my life."

"Of course you didn't. He's a cad and has got a spite against us, that's what it is. What's he going to do?"

"He says unless I take it to him by this time to-morrow, he'll send a policeman to take me up," and the unhappy youth's voice choked with the words.

Heathcote gave a long, dismal whistle.

"Whatever will you do?" he asked, in tones of deep concern.

"How can I take it back?" asked Coote, "if I hadn't got it. I wish to goodness I had got it!"

"You'll have to square him, somehow," said Georgie. "You're positive it hasn't dropped into your shoes, or anywhere, by accident."

The bare suggestion sent Coote up to the dormitory, where he undressed, and shook out each article of his toilet, in the hope of discovering the lost treasure.

Alas! high or low, there was no *sign* of it.

He spent a terrible afternoon, wondering where he should be that time to-morrow, or whether possibly Mr Webster would alter his mind, and send a policeman up forthwith.

He was in no humour for tennis, or a row in the Den, or a "Sociable" concert after school, and avoided them all. And to add to his troubles, Heathcote was detained two hours for some offence; so that he was deprived for an equal length of time of the consolation of that hero's sympathy and advice.

He spent the interval dismally in a retired corner of the field, where he hoped to be able to collect his shattered wits in peace. But it was no good. He could see no way through it.

"Oh!" thought he, for the hundredth time, "how I wish I had really taken it!"

He had just arrived at this conclusion, when a light step approaching, caused him to look up, and see Dick.

"Hullo, old man," said the latter, "how jolly blue you look. What's the row?"

Coote repeated his dismal story, and marked the dismay which crept over his leader's face as he told it.

"By Jove, old man," said Dick, "it's a mess. How ever are you to get out?"

"That's just what I don't know," groaned Coote. "If I only had the pencil it would be all right. But, really and truly, Dick, I never took it; did I?"

"All serene," said Dick. "But, I say, if you can't give him the pencil back, perhaps you can pay him for it."

"It cost thirty shillings; and I've only got seven-and-six."

"I've got ten shillings," said Dick. "That's seventeen-and-six. Perhaps if we gave him that, he'd wait for the rest."

"You're an awful brick," said poor Coote, gratefully. "If it hadn't been for you and Georgie, I don't know what I should have done."

Dick started and coloured.

"Is he in it? Does he know about it?" he asked.

"Yes, Dick," said Coote, feeling rather in a hobble. "I—thought, you know, I'd better tell him."

"What did he say?"

"Oh, not much; that is, he said he'd help me if he could. But—I don't see how he can."

"He might be able to lend you enough to make up the price," said Dick, after a pause.

"I know he would, he's such a brick—that is," added the wretched Coote, correcting himself, "you're both such bricks."

Dick made no answer, but walked off, musing to himself.

"Both bricks!" And yet poor Coote had to blush when he mentioned the name of one brick to the other! Dick was getting tired of this.

He retired to the school, to think over what could be done, and was about to ascend the stairs, when the familiar form of Georgie appeared coming to meet him.

"Georgie, Coote's in an awful mess; I vote we back him up."

"So do I, rather, old man."

And they went off arm-in-arm to find him.

Check to you, Pledge!

Chapter Twenty One
How our heroes fall out of the
frying-pan into the fire

Templeton opened its eyes as it saw David and Jonathan walking together across the fields that afternoon. The Den, with native quickness of perception, instantly snuffed a battle in the air, and dogged the heels of the champions with partisan shouts and cheers.

"Dick will finish him in a round and a half," shouted Raggles.

"Don't you be too cock-sure," cried Gosse, "Georgie's got a neat 'square-fender' on him, and I rather fancy him best myself."

Gosse had not the ghost of a notion what a "square-fender" was; nor had anyone else. But the word carried weight, and there was a run on Georgie accordingly.

Raggles, however, was not to be snuffed out too easily.

"Bah!" shouted he, "what's the use of a 'square-fender,' when Dick can get down his 'postman's knock' over the top, and blink his man into fits."

After that Georgie was nowhere. A fellow who can "blink" his man with a "postman's knock," no matter what it means, is worth half-a-dozen "square-fenders." And so Dick became a favourite, and the event was considered as good as settled.

Which was just as well; for our heroes, as they walked in search of Coote, could not be so engrossed either in their newly-healed alliance, or in the affliction of their friend, as to be unaware of the commotion at their heels. And it was not till Dick had ordered the foremost of the procession to "hook it," enforcing his precept by one or two impartially-distributed samples of his "postman's knock," that it dawned on the Den there was to be no fight after all.

Whereupon they yapped off in disgust, with their noses in the air, in search of some better sport.

Left to themselves, our heroes, with a strange mixture of joy and anxiety in their hearts, broke into a trot, and presently sighted Coote.

That unhappy youth, little dreaming of the revolution which his scrape was destined to effect in Templeton, was still sitting where Dick had left him, ruefully meditating on his near prospect of incarceration. The vision of Dick and Heathcote advancing upon him by no means tended to allay the tumult of his feelings.

"I'm in for it now," groaned he to himself. "They're both going to pitch into me for telling the other. What a mule I was ever to come to Templeton."

But Dick's first words dispelled these gloomy forebodings effectually.

"Keep your pecker up, old man, Georgie and I are both going to back you up. We'll pull you through somehow."

"I've got ten bob," said Georgie. "That's twenty-seven-and-six. Perhaps he'll let you off the other half-crown."

Considering he had not abstracted the pencil at all, Coote inwardly thought Mr Webster might forego this small balance, and be no loser. And he half-hinted as much.

"It's an awful shame," said he, "not to believe my word. I really don't see why we ought to stump up at all."

But this proposal by no means suited his ardent backers-up, who looked upon the whole affair as providential, and by no means to be burked.

"Bound to do it," said Dick decisively. "Things look ugly against you, you know, and it would be a terrible business if you got locked up. It would cost less to square Webster then to bail you out; wouldn't it, Georgie?"

"Rather!" said Georgie. "Besides, it looks awkward if it gets out that you've been to prison.—Our 'Firm' oughtn't to get mixed up in that sort of mess."

After this, Coote resigned all pretensions to the further direction of his own defence, and left his case unreservedly in the hands of his two honest partners.

They decided that very evening, with or without leave, to go down with the twenty-seven-and-six to Mr Webster.

Dick was the only one of the three who got leave; but his two friends considered the crisis one of such urgency that even without leave they should brave all consequences and accompany him.

Mr Webster was in the act of putting up his shutters when the small careworn procession halted before his door, and requested the favour of an interview.

The bookseller was in a good temper. He had rather enjoyed the day's adventure, and reckoned that the moral effect of his action would be good. Besides, the looks of the culprit and his two friends fully justified his suspicions. They had doubtless come to restore the pencil, and plead for mercy. They should see that mercy was not kept in stock in his shop, and would want some little trouble before it was to be procured.

So he bade his visitors step inside, and state their business.

"We've come about the pencil, you know," said Dick, adopting a conciliatory tone to begin with. "It's really a mistake, Webster. Coote never took it."

"No. We've known Coote for years, and never knew him do such a thing," said Heathcote.

"And they've turned out every one of my pockets," said Coote, "and there was no sign of it."

Mr Webster smiled serenely.

"Very pretty, young gentlemen; very pretty. When you have done joking, perhaps, you'll give me what belongs to me."

"Hang it!" cried Dick, forgetting his suavity. "It's no joke, Webster. I tell you, Coote never took the thing."

"You were here in the shop, of course, and saw him?" said the tradesman.

"No, I wasn't," said Dick; "you know that as well as I do."

"Coote," said Heathcote, feeling it his turn to back up—"Coote's a gentleman; not a thief."

"I'm glad to hear that," said Mr Webster. "He's sure he's not both?"

"I'm positive," said Coote.

"And is that all you've come to say?" said the bookseller.

"No," said Dick. "It's an awful shame if you can't believe us. But if you won't—well, we'd sooner pay you for the pencil and have done with it."

Mr Webster was charmed. He had always imagined himself a sharp man and he was sure of it now. For a minute or two the boys' joint protestations of innocence had staggered his belief in Coote's guilt; but this ingenuous offer convinced him he had been right after all.

"Oh, you didn't steal it, but you're going to pay for it, are you? Very pretty! What do you think it was worth?"

"Thirty shillings," said Dick, "that was the price marked on it."

"And yet you never saw it."

"Of course I didn't," retorted Dick, beginning to feel hot. "I've told you so twice—Coote saw it."

"Yes," said Coote, "there was a tiny label on it."

"We can't make up quite thirty shillings," said Heathcote; "but we've got twenty-seven shillings and sixpence. I suppose you'll make that do?"

"*Do* you suppose I'll make it do?" said Mr Webster, beginning to feel hot, too. "You think you can come to my shop, and pilfer my things like so many young pickpockets; and then you have the impudence to come and offer me part of the price to say nothing about it. No, thank you. That's not my way of doing business."

"There's nothing else we can do," said Dick.

"Oh, yes, there is. You can march off to the lockup—all three of you if you like; but one of you, anyhow. And so you will, as sure as I stand here."

"Oh, Mr Webster, I say, please don't say that. He never took it, really he didn't."

"Come, that'll do. Twelve o'clock to-morrow, unless I get the pencil, you'll get a call from the police. Off you go. I've had enough of you."

And the bookseller, whose temper had gradually been evaporating during the visit, bustled our heroes out of the shop, and slammed the door behind them.

"It's all up, old man," said Heathcote, lugubriously. "I did think the cad would shut up for twenty-seven shillings and sixpence."

"I'm afraid he wants me more than the money," said Coote. "Whatever *can* I do?"

"You can't prove you didn't take it; that's the worst," said Dick.

"He can't prove I did. He only thinks I did. How I wish I *had* that stupid pencil."

With which original conclusion they returned to Templeton. Dick, under cover of his *exeats* marched ostentatiously in. The other two, in a far more modest and shy manner, entered by their hands and knees, on receipt of a signal from their leader that the coast was clear.

Heathcote deemed it prudent not to exhibit himself in the Den, and therefore retired to Pledge's study as the place least likely to be dangerous.

Pledge was there working.

"Hullo, youngster," said he, "what's been your little game this evening? Been to a prayer meeting?"

"No," said Heathcote laconically.

It was no part of Pledge's manner to appear inquisitive. He saw there was a mystery, and knew better than to appear in the slightest degree anxious to solve it.

He had as yet heard nothing of the newly-formed alliance in low life, and attributed Heathcote's uncommunicativeness either to shame for some discreditable proceeding, or else to passing ill-humour. In either case he reckoned on knowing all about it before long.

Heathcote was very uncomfortable. It had not occurred to him till just now that Pledge would resent the return of his allegiance to Dick as an act of insubordination. Not that that would keep him from Dick; but Heathcote, who had hitherto admired his old patron as a friend, by no means relished the idea of having him an enemy. He therefore felt that the best thing he could do was to hold his tongue, and if, after all, a row was to come, well—it would have to come.

He sat down to do his own preparation, and for half an hour neither student broke the silence.

Then Pledge, who had never known his *protégé* silent for so long together before, felt there must be something the matter which he ought to be aware of.

So he leaned back in his chair and stretched himself.

"You're a nice boy, George!" said he, laughing; "you've been sitting half an hour with your pen in your hand and haven't written a word."

Georgie coloured up.

"It's a stiff bit of prose," said he.

"So it seems. Suppose I do it for you?"

"No, thanks, Pledge," said the boy, who, without having any particular horror of having his lessons done for him, did not like just now, when he was conscious of having revolted against his senior, to accept favours from him.

"No? It's true, then, Georgie is joining the elect and going to take holy orders?"

"No, I'm not," said Georgie.

"Then Georgie is trying to be funny and not succeeding," said the monitor, drily, returning to his own books.

Another silent quarter of an hour passed, and then the first bed bell rang.

"Good-night," said Heathcote, gathering together his books.

"Good-night, dear boy!" said Pledge, with the red spots coming out on his cheeks; "come down with me to the 'Tub' in the morning."

"I'm going down with another fellow," said Georgie, feeling his heart bumping in his chest.

"Oh!" said the monitor, indifferently; "with a *very* dear friend?—the saintly Dick, for instance?"

"Yes," said Heathcote, and left the room.

Pledge sat motionless, watching the closed door for a full minute, and, as he did so, an ugly look crept over his face, which it was well for Heathcote he did not see. Then he turned mechanically to his books, and buried himself in them for the rest of the evening.

The "Tub" next morning was crowded as usual, and it needed very little penetration on Pledge's part to see that the triple alliance between our three heroes was fast and serious.

They undressed on the same rock, they dived side by side from the spring-board, they came above water at the same moment, they challenged collectively any other three of the Den to meet them in mortal combat in mid-Tub, and they ended up their performance by swimming solemnly in from the open arm-in-arm, Coote, of course, being in the middle.

All this Pledge observed, and marked also their anxious looks and hurried consultations as they dressed. He guessed that there must be some matter of common interest which was just then acting as the pivot on which the alliance turned, and his taste for scientific research determined him, if possible, to discover it.

So when, after "Tub," the three friends marched arm-in-arm down town, Pledge casually strolled the same way at a respectful distance.

It was clear the "Firm" was bound on a momentous and unpleasant errand.

Coote every other minute was convulsed by the brotherly claps which the backers-up on either side bestowed upon him; and the long faces of all three, as now and then they stopped and scrutinised the shop-window of some silversmith or pawnbroker, betokened anything but content or high spirits.

At length Pledge saw them enter very dejectedly at Mr Webster's door, where, not being anxious to disturb them, he left them and took a short turn down the shady side of High Street, within view of the stationer's shop.

Their business was not protracted, for in about three minutes he saw them emerge, with faces longer than ever, and turn their steps hurriedly and dismally towards Templeton.

When they were out of sight, Pledge crossed the road and casually turned in at Mr Webster's door.

"Well, Webster, anything new?"

"No, sir; nothing in your line, I'm afraid," said the shopman.

"By the way," said Pledge, carelessly, "was that my fag I saw coming out here just now?"

"Mr Heathcote?" said Webster, frowning. "Yes, that was he, sir, and two friends of his. I'm afraid he's getting into bad company, Mr Pledge."

"Are you? What makes you think that?"

"It's an unpleasant matter altogether," said Mr Webster, "and likely to be more so. The fact is, sir, I've been robbed."

And he proceeded to give Pledge an account of the loss of the pencil-case, and of the efforts of the boys to get the matter hushed up.

Pledge heard it with an amused smile.

"They've just been here to try and buy me off," said the indignant shopkeeper, "but I'm going to make an example of them. I'm sorry to do it, Mr Pledge, but it's only fair to myself, isn't it, sir?"

"I don't know," said Pledge; "I don't see that it will do you much good. You'd better leave it to me."

"Leave it to you?"

"Well, I expect I can get back your pencil as easily as you can, if they've got it. You're sure they have got it?"

"I'm certain Master Coote took it; certain as I stand here. What they've done with it among them I can't say."

"Well, don't be in a hurry. I'm a monitor, you know, and it's as much to my interest to follow the thing up as to yours. If you'll take my advice, you won't be in a hurry to prosecute. Wait a week."

"Very good, sir," said the bookseller, to whom it was really a relief to postpone final action for a day or two, at least. If Pledge, meanwhile, should succeed in bringing the culprit to book, it would still rest with Mr Webster to decide whether to make an example of him or not Pledge departed, and the bookseller turned to dust his shop out for the day. In this occupation he had not proceeded far, when his brush, penetrating into a crack in his counter, caused something within to rattle. Being a tidy man, and not favouring dust or dirt of any sort, even out of sight, he proceeded to probe the hole in order to clear away the obstruction, when, to his amazement and consternation, he discovered, snugly lying in the hollow, the lost pencil-case!

Mr Webster's first thought was, "Artful young rogues! They've brought it back, and hidden it here to escape punishment!"

And yet, when he came to think of it, all the dust in that hole could not have settled there during the last half-hour; nor—and he was sure of this— had either of the boys, on their last two visits, been anywhere near that side of his shop.

After all, he had "run his head against a stone wall," and narrowly escaped ruining himself as far as Templeton was concerned. For he knew the young gentlemen of that school well enough to be sure, after a blunder like this, that the place would soon have become too hot to hold him.

Mr Webster positively gasped at the thought of his narrow escape, and forgot all about Pledge, and the culprit, and the culprit's friends, in his self congratulation.

About mid-day, however, he was suddenly reminded of them all, by the vision of Dick darting into the shop.

"Webster," said that youth, in tones of breathless entreaty, "*do* let us off this once! Coote really never took the pencil, and if you have him taken up, it will be ruination! I shall get in a row for coming down now, but I couldn't help. We'll do anything if you don't take Coote up. I'll get my father to pay you what you like. Will you, please, Webster?"

The boy delivered this appeal so rapidly and earnestly that Webster had no time to stop him; but when Dick paused, he said:—

"Make yourself comfortable, Mr Richardson, I've found the pencil."

Dick literally shouted, as he sprang forward and seized the bookseller's hand:—

"Found it! Oh, what a brick you are!"

"Yes; it had fallen into that hole, and I just turned it out. Lucky for you and your friend it did. And I'm not sorry, either, for I'd no fancy for putting any of you to trouble; but I was bound to protect myself, you see."

"Of course, of course. You're a regular trump, Webster," cried Dick, too delighted to feel at all critical of the way in which the bookseller was extricating himself from his dilemma. "I'm so glad; so will they be. Thanks, awfully, Webster. I say, I must get a *Templeton Observer* for the good of the shop."

And he flung down a sixpence in the bigness of his heart, and taking the newspaper, darted back to Templeton in a state of jubilation and happiness, which made passers-by, as he rushed down the street, turn round and look after him.

In ten minutes Coote and Heathcote were as radiant as he; and that afternoon the Templeton "Tub" echoed with the boisterous glee of the three heroes, as they played leap-frog with one another in the water, and set the rocks almost aglow with the sunshine of their countenances.

But Nemesis is proverbially a cruel old lady. She sports with her victims like a cat with a mouse. And just when the poor scared things, having escaped one terrible swoop of her hand, take breath, she comes down remorselessly with the other hand, and dashes away hope and breath at a blow.

And so it fared with our unlucky heroes. No sooner had they escaped the fangs of Mr Webster, than they found themselves writhing in the clutches of a new terror, twice as bad and twice as awkward.

In the first flush of escape, Dick had crammed the *Templeton Observer*, which he had paid sixpence for in celebration of the finding of the pencil, into his pocket, and never given it another thought. During the evening, however, having occasion to search the pocket for another of its numerous contents, he came upon it, and drew it out.

"What's that—the *Templeton Observer*?" asked Heathcote, becoming suddenly serious. "Anything in it?"

"I haven't looked," said Dick, becoming serious, too, and inwardly anathematising the public press.

"May as well," said Heathcote.

"Perhaps there'll be something about the All England Tennis Cup in it," said Coote.

Dick opened the paper, and his jaw dropped at the first paragraph which met his eye.

"Well," said Heathcote, reflecting his friend's consternation in his own looks, "whatever is it?"

"Has Lawshaw won it, or Renford?" inquired Coote.

Dick passed the paper to Georgie, who read as follows:—

The mysterious disappearance of a Templeton boat.—The boatman Thomas White was arrested yesterday at Glistow, and will be charged before the magistrates on Saturday with fraudulently pawning the boat *Martha*, knowing the same to be only partially his own property. The case is attracting much interest in the town. No news has yet reached us of the missing boat, but we hear on good authority that circumstances have come to light pointing to White himself as the thief, and we believe evidence to this effect will be offered at Saturday's examination. The police are reticent on the subject.

"What was the score of sets?" asked Coote, as Heathcote put down the paper.

The latter replied by handing the paper to the questioner and pointing to the fatal paragraph.

Coote read it in great bewilderment. Of course he knew all about Tom White's row and the missing *Martha*. Every Templeton fellow, from Mansfield down to Gosse, knew it. But why should Dick and Heathcote look so precious solemn about it?

"By Jove!" said he, "I wish they'd catch the fellow. What's the use of the police being reticent?"

"Coote, old man," said Dick, in a tone which made the youth addressed open his eyes, "do you know how the *Martha* got lost?"

"Stolen," said Coote, "by a fellow who was skulking about on the sands."

"Wrong. She was turned adrift; someone loosed the anchor rope when the tide was coming in."

"How do you know that?"

"Because I was the fellow."

"And I helped," said Heathcote.

"My eye! what a regular row!" said Coote.

Whereupon the "Firm" swore eternal friendship, and resolved to sink or swim together.

Chapter Twenty Two
The Hermit comes out of his cell

Mansfield never flattered himself that Templeton would right itself by a single turn of his hand, nor did he flatter himself that Templeton would ever love Jupiter as they had loved the old Saturn who had preceded him. And in neither expectation was he out of his reckoning.

After a week or two the sole result of the new *régime* seemed to be that the bad lot had plunged further into their evil ways. The "Select Sociables" had increased the number of their members to thirty, and made it an indispensable qualification for every candidate that he should have suffered punishment at the hands of the masters or monitors. It got to be known that it was war to the knife, and fellows flocked to the post of danger and begged to be admitted to the club.

All this Mansfield saw, but it did not disconcert him. He was glad to see a clear line being drawn, which made it impossible for any but the practised hypocrites to hang out false colours and pretend to be what they were not. It was half the battle to the Captain to know exactly who were friends and who were enemies.

He may sometimes have thought, with a passing sigh, of the affection which everybody, good and bad, had had for dear old Ponty, and wished he could expect as much. But he dashed the thought aside as folly. His duty was to make war on rebels, not to win them over by blandishments.

So he set his face like steel to the work, and made the name of monitor a caution in Templeton. And, it is fair to say, he was well backed up. Cresswell, Cartwright, Swinstead, and others of their sort rallied round him, and, at the risk of their own popularity, and sometimes against their better judgment, took up the rule of iron. Even the hermit Freckleton came out of his den now and then on the side of justice.

The cad Bull, who had neither the wit nor the temper to play a double part, threw up his monitorship in disgust and went over to the enemy, carrying with him one or two of the empty heads of the Fifth. Pledge alone looked on the whole revolution as a joke.

But even Pledge found it hard to make a case against the new rulers; for, if their severity was great, their justice was still greater. If they spared no one else, neither did they spare themselves. There was something almost ferociously honest and upright about Mansfield, and his lieutenants soon caught his spirit and made it impossible for anyone, even for Pledge, to point at them and say that either fear or favour moved them.

It was probably on this very account that Pledge deemed it well to treat the new state of things as a comedy, and not with serious attention.

A monitors' meeting was summoned for the morning after Pledge's call on Mr Webster, and he attended it with a pleasant smile on his face, as one who was always glad to come and see how his schoolfellows amused themselves.

The rest of the meeting was grim and serious.

"It's time we did something to put down this Club," said Mansfield. "They are drawing in all sorts of fellows now, and the longer we put it off the worse it will be."

"What shall we do?" asked Freckleton.

"I think we ought to be able to do it without going to Winter about it," said Cresswell.

"Would it do to start an opposition club?" suggested Swinstead.

"Or make it penal for any fellow to belong to it," said Cartwright.

"Or send a deputation," said Pledge, laughing, "and ask them please not to put the Sixth in such an awkward fix!"

"You see," said the captain, ignoring, as he usually did, Pledge's sarcasms, "whatever we do, some are sure to be irreconcilable. I would like to give any who wish a chance of coming out, and then we shall know what to do with the rest. Does anyone know when they meet?"

"I believe there's a meeting this evening," said Cartwright; "at least, my fag Coote told me a couple of days ago that he had a particular engagement this evening, and was sorry he couldn't say what it was, for he'd promised never to speak of the Club to anyone, least of all to a monitor."

There was a general smile at the expense of the artless Coote, and then Mansfield said:—

"Well, one of us had better go there and give them a caution. Will you go, Freckleton?"

"I?" exclaimed the Hermit, aghast.

"Yes, please, old man," said the Captain; "you'd do it better than anyone."

"Wouldn't you like me to go?" asked Pledge.

"There's one other thing I want to speak about," said Mansfield. "There's been a lot of breaking bounds lately among the juniors. I caught your fag yesterday, Cresswell, and gave him lines. Your fag too, Pledge, I have seen several times lately going out without leave."

"Dear me! how shocking!" said Pledge.

"If monitors don't see that their own fags keep the rules," said Mansfield, "there's not much chance of getting the school generally to keep them. In your case, Pledge, I happen to know you yourself gave Heathcote leave to go out more than once this term. I'm going to put a stop to that."

"Are you really?" said Pledge.

"Yes," said Mansfield, flashing with his eyes, but otherwise cool.

Whereupon the meeting broke up.

Freckleton had by no means a congenial task before him.

All this term he had been unable to settle down in his hermit's cell. Mansfield had always been bringing him out for this and that special duty, till he was becoming quite a public character; and, unfortunately for him, he had done the few services for which he had been told off so well, that Mansfield had no notion whatever of letting him crawl back to obscurity.

The Captain knew what he was about in selecting the Hermit to open the campaign against the "Select Sociables." A secret lawless society in a school is like a secret lawless society in a country—a pest to be dealt with carefully. Mansfield knew well enough that he himself was not the man to do it; nor was the downright Cresswell, nor the hot-headed Cartwright. It needed the wisdom of the serpent as well as the paw of the lion to do it, and if anyone was likely to succeed, it was Freckleton.

For Freckleton, hermit as he was, seemed to know more about every fellow in Templeton than anyone else. Where and when he made their acquaintance, no one knew and no one inquired. But certain it was no one knew the weak points of this boy and the good points of that better than he. And, as we have seen already, he was a "dark" man; hardly anyone knew him. They knew he had won the Bishop's Scholarship and was reputed prodigiously learned. For the rest, except that he was harmless and kindly, fellows hardly seemed to know him at all. The "Select Sociables" were in full congress. They had instituted a fine of a penny for non-attendance, which had worked wonders. And to-night every member was in his place, except only Heathcote and Coote, who, as the reader knows, had something else to think of just then.

The behaviour of these two young gentlemen was giving the club some uneasiness. They were not alive to their duties as "Sociables." And they had got into the abominable habit of obeying monitors and associating with questionable characters, such as Richardson, Aspinall, and the like.

A motion had just been passed calling upon the two delinquents to appear at the next meeting and answer for their conduct, when the door opened and Freckleton entered.

"Good evening, gentlemen," said he. "I'm not sure if I'm a member, but I hope I don't intrude."

The "Sociables" stared at him, half in anger, half in bewilderment, as he helped himself to a chair and sat down with his back to the door.

"The fact is," said he with a weary look, "I've lived such a retired life here, I hardly know where to find fellows I want. I've been hunting high and low for half a dozen fellows with brains in their heads, and someone told me if I came here I should find plenty."

There was a titter not unmingled with a few frowns, as the Hermit spread himself comfortably on his chair and looked round him.

"It's as hard to find a fellow with brains nowadays as it was for Diogenes to find an honest man, once. You know who Diogenes was, don't you, Gossy?" added he, turning suddenly on that young bravo.

Gosse blushed crimson at finding himself so unexpectedly singled out; and faltered out that he had forgotten.

"Forgotten?" said Freckleton, joining in the general laugh at Gosse's expense; "and you knew so well once! Ask Bull; he knows; he's in the Sixth, and *very* clever. Why, Bull (I hope he's not present)—"

Another laugh. For Bull sat in his place the size of life, with his bloated face almost as red as Gosse's.

"Bull actually found the Sixth so dull and unintellectual that he left us, in order to cultivate the acquaintance of Culver, and fellows of culture and scholarship like him. It was a great loss to us. We've hardly had an idea in the Sixth since Bull left."

This double hit greatly delighted the majority of the "Sociables;" scarcely less so than Bull's red cheeks, and the gape with which Culver received the reference to himself.

"You're not wanted here," Bull exclaimed; "get out!"

"There! Isn't that clever?" said the Hermit, in apparent admiration. "Did ever you hear a sentence so well put together, and so eloquently delivered. Why, not even the 'too-too' Wrangham (I hope Wrangham's not here)—"

Blushing was the order of the day. Wrangham tried hard to look unconcerned, but as the eyes of the Club turned round in his direction, the tell-tale roses came on his cadaverous cheeks and mounted to his forehead.

"The 'too-too' Wrangham, who loves lilies because they are pure, and calls teapots 'consummate' because—well, I don't exactly know why—he couldn't have put his one idea so neatly—"

"Look here, Freckleton," said Spokes, feeling it due to the dignity of the Club to put an end to this scene; "this is a private meeting. You've no right to be here. Nobody wants you."

"Dear me! was that the silvery voice of toffee-loving Spokes?" said the Hermit, amid a shout of laughter; for everyone knew Spokes's weak point. "He says 'Look here!' Really I cannot, until a sponge has been passed over the honest face and shorn it of some of its clinging sweetness. But, gentlemen of the 'Select'—'Select' is the word, isn't it?"

"If you don't go out, you'll get chucked out," said Bull.

"Oh, wonderful English! wonderful elocution!" said the Hermit. "Ah, it is good to be here. Ah! he comes, he comes!"

It was a critical moment as the burly Bull came down the room. Had he done so five minutes sooner Freckleton might have found himself single-handed. But already his genial banter had told among the more susceptible of his hearers, and he could count at any rate on fair play. For the rest, he had little anxiety.

"Wait a moment," said he, rising to his feet, and motioning to Bull to wait: "Sociables, Bull wants to fight me. Do you want me to fight him?"

"Yes, yes," shouted every one, delighted at the prospect of a fray, and many of them quite indifferent as to who conquered.

"Very well, gentlemen," said the Hermit; "I will obey you on one condition, and one only."

"What is it?" they shouted eagerly.

"This: that if I beat Bull, you make me your president; or, if you think it fairer, if I beat Bull first and then Spokes, you elect me. What do you say?"

The Hermit was staking high with a vengeance. Little had he dreamed, when he came down to have a little talk with the "Select Sociables," of such a proposal. It was the sight of Bull walking down the room which had furnished the inspiration, and he was daring enough to seize the chance while he had it and risk all upon it.

In his secret heart he was not absolutely sure of vanquishing his opponent. For Bull was a noted fighting man, and had made his mark in Templeton. The Hermit had never fought in his life. And yet he knew a little about boxing. He was strong, cool, and sound of wind; and knew enough of human nature to avoid the least appearance of doubt or hesitation in a crisis like this.

"What do you say?" asked he.

"Rather! If you lick, we'll make you president," shouted the Club.

"As it is a business matter," said Freckleton, "and will have to go on the minutes, wouldn't it be well for someone to propose and second it?"

Whereupon Braider proposed and someone else seconded the proposal, which was put to the meeting with due solemnity and carried unanimously.

"Now," said the Hermit, slowly divesting himself of his coat when the ceremony was concluded, "I'm at your service, Bull."

There was breathless silence for a moment as all eyes turned on the ex-monitor.

The blushes had left his cheeks, and a pallor rather whiter than usual was there in their place. He stood, in a fascinated sort of way, watching Freckleton as he rolled the sleeves up above his elbows and divested himself of his collar. He had never imagined the "dark man" would face him, still less challenge him thus before the whole Club.

The coward's heart failed him when the moment came. He didn't like the look of things. For an instant the crimson rushed back to his face, then, turning his back, he walked away.

Instantly a storm of hissing and hooting rose from the club, such as had rarely been heard in the walls of Templeton. None are so indignant at cowards as those who are not quite sure of their own heroism, and Bull found it out.

"Do I understand," said Freckleton, as soon as he could get in a word, "that the Bull declines?"

The Bull made no answer.

"He funks it. Turn him out!" cried Gosse.

The Hermit could not prevent a smile.

"Does anyone second Mr Gosse's motion?"

"I do," shouted Spokes, amid derisive laughter.

"Then," said Freckleton, opening the door, "we needn't detain you, Bull, unless, on second thoughts—"

Bull slunk out, followed by another howl, which drowned the Hermit's words. When he had gone the latter put on his coat, and, walking up to the chair, which Spokes had prudently vacated, called the club to order and said:—

"Gentlemen,—I beg to thank you for appointing me your president. I know it will be hard to follow worthily in the footsteps of the gentleman who has just left the room—(groans)—and of the gentleman who has just vacated this chair, leaving some of his sweetness behind him. (Derisive cheers.) Still, I would like to do something to help make this club a credit. I think we might look over the rules and see if we can get anything in which will keep cowards and cads out of the club. Of course that wouldn't affect any of you, but it would help to keep us more select for the future. (Cheers.) In fact, I don't see, gentlemen, why we shouldn't make the club big enough to take in any fellow who, like all of you, hates cowardice, and meanness, and dirtiness, and that sort of thing. (Cheers, not unmixed with blushes.) We may not all think alike about everything, but, if we are all agreed it's good form to be gentlemen, and honest and brave, I don't see why we can't be 'Select Sociables' still. We pride ourselves at Templeton on being one of the crack schools in the country. (Loud cheers.) Well, any lot of fellows who set up for the 'Select' here ought to be the crack of the crack—like you all, for instance. However, these are only suggestions. Now I'm your president I mean to work hard for the club and do my best—(cheers)—and I ask you to back me up. (Cheers.) I think, by way of a start, we might appoint a committee of, say, half a dozen, to look into the rules and see how they can be improved, and how the club can be made of most use to Templeton. What do you say?"

Cheers greeted the suggestion, and several names were proposed. The six elected included Spokes and Braider, and it was evident, from the half-nervous, half-gratified manner in which these two undertook their new responsibilities, that the Hermit had found out the trick of bringing out the good points even of the most unpromising boys.

The Club separated with cheers for the new president, and scarcely yet realising the transformation scene which he had made in their midst. A few, such as Wrangham, skulked off, but the majority took up the new order of things with ardour, and vied with one another in showing that they at any rate were bent on making the Club a credit.

Freckleton meanwhile retired to report the success of his mission to Mansfield.

"Well, have you got their names and cautioned them?" asked the Captain.

"I'm very hot and thirsty," said the Hermit, flinging himself down on a chair.

"Yes, yes; but what about this bad club?"

"Call it not bad, Jupiter, for I am its president."

"What! you its president!" cried the Captain, taking in the mystery at a bound. "You mean to say you've talked them over! By Jove! Freckleton, you ought to be Captain of Templeton."

"Thank you; I've quite enough to do as president of the 'Select Sociables.'"

And he then proceeded to give a modest history of the evening's proceedings.

Mansfield was delighted at every particular.

"But suppose Bull had fought you," said he, "where would you be now?"

"Better off, I think," said the Hermit. "It would have told better if I could really have knocked him down. However, I fancy it's as well it didn't come to a brush."

"But *can* you box, old man?"

"We must try one fine day. But now about the Club. I want you to help me draw up a scheme for my committee."

And the two friends spent the rest of the evening in one of the most gratifying tasks that ever fell to the lot of two honest seniors.

A very different conversation was taking place a few studies away, where Pledge found himself alone with his fag for the first time since the boy had avowed his reconciliation with Dick.

"Ah, Georgie, I don't see much of you now. My study's badly off for dusting."

"I'm very sorry, Pledge; I really hadn't time."

"No? Busy reading the police news, I suppose, and seeing how young gentlemen behave themselves in the dock?"

Heathcote flushed up, though from a very different cause from that which his senior suspected. In the new terror about Tom White, the youngster had forgotten all about Webster's pencil-case.

"You're going it, Georgie," said the monitor; "the inevitable result of bad company. You'll want me to go bail for you after all."

"I don't know what you are talking about," said the boy, with a confusion that belied the words.

"Well, I may be able to pull you through it better than you think, though, of course, I'm not such a great gun as Dick. However, what I want you for now is to go and post this letter at the head office."

"Why, it's half-past eight," said Heathcote.

"Wonderful! and the post goes at nine!"

"But I mean I shall get in a row for going out."

"Wonderful again! If anyone asks you, say I told you to go. Look alive!"

Heathcote took the letter mechanically and went. He was too dazed to argue the matter, and too much disturbed by Pledge's apparent knowledge of the scrape which was weighing on him and his friends to care to run the risk of offending him just now.

As he was creeping across the Quadrangle, a door opened, and Mansfield confronted him.

"Where are you going?"

"To the post. Pledge gave me leave."

"Go back to your room," said Mansfield, shutting the door.

"He's forgotten to give me lines," said Georgie to himself. "By Jove! I hope he's not going to send me up to Winter!"

To Georgie's surprise, he got neither lines nor a message to go to Dr Winter. But, as he was about to retire to rest, he received a summons from the Captain to go and speak with him in his study.

His sentence was as short as it was astounding "Heathcote, in future you fag for Swinstead, not Pledge. Good-night."

Chapter Twenty Three
Which treats of Law and Justice

While Pledge was dressing on the following morning, the Captain's fag brought him a note.

"There's no answer," said the junior, tossing it down on the table, and departing, whistling. Pledge opened it and read:—

"As you are determined to defy the rules, and make others do the same, I send this note to say Heathcote is no longer your fag, and that you will have to do without one for the future. I also wish to say that unless you are prepared to abide by school rules, it will save trouble if you send in your resignation as a monitor at once.—E. M."

His first impulse on reading this letter was to laugh, and toss the paper contemptuously into the hearth. But on second thoughts, his amusement changed to wrath, not quite unmixed with dismay.

He knew well enough last night, when he sent Heathcote out, that he was bringing matters between himself and the Captain to an issue. And he had been too curious to see what Mansfield's next move would be, to calculate for himself on what it was likely to be. And now he felt himself hit in his weakest point.

Not that the "Spider" was desperately in love with Heathcote. As long as that volatile youth had owned his allegiance and proved amenable to his influence, so long had Pledge liked the boy and set store by his companionship.

But lately Heathcote had been coming out in an unsatisfactory light.

For no apparent reason he had upset all his patron's calculations, and spoiled all his carefully arranged plans, by going over to Dick and placing Pledge in the ridiculous position of a worsted rival to that noisy young hero. And, as if that were not enough, he had let himself be used by the Captain as a means of dealing a further blow. For, when Pledge came to think of it, Heathcote had made prompt use of his new liberty to absent himself from his senior's chamber that very morning.

He left his study door open, and watched the passage sharply for the deserter.

He saw him at last, labouring under a huge pile of books, which he was carrying to his new lord's study.

"Ah, Georgie!" cried Pledge, with studied friendliness, "you'll drop that pile, if you try to carry all at once. Put some down here, and make two loads of it. So you've been promoted to a new senior?"

"It's not my choice; Mansfield moved me," said Heathcote, feeling and looking very uncomfortable.

"And I fancy I can hear the fervour with which you said, 'God bless you, for saving me from Pledge, Mansfield,' when he moved you."

"I said nothing of the sort. I knew nothing about it, I tell you, till he told me."

"Quite a delicious surprise. But you really mustn't be seen here," said Pledge, with a sneer. "The holy ones will think I am luring you back to perdition."

"I don't care what they say," said the boy.

"Oh, Georgie! How ungrateful! how sinful of you! Go to them. They may even be able to tell you how to enjoy yourself in a police cell."

It was gratifying to the senior to see the gasp with which the boy received this random shot.

"What do you mean?" faltered the latter.

"Really, hadn't you better ask Swinstead? He's your protector now. I have no business to interfere."

"Do tell me what you mean?" said the boy, imploringly.

But just at that moment a step sounded in the passage outside, and Mansfield entered the study.

Heathcote promptly vanished, and Pledge, face to face with his antagonist, had something else to think about than Mr Webster's pencil. The Captain, who had great faith in striking the iron while it is hot, had come down on the heels of his letter, determined that if any understanding was to be come to between him and Pledge, it should be come to promptly.

"You've had my note?" said he.

"Really, Mansfield," began Pledge, "I've no doubt it's an honour to receive a call from the Captain, but you seem to forget this is my study, not your's."

"You sent Heathcote out last night on purpose," said Mansfield, ignoring the protest, "and what I want to know now is whether you are going to resign your monitorship or not?"

Pledge's eyes blazed out as he met the Captain's determined face and cool eyes.

"You don't seem to have heard what I said?" he replied.

"I heard every word, and you heard my question?" answered the Captain.

"And suppose I don't choose to answer your question?"

"Then I'll answer it for you. If you choose to resign, you may. If you don't—"

"Well?"

"You cease to be a monitor, all the same."

"Who says so?" asked Pledge, sharply, and with pale lips.

"I say so, as Captain here," said Mansfield, coolly.

"You! You're not Templeton. You may be a great man in your own eyes, but you're only a schoolboy after all. I always understood Dr Winter was head master here, and not the boy Mansfield."

"You prefer to appeal to Winter, then?"

"Dear me, no! Dr Winter is so well drilled into what he has to say and do here, that it would be a pity to put him to unnecessary trouble."

"You can do as you like," said the Captain, drily. "There's to be a monitors' meeting at twelve. If you like to come and resign, do so; or if you like to come and hear your name taken off the list, you can."

And Mansfield turned on his heel, and went Pledge did not often fly into a passion; but as he locked his door, and heard the Captain's steps retreating down the passage, he gave vent to a fit of uncontrolled fury.

He was a coward. He knew it. He knew he dared not meet the enemy face to face, and fight for his good name in Templeton. He knew everyone hated him—everyone except, perhaps, Heathcote. And Heathcote was drifting from him, too. Should he appeal to Winter? He dared not. Should he let himself be expelled from the monitorship? If he could have counted on any one who would feel an atom of regret at the step, he might have faced it. But there was no one. Should he resign? and so relieve the monitors of their difficulty, and own himself beaten? There was nothing else to do.

Of the three alternatives it was the least dangerous. So he sat down and wrote:—

"Dear Mansfield,—As you appear to have set your mind upon my resigning my monitorship, and as I am always anxious to oblige the disinterested wishes of those who beg as a favour for what they know would come without asking, I take the opportunity to carry out what I have long contemplated, and beg to resign a post of which I have never been proud. At the same time I must ask you to accept my resignation from the Football Club, and the Harriers.—Yours truly, P. Pledge."

It was a paltry letter, and Pledge knew it. But he could not help writing it, and only wished the words would show half the venom in which his thoughts were steeped. The sentence about the Football Club and the Harriers was a sudden inspiration. Templeton should have something to regret in the loss of him. He knew they would find it hard to fill his place in the fields, however easily they might do without him in school.

Mansfield read the letter contemptuously, as did all the monitors who had the real good of Templeton at heart. A few pulled long faces, and wondered how the Fifteen was to get on without its best halfback; but altogether the Sixth breathed more freely for what had been done and were glad Mansfield had taken upon himself a task which no one else would have cared to undertake.

Meanwhile, our three heroes were spending an agitated Saturday half-holiday.

For Dick had decided two days ago that his "Firm" would have to look after Tom White.

"You know, you fellows," said he, "we're not exactly in it as far as his pawning the boat goes, but then if we hadn't lost her, the row would have never come on."

"And if he hadn't robbed us, we should never have interfered with the boat."

"And if we hadn't gone to the Grandcourt match," said Dick, who was fond of tracing events to their source, "he wouldn't have robbed us."

Whereat they left the pedigree of Tom White's "row" alone, and turned to more practical business.

"What can we do?" said Georgie. "We can't get him off."

"We're bound to back him up, though, aren't we?"

"Oh, I suppose so, if we only knew how."

"Well, it strikes me we ought to turn up at the police court to-morrow, and see how things go," said Dick.

The "Firm" adopted the motion. The next day was a half-holiday; and a police court is always attractive to infant minds. And the presence of a real excuse for attending made the expedition an absolute necessity.

As soon as Saturday school was over, therefore, and at the very time when the Sixth were considering Pledge's "resignation," our three heroes, having taken a good lunch, and armed themselves each with a towel, in case there might be time for a "Tub" on the way back, sallied forth arm-in-arm to back up Tom White.

They found, rather to their disgust, on reaching the police court, that they were not the only Templetonians who had been attracted by the prospect of seeing the honest mariner at the bar. Raggles and Duffield were there before them, waiting for the public door to open, and greeted them hilariously.

"What cheer?" cried Raggles. "Here's a go! Squash up, and we shall bag the front pew. Duff's got five-penn'orth of chocolate creams, so we shall be awfully snug."

This last announcement somewhat mollified the "Firm," who made up affectionately to Duffield's. "Old Tom will get six months," said Duffield, as soon as his bag of creams had completed its first circuit. "Rough on him, ain't it?"

"I don't know. I say, it'll be rather a game if it turns out he stole his own boat, won't it? Case of picking your own pocket, eh?"

"I don't know," said Dick. "I don't think he did steal it. But even if he did, you see it didn't belong to him."

"It's a frightful jumble altogether," said Georgie. "I think law's a beastly thing. If the pawnbroker chooses to *give* money on the boat—"

"Oh, it's not the pawnbroker—it's the fellows the boat belonged to."

"But, I tell you, Tom's one of the fellows himself."

"Well, it's the other fellows."

"We may as well have another go of chocolates now, in case they get squashed up going in," suggested Coote, who avoided the legal aspect of the case.

The door opened at last, and our heroes, some of whom knew the ways of the place, made a stampede over the forms and through the witness-box into the front seat reserved for the use of the public, where they spread themselves out luxuriously, and celebrated their achievement by a further tax on the friendly Duffield's creams.

The court rapidly filled. The interest which Tom White's case had evoked had grown into positive excitement since his arrest, and our heroes had reason to congratulate themselves on their punctuality as they saw the crowded forms behind them and the jostling group at the door.

"There's Webster at the back; shall you nod to him?" asked Heathcote.

"Yes—better," said Dick, speaking for the "Firm."

Whereupon all three turned their backs on the bench and nodded cheerily to Mr Webster, who never saw them, so busy was he in edging his way to a seat.

Having discharged this public duty our heroes resumed their seats just in time to witness the arrival of the usher of the court, followed by a man in a wig, and a couple of reporters.

"It's getting hot, I say," said Dick, speaking more of his emotions than of the state of the atmosphere.

It got hotter rapidly; for two of the Templeton police appeared on the scene and looked hard at the front public bench. Then the solicitors' seats filled up, and the magistrates' clerk bustled in to his table. And before these alarming arrivals had well brought the perspiration to our heroes' brows, the appearance of two magistrates on the bench sent up the temperature to tropical.

"Order in the court!" cried the usher.

Whereupon Duffield, in his excitement, dropped a chocolate on the floor and turned pale as if expecting immediate sentence of death.

However, the worst was now over. And when it appeared that the two magistrates were bluff, good-humoured squires, who seemed to have no particular spite against anybody, and believed everything the clerk told them, the spirits of our heroes revived wonderfully, and Duffield's bag travelled briskly in consequence.

To the relief of the "Firm," the first case was not Tom White's. It was that of a vagrant who was charged with the heinous crimes of begging and being unable to give an account of herself. The active and intelligent police gave their evidence beautifully, and displayed an amount of shrewdness and heroism in the taking up of this wretched outcast which made every one wonder they were allowed to waste their talents in so humble a sphere as Templeton.

The magistrates put their heads together for a few seconds, and then summoned the clerk to put his head up, too, and the result of the consultation was that the poor creature was ordered to be taken in at the Union and cared for.

Duffield's bag was getting very light by the time this humane decision was come to. Only one round was left, and that was deferred by mutual consent when the clerk called out "Thomas White!"

Our heroes sat up in their seats and fixed their eyes on the dock.

In a moment Tom White, as rollicking as ever, but unusually sober, stood in it, and gazed round the place in a half-dazed way.

As his eyes came down to the front public bench, our heroes' cheeks flushed and their eyes looked straight in front of them.

Duffield and Raggles, on the contrary, being the victims of no pangs of conscience, after looking hurriedly round to see that neither the magistrates, the police, nor the usher observed them, winked recognition at their old servant in distress.

This was too much for Dick. These two fellows who weren't "in it" at all were backing Tom up in public, whereas his "Firm," who were in it, and had come down for the express purpose of looking after the prisoner, were doing nothing. "Better nod," he whispered.

And the "Firm" nodded, shyly but distinctly.

Tom White was not the sort of gentleman to cut his friends on an occasion like this, and he, seeing himself thus noticed, and recognising, in a vague sort of way, his patrons, favoured the front public bench with five very pronounced nods, greatly to the embarrassment of the young gentlemen there, and vastly to the indignation of the police and officials of the court.

"Order there, or the court will be cleared!" cried the clerk, in a tone of outraged propriety; "How dare you?"

Our heroes, not being in a position to answer the question by reason of their tongues being glued to the roofs of their mouths, remained silent, and tried as best they could to appear absorbed in the shape of their own boots.

"If such a thing occurs again," persisted the clerk, "their worships will take very serious notice of it."

"Their worships," who had not a ghost of an idea what the clerk was talking about, said "very serious," and asked that the case might proceed.

It proceeded, and under its cover our agitated heroes gradually raised their countenances from their boots, and felt their hearts, which had just now stood still, beating once more in their honest bosoms.

For any one not personally interested, the case was prosy enough.

A solicitor got up and said he appeared for Tom's three partners, who charged him with pledging the *Martha* and appropriating the money, whereas the *Martha* belonged to the four of them, and Tom had no right to raise money on her except by mutual consent.

The three partners and the pawnbroker were put into the witness-box, and gave their evidence in a lame sort of way.

Tom was invited to ask any questions he desired of the witnesses, and said "Thank'ee, sir," to each offer. He had nothing that he "knowed of to ask them. He was an unfortunate labouring man that had lost his living, and he hoped gentlemen would remember him."

He accompanied this last appeal with a knowing look and grin at the occupants of the front public bench, who immediately blushed like turkey cocks, and again dropped their heads towards their boots.

"Have you anything to say about the disappearance of the boat?" said the clerk, shuffling his notes.

"Only, your worship," said the solicitor, "that on the 4th of June last the *Martha* disappeared from her berth on the beach, and, as White disappeared at the same time and refuses to give an account of himself at that particular time, the prosecutors are convinced he removed the boat himself."

In support of this very vague charge a policeman was called, who gave a graphic account of the beauties of the moonlight on the night in question, and of how he had seen, from his beat on the Parade, a figure move stealthily across the sands to the place where White's boat was supposed to be. He couldn't quite, swear that the figure was White or that the boat was the *Martha* but he didn't know who either could be if they were not. The figure might have been a boy, but, as he was a quarter of a mile off, he couldn't say. He never left his beat till one in the morning. By that time the tide was in. He didn't actually see Tom White row off in the *Martha* but neither of them was to be seen in Templeton next day.

After this piece of conclusive evidence the public looked at one another and shook their heads, and thought what wonderful men the Templeton police were for finding out things.

"Have you any questions to ask the witness?" demanded the clerk of Tom.

"Thank'ee, no, sir; it's all one to me," said Tom. "Bless yer! I never knows nothing about it till a young gentleman says to me, 'They're after you,' says he; 'scuttle off.' So I scuttled off. Bless you, sir, I didn't know I was doing harm."

Under this thunderbolt Dick almost collapsed. Fortunately, Tom's short memory kept him from recognising him in the matter any more than the other occupants of the seat. He nodded generally to the young gentlemen as a body—a most compromising nod, and one which included all five in it meaning.

One of the magistrates who saw it looked up and asked genially:—

"You don't mean to say it was one of those young gentlemen, prisoner?"

"Bless you, sir, likely as not. They young gentlemen, sir, always spare a trifle for a honest—"

"Yes, yes; we don't want all that! If you have no more questions to ask the constable, the constable may stand down."

The constable stood down, and a brief consultation again ensued between the Bench and the clerk which Dick, firmly believing that it referred to him, watched with terrible interest.

"Yes," said the magistrate, looking up, "we remand the case for a week."

Dick breathed again. The storm had blown over after all. Not only had he himself escaped punishment for conspiring against the ends of justice, but Tom White had still another week during which something might turn up.

The court emptied rapidly as the case ended.

"Rather hot! wasn't it?" said Duffield, as the five found themselves outside, solacing themselves with the last "go" of the creams.

"Awful!" said the "Firm" from the bottom of their hearts, and feeling that many afternoons like this would materially shorten their days.

Chapter Twenty Four
How our heroes turn their attention to the chase

During the few days which followed their gallant but unsuccessful attempt to "back up" Tom White, the "Firm" found plenty to think about nearer home.

The rumour of the revolution in the "Select Sociables" spread rapidly over Templeton, and Freckleton was almost mobbed more than once by his new admirers. However, he kept his head, and steered his new ship craftily and carefully. By appealing to the patriotism and honour of his "Sociables," he succeeded in getting the rules so amended and purified, that in a few days, instead of being a select Club of the worst characters in Templeton, its constitution was open enough to admit any boy who in any way proved himself a credit to the school.

A still more important step was the voluntary disbanding of the old Club for the purpose of placing the new rules before a meeting of the whole school. This was not an easy thing to accomplish, for the old members knew, most of them, that their qualifications were the reverse of those which would make them eligible for membership according to the new rules. They therefore clung tenaciously to their hold, and it was not until Freckleton compromised the matter by promising to hold them eligible for election to the new Club, and exempt them from the conditions other fellows would have to fulfil to become eligible, that they finally gave way.

It was a great day when, by virtue of a personal invitation to each boy in the Hermit's name, Templeton met together in the Great Hall to put the new Club on its feet.

It was remarked at this meeting that the Sixth took their places as ordinary Templetonians in the body of the hall, and not on the dais, and that the Den, which usually herded together at the lower end, was distributed here and there impartially.

In fact, everyone was equal to-day, and the very knowledge of the fact seemed to put dignity and order into the assembly.

After rather an awkward pause, during which it seemed doubtful how the business ought to begin, Freckleton stepped up on to the platform. His appearance was greeted by cheers, which, however, he immediately extinguished.

"I think," said he, quietly, "as this is quite a private meeting, you will all see cheering is hardly the thing. Suppose we do without it. It is very good of you fellows to come here in such numbers, and I only hope you'll not hesitate to say what you think about the proposal I am going to make—for the question is one which the whole school ought to decide, and not any one particular clique or set among us. (Hear, hear.) You, all of you, know I believe, what the object of the meeting is. Up till quite recently we had a Club in Templeton which rejoiced in the name of the 'Select Sociables.' (Laughter.) It wasn't a public Club—(laughter)—but most of the school, I fancy, had heard of its existence. (Laughter.) Gentlemen laugh, but I assure them I am telling the truth, and have good reason to know what I am talking about, as I happened to be the president of the 'Select Sociables.' (Hear, hear.) We found the Club wasn't altogether flourishing. (Laughter.) Some of the rules wanted looking to, and a few of the members were not exactly the best specimens of Templeton form. (Loud laughter.) Gentlemen think there was a joke in that, I suppose. I didn't see it myself. We put our heads together to see how the Club could be improved, and I am bound to say the old members came forward most patriotically and gave up their undoubted rights, in order to make the Club a thoroughly Templeton affair."

Cheers were raised here for the old "Sociables," who never felt so virtuous in all their lives.

"Now you want to hear what our proposal is. You'll understand it best if I read the rough rules which the committee has drawn up:—"

1. That the Club be called the "Select Sociables."

2. That the number of members be limited to thirty.

3. That not more than six members be chosen from any one Form.

"This is to prevent the Club getting crowded out with Sixth-form fellows—(loud cheers from the juniors)—or fellows from the Junior Third. (Laughter from the seniors.) It will insure each form getting represented on it by half a dozen of its best men."

4. That all Templetonians are eligible who have either—

(*a*) Gained any prize or promotion in the school examinations.

(*b*) Played in any of the school-house matches, senior or junior. (Cheers.)

(*c*) Won any event at the school sports.

(*d*) Run through any hunt with the Harriers. (Cheers.)

(*e*) Swum round the Black Buoy. (Loud cheers.)

(*f*) Done anything which, in the opinion of the school, has been for the good of Templeton.

5. That all elections take place by ballot.

6. That the first thirty members be elected by ballot by the whole school, and future vacancies be filled up by the Club.

7. That all the original members of the old Club shall be considered eligible for election whether they have complied with any of the conditions named or not. (Laughter and blushes.)

8. That if there are less than six fellows eligible in any Form, the number may be filled up from eligible candidates in the Form below.

"There, that's—roughly speaking—how it is proposed the new Club should be formed."

"We should like to know," said Cresswell, rising, "what the Club will do, when it will meet, and so on?"

"Well," said Freckleton, "we thought we could get leave to use the library every evening; and, being a Sociable Club we should try to afford to take in a few of the illustrated and other papers, and manage supper together now and then, and make ourselves as comfortable as possible,"—(laughter and cheers, especially from the youngsters). "If we got talent enough in the Club, we might give the school a concert or a dramatic performance now and then, or, in the summer, try our hand at a picnic or a fishing cruise. If Cresswell gets elected himself—and he'd better not be too sure—he'll find out that the 'Sociables' will have a very good idea of making themselves snug." (Laughter.)

"Is there to be any entrance-fee or subscription?" asked Birket. "We think fellows might be asked to subscribe half-a-crown a term. It's not very much; and as the juniors usually have twice as much spare cash as we seniors, we don't think they will shy at the Club for that,"—(loud cheers and laughter from the juniors).

"There's just one other thing, by the way," continued the Hermit. "It's only, perhaps, to be talking about turning fellows out of the Club, but we think we ought to protect ourselves by some rule which will make any member of the Club who does anything low or discreditable to Templeton liable to be politely requested to retire. I don't mean mere monitors' rows, of course. Fellows aren't obliged to get into them, though they do. But I don't think we ought to be too stiff, and turn a fellow out because he happens to get a hundred lines from Cartwright, for climbing one of the elms. (Laughter, and 'hear, hear,' from Cartwright.) He's no business to climb elms, and it's quite right to give him lines for it. But as long as he doesn't do that sort of thing systematically, in defiance of rules, then, I say, let him find some place other than the club-room, to do his lines in—(hear, hear). The fellows the Club will want to protect itself against are the cads and sneaks and cheats, who may be knowing enough to keep square with the monitors, but are neither Select nor Sociable enough for a Club like ours. There, I never made such a long speech in all my life; I'm quite ashamed of myself."

Templeton forgot its good manners, and cheered loudly at this point.

There was something about the genial, unassuming, straightforward Hermit which touched the fellows on their soft side, and made them accept him with pride as a representative of the truest Templeton spirit. They might not, perhaps, love him as fondly as they loved dear old lazy Ponty, but there was not one fellow who did not admire and respect him, or covet his good opinion.

As soon as silence was obtained, Mansfield rose.

It was a self-denying thing to do, and the Captain knew it. There was very little affection in the silence which fell on the room. He had given up, long since, expecting it. It said much for him that its absence neither soured nor embittered him. It made him unhappy, but he kept that to himself, and let it influence him not a whit in the path of duty he had set before him—a path from which not even the hatred of Templeton would have driven him.

"I'm sure we are all very grateful to Freckleton," he said. "It will be an honour to anyone to get into the Club, and for those who don't get on at first, it will be something to look forward to and work for. I don't think a better set of rules could have been drawn up. It will be a thoroughly representative Club of all that is good in Templeton. It doesn't favour any one set of fellows more than another. Fellows who are good at work, and fellows who are good at sports have all an equal chance. The only sort of fellows it doesn't favour are the louts and the cads, and the less they are favoured anywhere in Templeton the better. It's a shame to trouble Freckleton with more questions, but some of us would like to know when the ballot for the new Club is to take place, and how he proposes we should vote?"

There was a faint cheer as the Captain sat down. Templeton, whatever its likes and dislikes were, always appreciated generosity. And the Captain's honest, ungrudging approval of a comrade who had already distanced him in the hold he exercised over Templeton, pleased them, and told in the speaker's favour.

"I think the best way would be," said Freckleton, "for every fellow to make a list of the thirty fellows he thinks most eligible, between now and to-day week. If he can't think of thirty, then let him put down all he can, remembering that there are not to be more than six in any form. To-day week we'll have the ballot, and fellows will drop their lists into the box, and the highest thirty will be elected."

"Hadn't we better have a list posted up somewhere of the names of fellows in each form who are eligible?" asked someone.

"Certainly. I'll have one up to-morrow, and if there are any corrections and additions to make, there will be time to make them, and get out a final list two days before the election."

Among the crowd which jostled in front of the list on the library door, next day, might have been seen the eager and disconsolate faces of our three heroes.

Alas! not one of their names was there! Everybody else's seemed to be there but their's. Aspinall's was there, of course, for Aspinall had won his remove with honour last term. Raggles was there, for Raggles had played in the junior tennis fours of Westover's against the rival houses. Spokes was there, for Spokes had swum round the Black Buoy, and become a "shark." Even Gosse was there, for Gosse had "walked over" for the high jumps for boys under 4 foot, 6 inches, last sports.

Dick gulped down something like a groan, as he strained his eyes up and down the cruel list, in the vague hope of finding his name in some corner, however humble.

But no. He turned away at last, with his two disconsolate friends, feeling more humiliated than he had ever felt in his life.

He had done nothing for Templeton—he, who had passed for a leader among his compeers, and for a hero among his inferiors!

His record was absolutely empty. In school he had failed miserably; out of school he had shirked sports in which he ought easily to have excelled and "rotted" when he might have been doing good execution for Templeton. He scoured his memory to think of anything that might savour of credit. There was the New Boys' Race. He had won that, but that was all, and it didn't count. He had thrashed Culver and been patted on the back for it, but that hadn't got him on to the list.

And, except for these two exploits, what good had he done? Nay, hadn't he done harm instead of good? He had dragged Heathcote after him, and

Heathcote and he had dragged Coote; and here they were all left out in the cold.

Dick remembered the Ghost's letter, and could have kicked himself for being so slow to take its advice.

"We're out of it," said Georgie, dismally, as the three walked down the shady side of the fields. "I did think we might have scraped in somehow."

"Whatever could you have scraped in for?" asked Dick sharply. "Hadn't you better give in we've been a pack of fools at once?"

"So we have," said Coote. "I'd have liked awfully to get in the Club. How stunning the picnics would be!"

"Young ass!" said Dick, "the grub's all you think about. Even if you got on the list, it doesn't follow you'd be elected."

"It would be something, though, to get on the list," said Georgie. "It makes a fellow feel so small to be out of it. Think of that howling young Gosse being on!"

"Yes, and Raggles!" said Coote.

"Look here, I say," exclaimed Dick, suddenly stopping short in his walk, his face lighting up with the brilliancy of the inspiration, "what asses we are! There's the first Harrier hunt of the season to-morrow. Of course, we'll go and run through!"

Heathcote whistled.

"They sometimes run a twelve-miler," said he.

"Never mind if they run twelve hundred," said Dick. "We're bound to be in it, I tell you; it's our only chance."

"Birket told me hardly anyone ever runs in it below the Upper Fourth."

"Can't help that," said Dick, decisively; "there's nothing to prevent us."

"Oh, of course not," said Heathcote, who inwardly reflected that there was nothing to prevent their jumping over the moon if they only could.

"You're game, then?"

"All right," replied the two pliable ones.

"Hurrah! You know, we may not keep close up all the way, but if we can only run it through it's all right. By Jove! I am glad I thought of it, aren't you?"

"Awfully," they said.

Templeton opened its eyes that evening when it saw the "Firm" solemnly go to bed at half-past seven.

It wasn't their usual practice to shorten their days in this manner, and it was evident this early retirement meant something.

Speculation was set at rest next morning when, immediately after morning school, they appeared in their knickerbockers and running shoes and bare shins.

"Hullo!" said Cresswell, who was the first to encounter them in this trim, "are you youngsters going to have a little run of your own?"

Cresswell was in running costume, too—a model whipper-in— determined to do his part in the long afternoon's work which he had cut out for himself and his Harriers.

"We're going to run in the big hunt," said Dick, modestly.

"What!" said the senior, laughing; "do you know what the run is?"

"About twelve-miles, isn't it?" said Coote, glad to air his knowledge.

"Yes. I'm afraid it will be hardly worth your while to take such a short trot," said Cresswell, with a grin.

"We're going to try," said Dick, resolutely. "Who are the hares, Cresswell?"

"Swinstead and Birket; good hares, too. But, I say, youngsters, you'd better not make asses of yourselves. If you like to come the first mile or two, all right, but take my advice and turn back before you're too far from home."

"We're going to run it through," said Dick, "if we possibly can."

"We want to get on the Sociables' list," blurted out the confiding Coote; "that's why."

Dick and Heathcote blushed up guiltily, and rushed their indiscreet chum off before he had time to unbosom himself further.

Cresswell, with the grin still on his honest face, turned into Freckleton's study.

"By Jove! old man," said he, "you'll have a lot to answer for, the rate you're going on. There are three youngsters—my fag Dick and his two chums—going to run this hunt through, because their names are not on your precious list. They'll kill themselves."

"Hurrah!" cried the Hermit. "I'm delighted—not, of course, about the killing, but I like spirit. I hope they'll scramble through. Mark my word, Cress., those three partners will make their mark in Templeton yet."

"They're likely to make their mark at a coroner's inquest," said Cresswell. "Did *you* ever run in a twelve-mile hunt?"

"No, thank you," said the Hermit. "Well, I only hope they'll cool down before they go too far, that's all," said the whipper-in. "They don't know what they're in for."

"They're in for the 'Sociables,' and more power to them, say I," said the Hermit. When Cresswell arrived at the meet, he found our heroes the centres of attraction to the crowd who usually assembled to see the hounds "throw off."

They bore their honours meekly, and affected an indifference they were far from feeling to the chaff and expostulations which showered upon them from all sides.

"All show off!" cried Gosse. "They'll sit down and have a nap under the first hedge, and make believe they ran it through."

"Come, youngsters," said Cartwright, "you've had a jolly little game. Better go home and put on your trousers, and not try to be funny for too long together."

"Is it true," said someone else, with a significant jerk of his head in the direction of the "Firm," "that the hares are going to make a twenty-mile run of it, instead of twelve?"

"Of course we go through Turner's field, where the mad bulls are?" said another.

Our heroes began to think the delay in starting was getting to be criminal. Everyone had turned up long ago. Whatever was keeping the hunt from beginning?

Ah! there was Cresswell calling up the hares at last. Thank goodness!

Swinstead and Birket, *par nobile fratrum*, were old stagers in the Templeton hunts, and fellows knew, when they buckled on their scent bags and tied their handkerchiefs round their waists, that the Harriers would have their work cut out for them before the day was over.

"All ready?" asked the whipper-in, taking out his watch.

"All serene!"

"Off you go then!"

And off went the hares at a long easy swing, out of the fields and up on to the breezy downs.

"Now then, Harriers, peel!" said the whipper-in, when the hares had disappeared from view, and his watch showed seven minutes to have elapsed.

Our heroes nervously obeyed the order, and confided their outer vesture to Aspinall's custody.

Then steeling their ears and hearts to the final sparks of chaff which greeted the action, they moved forward with the other hounds and waited Cresswell's signal to go.

It seemed ages before those three minutes crawled out. But at last the whipper-in put his watch back, and blew a blast on his bugle.

"Forward!" shouted everybody.

And the hunt was begun.

Chapter Twenty Five
How our heroes make their record

If I were a poet, I should, at this point, pause to invoke Diana, Apollo, Adonis, and the other deities who preside over the chase, to aid me in describing the famous and never-to-be-forgotten run of the Templeton Harriers that early autumn afternoon. How they broke in full cry out of the fields up on to the free downs. How, with the fresh sea scent in their faces, they scoured the ridge that links Templeton with Blackarch, and Blackarch with Topping. How at the third mile they cried off inland, and plunged into the valley by Waly's bottom and Bardie's farm, through the pleasant village of Steg, over the railway, and along the fringe of Swilford Wood, to the open heath beyond. How half the hunt was out of it before they went up the other side of the valley, and scattered the gravel on the top of Welkin Beacon. How those who were left dropped thence suddenly on Lowhouse, and swam the Gurgle a mile above the ford. How from Lowhouse they swerved eastward, and caught the railway again at Norton Cutting. How they lost the scent in Durdon Copse, but found it again where the wood and the gravel pits met. How the six who stayed in blistered their feet after that on the gritty high road, till Cresswell hallooed them over the hedge, and showed them the scent down the winding banks of the Babrook. And once again, how they dived into the queer hamlet of Little Maddick, and saw the very loaf and round of cheese off which the hares had snatched a hasty meal not five minutes before. How Mansfield and Cresswell made a vow to taste neither meat nor drink till they had run their quarry down; and how the ever-diminishing pack sighted the hares just out of Maddick, going up the Bengle Hill. Over Bengle Hill, down into the valley beyond, and up the shoulder of Blackarch ridge, how they toiled and struggled, till once more the sea burst on to their view, and the salt breezes put new life into their panting frames. How along the ridge and down towards Grey Harbour the leaders gained on the hares, hand-over-hand. And how, at last, in that final burst along the hard, dry sand, the hares were caught gloriously, half a mile from home, after one of the fastest runs Templeton had ever recorded.

But my muse must curb her wings, and descend from poetry to prose, in order to narrate the particular adventures of our three modest heroes.

For the first half-mile, be it said to their glory, they led the hunt.

Being convinced that their only hope was to get a good start, and shake off the field from the very beginning, they dashed to the front on Cresswell's cry of "Forward!" at the rate of ten miles an hour, and for five minutes showed Templeton the way.

Then occurred one of those lamentable disasters which so often befall youthful runners on the exhaustion of their first wind: Coote's shoe-lace came undone! That was the sole reason for his pulling up. To say that he was blown, or that the pace was hard on him was adding insult to calamity; and doubtless the redness of his countenance as he knelt down to make fast the truant lace was solely due to indignation at the possibility of such a suggestion.

Dick and Heathcote, as they stood one on each side of him, really thankful for the pause, professed to be highly impatient at the delay.

"Come on," said Dick, "here they all come."

"What a brutal time you take to do up that beastly lace!" cried Georgie, "we might have been in the next field by this time."

"I think it will hold now," said Coote, rising slowly to his feet, as the pack came up in full cry.

"Blown already, youngsters?" asked Cresswell. "Better go home."

"We're not blown at all," said Dick, trotting on abreast of the whipper-in; "Coote's lace came undone, that was all."

"Yes; we should have been in the next field if it hadn't," said the owner of the luckless lace.

The Harriers smiled, and for a minute or two the pack swung in an even line across the field.

Then Coote, anxious not to crowd anyone, let half a dozen or so of the Fifth go in front; and Dick and Georgie, generously considering that it would be rather low to leave their short-winded comrade in the lurch, dropped behind the leading rank in order to be nearer him.

In a minute more all anxiety Coote may have felt as to crowding any one was at an end. He was a yard or two in the rear of the last man, with a stitch in his side, beginning in his inmost soul to wonder whether the new "Sociables" Club was such a very good thing after all.

Dick and Georgie, as they gradually sacrificed their prospect of being in at the death, and fell back to the support of their ally, waxed very contemptuous of stitch in a fellow's side. They knew what it meant. It was a pity Coote had started if he was liable to that sort of thing. His stitch had cost the "Firm" a whole field already. However, they were not selfish; they must back him up even if it meant coming in at the tail of the hunt; though, to be sure, the pace Mansfield, Cresswell, and a few others were going at was one which couldn't be kept up, and the "Firm," as soon as the stitch was out, might be in the running after all.

By dint of persuasions, threats, and imputations, Coote's stitch did come out; but before it was gone the last of the pack were seen going over the ridge.

"We're out of it," said Georgie, despondently.

"Not a bit of it," said Dick, who was getting his second wind and felt like holding on. "We're bound to pull up on them if Coote only keeps up."

So they held on gallantly.

They could not long keep up the fiction of being in the hunt. No amount of self-deception could persuade them, when the end of the straggling line of fellows going up the ridge was a clear half-mile ahead, that they were in it. Still every minute they held on they felt more like staying, and when they reflected that it was possible to run through the hunt without being in at the death, they took comfort, and determined Templeton should not say they had turned tail.

"We shall have to follow the scent now," said Dick, when the pack suddenly disappeared to view over the ridge. "Thank goodness, it's all white paper, and plenty of it. Come on, you fellows, we'll run it through yet."

"I feel quite fresh," said Coote, mopping his head with his handkerchief. "How far do you think we've gone—six miles?"

"Six! we've not done a mile and a half yet."

Coote put away his handkerchief, and gave the buckle of his running drawers a hitch; and the "Firm" settled down to business.

Having once found out their pace, and got their second wind, they felt comparatively comfortable. The scent lay true up the ridge, and as they rose foot by foot, and presently breasted the bluff nor'-wester, they felt like keeping it up for a week.

"Hullo, I say," cried Georgie, when the top of the ridge was gained, "there they go right under us; we might almost catch them by a short cut."

"Can't do it," said Dick, decisively. "We're bound to follow the scent, even if the hares doubled and came back across this very place."

"Would real harriers do that?" asked Coote. "If I was a real harrier, and saw the hare close to me, I'd go for him no matter what the scent was."

"All very well, you can't do it to-day—not if you want to get on the list," said Dick. "They've taken a sharp turn, though, at the bottom."

Trotting down a steep hill is not one of the joys of the chase, and our heroes, by the time they got to the level bottom, felt as bruised and shaken as if they had been in a railway accident.

However, a mile on the flat pulled them together again, and they plodded on by Bardie's Farm, where the scent became sparse, and on to Steg where, for the first time since leaving Templeton, they came upon traces of their fellow-man.

The worthy inhabitants of Steg, particularly the junior portion of them, hailed our three heroes with demonstrations of friendly interest. They had turned out fully half an hour ago to see the main body of the hunt go by, and just as they were returning regretfully to their ordinary occupations, the cry of "Three more of 'em!" came as a welcome reprieve, and brought them back into the highway in full force.

Fond of their joke were the friendly youth of Steg, and considering the quiet life they led, their wit was none of the dullest.

"Hurrah! Here's three more hounds!"

"They's the puppies, I reckon."

"Nay, one of 'em's got the rickets, see."

"If they don't look to it, the hares will be round the world and catching them up."

"Hi! Mister puppy, you're going wrong; they went t'other way."

"Shut up!" cried Dick.

"Go and give your pigs their dinner," shouted Heathcote.

Coote contented himself with running through the village with his tongue in his cheek, and in another three minutes the trio were beyond earshot and shaking the dust of Steg from their feet.

"How many miles now?" asked Coote, with a fine effort to appear unconcerned at the answer, which he put down in his own mind at six or seven miles.

"Three and a half, about—put it on, you fellows."

It was a long trot along the springy turf outside Swilford Wood. Once or twice the scent turned in and got doubtful among the underwood, but it came out again just as often, and presently turned off on to the Heath.

Our heroes ploughed honestly through the bracken and gorse which tangled their feet and scratched their bare shins at every step. That mile over the Heath was the most trying yet. The hares seemed to have picked out the very cruellest track they could find; and when, presently, the "Firm" caught sight of the ruthless little patches of paper going straight up the side of Welkin Beacon, Coote fairly cried for quarter and announced he must sit down.

His companions, though they would not have liked to make the suggestion themselves, were by no means inexorable to the appeal.

"Why, we've hardly started yet," said Dick, throwing himself down on the ground; "you're a nice fellow to begin to want a rest!"

"Only just started!" gasped Coote; "I never ran so far in my life."

"We came that last bit pretty well, considering the ground," said Heathcote, anxious to make the halt as justifiable as possible.

"I wonder where the hares are now?" said Dick, rather pensively.

"Back at Templeton, perhaps," said Heathcote, "having iced ginger-beer, or turning into the 'Tub.'"

"Shut up, Georgie," said Dick, with a wince. "What's the use of talking about iced ginger-beer out here?"

They lay some minutes, each dreading the first suggestion to move. Coote feigned to have dropped asleep, and Heathcote became intensely interested in the anatomy of a thistle.

Dick was the only one who could not honestly settle down, and the dreaded summons, when at last it came, came in his voice:—

"You lazy beggars," cried he, starting up, "get up, can't you? and come on."

Rip Van Winkle never slept more profoundly than did Coote at that moment. But alas! Rip had the longer nap of the two.

An unceremonious application of the leader's toe, and a threat to go on alone, brought the "Firm" to their feet in double-quick time, and started them up the steep side of the Beacon Hill.

Demoralised by their halt, they fared badly up the slope, and had it not been for Dick's almost vicious resolution, which kept him going and overcame his own frequent inclination to yield to the lazier motions of his companions, they might never have done it. Dick saw that the effort was critical, and he was inexorable. Even Georgie thought him unkind, and Coote positively hated him up that slope.

Oh, those never-ending ridges, one above the other, each seeming to be the top, but each discovering another beyond more odious than itself!

More than once they felt they had just enough left in them to make the peak that faced them; and then, when it was reached, their endurance had to stretch and stretch until it seemed that the point of breaking must come at each step.

If nothing else they had ever done deserved the reward of the virtuous, that honest pull up the side of the Welkin Beacon did; and Freckleton, had he seen them making the last scramble, would have put their names down on his list without further probation.

The cairn stood before them at last, and as they rushed to it, and planted themselves on the topmost point, where still a few scraps of the scent lingered, all the fatigue and labour were forgotten in an exhilarating sense of triumph and achievement.

"Rather a breather, that," said Dick, his honest face beaming all over; "you chaps took a lot of driving."

"I feel quite fresh after it," said Coote, beaming too.

"You didn't feel fresh ten minutes ago, under the last shoulder but one, my boy. If you feel so fresh, suppose you trot down and up again while Georgie and I sit here and look at the view."

Coote declined, and after a short rest they dropped down the long slope, with the scent in full view, on to Lowhouse, where the Gurgle, slipping clear and deep between its banks, seemed to them one of the loveliest pictures Nature ever drew.

The scent lay right along the bank, sometimes down on the stones, sometimes on the high paths above the tree tops, until suddenly it stopped.

"By Jove, we shall have to swim for it, you fellows," cried Dick, delighted. "Chuck your shoes and things across, and tumble in."

With joy they obeyed. They would fain have spent half an hour in the delicious water, so soft and cool and deep. But Dick was in a self-denying mood, and would not allow his men more than ten minutes. That, however, was as good as an hour's nap; and when, after dressing and picking up the scent, they took up the running again, it was like a new start.

Half-a-mile down, they came on to the country road, and here suddenly the scent vanished. High or low they could not find it. It neither crossed the road, nor went up the road, nor went down the road. They sniffed round in circles, but all to no good—not a scrap of paper was anywhere within twenty yards, except at the spot where they had struck the road.

They had gone, perhaps, half a mile with no sign yet of the scent, and were beginning to make up their minds that, after all, they should have turned up the road instead of down, when a horseman, followed by a groom, turned a corner of the road in front of them and came to meet them.

"Hurrah!" cried Dick, "here's a chap we can ask."

The "chap" in question was evidently somewhat perplexed by the apparition of these three bareheaded, bare-legged, dust-stained youngsters, and reined up his horse as they trotted up.

"I say," cried Dick, ten yards off, "have you seen the Harriers go by, please?—Whew!"

This last exclamation was caused by the sudden and alarming discovery that the "chap" thus unceremoniously addressed was no other than one of the two magistrates before whom, not three days ago, Tom White had stood on his trial in the presence of the "Firm."

"What Harriers, my man?" asked the gentleman.

"Oh, if you please, the Templeton Harriers, sir. It's a paper-chase, you know."

"Oh, you're Templeton boys, are you? Why, I was a Templetonian myself at your age," said the delighted old boy. "No; no Harriers have gone this way. You must have lost the scent."

"We lost it half a mile ago. If you're going that way, we can show you where," said Dick.

"Come on, then," said the good-humoured squire; "we'll smell 'em out somewhere."

So the "Firm" turned and trotted in its very best form alongside the worthy magistrate until they reached the point where the scent had struck the road.

The old Templetonian summoned his groom, and, dismounting, joined the boys, with all the ardour of an old sportsman, in their search for the scent. He poked the hedges knowingly with his whip, and tracked up the ditches; he took note of the direction of the wind, and ordered his groom to take his horse a wide sweep of the field opposite on the chance of a discovery.

The boys, fired by his example, strained every nerve to prove themselves good Harriers, and covered a mile or more in their circuits.

At length the old gentleman brought his whip a crack down on his leggings and exclaimed:—

"I have it! Ha! ha! knowing young dogs! Look here, my boy! look here!"

And, taking Dick by the arm, he led him to the point where the scent touched the road.

"Do you see what they've done?—artful young scamps! They've doubled on their own scent. Usen't to be allowed in my days."

And, delighted with his discovery, he led them back along the scent for a hundred yards or so up the field, where it suddenly forked off behind some gorse-bushes, and made straight for the railway at Norton.

"Ha! ha! the best bit of sniffing I've had these many years. And, now I come to think of it, with the wind the way it is blowing, they may have dropped their scent fair, and the breeze has taken it on to the old track. Cunning young dogs!"

"Thanks, awfully," said Dick, gratefully; "we should never have found it."

The other two echoed their gratitude, and the delighted old gentleman valued their thanks quite as much as his Commission of the Peace.

"Now you've got it," said he, "come along and have a bit of lunch at my house; I'm not five minutes away."

"Thanks, very much," said Dick, "but I'm afraid—"

"Nonsense! come on. You're out of the hunt; ten minutes won't make any difference."

Of course they yielded, and enjoyed a sumptuous lunch of cold meat and bread and cheese, which made new men of them. It took all their good manners to curb their attentions to the joint; and their chatty host spun out the repast with such stories of his own school days, that the ten minutes grew to fully half an hour before they could get away.

Before they did so Dick, who for a quarter of an hour previously had been exhibiting signs of agitation and inward debate, contrived to astonish both the "Firm," and his host.

"We saw you at Tom White's trial the other day, sir," said he, abruptly, at the close of one of the Squire's stories.

"Bless my soul! were you there? Why, of course—all three of you; I saw you. They didn't let the youngsters do that sort of thing in my day."

"We were rather interested about White, you know," said Dick, nervously.

"A good-for-nothing vagabond he is!" said the very unprofessional magistrate.

"We rather hope," said Dick, turning very red, "he'll get let off."

"Eh? what? Do you know, you young scamp, I can— So you want him let off, do you? How's that?"

"Because he didn't take the boat away," said Dick, avoiding the horror-struck eyes of his "Firm."

"We—that is I—let it go."

"What do you say?" said the Squire, putting down his knife and fork and sitting back in his chair.

Whereupon Dick, as much to stave off the expected storm as to justify himself, proceeded to give a true, though agitated, story of his and Georgie's adventures on the day of the Grandcourt match, appealing to Georgie at every stage in the narration to corroborate him. Which Georgie did, almost noisily.

The magistrate heard it all out in silence, with a face gradually becoming serious.

"Do you know what you can get for doing it?" he asked.

Dick's face grew graver and graver.

"Shall we be transported?" he asked, with a quaver in his voice.

The magistrate took a hurried gulp from the tumbler before him.

"You've put me in a fix, my man. You'd no business to get round me to prevent me doing my duty."

"I really didn't mean to do that," put in Dick.

"No—we wouldn't do such a thing," said Georgie.

"Well, never mind that. Whatever Tom White did to you, you'd no right to do what you did. You've put me in a fix, I say. Take my advice and write to your father, and tell him all about it, and get him to come down. If Tom White's partners and the pawnbroker get their money, they may stop the case, and there'll be an end of it. If they don't, Tom must take his chance. Dear, dear, things have changed in Templeton since my day. Confound it,

I wish the Harriers would choose some other run! A nice fix I'm in, to be sure—young rascals!"

Late that evening a crowd assembled in the Quadrangle of Templeton. The hunt had been in three hours ago, and all the hounds but three had turned up and gone to their kennels. It was to welcome the remaining three that the crowd was assembled. They had already been signalled from the beach, and the faint hum in the High Street told that they had already got into their last run.

Nearer and louder grew the sound, till the hum became a shout, and the shout a roar, as through the great gate of Templeton three small travel-stained figures trotted gamely into the Quad, with elbows down and heads up.

They hardly seemed to hear the cheers or notice the crowd, but kept their faces anxiously towards where Cresswell—book in hand—stood at the door of Westover's to receive them.

"Have you run right through?" he asked as they came up.

"Yes, every step," gasped Dick.

Five minutes later, the "Firm" was in bed and fast asleep.

And two days later, when the revised list of candidates eligible for election to the "Select Sociables" was displayed on the library door, it included the names of Richardson, Heathcote, and Coote.

Chapter Twenty Six
How the sword of Damocles still
hangs over our heroes

Dear Father,—Please come down here as soon as you can. We're in a regular row. I'm awfully afraid fifty pounds will not quite cover it.

Please try and come by the next train as the case comes on on Saturday, and there's not much time. We saw the magistrate yesterday, and made a clean breast. I hope they won't transport us. He was very jolly helping us find the scent, and gave us a stunning lunch. We ran the big hunt right through, and are pretty sure to get our names on the "Sociables" list. I wish you and mother could have seen the view on the top of Welkin Beacon. The awkward thing is that Tom White may get transported instead of us, and it would be jolly if you could come and get him off. Coote wasn't in it, but he's backing us up. How is Tike? I hope they wash him regularly. If I'm not transported, I shall be home in eight weeks and three days and will take him out for walks.

Love to mother, in which all join,—Your affectionate son, Basil.

P.S.—If you come, don't take Fegan's cab—he's a cheat. Old White will drive you cheap. He's Tom's father. Georgie sends his love.

The reader may imagine, if he can, the consternation with which Mr and Mrs Richardson read this loving epistle at breakfast on the Friday morning following the great hunt.

They gazed at one another with countenances full of horror and terror, like people suddenly brought face to face with a great calamity. At length Mr Richardson said:—

"Where's the Bradshaw, Jane?"

"Oh, the train goes in half an hour. You have just time to catch it. Do go quickly. My poor, poor boy!"

The father groaned; and in another five minutes he was on his way to the station.

That morning, while school was in full swing, the porter entered the third class room with a telegram in his hand, which he took straight to the master.

"Richardson," said the master, "this is for you."

Dick, who was at the moment engaged in drawing a circle on his Euclid cover with a pencil and a piece of string, much to the admiration of his neighbours, jumped up as if he had been shot, and with perturbed face went up to receive the missive.

He tore it open, and, as he glanced at its contents, his anxious face relaxed into a complacent grin.

"From G. Richardson, London. I shall reach Templeton at 3:5 this afternoon. Meet me, if you can."

"Huzzah, Georgie!" said he, as he returned to his seat. "Father's coming down by the 3:5. Let's all go and meet him."

The "Firm" said they would, and, accordingly, that afternoon after dinner the trio sallied forth in great spirits and good-humour to give the anxious father a reception.

With the easy memory of youth, they forgot all about the probable object of his visit; or, if they remembered it, it was with a sort of passing feeling of relief that the Tom White "row" was now as good as over—at any rate, as far as they were concerned.

When Mr Richardson, haggard and anxious, descended from the carriage, it was a decided shock to encounter the beaming countenance of his son and hear his light-hearted greeting.

"Hullo, father—jolly you've come! Old White's cab is bagged, but Swisher's got a good horse to go. Here's Georgie and Coote—you know."

The bewildered gentleman greeted his son's friends kindly, and then, disclaiming all intention of taking anybody's cab, drew his son aside.

"What is all this, my boy? Your mother and I almost broke our hearts over your letter."

"Oh, it's all serene—really, father," said the boy, a little disturbed by his father's anxious tones. "We really wouldn't have sent if the magistrate hadn't said we'd better—would we, Georgie?"

"No; he said that was our only chance," replied Georgie.

"If your two friends will take my bag up to the 'George,'" said Mr Richardson, despairing of getting any lucid information out of the "Firm" as a body, "I should like a walk with you, Basil, on the strand."

Coote and Georgie departed with the bag, and the father and son being left alone, Dick gave a simple and unvarnished narrative of the legal difficulties in which he and his friends were involved.

Mr Richardson's heart beat lighter as he heard it. The scrape was bad enough, but it was not as bad as he had imagined, nor was the foolish boy at his side the monster of iniquity his letter had almost implied. They had a long talk, those two, that afternoon as they paced the hard, dry strand at the water's edge and watched the waves tumbling in from the sea. They talked about far more than Tom White and his boat. Dick's heart, once opened, poured into his father's ears the story of all his trials and temptations, and hopes and disappointments, at Templeton.

The narration did him good. It cleared and strengthened his mind wonderfully. It humbled him to discover in how many things he had been wrong, and in how many foolish; and it comforted him to feel that his father understood him and judged him fairly.

It was late in the afternoon when their walk came to an end. Then Mr Richardson said:—

"Now, I suppose you and your friends have decided that I am to give you high tea at the 'George'—eh?"

"Thanks," said Dick, who had had a dim prospect of the kind.

"Well, I'll come up to the school and see if I can get Dr Winter to give you leave."

"Dr Winter doesn't know about Tom White's boat, you know," said the boy, as they walked up. "I didn't like to tell him."

Dr Winter was easily persuaded to allow the "Firm" to spend the evening with Mr Richardson at the "George."

The small party which assembled that evening at the table of the worthy paterfamilias did not certainly look like one over which hung the shadow of "transportation." The talk was of "Tubs" and Harriers, of tennis and "Sociables," of Virgil and Euclid; and as the first shyness of their introduction wore off, the "Firm" settled down to as jovial an evening as they had spent for a long time.

Only once did the shadow of their "row" return, when Mr Richardson, at eight o'clock, said:—

"Now, boys, good-night. I have a solicitor coming here directly."

"About the trial, father?" asked Dick, with falling countenance.

"Yes, my boy. As the case comes on to-morrow, there is no time to be lost."

There certainly was not; and Mr Richardson, before he went to bed that night had not only seen a good many persons, but had materially lightened his pockets.

Buying off the law, even in the most straightforward way, is an expensive luxury. The prosecutors, of Tom White, seeing that their victim had an unexpected backer, became very righteous and high-principled indeed. They could not think of withdrawing the case. It was a public duty—painful, of course, but not to be shirked. It pained them very much to bring trouble on any one, particularly an old shipmate; but they owed it to society to see he got his deserts.

They were, of course, wholly unaware of Mr Richardson's special interest in the matter. Otherwise, they might have been even more virtuous and high-principled than they were. They looked upon him as a benevolent individual, bent on getting the half-witted vagabond out of trouble, and, as such, they knew quite enough of fishing to see that he was in their net.

Their own solicitor, too, knew something about this sort of fishing, and the unfortunate father spent a very unhappy morning floundering about in the net these gentlemen provided for him—extremely doubtful whether, after all, he would not be obliged publicly to incriminate his son, in order to solve the difficulty.

However, by dint of great exertion, he contrived to get the case adjourned for three days more. The prosecutors were, of course, shocked to see the course of the law delayed for even this length of time. It meant expense to them, as well as inconvenience. Of course Mr Richardson had to act up to this broad hint, and promising, further, not to make any attempt to bail their prisoner, he obtained their reluctant consent to a postponement till Wednesday, greatly to the disgust, among other persons, of Duffield and Raggles, who, mindful of their pleasant morning last Saturday, had come down with another five-pennyworth of chocolate creams, to watch the case again.

"Beastly soak it was," said Raggles that afternoon, to Dick, who, acting on parental orders, had abstained with the "Firm" from visiting the Court.

"They say there's some idiot come all the way from London to stop the case. I'd like to kick him. What business has he to come and spoil our fun?"

"Look here!" said Dick, with a sudden warmth which quite took away the breath of Master Raggles. "Shut up, and hold your row, unless you want to be chucked out of the Quad."

"What on earth is the row with you?" asked the astounded Raggles.

"Never you mind. Hook it!" retorted Dick.

Raggles departed, not quite sure whether Dick had not had too much "swipes" for dinner, or whether his run after the Harriers yesterday had not been too much for his wits.

Dick felt rather blue that afternoon as he watched the train which carried his father steam out of Templeton station.

He had somehow expected that this visit would settle everything. But instead of doing that, Mr Richardson had left Templeton almost as anxious as when he entered it. Dick couldn't make it out, and he returned rather dismally to Templeton.

Here, however, he had plenty to distract his attention. The fame of the "Firm's" exploit on the previous day was still a nine days' wonder in the Den, and he might, had he been so inclined, have spent the afternoon in discoursing to an admiring audience of his achievement. But he was not so minded. He was more in the humour for a football scrimmage, and as to-day was the first practice day of the season, he strolled off to the fields, and relieved his feelings and recovered his spirits in an hour's energetic onslaught on the long-suffering ball.

Rather to his surprise, Georgie did not join him in this occupation. That young gentleman, to tell the truth, was very particularly engaged elsewhere.

His proceedings during the last few days had not been unnoticed by his old patron, Pledge.

That senior, after his unceremonious deposition from the monitorship by Mansfield, had been considerably exercised in his mind how to hold up his head with dignity in Templeton.

He was acute enough to see that his chief offence in the eyes of these enemies had been, not open rebellion, or a flagrant breach of rules, but his influence over the juniors with whom he came into contact.

Over George Heathcote's soul, especially, he saw that a great battle had been waged, and was still waging, in which, somehow or other, the two great parties of Templeton seemed involved.

So far, the battle had gradually gone against Pledge. Just when he had considered the youngster his own, he had been quietly snatched off by Dick, and before he could be recovered, the monitors had stepped in and taken Dick's side, and left him, Pledge, discomfited, and a laughing-stock to Templeton.

Had they? Pledge chuckled to himself, as he thought of Mr Webster's pencil, and of the toils in which, as he flattered himself, he still held both Heathcote and Dick. They were sure of their darling little *protégés*, were they? Not so sure, reflected Pledge, as they think. They might even yet sue for terms, when they found that by a single word he could change the lodgings of the two sweet babes from Templeton to the county jail.

He, therefore, in moderately cheerful spirits, allowed a day or two to pass, avoiding even a further visit to Webster; and then casually waylaid his old fag as he was returning, decidedly depressed in mind, from saying good-bye to Mr Richardson.

"Why, Georgie, old man," said Pledge, "how festive you look! The change of air from my study to Swinstead's has done you good. Where have you been all the morning?"

"I've just come up from the town," said Heathcote, wishing he could get away.

"Ah, trying to square somebody up, eh? It's not quite as easy as one might think; is it?"

Heathcote looked doubtfully up at his old senior's face, and said nothing.

"It's a wonder to me, you know," said Pledge, turning his back and looking out of the window, "that your new angelic friends don't somehow do it for you. There's Mansfield, you know. One word from his lips would do the business. Everyone knows he never did anything low."

"Mansfield never speaks to me," said Georgie, more for the sake of saying something than because he considered the fact important.

"Really! How ungrateful of him, when you have been the means of enabling him to kick me out of the Sixth. Very ungrateful!"

"I never had anything to do with that," said Georgie.

"No! You don't, then, believe a fellow can make use of you without your knowing it. You can't imagine Mansfield saying to his dear friends, 'I'd give anything to get at that wicked Pledge, but I daren't do it straight out. So I must pretend to be deeply interested in that little prig, Heathcote, and much concerned lest he should be corrupted by his wicked senior. That will be a fine excuse for having a slap at Pledge. I'll take away his fag, and then, of course, he'll resign, and we shall get rid of him!'"

"I don't believe he really said that," said Heathcote, colouring up.

"'And then,' he would say, 'to bribe the youngster over, and keep him from spoiling all and going back to his old senior, we'll manage to fool him about our precious new Club, and put his name on the list.'"

This was rousing Georgie on a tender point.

"If my name gets on the list, it will be because Dick and Coote and I ran through the hunt; that's why!" he said, rather fiercely.

"Ha, ha! If they could only humbug everybody as easily as they do you. So you are really going to get into the Club?"

"I'll try, if our names get on the list."

"And you think they are sure to elect you? Of course you've done nothing to disgrace Templeton, eh?"

The boy's face fell, and Pledge followed up his hit.

"They'd like you all the better, wouldn't they, if they heard you and your precious friends are—well, quite a matter of interest to the Templeton police; eh, my boy?"

"We're not," stammered Georgie, very red. "You needn't say anything about that, Pledge."

"Is it likely? Don't I owe you too much already for cutting me, and talking of me behind my back, and letting the monitors make a catspaw of you to hurt me? Oh, no! I've no interest in telling anybody!"

"Really, Pledge, I never talked of you behind your back, and all that. I didn't mean to cut you. Please don't go telling everybody. It's bad enough as it is."

Pledge chuckled to himself, and began to get his tea-pot out of his cupboard.

"You see I have to help myself now," said he.

Georgie's heart was touched. What with dread of the possible mischief Pledge could do him, and with a certain amount of self-reproach at his desertion, he felt the least he could do would be to fall into his old ways for this one evening.

It was just what Pledge wanted. How he longed that Mansfield and Cresswell and Freckleton could all have been there to see it.

"Mansfield is hardly likely to trouble his head about every errand even such an important personage as you run," said he, in reply to one feeble protest from the boy. "Call yourself Swinstead's fag by all means. You can still fag for me. However, it doesn't matter to me. I can get on well enough without."

"Oh, yes, I'll try," said Georgie.

That was enough. Pledge felt that too much might overdo it. So with this triumph he dismissed his youthful perturbed *protégé* for the night, and dreamed sweetly of the wrath of his enemies, when they discovered that after all he (Pledge) was master of the situation in spite of them.

Chapter Twenty Seven
How the "Martha" comes home to her bereaved friends

Pledge did well to sleep sweetly and enjoy his triumph while it lasted, for the battle which raged over the soul of George Heathcote was by no means ended yet.

"I say, Georgie," said Dick, next day, as the "Firm" took a Sunday afternoon stroll along the cliffs. "Where on earth did you get to yesterday? You never turned up at football practice, and skulked all the evening."

Georgie coloured. His conscience had already smitten him for detaching himself from his leader at a time of danger like the present; still more, for deserting him for a fellow like Pledge.

One result of Dick's sovereignty had been that the "Firm" had contracted a habit of telling the truth to one another on all occasions. It was found to be the shortest cut to friendship, and a vast saving of time and trouble.

Georgie, therefore, however much his inclination, as moulded by Pledge, may have led him to prevaricate, replied, "I was in Pledge's study."

Dick whistled, rather a dismayed whistle.

"I thought you were out of that," he said.

"So did I; but, I don't know, Dick. He's got to know all about our row, and if I don't be civil to him he'll let out on us."

"How does he know? Who's told him?"

"I never did," said Coote.

"I can't fancy how he heard. But he knows all about it, and he as good as says he'll spoil our chance for the 'Sociables' if I don't fag for him."

"Beastly cad!" murmured Dick.

"He says, you know," pursued George, "that it was all a spite of Mansfield's against him—that making me Swinstead's fag. They knew it would make him resign. It is rather low, isn't it, to humbug me about just for the sake of spiting someone else?"

"It's all a lie, Georgie. Pledge is one of the biggest cads in Templeton. I heard lots of people say so. Webster said so. He says he'd no more let a boy of his go near Pledge than he'd fly; and Webster's not particular."

"And I heard Cartwright say," said Coote, by way of assisting the discussion, "that Pledge has done his best to make a cad of you, and nearly succeeded."

"He said that?" said Georgie, hotly; "like his cheek! Has he done so, Dick?"

"Not much," said Dick, frankly.

"I don't feel myself a cad," said poor Heathcote.

"Perhaps fellows can't always tell, themselves," said Coote.

There was a pause after this, and the "Firm" walked on for some distance in silence. Then Dick said:

"You'll have to jack him up, Georgie, that's all about it."

"But I tell you he'll let out on us," pleaded Georgie, "and really I've only said I'll fag now and then for him."

"Can't help, Georgie; We don't want to have you made a cad of. It would smash up our 'Firm,' wouldn't it, Coote?"

"Rather," said Coote.

"Besides," said Dick, "he's such a cad, no one would believe him if he did tell of us. My father would shut him up. He'll be down, you know, on Tuesday."

Heathcote breathed hard. But when it came to a question of choosing between Pledge and the "Firm," it needed no very desperate inward battle to decide.

"What had I better do?" he asked.

"Cut him," said Dick.

"But suppose I've promised him?"

"That's a nuisance. Never mind, we're all in it, so we'll send him a letter from the 'Firm' and tell him you cry off. It's a bad job, of course, but it can't be helped, and we'll back you up, won't we, Coote?"

"I should rather say so," replied the genial junior partner.

So, that quiet Sunday afternoon, in an unpretentious and unsentimental way, a very good stroke of work was done, not only for the soul of Georgie Heathcote, but for Templeton generally.

The "Firm" were by no means elated at their decision, for they had yet to learn what revenge the senior would take upon them. Still, the effort and the common peril knit them together in bonds of closer brotherhood, and enabled them to face the future, if not cheerily, at least, with grim determination.

Pledge was considerably astounded that evening, just as he was speculating on the reason of Heathcote's non-appearance, to see Coote's round head suddenly thrust in at the door, and a small billet tossed on to the table.

Pledge was getting used to small billets by this time, and was rather tired of them. Coote, as he knew, was Cartwright's fag; he therefore concluded that Cartwright was the writer of the note, and that being so, he pitched the paper unopened into the empty fireplace with a sneer.

He waited for another half-hour, and still Heathcote did not appear. Pledge didn't like it, and began to grow concerned. Was it possible, after all, he had made too sure of his young friend?

Partly to pass the time, and partly with the vague idea that might throw some light on the matter, he had the curiosity to pick the neglected billet out of the hearth and open it.

His face went through a strange series of emotions as he read its extraordinary contents:—

> Our Dear Pledge,—We think you will like to hear that Heathcote can't fag for you. He doesn't believe he really promised, but must be excused. We've made him do it because we don't want him to be made a cad. He is very sorry, and hopes you won't be a cad and let out about the row we are in. Excuse this short letter, and, with kind regards, believe us, our dear Pledge, your affectionate young friends, B. Richardson, G. Heathcote, A.D. Coote. Sunday afternoon.

This masterpiece of conciliatory firmness, which had cost the "Firm" an hour's painful labour to concoct, brought out the angry spots on Pledge's cheeks and forced some bad language from his lips.

The letter he had received from Mansfield a week ago had been nothing to this. Mansfield and he were equals, and a reverse at Mansfield's hands was at least an ordinary misfortune of war.

But to be coolly flouted, and to have all the work of a term upset by three wretched youngsters, who called themselves his affectionate young friends, was a drop too much in the bucket of the "spider's" humiliation.

He stared at the letter in a stupid way, like one bewildered. Even its quaint phrases and artless attempts at conciliation failed to raise a sneer on his lips. Something told him it was the hardest hit yet, and that out of the mouths of these honest babes and sucklings his confusion had reached its climax.

If Richardson, Heathcote, and Coote snapped their fingers at him in the face of all Templeton, who else would care a fig about him?

The one grain of comfort was in the possession of the secret of Mr Webster's pencil, to which Pledge clung as his last and winning card.

How to make the most of it was the important question Pledge decided not to be impatient. Wednesday was to be the great election for the "Sociables," and, if our heroes' names appeared on the list, as rumour already said they would, his blow would tell best if held over till then.

So he sat down, and acknowledged the "Firm's" note as follows:—

> My Dear Richardson, Heathcote, and Coote,—Pray do as you like. Promises are never made to be kept by "Select Sociables" of your high character. I do not understand what you mean about your row. What row are you in? *Are* you in a row? You don't call that little matter that I am expecting to talk to the "Sociables" about on Wednesday a row, do you? Please give my kind regards to Georgie Heathcote, and tell him he will need to beg hard before I trouble him to lay my cloth. No doubt he has given you many interesting stories of the miserable week he spent with me last holidays in London. I'm not surprised at his turning against me after that. I hope I shall not have to tell anyone some of the stories he has told me of Richardson and Coote. Excuse this long letter, and believe me, my dear young jail-birds, your "affectionate" P. Pledge.

This bitter effusion was read next morning by the "Firm" as they walked down to the "Tub." Its full sting did not come out till after three or four careful perusals, and then the "Firm" looked blankly at one another with lengthened faces.

"I couldn't believe any fellow could be such a cad," said Dick.

"It's jolly awkward!" said Heathcote. "You know he was awfully civil to me in London, and it does seem low to be cutting him now."

"Civil, be hanged!" said Dick. "He tried to get hold of you to make a cad of you, that's what he did; and you were precious near being one, too, when you came back, weren't you?"

"Was I?" asked the humble Georgie.

"Rather," said Coote; "everybody said so."

"Well, of course," said Georgie, "if that's what he was driving at, it doesn't matter so much."

"Except that it makes him all the bigger a cad."

"What on earth shall we do about the other thing?" asked Georgie.

"The row? We must cheek it, that's all. If he does us over the 'Sociable' election, we can't be helped."

"And suppose he gets us transported?"

"Can't do it, I tell you; my father will be up here, you know."

There was a pause, and the "Firm" walked on. Then Georgie said:—

"I say, what does he mean about the stories I told about you and Coote. I never told any stories, that I remember. I never had any to tell."

"Ah, I was wondering what that meant," said Dick. "He speaks as if you'd been blabbing all sorts of things."

"I really don't think I ever did," said Heathcote, ransacking his memory. "I may have said once I thought Coote was rather an ass, but that was all."

"What made you tell him that?" said Coote.

"He asked me if I didn't think so," said Georgie, apologetically, "and of course I was bound to say what I thought."

"Rather," said Coote.

"But he's telling crams about you, Dick," said Georgie; "I'm quite sure of that. He used to try and make out you were a sneak and a prig; and perhaps I believed him once or twice, but that was while I was a cad, you know."

"Oh, yes, that's all right!" said Dick, putting his arm in that of his friend.

Pledge would have had very little consolation out of this short discussion, and if for the next two days he sat up in his study expecting that every footstep belonged to the "Firm" on its way to capitulate, he must have been sorely disappointed. Capitulation was the one consideration which had never once entered the heads of the honest fraternity.

That afternoon the town of Templeton was startled by an incident, which had it come to the ears of our heroes, as they sat and groaned over their "Select Dialogues of the Dead," would have effectually driven every letter of the Greek alphabet out of their heads for the time being.

The event was nothing else but the arrival in port of the collier brig, *Hail! Columbia* with a cargo of coals from the Tyne, and *mirabile dictu*! with the *Martha* lying comfortably, bottom upwards, safe and sound, on her deck.

The collier, according to the account of the skipper, had been running across the head of the bay on the 5th of June last, in half a cap of wind from the shore, when it sighted the *Martha* drifting empty out to sea. Having sent one of his men after her to capture her, and being convinced by the absence of oars or tackle that she must have drifted from her moorings empty, he took her on board; and, as he was bound to deliver his cargo by a certain day, and the wind being against his putting into Templeton, he stowed his prize comfortably away amidships, where she had been ever since, awaiting his next call at Templeton.

With the free-and-easy business ways of his craft, he had neglected to send any letter or message announcing the safety of the *Martha* to her afflicted friends; and having been detained in this place and that by stress of weather or business, he had now, after more than three months' absence, his first opportunity of restoring the lost property to its rightful owner.

If the simple fishermen of Templeton had been inclined to believe in miracles, the strange reappearance of the missing *Martha* at this particular time must have savoured of something of the sort. But being matter-of-fact folk, they contented themselves with lounging round the boat as she lay once more on the beach, staring at her, and wondering between their whiffs what the solicitors and judges would say now.

The skipper of the *Hail! Columbia* had neither the time nor the patience to discover who just now was the lawful owner of the boat. Some said Tom White; some said Tom White's partners; some said the pawnbroker.

The master disposed the problem off his mind very simply by setting down the *Martha* on the beach, and letting those who chose to claim her settle their squabble among themselves.

The news of the return of the prodigal was not long in spreading; and by the time the Templeton boys came down for their afternoon bathe it was common property.

Our heroes heard it in the water, from Raggles, and immediately landed and dressed. They scarcely exchanged a word till they stood at the side of the *Martha*, where she lay in almost the same spot where two of them had seen her three-and-a-half months ago. Then Dick said:—

"Think of her turning up at last!"

"I half guessed she would," said Georgie, "though I never expected it. I say, this settles our row, doesn't it?"

"Pretty well. But of course Tom White may catch it for pawning the boat. He collared the money, you know."

"Ah, but that's not got much to do with us," said Heathcote.

"Well," said Dick, "we ought to back him right up, while we are at it. Besides, you know, we may still get into a row for letting her go, though she *has* turned up."

Altogether the "Firm" were not very sure how far their position was improved by the recovery of the *Martha*. If Pledge, or any one, chose to tell tales, or if they themselves, in order to extricate Tom White, had to tell tales of themselves, all might yet go wrong. The one good thing, they decided, was that Mr Richardson, when he came to-morrow, would be saved the expense of buying at least one new boat for somebody.

Our heroes, as in duty bound, were at the station to meet the 3:5 train, and give the worthy paterfamilias a reception.

"Hullo, father," cried Dick, as if he had only parted with his parent five minutes ago, "they've found her, I say. Do you see that two-masted collier in the harbour? She picked her up, the day after we slipped her. Isn't it jolly?"

Mr Richardson certainly looked surprised, and a trifle relieved; but the matter did not yet occur to him in a "jolly" light.

"It's a good thing she has come back," said he; "and now, as I have a great deal to do, I'll say good-bye for the present. I have sent a note to Doctor Winter, to ask him to let you breakfast with me at the 'George,' in the morning."

"Thanks, awfully, sir," said Coote, beaming all over.

Mr Richardson laughed.

"I'm afraid I only mentioned Basil in my note," said he, "but I daresay we shall be able to have a meal together later in the day. Good-bye."

"Rather cool cheek of you, Coote," said Dick, as the "Firm" returned to the school, "cadging my father that way for breakfast."

"Very sorry," said Coote, humbly. "I thought we were all in it, that's all."

The evening passed anxiously for the boys, and no less so for poor Mr Richardson, who was buffeted about from pillar to post, from lawyer to lawyer, from boatman to pawnbroker, in his honest efforts to extricate his son from his scrape.

The recovery of the *Martha*, he found, made very little improvement in his prospects. For now she had come back, everybody seemed to be calculating the amount of money she would have brought in had she remained at Templeton during the busy season. This loss was estimated at several times the value of the boat, and the high-principled prosecutors would hear no suggestion of withdrawing the case until each one of them — partners, pawnbroker, and all — had been refunded the entire sum.

Then, when that was done, the lawyers pulled their bills out of their desks, and hinted that some one would have to settle them; and as neither the partners, nor the pawnbroker, nor Tom White, saw their way to doing so, Mr Richardson had to draw his own inferences and settle them himself. Then, when all seemed settled, the police recollected that they had had considerable trouble in looking after the case. They had made several journeys, and spent several hours on the beach looking out for the supposed thief. They had also had charge of Tom White for a fortnight; and what with postages, telegrams, and office fees, they were decidedly out of pocket over the whole business.

The long-suffering father put them in pocket, and after subscribing to several local charities, and consoling the reporters of the *Templeton Observer* and other such outsiders, he retired, jaded, but comforted, to the "George," feeling that if his mission had been successful, it had cost him an amount of generosity which he could hardly have believed was in him.

When Dick, "with shining morning face," presented himself next morning for breakfast, he little imagined how much of his father's money was at that moment scattered about in Templeton.

"Huzza! father," said he, when his parent presented himself in the coffee-room. "Such a game! Cresswell says he'll give us his study this evening, so our 'Firm's' going to give you a spread. Coote and Georgie are out ordering the tucker now — kidneys and tea-cake. I asked Winter when I went for my *exeat* if we might have you, and he said, 'Yes; he'd be very glad.' Mind you come. It'll be a stunning spread, and Georgie and Coote are sure to pick out good things. I wish mother could come too."

In the face of this hospitable outburst, Mr Richardson could hardly expatiate on the cost and anxiety of his mission to Templeton. A calmer moment must do for that. Meanwhile he delighted his son's heart by accepting his invitation on the spot.

He allowed Dick and his two friends, if it fitted in with school rules, to be present in the Court to hear the end of Tom White's case—a permission they were not slow to avail themselves of, although this time they occupied a modest seat at the back, and attempted no public manifestations of encouragement to the prisoner in court.

The case ended very simply. When it was called on, and Tom, as friendly as ever, was ushered into the box, no one appeared to accuse him, and the magistrates, rightly concluding this to mean that the prosecution had retired, dismissed the case accordingly.

Tom said, "Thank'ee, sir," and looked quite bewildered on being told he might walk out of court a free man.

Our heroes, who had already got outside before he reached the door, deemed it their duty to complete their efforts in his favour by congratulating him on his escape.

"Jolly glad we are, Tom White," said Dick, as the worthy mariner came towards them. "It was hard lines for you, and it wasn't all your fault. It's my father got you off, you know."

"Thank'ee, young gentleman. It's very hard on a hard-working mariner not to have his living. If you could spare a trifle and tell the gentlemen, I'd thank you kindly."

"We haven't got any tin to spare now," said Dick, who knew that the resources of the "Firm" had been well-nigh exhausted in preparation for the spread in Cresswell's study that evening; "but we won't forget. Good-bye, old man. Jolly glad you've got out at last!"

Chapter Twenty Eight
How Nemesis makes her final call

Our heroes, as they returned arm-in-arm from the trial of Tom White, were conscious that in proportion as the troubles behind them diminished, those ahead loomed out big and ominous.

They had escaped transportation; at least, so they told one another; and although, when all was said and done, they had not done much towards righting Tom White or recovering the *Martha* still, somehow, Nemesis had been "choked off" in that direction.

But when they turned their faces from what lay behind to the immediate future, their hearts failed them. They had staked high for the "Sociables." Their run with the Harriers had been no trifle: and far more important was the general attention it had drawn to themselves, and to their efforts to get into, the select company. Their candidature was a master of public notoriety, and if Pledge should at the last moment carry out his threat, their fall would be sad in proportion.

When they reached Templeton they found the place in a ferment. Fellows were going about with pencils and paper, making up their lists.

"I say," said Pauncefote, waylaying our heroes as they entered the Den; "vote for us, I say. I'll vote for you."

"Oh, ah!" said Dick; "that means we give you three votes, and you only give us one. See any green? You get a couple of other chaps to stick us down, and then we'll do it."

Pauncefote, rather bewildered by this way of putting the matter, went off immediately, and canvassed actively among his particular friends on behalf of the "Firm;" which was very kind of him, as several fellows told him.

"Look here, you fellows," said Gosse, approaching the "Firm" with a troubled face, "*do* you know anybody in the lower Fourth who isn't a cad? I've got down all the other forms, but I can't get a single decent name for the lower Fourth."

"Aspinall," said Dick.

"But he's such a muff. I'd be ashamed to put him down."

"Aspinall would lick you left-handed at tennis, and knows more Greek than you know English," said Dick, hotly; for he always looked upon the Devonshire boy as a credit to his protecting arm. "If you call that being a muff, well, he is one, and you aren't, that's all."

Gosse received this judgment with attention, and went off to have a private look at Aspinall at close quarters.

"Oh, I say, Dick," said Raggles, whom our heroes presently found absorbed in the deepest study; "here's a go! We've only got to put down six in each form, and I've got a dozen down for ours, and don't see I can cut any of them out."

"Let's hear their names," said Dick.

"All serene! Raggles—"

"By Jove, that's modest! You're determined *he's* to have one vote."

"Oh, you know, I believe I'm safe; but, of course, everybody votes for himself."

"Go on. Who are the rest?"

"Raggles, Culver, Pauncefote, Smith, Gosse, Starkey, Crisp, Calverly, Strahan, Jobling, Cazenove, and—well, I thought of sticking down one of you three for the twelfth."

"Thanks," said Dick. "We aren't particular, are we, you chaps?"

"I'm not," said Coote. "You can stick me down if you like, Rag."

Raggles, finding not much assistance forthcoming to help him in his difficulty, retired to a quiet corner, and privately tossed up for each name in succession. As his penny came down "tails" persistently both for himself and everybody else, except Gosse, he resorted to the less risky method of shutting his eyes, and dropping six blots on his paper. This happy expedient was only partially successful, as none of the blots fell anywhere near any of the names. Finally, as time was growing short, he put down his own name on the paper, and resolved to sacrifice his other votes. And when he had done it, he rather wondered the idea had never struck him before.

Our heroes meanwhile were busy with their own lists, which, under Dick's guiding influence, rapidly filled up with a set of good names. When it came to their own Form they agreed that, being a "Firm" and all "in it," they were entitled each of them to vote for the "Firm" as a body; which they did amid much mutual rejoicing.

At a quarter to four the big Hall began to fill. Everybody was there. Fellows who were on the list, sanguine, anxious, touchy; fellows who were not on the list, cross, sarcastic, righteous. Nearly every one had his paper in his hand, which he furtively glanced through for the last time before the summons to deposit it in the basket on the platform.

As before, the Sixth took rank as ordinary Templetonians, and no distinction was made between monitor and junior, eligible and non-eligible.

When the clock struck there were loud cries for Freckleton, who accordingly ascended the dais, and, after waiting patiently for order, proceeded to explain the order of election.

"I suppose," said he, "all of us who mean to vote have by this time filled up our papers with the names of the fellows we think most worthy to be elected on the new Club. You'd better have a last look to see you haven't put down more than thirty names altogether, and that there are not more than six in any one Form. Also make sure you have none of you signed your names to the papers, as this is secret voting, and it's not supposed to be known how any one has voted. Now, will fellows come up by benches and drop their papers into the basket?"

The front bench, consisting chiefly of Sixth-form fellows, obeyed the invitation, and deposited their papers in the receptacle. The rest of the meeting could not forbear the luxury of a few cheers as popular and unpopular seniors presented themselves; but, on the whole, the ceremony was gone through rapidly and in an orderly fashion.

Among the juniors, the Firm walked solemnly up the room amid cheers and cries of "Well run, puppies!" and gave in their votes. They glanced nervously round at Pledge, where he sat with a sneer on his face, and did not like the looks of him. The sneer they would have thought nothing of, but there was a serious, half-determined look about him which was ominous.

"The beast!" whispered Dick. "He's going to do something."

"Ugh!" said Georgie, "to think I ever liked him!"

"Now," said Freckleton, when the voting was over, "to insure the counting being fairly done, I propose that three fellows who have not had the good luck to be on the list be asked to count. I dare say they won't grudge the trouble, and it will be satisfactory to everybody to know they see fair play for the rest." (Hear, hear.) "Will any three fellows volunteer?"

Five stood up.

"Will you five choose three among you?" said Freckleton.

This was soon done, and the scrutineers were in a few moments buried in their work, watched eagerly by many anxious eyes.

It took a good while, but to our heroes, as they sat and watched Pledge's ugly look, the end seemed to come all too soon.

There was a loud hum of excitement when the list, as finally made out, was handed solemnly to Freckleton.

"I think, if you don't mind," said the Hermit, passing it back, "as I am an interested party, it would be better if one of you read it."

"All right," said the obliging scrutineer. "Gentlemen,—Unaccustomed as I am to public speaking, I beg to read you the list of the Sociables' Club. I don't see my own name on the list, but perhaps you'll consider the fag we three have been put to this afternoon is a public service for the good of Templeton. If so, please remember the poor scrutineers at the next election." (Cheers and laughter.) "Now for the list."

"Better only read the names of the elected ones in each form, and not the number of votes," suggested Freckleton.

"Lucky Freckleton said so," remarked the scrutineer, "or I should have told you that his name is at the top of the poll by a very long start." (Tremendous cheers.) "But, as I'm not to let out figures, all I can say is, he's in. And so are Crossfield, Cartwright, Swinstead, Frith, and Mansfield for the Sixth-Form."

It was curious to notice the effect of this announcement on the meeting generally and on the boys specially concerned. As name followed name without that of the Captain, fellows looked round at one another in something like consternation. After all, the Captain of Templeton *was* the Captain of Templeton, and those who had not voted for him had made sure other fellows would. But when five names were read out, and it was found that even Swinstead and Frith were elected, a sudden tide of repentance set in, which found vent in an unexpected cheer as the Captain's name followed. Templeton felt it had had a narrow escape of making itself foolish, and the cheer was quite as much one of relief as of congratulation.

Mansfield may have understood it. He had kept his eyes steadily on the reader, with a slight flush on his quiet face, and fellows who watched him could not tell whether the peculiar gleam which passed his eyes as his name was read was one of triumph or vexation. Whatever it was, every one knew the Captain would be altered neither in purpose nor motive by the incident. Jupiter would be Jupiter still, whether in Olympus or out of it; and Templeton, on the whole, felt that, had the vote gone otherwise, it would have had quite as much blushing to do as the defeated hero.

The scrutineer continued his list in order of forms. Of our particular acquaintance, Birket, Hooker, Duffield, Braider, and Aspinall all got safely "landed," while Bull, Wrangham, and Spokes were passed over.

Templeton, in fact, was a very good judge of honour when it was put to the choice, and even the enemies of the new Club could not help admitting that the best men, on the whole, were the elected ones.

A grim silence fell on the Hall as the scrutineer said —

"Now, Gentlemen, the Upper Third. The following are elected: —

"Richardson."

Dick caught his breath and felt he dared not move a muscle. Pledge was looking that way, and, as the boy's eyes and his enemy's met, the cheers of the Den sounded feeble, and the shouts of the Firm were spiritless.

"Pauncefote."

Dick started again at this and shook off the spell that was upon him. How dared Pauncefote come between him and his Firm? If fellows voted for him—Dick—what on earth did they mean by not voting also for Georgie and Coote? He faced defiantly round towards the reader and waited for the next name.

"Smith."

Dick quailed as he listened to the mighty cheer with which Pauncefote welcomed his chum into the realms of the Select. Pauncefote and Smith were partners; they hunted in couples, they wrote novels together: and here they were side by side, while the "Firm" was cruelly severed member from member. Surely Nemesis was having a fling too many if this was her doing!

"Heathcote."

"Ah! about time, too," thought Dick, as he raised his voice in a defiant cheer. He'd like a quiet five minutes with the fellows who had dared to pass his chum by in the voting. But, at any rate, Georgie was safe, and, if only Coote came next, the "Firm" could afford to snap its fingers at its constituents.

"Cazenove."

What! fat Cazenove jammed in between the "Firm" and its junior partner! Dick and Georgie glared at him, scarcely able to repress a howl at the sight of his smiling expanse of countenance. It had never occurred to any of them that the ballot may part friends whom not even a sentence of transportation could have severed, and they looked on, now more than half bewildered, as the scrutineer read out the sixth name.

"For the sixth place," said he, "there appears to be a dead-heat. Calverly and Coote have both the same number of votes. What's to be done, mighty Lycurgus?"

"Say you retire!" shouted Dick to the astonished Calverly, on whom the announcement had fallen with as much surprise as it had on his friends.

"Don't you do anything of the sort," shouted Gosse; "you're are as good as that lot. Stick in!"

"Of course he will," shouted others.

So Calverly announced he would stick in, and Coote had better retire, a suggestion Coote did not even condescend to notice. He was in his "Firm's" hands, and the "Firm" were determined to fight the thing out till they had not a toe to stand on.

"The simplest way," said Freckleton, "is to vote again for the two. What do you say, gentlemen of the Den?"

"All right," roared the Den.

"What's it to be: ballot or show of hands?"

"Show of hands," shouted most of them.

"Do you agree to show of hands, you two," said Freckleton, "or would you sooner have ballot?"

"I'd rather have show of hands," said Calverly.

"So would Coote," shouted Dick and Georgie.

"Then those who vote for Calverly hold up one hand," said Freckleton.

It was a big show, and the scrutineers, as they went from bench to bench, counted 141.

"Now for Coote."

Every one could see it was a terribly close affair. As Dick and Georgie scanned the benches, their hearts sank at the sight of so many not voting.

"Another dead-heat, I expect," said Pauncefote.

The suggestion drove Dick almost frantic. Coote *must* come in, or the consequences would be awful.

"Now, you fellows," he cried, starting up and addressing Templeton generally, as the scrutineers started on their rounds, "all together for old Coote! Don't forget his trot with the Harriers!"

This simple election speech called forth a cheer, and, better still, sent up two or three more hands.

Loud cries of "Order" from the top end of the room prevented any further appeal, and amid dead silence the scrutineers finished their work.

"For Coote," announced the spokesman, "there are 146."

Then did the "Firm" go mad, and lose their heads. Then did they yell till their throats were hoarse, and wave their hands till their arms ached.

Then did they link arms, as they sat victorious, and forget the sorrows of a term in that one paean of victory.

"Very close," they heard Freckleton say, as soon as order was restored. "Are you satisfied, Calverly?"

Woe betide Calverly had he ventured to be otherwise!

"All right," he said, meekly, cowed by the mighty triumph of the "Firm."

"Then Coote is in," announced the scrutineers.

The election was over, and Freckleton was about to disperse the meeting, when it was noticed Pledge was on his legs, trying to speak.

A low hiss and groan went round the Hall, but curiosity to hear what the deposed monitor had to say at such a time restored order.

Three boys alone knew what it all meant, and their faces blanched, and their limbs shook, as they looked out from their retreat and awaited their fate.

"Perhaps," said Pledge, "as this is a public meeting, you will allow me, though I have not the proud honour of being a 'Sociable,' and although I believe I am not a monitor either, to ask a question. I assure you I do it in the interests of Templeton, and of your immaculate Club. I don't suppose any one will thank me for doing it, and I am glad to say I have ceased to expect thanks. You may attribute any motive you like to me; the worse it is, probably, the better you will be satisfied. I certainly shall not trouble to tell you my motive, except that it is for your good. All I want to ask is, whether this meeting is aware that three members of the new Club are at this moment under the eyes of the police, for a disgraceful act of theft committed in the town; and, if so, whether you think that fact increases their claims to become members of a Club which is to be a credit to Templeton?"

The speech was heard in dead silence. But as it closed, a storm broke forth from all quarters of the Hall.

"Name! Sneak! Cad! Name!"

The angry spots blazed out in Pledge's cheeks as he faced the storm and heard the cries.

"You want the names, do you? You think, perhaps, I do not dare to give them. I do dare, though I stand here single-handed. The three boys are Richardson, Heathcote, and Coote, and if you don't believe me, ask them."

Another dead silence followed this announcement, and all eyes turned to where the "Firm" sat, pale and quivering.

Before, however, they could say a word, Mansfield rose, and stepped up on to the platform.

"Pledge has, for reasons best known to himself, charged three boys here with theft. Unlike his usual manner, he makes the charge in public before the whole school; and that being so, it is only fair the whole school should hear from him and his witnesses, if he has any, what the theft is."

The Captain's words were greeted with cries of approval from the meeting, and every one turned now to Pledge.

He stood a moment irresolute, scowling at his arch-enemy, and longing to be able to include him in the accusation he brought against his *protégés*. Then, with a half-swagger, he stepped on to the platform.

"If the Captain thinks I'm afraid to do what he asks, he's mistaken. I don't believe in hole-and-corner business. And as he has challenged me to accuse his three young friends in public and bring my witness, I will do both."

"What witness?" groaned Heathcote, in a whisper to Dick.

"Don't talk to me," hissed Dick, between his teeth.

"Go on," said Mansfield, to the accuser.

"Thank you. So I will. A fortnight ago, gentlemen, a small boy went down to Templeton—"

"Wait!" interposed Mansfield, "we must have names. What boy?"

"A small boy named Coote," began Pledge.

Coote, at the sound of his name, half-bounded from his seat. He knew he was "in it." But what on earth had any proceedings of his a fortnight ago to do with the loss of the *Martha*?

"Went down to Templeton to a shop—"

"What shop?" demanded Mansfield.

"To Webster's shop," replied Pledge, beginning to be ruffled by the Captain's determined manner.

The "Firm" started suddenly. Whatever was coming?

"While spending his time in the shop, the young gentleman, as young gentlemen sometimes do, stole a silver pencil."

There was a pause, and every eye turned towards Coote, who gaped at the announcement and stared at his partners as if he had been confronted with a ghost.

On Dick's countenance a curious change was taking place. Horror had already given way to bewilderment, and bewilderment was in turn giving way to something which actually looked like a grin.

"The young gentleman," proceeded Pledge, "had two dear friends, called Richardson and Heathcote, to whom he confided his stroke of business, and who joined him in concealing or disposing of the stolen article."

Dick could remain silent no longer. To the horror of his Firm, and the bewilderment of every one else—most of all, Pledge—he burst into a laugh, which sounded weird in the dead silence.

"Order!" cried Mansfield, sternly. "Go on, Pledge."

"I heard of the theft from the—from Webster immediately after it occurred, and for the last fortnight have been watching the culprits—"

Here he was interrupted by a hiss, which the Captain immediately suppressed.

"And they have actually admitted their guilt in begging me not to tell of them to you."

At this point Dick started up excitedly, and began—

"I should like to say—"

But the Captain stopped him.

"You will be heard shortly. First of all we must hear Pledge's witness."

"Certainly. I told Webster to call up at half-past four. He doesn't know what for. You'd better have him in. I'll go and fetch him."

"No," said the Captain. "Aspinall, will you ask him to come in?"

Chapter Twenty Nine
How Templeton turns a corner

Aspinall was not absent three minutes altogether, but the interval seemed interminable.

Our heroes, as they sat huddled together, pale, defiant, but bewildered, dividing the attention of the meeting with their accuser, thought it a century. More than once Dick, boiling over, started to his feet and attempted to speak, but every time Mansfield quietly suppressed him, and told him to wait till the proper time came.

Coote was once more racked by doubts as to whether he had really taken the pencil after all. He was morally certain he had not, but Coote was a youth always open to conviction.

The door opened at last, and Aspinall appeared ushering in the bookseller, who looked like a man who suspected a trap and was prepared to defend himself at the first sign of attack.

He had received a note in the morning from Pledge—of whom he had seen or heard nothing since his visit to the shop a fortnight ago—asking him to be sure to call at the school at 4:30 on a matter of business.

When Aspinall summoned him, he concluded it was to go to Pledge's study. But when, instead of that, he found himself suddenly ushered into a congregation of the whole school, it was small wonder if he felt bewildered and sniffed treachery.

"Mr Webster," said Mansfield, "Pledge, here, has just been publicly accusing three boys of theft. He says they have robbed you, and we want you to hear his statement and tell us if it is true. Please repeat what you have to say, Pledge, in Mr Webster's hearing."

The stationer, with inquiring face, turned to Pledge, who, despite some vague doubts which were beginning to disturb his confidence, smiled affably and said—

"Oh, sorry to bring you up, Mr Webster, just at your busy time, but I was telling my friends here about that little affair of the pencil-case, you know, which was stolen from you; and as they don't seem inclined to believe me, I thought the best thing would be for you to tell them about it yourself."

The countenance of the bookseller underwent a marvellous transformation as the speech proceeded. When Pledge had ceased, he exclaimed—

"Pencil-case! Why, bless you, Mr Pledge, I found that a fortnight ago!"

This announcement was the signal for a howl such as Templeton had rarely heard. The pent-up scorn of an afternoon broke out against the accuser as he stood there, pale and stupefied, staring at Webster.

It was all Mansfield could do to restore order. The gust had to blow itself more than half out before even he was heeded.

"Look here, you fellows," said he, "don't let us lose our heads. We want to hear the rights and wrongs of the case fairly. Hadn't you better wait till that's done before you turn the place into a bear-garden?"

The rebuke told, and the meeting relapsed into silence.

"You never told me that," snarled Pledge. "You've been fooling me."

"You never asked me. Mr Richardson knew; he was in the shop just after I found it."

"Of course he was," sneered Pledge.

"He needn't have been, if that's what you mean. He'd nothing to do with it. Bless you, it's an old story now; I'd almost forgotten it."

"You forgot, too, that you asked me to recover it for you; and you let me go on while all the time you had it."

"You offered to get it back. I never asked you. You said you had an interest in the young gentlemen."

"And you never thought it worth while to tell me the thing had turned up?"

"I told Mr Richardson, and said I was sorry for the fright he and his two friends had had. It never struck me you'd go on bothering about it, or I'd have told you. Fact of the matter is, I've never seen you from that day to this."

"Is that all you want to say?" said Mansfield, turning to Pledge.

"I can only say this," said Pledge: "that I never saw three boys imitate guilt better. If they hadn't done it, I should like to ask them why they quaked in their shoes whenever they met me, and why they sent me a round robin, asking me not to tell about them?"

"I can tell you that!" shouted Dick, springing up.

"You needn't wait, Mr Webster," said Mansfield. "Thank you for coming up."

"Thank you, gentlemen," said the tradesman.

"I'm sorry to be mixed up in the matter. Mr Pledge can go somewhere else for his books. Good day, gentlemen."

"Good day," said several voices.

When order was restored, Dick was discovered, red in the face, mounted on a form, propped up on either side by his faithful allies.

"I can tell him that," he cried, "and all of you, too. We thought he knew about another row of ours—about Tom White's boat, you know. It was us let her go; at least I did, and Georgie was there, too, and Coote's been in it since he came up. Tom White robbed us coming back from Grandcourt, and we were awfully wild, and were cads enough to slip his boat on the beach. There's been a regular row, and we expected to be transported. We backed Tom White up all we could, and tried to get him off. I told the magistrate it was us did it, and he said I'd put him in a jolly fix. Pledge was always talking to us about the police, and the county gaol, and that sort of thing, and we made sure he'd found out all about it, and was going to do us over it. We never guessed he was running his head against that pencil business, or we could easily have put him right. We're awfully sorry about the boat, you know. My governor came down and squared most of the fellows, and it's all right now, and Tom's got let off. Pledge has got a spite against all our 'Firm,' because we're not going to let Georgie be made a cad of by him, and we told him so; didn't we, you chaps?"

"Yes, we did," shouted the "chaps."

"Yes, he thought," continued Dick, warming up, "he'd make Georgie go and fag for him again, by threatening him about this row; but we backed Georgie up, and wouldn't let him; and then he promised to show us up at the 'Sociables,' and so he has."

Dick's oration was too much for the feelings of his audience. They laughed and cheered at every sentence; and when finally he subsided between his two supporters, quite short of breath, and wondering at the length of his own speech, they forgot the Captain's rebuke, and finished their howl against Pledge to the bitter end.

"Does Pledge want to ask any more questions?" asked Mansfield.

Pledge laughed bitterly.

"No, thank you; I'm not quite clever enough for them."

"Perhaps you are right," said the Captain, drily. "And if you have nothing more to say, perhaps you would like to go."

Pledge hesitated a moment, amid the howls which followed the Captain's words. Then he coolly rose, and ascended the platform. His face was flushed, and his eyes uneasy; but otherwise impudence befriended him, and he stood there to all appearances neither humiliated nor dismayed.

"Gentlemen," he began; but a fresh storm arose, and drowned his voice.

The uproar continued till Mansfield called for order, and said—

"I think in ordinary decency you ought to treat everybody fairly on a day like this. It will do you no harm, and it will be more worthy of Templeton."

"Gentlemen," said Pledge, "thank you for being ordinarily decent, although it wouldn't break my heart if you didn't hear me. It's not as easy as you may suppose to stand up single-handed against a school full of howling enemies. It's easy for you to howl when everybody howls on your side. Suppose you change places with me, and try to speak when everybody's howling against you. However, I don't complain. Somebody must be on the losing side, and as all of you take care to be on the winning. I'll do without you."

Pledge certainly knew his audience. He had hit them cleverly on a weak point—the point of chivalry; and had he been content to rest where he was, he might even yet have saved a following for himself in Templeton. But he went on—

"Our three young friends have told you a pretty story, which has highly amused you. It amused me too. They told you I had a spite against them. I must say it's the first I've heard of it. As a rule Sixth-form fellows don't waste much time in plotting against boys in the Third; but Richardson evidently thinks he and his friends are considerably more important than other boys of their age and brains. Suppose I were to tell you that, instead of my having a spite against any one, somebody has, for the last year, had a spite against me, and that somebody is the holy Captain of Templeton? Suppose I told you that he dared not show it openly, but made use of my wretched fag and his friends to tell tales, and trump up stories about me? Suppose I told you he and his fellow-monitors resorted to a mean dodge to get me to resign my monitorship, and then got up this precious Club in order to soft-soap their own toadies for helping them to do it? What has Mansfield done for Templeton, I should like to know? Hasn't he done more harm than good by his hectoring manner and his favouritism and fussiness? Isn't he one of the most unpopular fellows in Templeton? Didn't he all but get ignominiously left out of his own wonderful Club? And what do you think of him when he gets up here and tries to pass as a model of justice, when as likely as not, he has pre-arranged the whole affair, and told every one what part he is to play in the farce?"

He sat down amid a dead silence, conscious he had overdone it. A little less, and he might have convinced some that what he said was true; but when he talked such palpable nonsense as that of the Captain having arranged the whole scene which Pledge himself had got up, the meeting took his whole tirade for what it was worth, and received it in mocking silence.

Freckleton, to the relief of everybody, got up and said—

"I did think we might be spared quite such a ridiculous speech as that to which we have just listened. However, I have nothing to say about its comic side. What I want to say is this. It is perfectly true Mansfield had a spite against Pledge. So had I; *so* had Cresswell. So had eleven out of twelve of all the other monitors. And I'll tell you why. When a fellow deliberately sets himself to corrupt juniors entrusted to his care, as he corrupted young Forbes (howls), when he sets himself to upset every vestige of order and good form in Templeton; when he tells lies of everybody, and never tells the same lie correctly twice running (laughter); when he cudgels his brains how he may make mischief between friends (cheers from the 'Firm'), and get the credit of being the only friend of the very fellows he tries to ruin; then, I say, it's no wonder if Mansfield, and you, and everybody has a spite against him. I don't say much for the Templetonian that hasn't. I don't mean the spite which would lead any one to kick him. Thank goodness, we can let him know what we think without wearing out our shoe-leather (laughter). He talks in noble strain about being single-handed, and on the losing side. Thank goodness he is single-handed, and on the losing side! Thank goodness, too, he is lonely, and finds no one ready to keep him company in his low ways! He talks about Mansfield," continued the speaker, waxing unexpectedly warm. "Gentlemen, if you knew Mansfield as well as I do, you would be as angry as I am to hear the lies this miserable cad tells. Mansfield, gentlemen, would, I know, risk his life for the good of Templeton. He may not be popular. He's told me, often and often, he knows he isn't. But, I say to him, and I think you will say too, 'Go on, old man,' (cheers). 'You've done more good to Templeton in a term than other Captains have done in a year; and if the only thing you had ever done had been to rid us of the cad, Pledge, you would have done the school a service that any one might be proud of,' (loud cheers). There, I've used hard words, I know, and almost lost my temper, but it's best to speak out sometimes. Pledge has heard what I've said, and I shouldn't say anything different behind his back."

The Hermit sat down amidst a roar of applause, in which the Sixth joined as heartily as any. The effect of his simple, straightforward speech was immediately apparent when Mansfield rose to dismiss the assembly.

For a moment he stood there, unable to speak for the cheers which greeted him. The honest indignation of his friend had touched a keynote, which suddenly awakened Templeton to the conviction that its Captain was a hero after all; and the almost pathetic reference to his unpopularity roused them to an enthusiasm of repentance which was almost startling.

At length silence reigned, and the Captain said, with the faintest suspicion of a tremble in his voice—

"I think we've all had enough of this, you fellows. There's the Chapel bell. This meeting is over."

By a curious sort of instinct, the meeting, instead of immediately dispersing, remained seated, while Pledge rose, and moved to the door. He had got half-way there before he noticed his isolation, and a sudden flush of scarlet in his cheeks betrayed his emotion at the discovery. It was too late to retreat to his seat, and too late to pretend not to notice his position. With a pitiful attempt at a swagger, he completed his passage to the door, and left the Hall.

As he reached the door, a low hiss rose from the middle of the assembly, but a sudden gesture of appeal from the Captain stifled it before it could spread, and the door closed behind the retreating figure amid a silence which spoke volumes.

The meeting waited a minute or two, and then quietly rose and dispersed, every one feeling that from that afternoon a new era in the history of Templeton had been inaugurated.

Our heroes, who in the midst of later excitements had half-forgotten their own share in the afternoon's proceedings, were among the first to get out into the Quadrangle; and once there, their manner changed from one of dignified solemnity to one of agitated expectancy.

In a quarter of an hour their guest was due in Cresswell's study, and between now and then, what had they not to do?

Who shall describe that wondrous spread, or the heroes that partook of it? How, when Mr Richardson arrived, punctual and hungry, he found a table groaning under every delicacy the ingenuity and pocket-money of three juniors could provide; how the kidneys were done to a turn and the tea-cake to a shade; how jam-pots stood like forts at each corner of the snowy cloth; how hot rolls and bath buns lorded it over white loaf and brown; how eggs, boiled three minutes and five seconds by Heathcote's watch, peeped out among watercress and lettuces; how rosy apples and luscious pears jostled one another in the centre dish; and how tea and coffee breathed forth threatenings at one another from rival pots on the same tray?

It was a spread to make the mouths in Olympus water, and drive Hebe and Ganymede to despair. Mr Richardson, who, in the guilelessness of his heart, had brought a small plum-cake as a contribution to the feast, positively blushed as he saw that table, and hid his poor mite back in his pocket for very shame.

The "Firm," when they did go in for a thing, did it well, and no mistake; and, if Mr Richardson had paid up royally for them during the day, he should find that more than one could play at that game, and that they would pay up royally at night.

Like a brave man, the good father expanded his appetite, and, regardless of consequences, took a little of everything. The "Firm" took a great deal of everything, and never was a more jovial meal.

Coote's cup seemed to be always on the road to or from the pot, and Georgie was for ever mistaking the dish of tea-cake for his own private plate; while Dick, bolder than any of them, insisted on giving his parent ocular demonstration of the wholesomeness of each several dish, until that good gentleman began to think it was a good thing he was not a daily visitor at Templeton.

"Jolly brickish of old Cress, giving us his study, isn't it, you chaps?"

"Rather!" said Georgie. "I think we might almost leave him out something."

"I don't particularly want this *egg*," said Coote, who had already accomplished two and was gently tapping a third, "if you think he'd like that."

"How would it be to ask him in? Would you mind, father?"

"Not at all," said Mr Richardson, really relieved at the prospect of a fifth appetite to help off the banquet.

So Dick went in search of his senior, and found him in Freckleton's study. He felt constrained to invite both seniors to join their party, and, somewhat to his alarm, they both accepted gladly.

Dick need not have been alarmed, though, for both the provisions and the company held out wonderfully.

Mr Richardson was delighted with his boy's seniors, and they were no less delighted with him. The whole story of Tom White's boat was rehearsed again, as were also the other stories of the term, finishing up with the eventful assembly of the afternoon.

"It wasn't a pleasant affair at all," said Cresswell, "but thunderstorms do clear the air sometimes, and I think Templeton understands itself better now."

"Of course we shall have Pledge still," said Freckleton, "but, as long as fellows know what he is, he's not dangerous. It's when he gets hold of young greenhorns like Heathcote and Coote he does mischief."

"He never got hold of me," said Coote.

"I was an ass to let him make a cad of me," said Heathcote. "I had warning, you know; the Ghost wrote to me before I'd been here a fortnight."

"What Ghost?" asked Mr Richardson.

Cresswell laughed.

"Nobody knows," said he, "though some of us guess."

"Who? Was it you?" asked Dick. "I got a letter too, you know."

"No; it wasn't I."

"Then, by Jove! it must have been Freckleton," exclaimed Dick, interpreting the guilty look on the Hermit's face. "Was it, I say?"

"'*Dominat qui in se dominatur*'!" said the Hermit in a sepulchral tone. "Yes, my boy; but keep it mum. I shan't waste my Latin over you again in a hurry."

"Your letter really made me sit up," said Dick, gravely.

"Well, I expect," said Cresswell, "if Templeton goes on as she's doing now, the poor Ghost will be hard up for a job. Mansfield is the right man in the right place, and he's more right than ever now."

"That he is," said Freckleton, warmly. "I can tell you fellows that, in spite of his iron hand, he's one of the humblest fellows that ever lived. I believe he prays for Templeton night and morning, and that's more than a lot of us do, I fear."

"After all," said Mr Richardson, "that's the best sort of Christian. A man who lives up to what he believes will lead fifty, where a man who believes more than he acts up to will barely lead one."

"It strikes me," said Freckleton, "it's no joke to be a leader of men, or boys either; is it, Dick?"

"Oh, I don't know," said Dick. "It's no good as long as you don't go quite straight yourself. You've got to go square yourself, I suppose, before any one else will back you up."

"Yes," said Coote; "we couldn't back you up, you know, while you were going on as you were, could we, Dick?"

"Didn't look like it," said Dick, with a grin.

"But I expect Dick thinks it was worth his while to have to go steady," said Cresswell. "It's done your 'Firm' no harm, has it?"

"Rather not!" said the "Firm," returning to their supper.